P9-DUX-660

Seekers of the Chalice

TOR®

A TOM DOHERTY
ASSOCIATES BOOK
NEW YORK

Brian Cullen

Seekers of the Chalice

This is a work of fiction. All of the characters, organizations, and events portrayed in this novel are either products of the author's imagination or are used fictitiously.

SEEKERS OF THE CHALICE

A Tor Book
Published by Tom Doherty Associates, LLC
175 Fifth Avenue
New York, NY 10010

www.tor.com

Library of Congress Cataloging-in-Publication Data

Cullen, Brian.
Seekers of the chalice / Brian Cullen.—1st ed.
p. cm.
"A Tom Doherty Associates book."
ISBN-13: 978-0-7653-1473-4
ISBN-10: 0-7653-1473-8
I. Title.
PR6053.U372S44 2008
823'.914—dc22
2007041820

First Edition: February 2008

Printed in the United States of America

0 9 8 7 6 5 4 3 2 1

From the Author to the Reader

This is a work of fiction. License has been taken with Ancient Irish myth to create a different world. Anyone trying to make something more of it will suffer the Ancient Curses.

for Rennie Shattuck

To Cruachan Connor sent the three,
Cucullen, Conall, and Leary,
For Maeve to choose which one
Would be the Red Branch champion.
A cup of bronze with silver eagle
At the bottom went to Leary.
A cup of silver with a gold eagle
At the bottom went to Conall.
But to Cucullen went the champion's
Cup of gold with a flawless ruby
Carved in the shape of a raven
And around its base in Old Tongue graven
"I am made of Air, Fire, Land, and Sea
Only the Just may drink from Me."

—Translated from *Annals of the Red Branch*
by Aruadh the Wise in the Year 369 Tír Na Og

But I who have written this story (*historia*), or rather this fable (*fabula*), give no credence to the various incidents related in it. For some things in it are the deceptions of demons, others poetic figments; some are probable, others improbable; while still others are intended for the delectation of foolish men.

—Translated from *Annals of the Red Branch*
by Aruadh the Wise in the Year 369 Tír Na Og

Seekers of the Chalice

IN THE BEGINNING . . .

From the mists of time before time was known, five Grecian tribes set forth in search of a new world. They came together upon the shores of Erin and became the Tuatha De Danann, the Children of Danu, a goddess who has disappeared into time. The Tuatha De Danann, the direct descendants of Nemed, a king of Erin who fought three wars against the cruel Fomorians, brought five treasures with them to Erin: the Lia Fail, a stone that utters a shriek at the crowning of the rightful king; the invincible Spear of Lugh; Casurairmed, the deadly Sword of Nuada; the ever-plentiful Cauldron of The Dagda; and the Chalice of Fire, the Bladhm Caillis, that brought peace to those who held it and immortality to those worthy who drank from it.

In the forges of the Tuatha De Danann, deep within the Mountains of Maylor, the smith Goibniu had made the Chalice of Fire with gold taken from deep within the mines on Teach Duinn, the House of Donn, the King of the Dead. Goibniu worked all that was good into the Chalice and more, but he could not work all needed to guard the Chalice from pride and desire for power that filled those who served the fallen god, Ragon Garg-Fuath, whose name means "hatred for all": he who was cast from the Hall of the Pantheon by Lugh Longarm for wanting the power of The Dagda. Ragon fell through darkness visible until he came to the frozen lake of fire in the Underworld where he plunged into the flaming waves and emerged burnt black and filled with a poisonous desire to conquer and rule both Earthworld and Otherworld.

Slowly, Ragon gathered others around him with promises of great wealth and a place above those in the Otherworld. A great war began in the Otherworld between Ragon and his forces and the armies from the Otherworld. Ragon was defeated and sentenced to Ifreann, an island in the Western Seas hidden by enchantment; an island of ice and fire made by Samach, the Great One, who created all gods before quietly slipping away to become a part of the cosmos.

A blood-red ruby carved into the likeness of a raven fell from Ragon's forehead during his fall and was found by Boand in one of the rivers she guarded. Boand gave the ruby to Goibniu, who placed it in the bottom of the Chalice of Fire as a talisman to guard the seekers of truth.

First, the gods drank from the Chalice to become immortal. Then, the Chalice was given to the elves, who lived in the tree houses they built in the forests, and the dwarfs, who lived in the Great Halls they built deep within the mountains. Then the Chalice was secretly buried by The Dagda, the god-king, on the Island of Shadows, where it was guarded by Scathach Buanand, the Woman of Victory. Only the bravest of the brave could reach the Island of Shadows and what lay beyond by making their way through the gray Mountains of Mourne to the Giant's Causeway, where they could cross the Misty Sea to the island.

In time, the Pantheon of Gods decided that the heroes of men should receive the Chalice so that they too could become immortal. But only those worthy of drinking from the Chalice would become like gods. Those who were unworthy would enter the World of Dreams, where they would walk through the ancient fires of the Fomorians and where their flesh would blister from the dreadful heat and the hair be singed from their bodies until only black stubble remained. They would see the fire from the Blood Raven sweep up to the night sky and would weep for that which they could not become.

The gods gave the Chalice to Fand, the wife of the sea-god Mannanan Mac Lir, and directed her to take the Chalice to man. This she did, and in time, the Chalice made its way to the Land of Connacht, where it came into the hands of the warrior-queen Maeve. But Maeve could not receive the glory of the Chalice as she desired power over the land for herself. Still, she kept it until the great champion of the Red Branch in Ulster, Cucullen, came to her court in Cruachan Ai. Desiring him for her own, Maeve gave the Chalice to him, but Cucullen ignored her sultry ways meant to seduce him and took the Chalice back to the Red Branch.

The Chalice was meant to bring peace to the land, but men did not want peace, as they showed in their cruelty toward Macha. Macha pleaded with Connor that she not be forced to race against his horses since she was pregnant, but Connor refused to be swayed. Although she defeated Connor's team in a footrace, the trial brought about the birth of twins, and afterward she cursed Ulster and the Red Branch. During times of severe crisis, the Ulstermen and all of their generations would suffer her identical pains for five days and four nights.

And then the Chalice was stolen and came into the hands of the servers of darkness.

And although the dark servants could not bend the powers of the Chalice to their will, they could deny the powers to those worthy of the Chalice. And this they did while they quietly searched for one who could be bent to their ways.

And so they discovered Bricriu.

The Theft

Fog blanketed Emain Macha, spreading thickly around the Red Branch Hall, the home of the heroic knights who protected Ulster under their king, Connor. The fog smelled dank, wrapping itself around them with clammy arms from the Home of the Dead, and within the fog, Bricriu Poisontongue crept quietly, making his way into the hall where the knights slept in their rooms, sated from the ale-feast in celebration of Beltaine, the celebration of spring when the ground grows fertile. Carefully, Bricriu stepped over the sleeping servants who curled up in blankets on heavy pallets on the floor outside the rooms of the knights they served.

He made his way to Connor's treasure room and carefully lifted the wooden latch and slipped inside. He ignored the heaps of jewels and swords and shields and made his way to the back of the room, where a small box made out of red oak rested on a blackthorn table. He opened the box and stared at the golden Chalice with a blood-red ruby carved in the figure of a raven at the bottom of the cup. Around the base of the Chalice was a legend:

I am made of Air, Fire, Land, and Sea
Only the Just may drink from Me

His dark face split into a wolfish grimace as he closed and latched the wooden box and carefully placed the box in a leather bag slung crosswise over his body. Then, his face closed tightly with bitter anger as he remembered the insult heaped upon him by the Red Branch knights, who had refused to invite him to the feast as he had a tongue of acid and took great glee in twisting words to pit one knight against another.

Now, he thought, I have the Chalice of Fire, given to the greatest warrior of the Red Branch, Cucullen, by Maeve, the warrior-queen of Connacht, before his death. The Chalice had brought peace and prosperity to the lands of Emain Macha and made Ulster the strongest of the Four Provinces—Ulster, Munster, Meath, and Connacht. It was the most valued treasure of the Red Branch, for without it, Ulster would never know peace.

He chortled silently, recalling Macha's curse, which decreed that during times of severe crisis, all generations of Ulstermen would suffer her pains of childbirth for five days and four nights.

Bricriu turned and left the treasure room and began to retrace his steps. The fog would not last long; he did not have the skills to maintain it indefinitely. But the hall was dark, lit only by a torch burning faintly at the far end. He did not see the knife a careless servant had not retrieved when it slipped to the floor from a platter the servant was removing from the feast hall to the kitchen. Bricriu's foot slid when he stepped on the knife. He stumbled and fell against the wooden wall, knocking a spear and shield from the pegs upon which they had been hung. The clatter woke the servants, who stared in confusion at the dark figure in front of them.

"It's Bricriu," whispered one.

Bricriu snarled and ran from the hall. Outside, the fog was lifting, and he hurried to the front gate and slipped through, disappearing into the dark as he raced to the deep woods at the far end of the clearing. He laughed wildly as he disappeared into the woods, his hand clutching the leather bag, gripping the wooden box.

In the middle of the woods, he paused to rest when he came upon a sylvan stream filled with leaping salmon. Thirsty, he scooped water with the Chalice of Fire and upended it, drinking.

Immediately an iron band tightened around his head and he fell to the ground, screaming in pain. Through eyes tightened in agony, he watched as a pillar of fire rose up from his breast, and from that pillar, a beautiful bird with red and green and yellow and blue plumage leaped upward into the night, disappearing into a brilliant rainbow that suddenly arched across the black vault of the sky. His throat constricted and water vomited forth upon the ground. He fell back against the earth as the band eased. He panted and lay quietly, gathering his strength.

In time, he levered himself up on his elbows and glared at the Chalice of Fire, made from red gold with a silver luminescence surrounding it. Cautiously he touched the Chalice and jerked his hand back as blisters formed immediately on the tips of his fingers. He plunged his hand into the stream to cool it.

"Damn you," he said softly through gritted teeth to the Chalice. "Damn you. If I can't have you, no one shall. Least of all, the Red Branch."

He cupped his hands and drew water and splashed it on the Chalice over and over. Slowly, the luminescence disappeared, and when it was gone, he touched the Chalice again and this time it was cool to the touch.

He took it cautiously, wrapped it in a piece of cloth he tore from his cloak, and placed it in the leather bag hung over his shoulder.

Then, he rose and crossed the stream and moved ever deeper into the piney woods, heading west toward the Land of Connacht, Ulster's mortal enemy.

1

Heavy waves swept across the gray sea in the Otherworld, reflecting the turmoil of the Earthworld. Mannanan Mac Lir watched grimly from his sea home as his silver-hoofed horses pulled his jeweled chariot, skimming over the moonlit waves, carrying his wife, Fand, the Pearl of Beauty, long golden tresses flying behind her, to the sandy shores. Mannanan was not in favor of her journey. The Otherworld, he was adamant, needed to stay out of the affairs of the Earthworld as much as possible. But, he reflected sourly, that didn't seem to matter to Fand. She had dabbled in the affairs of the Earthworld ever since she had fallen in love with Cucullen, the boy warrior who alone had held off the Connacht army from Ulster's borders. Fand had him brought to the Otherworld, where they remained lovers until Mannanan had shaken his many-colored cloak between them, sending Cucullen back to the Earthworld. But Fand had become with child during her dalliance with Cucullen, and she soon gave birth to a son she named Cumac, the son of Cucullen.

The thing was, Mannanan thought, he liked the boy; it was the father that he had disliked. But he shouldn't begrudge Fand for doting on her son. Especially now.

Mannanan ran his fingers through his flowing blue-green beard as he directed his gaze toward the Earthworld, overcast and wet. Many Sword-wanderers roamed the forests, looking for victims. The Seven Seals that the Tuatha De Danann had used to close the Great Rift, the gateway between the Darkworld and the Earthworld, were breaking, loosing the Grayshawls, wizards from the Cultas Dubasarlai, the Cult of Black Sorcerers, and their followers, the Nightshades or the "Black Riders," ancient warriors who followed Ragan in his war against the Pantheon of Gods and were cast into the Great Rift along with him after the Battle of Moytura. They were forms more than flesh and blood and wore flowing black robes over gray cloth. Hands and forearms were protected by black gauntlets made from iron. They carried black swords and daggers whose slightest scratch unleashed a terrible poison that flooded their veins.

Along with them came the Fomorians, a race of demons, hideous and evil, in darkness. The Great Rift was once again open and now Maliman, the Dark One, the strongest wizard and leader of the Fomorians, once again began to work his will in the Earthworld.

He sighed. The work of the Pantheon had been thoroughly undone with the theft of the Chalice of Fire from the Red Branch. He had warned against giving the Chalice, created by The Dagda, to the mortals, but Fand had given the Chalice to Maeve, She-Who-Intoxicates, as an award for Fand's former lover, Cucullen. Since then, Ulster had been at peace and the land had grown fruitful and the people prosperous. But now, now—he sighed again. The land had fallen into ruin, and the people had become warlike. The old feud between Connacht and Ulster had broken out once again, and warriors raided along their border.

Women! he thought sourly. Always thinking they had the answer to the problems of the Otherworld and the Earthworld. Well, he'd just wash his hands of the whole affair and leave the problem to Fand—and those of the Pantheon who had backed her when he had disagreed with sending a hero to aid the Red Branch after their greatest hero, Cucullen, had been killed.

Women!

Scowling, he scrubbed his hands over his face and looked broodingly into the distant waves, where white horses danced on top of the gray water. He shook his head wearily as he remembered the nearly violent argument among the Pantheon when Lugh had proposed sending his son to find the Chalice, stolen by Bricriu Poisontongue. Midir, the Proud and the Haughty, had objected strenuously to the sending of one to find the Chalice, and others followed him, arguing until The Dagda threatened to cast Midir and his host into the Great Rift, where the mighty furnace made by Goibniu, the blacksmith of the gods, burned with a fierce heat that blistered even the spirits cast into its depths, where they would be banished forever.

EVENING fell and the weather turned sunny and golden by the time Fand crossed the waves of the Eternal Sea and came to the shores of the Otherworld. She left the white horses and jeweled chariot by the sea and walked inland, her white gown and cloak swirling around her like mist. She was pale-faced and golden-haired, and when she walked over the earth, water lilies appeared in tiny ponds wherever her feet touched and crickets began to sing. Under her arm she carried a bundle wrapped in finely dressed white leather with ancient signs and symbols, whose meaning was lost in the ages, embroidered in fine gold thread.

She remembered fondly the time when she had been forced to go to the Earthworld to beg Cucullen to come to the Otherworld and fight the three demons that were threatening the Pantheon. At first, Cucullen had refused, as he had heard tales of what happened to those from Earthworld who had entered the Otherworld and never came back. In desperation, she had offered to reward him with her love, and, if the truth be told, she was not reluctant to make such an offer, as she was already under the spell of the handsome Cucullen.

And Cucullen had gone with her to the Otherworld, where he handily defeated the three demons and spent a month lazing beside the crystal stream Misha, which circles the Pantheon before emptying into the wine-dark sea to the west. But after that month, Cucullen's wife, Emer, came to Fand's pool and cast her jewelry into the waters, begging Fand to allow Cucullen to return to her. With a pang, Fand realized that Cucullen could never love her as much as he did Emer and sent her lover back to the Earthworld. After he left, however, Fand discovered she was pregnant and gladly with a son whom she named Cumac, the Son of the Hound.

She came to the house that Lugh Longarm had made for his grandson and entered, searching for Cumac. The house was made from polished oak. The walls had a soft golden sheen to them, and the pegged floor was burnished to a red glow. A cobblestone fireplace, the ashes cool to the touch, had been built at the far end of the Great Room, where stood a dining table and chairs made from thin slats of hickory bound tightly together.

She searched the house, but Cumac wasn't there. A frown pinched the space between her fine eyebrows, and she left the house and stood outside on the path that wound through Cumac's scented garden.

A thought came to her, and she made her way up the hill swathed with green grass behind the house to where a mimosa tree flowered on the crest. Beneath the tree Cumac sprawled lazily, his fingers gently touching the strings of a harp. He wore a white tunic edged with a narrow red band, leather pants, and calf-high boots dyed black. A red cloak had been tossed carelessly on the ground beside him. Notes tinkled softly from the harp, and wrens twittered cheerfully from the limbs overhead in harmony.

She smiled fondly when she saw her son and called, "Cumac!"

Cumac, the Hound's Son, sat up and brushed his hair—shoulder-length and black with a silver streak down the center—back from his forehead and set the harp aside. He smiled back.

"Mother! What brings you to land?"

She came to sit beside him. She sighed and placed the leather-wrapped package on the ground between them. Cumac eyed the package but made no move to open it.

"You have been well," Fand said. It was not a question but Cumac answered it anyway.

"Yes, I have," he said. He grinned mischievously. "And I have been busy. Learning."

Fand sniffed. Cumac had been sent to land in the Otherworld to study under The Dagda and Lugh, the Sun God, and Deroi, but his studies also included surreptitious nights with the woodland nymphs and selkies, who came ashore in early night when the orange-colored full moon began to peek over the horizon and shed their sealskins to become beautiful women who dallied with mortals and immortals alike.

"Perhaps it would be better if you spent more time with your teachers and less playing will-o'-the-wisp by day," she said.

Cumac laughed. "There are lessons and then there are lessons, Mother. Should I not learn whatever I can?"

"Yes, I suppose you should," she said. Then, she could not help herself and burst out laughing as a wide smile curved Cumac's cheeks into deep dimples. "You are the most irritating son any mother could have."

"I know," he said modestly, placing his hand upon his heart. "I do try to live up to your expectations. But, you did not come here to check on my studies, did you, Mother?"

She shook her head. "No. I did not."

"As I thought," he said. He leaned back against the tree, his eyes somber.

"Your father's Chalice, the Bladhm Caillis, has been stolen," she said. "The Great Rift has been opened, and the Earthworld is becoming a wasteland. The Fomorians are free," she added grimly. "And you know what that means."

He sobered instantly and nodded. The Fomorians had ruled the land from their island with a powerful grip before the Tuatha De Danann came. The forces of darkness favored the Fomorians at first in the ensuing battles, but the Dananns defeated the Fomorians in the First Battle of Moytura and then again in the Second Battle of Moytura. The Fomorians were imprisoned in the bottom of the Great Rift and the entrance sealed with seven seals, one each of gold, silver, lead, iron, bronze, oak, and hazel. But now, the seals were being broken one by one, releasing those who had been confined in the Great Rift's depths.

"War is everywhere," she continued. "I fear that there will never be peace upon Ulster's land if the Chalice is not returned to Emain Macha." She hesitated. "The Earthworld and the Otherworld depend upon each other. The temper of the time in the Earthworld is measured as well in the Otherworld. Each is woven from the same fabric. Now, the Grayshawls and the Nightshades have come forth from the Great Rift with the Fomorians and are spreading their evil across the land. I have spoken to The Dagda and the others of the Pantheon. Now, I come to speak with you."

Cumac frowned. He knew the story of his father. His mother had seen the warrior champion Cucullen and envied his marriage to Emer. She had had his spirit brought to the Otherworld and had enchanted him to make him forget his mortal life and wife until Emer had entreated Fand to return Cucullen's spirit to her. He had left Fand pregnant with Cumac, a demigod, half mortal, half immortal, whose mortal self was thinking about what his mother had said and feeling a draw toward the Earthworld.

Fand covertly watched the play of emotions over her son's face and knew the thoughts running through his mind, felt the pull of her remembered love for his father. She took a deep breath and slowly let it out. The son was more handsome than his father, with his broad shoulders and trim waist. His forehead was high and his eyes gray and clear. She could understand why women sighed when he passed them.

"What would you have me to do, Mother?" he asked quietly.

"What your heart tells you," she answered. "You are your father's son. What would he do in such a time? The Red Branch is without a hero," she added. "At least, without a hero that can be spared to find the Chalice and return it to Emain Macha."

"You think I should go?" he asked. She didn't answer him. He nodded slowly. "Yes. I should go." He laughed. "Ah, but it will be a grand adventure."

She felt relieved. She reached for the white leather package and laid it upon his lap. He glanced at her quizzically.

"It is a gift from Boand of the Waters, to whom it must be returned when the wearer is finished with it."

Cumac unfolded the leather wrapping and revealed a sword with a bone-white handle in a triple-folded red leather scabbard. Down the center of the scabbard a legend had been laid in Ogham, the Old Tongue: ᚛ᚉᚐᚂᚐᚇᚁᚑᚂᚌ—The Rainbow. He withdrew the sword and revealed a blade of a curious steel that reflected light like a prism. The sword was longer than others by a good six inches. He swung it, testing its balance, and a many-colored arch followed the movement, springing from the beginning of his swing to the nesting at the end.

"It is called Caladbolg and was given to your father by Fergus, who received it from Boand when he was king of the Red Branch before Connor. After your father defeated the Connacht armies when they tried to capture the Brown Bull of Cooley, he had need of a new sword. The blade will never dull or break. It was forged by Goibniu, the smith of the Dananns."

Cumac rose and swung the sword. It sang musically through the air. The weight balanced well in his hand. He laughed and began the movements that he had been taught by his grandfather, Lugh Longarm, the Sun God, the Golden Warrior. Cumac moved smoothly through the Apple Feat, the Edge Feat, the complicated Crescent Feat that left most twisted and contorted on their own feet and legs, and the Scythe Feat.

"I thank you, Mother. Thank Boand for me," he said, pleased with the gift. He picked up his cloak and pinned it around his shoulders. He replaced the sword in its scabbard and hung it over his shoulders, the haft sticking up above the right. The blade dropped down to mid-calf on him, a good foot more than it would on any other warrior.

She smiled as she considered the breadth of his shoulders that made him look shorter than he was. A deception that made others dismiss him as a boy just growing into manhood.

How like his father, she thought. Then she sighed.

"You should travel first to Ce-Aehd's Sidhe in Connacht to enter the Earthworld. That is the safest way for now, although we cannot predict if it will remain safe for long. Evil has come to rest in Ulster, and to enter the Earthworld there, I suspect, would be dangerous. I do not think the Chalice is in Connacht, but that is where it came from before your father took it to Ulster. Things have a way of returning to their beginnings. But be wary. There is much danger in the Earthworld, now. Much. And," she added meaningfully, "you are half mortal."

She reached and ruffled his hair affectionately. He grinned recklessly. He knew that once he entered the Earthworld, he would become mortal.

"I'll charm the danger with my harp," he said. Again he slipped the sword from its sheath and lifted it high. It gleamed and shimmered like silver breastmail made by the mysterious Tuatha De Danann before they disappeared from the Earthworld. "Or with Caladbolg."

"Do not rely solely upon the sword," Fand cautioned. "Your father did, and he died by the sword. Use it wisely. But choose wisely before you use it. You must live by your wits as well as your strong right arm. You have not yet been tested in battle. Lessons are lessons, but grim war is different. Remember this."

"I shall."

Fand's eyes suddenly became misty. She caressed Cumac's cheek with her hand. No beard bristle scraped over her palm. Like his father, she thought. No beard to mar his features.

"You worry too much, Mother," Cumac said. He replaced Caladbolg in its sheath. "Crafty Lugh taught me well in the use of the sword. Remember, he went to the aid of my father on the cattle raid when Father was weak and wounded. No warrior is better."

"There is always someone better," she said sternly, admonishing him with a pull on his earlobe that made him wince. "It is the foolish man who lets his mouth do his thinking for him."

"It is the brave man who can make the brag stick," Cumac said in return. Deep dimples appeared again in his cheeks as he grinned at her. "In the Earthworld is that not the way of the men?"

She sighed and shook her head. Tiny lights glinted from her golden hair. "Youth. Always learning the hard way. Here." She handed him a leather bag. "Here is food and water for your beginning. It is no feast," she cautioned, "but it will sustain you on your journey. Go, then."

Cumac bent and kissed her. He grinned once more, and left, loping his way west.

She watched him leave with sadness.

And may The Dagda protect you, she thought and, turning, sadly returned to the chariot that had brought her over the waves of the sea.

2

It took five weeks for Cumac to reach the Tanglewood Forest, the ancient forest, dark and forbidding, that marked the entrance to the Great Rift he had to cross to get to Ce-Aehd's Sidhe. Moss hung like dark-green tapestry from the black limbs of the trees. A dank odor like rotted meat rose from the floor of the forest, and no birds sang. A dark canopy of moss and dead leaves draped over the hardpan path that led into the forest. He squatted on his heels and reached into the leather bag suspended on a wide strap from his shoulder. He removed a loaf of pannin bread given to him by the Sylvanian fairies when he passed through their flower-strewn land the week before, broke off a piece, and munched happily as he studied the path.

At the end of the first week, he had reached the land of the Sylvanians, a land filled with flowers and green trees and thick, lush, green grass where honeybees buzzed lazily around the glades. At first, they had greeted him with suspicion, but they could not stay suspicious for long as they led the way to their queen, Nefyn.

"Greetings, Cumac," Nefyn had said softly, her voice low and musical. Wild black tresses hung to her waist. She wore a neck-high white gown with periwinkles embroidered around the neck. Her eyes were a startling blue like bluebells.

"Greetings," Cumac had answered formally. "I travel to Ce-Aehd's Sidhe in Connacht and would cross your lands. I request hospitality in accord with the ancient laws. I will only stay the night," he added. "I do not wish to impose longer. I request a guide to lead me to the Tanglewood Forest."

A smile curved Nefyn's full lips, spreading into deep dimples in her cheeks. Her hazel eyes twinkled merrily. She gestured to the Sylvanians standing next to her.

"We do not get many travelers here," she said musically. "Surely you would not leave without enjoying our hospitality."

"Time is not on my side," he said.

"I will give you a guide," she said. "But first, we must celebrate your coming with a feast and dancing. I give you my word that we will not detain you."

With misgivings, he had agreed to her request and followed nymphs to a silver fountain where sparkling water trickled merrily over white stones and the air was perfumed with roses growing around the fountain.

Giggling, the nymphs took his clothes from where he dropped them. Hastily he entered the fountain, stretching back and letting the water bubble around him, washing away the strain of the journey.

By the time he had finished, his clothes had been returned, clean and fresh from washing in honeysuckle water. Self-consciously he dressed, turning away from the bold eyes of the nymphs who giggled again at his movements.

Then, he had followed them to a bee-loud glade, where a feast had been prepared and golden pitchers of honeyed wine stood on silver tables, draped with purple cloths edged in gold thread, laden with fish and fruits and candied sweets. Gratefully, he took a platter prepared for him and ate hungrily, washing down the portions with wine.

"You are hungry," Nefyn said.

Bright red burnt his cheeks, and he forced himself to slow his eating.

"I have not eaten for three days," he said.

"Is it to your enjoyment?" she asked innocently. "Have more wine."

Gratefully he took the chalice extended to him by a white hand and drained it.

Music came on a gentle breeze and a group of Sylvanians, clad in hyacinth and wild rose petals, slipped from among hawthorn trees to dance on the green grass. Their highly arched white feet seemed to whisper across the grass, and Cumac watched as they danced a dance that was old before the marking of time, their bodies seeming to slip between the notes of the music from a harp that lulled him into a sleepy peacefulness.

"You are tired," Nefyn had whispered after the dancers had finished.

"Yes," he said, yawning. "Yes, I am very tired."

"Then, come. I shall take you to your bed."

Rising, she took his hand and pulled him to his feet and led him into the twilight between a stand of trees heavy with golden apples. A soft bed of ferns covered with otter skins had been made ready for him and he fell sleepily upon it.

"Rest," Nefyn said and began to sing softly to him, her voice enchanting, and he fell into a deep sleep and dreamed of Nefyn slipping her gown from her shoulders and coming to bed with him.

When he awoke, he was alone on the bed, and a platter of fresh fruit and more wine had been placed beside him. He frowned and reached for an apple and bit into it, his mouth watering from the explosion of sweetness that burst within it.

Another day, he thought, can do no harm. Then you will be well rested for the remainder of your journey. He ate happily and sipped the wine and leaned back drowsily upon the bed.

"You are happy here?" Nefyn said, coming to his side with a bottle. She slipped his tunic from his shoulders and opened the bottle. Gently, she began to massage the oil into his skin. His muscles relaxed with the hypnotic movement.

"Yes," he said. "Yes. But I cannot stay."

"I know," Nefyn said. Her hands continued gently massaging the oil into his skin and muscles, and a drowsiness slipped over Cumac. Nefyn began singing to him:

Here among the Sylvanians
You will have no cares.
Beauty is here and love
And fragrances fill the air.

Love you will find here
And hives for the honeybee
And fairies dance for you
And kisses you'll have from me.

Tarry a while, there's no hurry
For your journey will always wait
While you take your ease
And enjoy the flowers and the trees.

And Cumac slept, and within his sleep he dreamed of the days and ways of the Sylvanians. Other men walked peacefully among the flowered glades and showed not a care among them. The men bathed in silver fountains and ate honeyed bread and honeydew and listened to the songs of the dancing fairies when evening cast its purple glow over the land.

Nefyn began to ask Cumac for little things: to gather the honey, to draw water for her to bathe, and to gather flowers for the elves to make scented garlands for their dances. Gladly he did her bidding as it seemed right to be serving the fairies for the peace they gave him.

Then one night he awoke from a deep sleep in the deep dark and suddenly realized he had forgotten to mark the passage of time while he had been enjoying himself. He wrinkled his brow as he tried to remember the days and counted the passing of two weeks. He rose from the bed and quietly gathered his things and a sack of pannin bread, and crept away from the land of the Sylvanians without the promised guide.

He ran lightly, ignoring the white mist that chilled the air until the sun burned it away. Green grass and wildflowers grew upon the land and songbirds sat in the occasional tree adding melody to the air. At times, brown deer slipped cautiously away from his path and rabbits scurried away. Then one day, a forest appeared in the distance, black and forbidding. A silence gathered around him like a dingy cloak, and the birds sang less and less. No deer or rabbits were seen, and he knew that he had come to the edge of Tanglewood Forest. Many paths ran through it, and Cumac knew that goblins and hobgoblins used them constantly.

There will be no Sylvanians in there, he mused while he ate. Hobgoblins for certain, perhaps Scytha fairies who believe in human sacrifices and lie in wait for travelers, but no Sylvanians. But what else will be in there? Since the opening of the Great Rift, many demons have slipped out and linger now on the border between the Earthworld and the Otherworld. The gray-shawled ones, those who had been sentenced to the rift by the Danann, undoubtedly had escaped the fires at the bottom of the dark and were either in the forest or out in the Earthworld—or both, he amended grimly. But the Nightshades worried him the most. Some of them had been the Fomorians, a race of demons, hideous and evil, who demanded two-thirds of the children of the Nemeds to sacrifice to their gods.

The Fomorians had been defeated by Lugh and the Nemeds, the warriors of the Tuatha De Danann. The Nemeds had lost so many numbers in battle that they slowly disappeared from the country.

The Dananns, however, drove the Fomorians into the Great Rift at the Second Battle of Moytura, where the Fomorians slowly slipped into shadow forms to do the bidding of the Grayshawls, whose bodies and souls had become so corrupted that they ceased to be human and now were only spirits, the strongest of Maliman's servants. They wore flowing gray hooded robes and carried deadly swords forged from molten steel, into which the poison of Rathtrees of Tanglewood Forest had been worked.

Cumac finished his bread and stood in one fluid motion. He reached over his shoulder and loosened Caladbolg in its scabbard and took a deep breath.

All journeys begin with the first step, he thought. And then all journeys flow into one, each road leading to another, each path linked to the first and to choice. To hesitate is useless—if one plans on choosing.

He stepped forward firmly, setting his feet on the path that wound into the mist and around the blackened trunks of poison Rathtrees that gleamed wetly. The forest closed quickly around him, as if it had been waiting for one foolish enough to venture within it. Fingers of mist touched his cheeks, leaving them clammy, and things rustled in the underbrush. Wings of shadow flapped at him. His senses straightened, seeking the danger that he knew was there, and the hackles on the back of his neck vibrated with intensity.

No sunlight slipped through the heavy moss and branches of the trees, only a stone-gray light that marked night from day, neither of which was filled with the sound of crickets or linnet wings. His eyes strained to see through the murk as he followed the path winding randomly through the forest. Nothing moved except black squirrels that ran up trees at his approach and watched him with red gleaming eyes. He heard nothing except the rustlings in the underbrush that seemed to become more ominous as he moved deeper into the forest. Tree branches loomed lower and at times, he was forced to push one away, feeling it vibrate in his hand as if it were alive, although no leaves clung to it.

Long, silver filaments began to appear dangling from the branches as he worked his way deeper into the forest. Occasionally when he would glance into the upper branches of the trees, he thought he saw red eyes watching him, but when he stopped and stared at them, trying to make them out, they disappeared.

Suddenly a coldness swept over him, and he smelled the sour stench of death. He frowned, his eyes sharp and watchful.

He rounded a bend and stopped. Standing before him was what appeared to be a broad-shouldered man, although he had the pointed ears of an elf. A scar ran down from the corner of one eye to his mouth, twisting his lips so they appeared to be set in a permanent sneer. His hair was red and long and greasy. He wore a gray jerkin and pants that seemed to be made from human skin. His wide black belt bristled with knives, and he gripped a short sword with a black blade in his right hand.

"You are trespassing," he said bluntly as Cumac stopped a swordlength from him.

"I am sorry," Cumac said. "I am just passing through. I mean no harm."

The other laughed, a cruel sound that grated on the ears like a file on rough iron. *Ark, ark, ark.*

"Passing through or staying is all the same to me. Like swamp gas. Just hangs in the air whether you're coming or going. There's a charge to be paid to Jack-in-Irons. That's me. And you?"

"My name is for myself," Cumac said, for to give one's name out to another in the Otherworld was to give him a hold over you.

Jack-in-Irons frowned at Cumac. "Too good to name yourself, eh? Makes no matter. Noname or Name, the tariff's the same."

"Wouldn't it be simpler to just let me pass? I promise not to tarry," Cumac answered.

"A fancy young sport like you can afford the tariff," Jack-in-Irons said, raising his sword menacingly. "Now, come across with the tariff, or I'll split you from throat to gizzard. Maybe I will anyway. Been a while since an outsider came through Tanglewood. My lovelies could use a meal of fresh meat."

"Your lovelies?" Cumac glanced around quickly, seeking a new threat.

Jack-in-Irons laughed. He gestured and suddenly four large rats, two feet high at the shoulder, appeared from the bushes at the sides of the path, baring long yellow teeth. Their eyes glowed with an yellow-orange light in the gloom. A loathing swept over Cumac. He reached over his shoulder and drew his sword. Jack-in-Irons's eyes narrowed.

"Not a wise move, young one," he said.

Suddenly he whistled and the rats jumped, springing for Cumac's throat. Cumac took two steps back, the blade blurring in his hand, and the rats lay twisting in their death throes on the ground in front of him as their heads bounced into the underbrush.

"My lovelies!" Jack-in-Irons shrieked. His eyes rolled in his head until the whites showed, and mad foam appeared at the corners of his mouth.

Jack-in-Irons leaped forward, his sword raised, but Cumac slipped to the side and brought his sword around in a Crescent Move, severing the head of Jack-in-Irons. Cumac stepped quickly away as black blood fountained from the neck stump. The head rolled twice down the path and came to rest, facing back toward him.

"A strong blow," the head spoke. Lips spread in a hideous grin. "You've well earned your passage. Go! But do not tarry so night comes upon you in the forest. The Truacs hunt at night, and their numbers are great. At the edge of the forest, before you enter the Great Rift, you will come upon Mandar's Well, He-Who-Makes-the-Waters in Tanglewood. Spend the night there and at first light, begin your journey through the Rift."

Cumac laughed and cleaned the blade of Caladbolg on Jack-in-Irons's jerkin before slipping it back in its sheath. "You are certainly bold enough without your head," he said.

At that, the body of Jack-in-Irons jerked and stood. Cumac watched with narrowed eyes as the body lurched forward, bent and retrieved the head, and set it on its shoulders. Cumac's hand raised again to his sword, but Jack-in-Irons stayed him by spreading his palms harmlessly.

"Now! Now!" he cried. "Enough is enough, and to do more would be to burn the biscuits! Go forward, but hasten your pace! Tanglewood is not a place to spend the night. Heed me well! You will come to a fork in the path. Take the right one! Remember, the right one!"

"You—" Cumac began, but Jack-in-Irons ignored him and stepped off the path into the trees and quickly disappeared, leaving only a breath like rotting meat where he had once stood.

Cumac hesitated, searching the underbrush with narrow eyes before turning once again onto the path. "Much trickery here!" he muttered, and quickened his pace.

The woods on either side became denser and the dried branches of dead hazelwood began to appear, weaving their way back into the forest. Somewhere a stream trickled, and although Cumac was immediately thirsty, he knew he should not drink any water that flowed through Tanglewood.

The gray light grew dimmer and dimmer, and he began to walk faster and faster. But every time he looked for the end of the forest as he rounded a bend in the path, the dark trees continued on to the next bend.

And then night fell quickly, as if a blanket had been thrown over the forest, and Cumac paused, eyes straining to see the path. At last, he was forced to halt.

"You may have been well-meaning, Jack-in-Irons," he said grimly. "But where is this fork of which you spoke? And where is the end of the forest?"

He moved cautiously to the side of the path, broke off branches from hazelwood, and carefully laid a fire. He took tinder and flint and steel from a pouch on his belt and struck sparks, igniting the tinder. He blew gently, but the hazelwood did not catch flame at first. Then, slowly, it began to burn with glowing embers, sending thick smoke upward.

Cumac coughed and moved back a little from the fire. "Better than nothing!" he muttered. "Although I don't know if a fire could be worse."

He drew his sword and wrapped his cloak around him, keeping his sword arm free, and settled down beside the fire. A drowsiness stole over him and before long, he slept, forgetting that he was to wait until he reached Mandar's Well before sleeping.

3

He came awake suddenly and fully, senses tensed. He lay still, trying to determine what had brought him out of his deep slumber. Slowly, he turned his head and searched the darkness around the small fire still glowing. He saw nothing but *felt* that something or someone was on the outskirts of the fire, waiting. His hand crept slowly down his side and closed on the hilt of his sword. He yawned and stretched, then leaped to his feet, clutching Caladbolg. The blade glowed blue and gray.

"Who's there?" he demanded. His eyes darted around the small clearing, seeking what his senses told him was there.

A low laugh came from the darkness at the edge of the clearing, then a woman stepped into the pale light of the fire. Her hair was long and blond and plaited in three braids. Her face had a narrow chin and a wide brow and two pitch-black eyebrows above eyes of bright blue sky. Her lips were as red as ripe strawberries and her teeth even and as white as pearls. Twin dimples appeared in her cheeks. She wore a loose hooded tunic, with an embroidered red design around the hem, that ended halfway down her thighs, golden tan and shapely and tapering into well-formed calves. Her feet were high-arched and covered with calf-high boots with gold buckles. Around her shoulders she wore a green cloak edged with white and red threads and held in place with a red-gold brooch shaped like a sunburst. Around her narrow waist was cinched a scarlet belt. A leather traveling bag hung from one hip. Over one shoulder a curved sword hung in its sheath, inlaid with seven rings of red gold. Over the other, a quiver of arrows, fletched with raven feathers. She carried a yew bow inlaid with silver crescents.

"Greetings, Cumac. Why do you tarry in Tanglewood Forest? Jack-in-Irons warned you about doing so. This is a place of spells and enchantments. The Merrows, ugly creatures who serve the Nightshades, live here, and when they appear to you, you will be enslaved by their enchanted beauty that hides their ugliness. They have mouths that drip foul gobbets of flesh and their breasts leak pus. Their legs are hairy and twisted. Their songs will lull you to sleep and then you will become their food," she said. "Or else," she added, "the Truacs will come upon you when least expected."

"You know me. But I do not know you," Cumac replied. His hands brought the sword to his side, held in readiness for the Disemboweling Blow. He watched her warily.

She laughed, and the notes of her laughter were as musical as the song of the lark.

"I am Fedelm of the Sidhe of Rath Cruachan," she said. "I have heard about your journey."

"One of the Danann. Then you have also heard about the need

for my journey," Cumac said. He slipped Caladbolg back into its sheath.

The smile slipped from Fedelm's face.

"I have that," she said soberly. "And for that, I come to help you."

"I don't need your help," Cumac said cautiously.

A tight smile played across her lips. "Can your two eyes watch front and back at once? Can your sword arm protect your front as well as your back? The way to Ce-Aehd's Sidhe in Connacht is long, and you are still in Tanglewood Forest. It will take you the better part of a fortnight to travel to the Sidhe. I know what Jack-in-Irons told you, and there is truth in what he said. But you must be wary of such truths, for truth may be twisted or left half told."

"By such as yourself?" Cumac asked.

"Yes. Perhaps," she said warningly. "But I can see that your way is a dangerous way and blood will have to be spilled before it is over."

Cumac's eyebrows shot up. "You have the *imbas forasnai,* the True Light of Foresight?"

She laughed and her eyes crinkled merrily. "I am from the Sidhe, the fairy-mound. I am of this world and the next. The trees and the grass, the wind and the waters. I know your mother."

The last startled him and he stared closely at her. "My mother? Did she send you to me?"

"Perhaps," Fedelm said. She grinned. "No woman tells all."

Then the smile slipped from her face.

"But this I *will* tell you: Maliman has been released as well."

Cumac shivered involuntarily. Maliman had nearly conquered the two worlds with his spells and enchantments before Nuada Silverhand defeated Maliman's forces with the rainbow sword Caladbolg, in the Final Battle against the Fomorians.

But the Final Battle had been very close.

Cumac sighed and ran his hand across his hair, smoothing it. Fedelm's eyes followed the movement, bright with interest. He caught her gaze and laughed and shrugged.

"All right," he said gaily. "Come with me. You will anyway, so we might as well travel together."

He slipped his sword into the sheath and bent and gathered his bag and hung it over a shoulder, leaving his sword arm free. She laughed and, turning, led the way down the path with a swinging, ground-gaining walk, her hair bouncing upon her shoulders with her movements.

4

Heat came down through the trees and left Cumac and Fedelm wet with perspiration as they made their way along the narrow path. Brambles threatened to snag their cloaks, and roots from the dark trees bulged up from the hard-packed earth at their approach, threatening to trip them up if they were careless. They were thirsty, but the only water they had encountered had been a small black pool that stank of sulphur and had tiny bones scattered around from the animals who had tried to drink from it.

By midday, rain began to fall, but it dripped through the heavy moss and they were afraid to catch it and drink it. The rain fell onto the ground and a foul, evil smell rose up from the dank earth.

Everywhere they went, they sensed eyes watching them, but although they looked vainly for them, turning rapidly in various directions at odd times, they could see nothing. Yet the feeling persisted as they made their way along the twisting path.

"I don't like this," Cumac said softly.

Fedelm glanced over her shoulder. "No one likes this. Since the Grayshawls and the Nightshades left the Great Rift, things are not what they once were. Things get worse when we near the Great Rift. The Grayshawls have released the Fomorians and hobgoblins. Whatever evil could be set upon the Earthworld is there, now. Thanks to Bricriu Poisontongue," she added harshly.

"Do we know where he is?" Cumac asked.

She shook her head. "No. There are many who will welcome him with the Chalice of Fire. Ulster's enemies. And they," she said ruefully, "number many. Your father made Ulster very wealthy before his death. Several kings have joined to push against Ulster's borders. Maeve has brought back her sons, the Maine—the seven sons of Maeve and Ailill: Fiedhlin, Cairbre, Eochaidh, Feargush, Sin, Ceat, and Daire—those, that is, who are left from when Maeve tried to take the Brown Bull of Cooley."

Cumac nodded. Although the cattle raid had taken place before his birth, he had heard the story many times while growing up.

The bulls, the Brown Bull of Cooley and the White Bull of Connacht, were magical bulls, whose coming was from a contest gone bad.

Once, there had been two pigkeepers, Rucht and Frucht, who began to argue about which one was the greatest spell-caster. Each began casting wicked spells upon the other's pigs. At last, their kings tired of their petty games and banned the pigkeepers from their courts. But by this time, Frucht and Rucht had built their argument into a seething hatred for each other. They turned themselves into birds of prey and continued fighting, but neither was able to harm the other. Then they turned themselves into carp, stags, warriors, phantoms, and dragons, constantly searching each other out and grimly fighting. Eventually, they turned into maggots. Rucht fell into a spring at Cooley where he was lapped up by a cow belonging to Daire, while Frucht fell into a Connacht spring and was lapped up by a cow belonging to Maeve. The two cows gave birth to bull calves, the Donn Cuailnge and Findbennach, each stalwart and strong, who tired of people teasing them as to which one had the greatest power. They were friends and would visit each other wherever the acorn mast was the best for the pigs.

One night in bed, Queen Maeve of Connacht quarreled with her husband, Ailill. They argued over who had the most wealth. Maeve taunted Ailill, saying he was a kept man. Ailill, who knew himself to be a *fer for ban thincur*—a man for all things—nonetheless challenged Maeve with a demonstration of each's wealth, and all were equal except for Ailill's magnificent white bull, Findbennach, which was the deciding factor in their measuring of possessions. Maeve became angry and stormed from the bedchamber, but her steward, Mac Roth, told Maeve of another equal to Ailill's white bull—the Brown Bull of Cooley. Maeve immediately dispatched Mac Roth to Cooley to borrow the Brown Bull for a year so the bull could sire a calf upon one of the heifers from her herd, promising Daire much gold until a calf was born.

Daire, the bull's owner, was agreeable to Maeve's proposal until Mac Roth and his party, drunk at the feast Daire held, revealed that had they not been allowed to borrow the bull, they would have taken it by force. Angry at this insult, Daire exiled them from Cooley without the bull. When they had returned home without the bull, Maeve decided to declare war on Cooley, a minor kingdom under Ulster's rule. But first, she commanded that the two who had caused Daire to refuse to loan her the Brown Bull have their lips sewn shut with waxed bowstrings and cast out of Cruachan to wander for the rest of their days.

Maeve and her army marched across Ulster's borders, and the men of Ulster immediately fell ill with labor pains, the result of

Macha's ancient curse. All, that is, except Cucullen, who was a youth and not from Ulster.

Alone, Cucullen defended Ulster, harassing Maeve's soldiers, swooping down again and again on their ranks, beheading any who strayed from the main force.

One by one, day after day, Cucullen defeated each champion, until eventually he faced Ferdia, his foster brother and friend. Cucullen pleaded with Ferdia to leave, but Ferdia refused, and for three days they fought. On the third day, Cucullen flew into a heedless killing rage and slew his friend.

Overcome by grief, Cucullen abandoned the fight. Maeve's army moved south with the stolen bull. The Ulstermen rallied and, with Cucullen in their ranks, gave chase, but they could not catch the Connachtmen and return with the Brown Bull. But the war between Ulster and Connacht had been devastating to the Connacht army, and although Connacht men had captured the prize, they lost the war for dominion over Ulster.

"Yes," Cumac said. "I remember the stories about my father and the other heroes of the Red Branch. But that was long ago."

Fedelm paused on the path and turned to face him. She shook her head.

"No, time does not mellow hatred. And Maeve has not forgotten the indignity of being defeated by Connor, her husband before Ailill."

Fedelm's eyes looked into the past, remembering. "I tried to warn her that attacking Ulster would be disastrous. But she would not listen. She sees truth as she wants it to be and tries to convince others that she is right with her friendly thighs and white breasts." She smiled wryly. "And she is successful with men. She intoxicates them with her beauty until they willingly follow her into the reign of Donn, the Death God. When we come to Cruachan, her fortress, you would do well to remember this, as I have no doubt that she will try to work her will upon you."

She glanced up at the canopy over their heads. "And now," she said, "if we hurry, I think we can be out of the forest by dark. There is a field before the Great Rift and the way to the Sidhe of Rath

Cruachan. I think it would be better if we entered the Earthworld there rather than at Ce-Aehd's Sidhe."

"My mother said—" he began, but Fedelm interrupted him.

"I know what your mother said," she said grimly. "But since that time, the Nightshades have taken the land around Ce-Aehd's Sidhe. Your mother warned you that this might happen. We would do better to enter at the Sidhe of Rath Cruachan. But," she cautioned, "we may find danger there as well. Still, there is more hope there than other Sidhes. That I know of," she amended. "I cannot know what has happened since I left to find you. It takes only a wink of time to weave a new thread into the fabric of the Earthworld."

She looked around carefully, then stiffened.

"What is it?" Cumac asked.

She drew a black-feathered arrow and nocked it. "Something, I think," she murmured. "I feel that which I should not feel here."

Cumac reached over his shoulder and drew Caladbolg. He stepped beside her, turning so he was facing away from her.

"What?" he whispered.

A low moaning came through the trees and seemed to sweep around them, pebbling the flesh of their arms.

"Nightshades!" Fedelm exclaimed softly. "We must hide!"

"Where?" Cumac asked. "There is no place."

"We shall have to leave the path," she answered. "Come!"

"But—" he started to argue, but Fedelm ignored him and stepped off the path, slipping through brambles, moving swiftly between the trees.

Hastily, he followed the path she was making.

The forest closed around them, drawing them into a clammy embrace. Deeper and deeper they ran, dodging gray moss curtains and spider filaments. The moaning seemed to follow them, but Fedelm ran grimly on, moving ever deeper into the forest.

And then the moaning faded, and she slowed and stopped when she came into a glade covered with black grass. She stood, breathing deeply, her breasts rising and falling with each breath, her forehead dotted with perspiration. Cumac paused and leaned on his sword as he drew in deep, ragged breaths.

"I think we have lost them," she said. She sighed and looked around. "But I don't know where we are, now."

"Out of the pan and into the fire," Cumac said, looking around nervously.

"Something like that," she said, biting her lip.

"What are we going to do now?"

She shrugged. "Rest here. It is too late to go bumbling our way farther through the trees. Best to wait until full light. Here, we can guard ourselves. Among the trees we can be surprised by whatever is there."

Cumac nodded and sheathed Caladbolg. He squatted on his heels and took a leather waterskin from around his neck and offered it to her.

"It is the last of our water," he warned.

She took a swallow and handed it back. He took two cautious swallows and firmly worked the wooden stopper back into the neck of the skin.

"We need a fire," she said. "Not just for warmth, but to light up the glade so we will know if something comes for us."

Cumac rose and started for a stand of brown bramble bushes at the edge of the clearing.

"Do not use the brambles," she cautioned as she saw his direction. "It is the month of Dumannios. Use the blackthorn."

He stopped and looked questioningly at her.

"The brambles will have been steeped in a foul sap. But the blackthorn will be dried wood," she said.

Obediently he stepped past the brambles and gathered dead branches of blackthorn and carried them back to the glade. Carefully he built a fire, and when flames danced around the clearing, lighting it, he took a loaf of pannin bread from his pouch, broke it in half, and handed a piece to Fedelm.

"What will we do at light?" he asked, munching the sweet bread.

"Let us wait for light to see," she answered. "Tonight, I will sleep the sleep of *imbas forasnai* for the gift of prophecy. Perhaps the answer will come to me."

5

A dull gray light awoke Cumac suddenly, senses alert, hand grasping the hilt of his sword. He glanced over at Fedelm and saw the woman from the Sidhe still wrapped in her cloak, asleep, her face composed but white, her hands folded upon her breast. He cursed and leaped to his feet, turning quickly around the small clearing where they had made camp.

"Fool!" he said angrily to himself. "Sleeping on guard like a boy tending sheep!"

A soft moaning came to him through the trees. He frowned, gripping the haft of his sword, and shook Fedelm awake.

Instantly she was on her feet, bow in hand, arrow nocked.

"What is it?" she whispered. Then she heard the moaning and frowned.

"I don't know," Cumac whispered. "But I do know that nothing good has come in this forest yet."

"I sense something beneath the sound," Fedelm said. "But what? What?"

She closed her eyes, concentrating, but a soothing calm came over her senses and she could not see into the shadows that lurked in her mind. She opened her eyes and shook her head, fighting the calm.

"I cannot see," she whispered to Cumac. "I am feeling drowsy and curtains are trying to slip over me."

"As me," he answered softly. She looked at him; he was fighting to keep his eyes open. "It is an enchanting song."

"Ignore the song!" Fedelm said, desperately trying to follow her own advice. "You must fight giving in to its melody."

Cumac shook himself and gripped the haft of his sword tightly until the tendons in his hand cracked from the strain. Slowly, the curtain of comfort slipped away from him. He turned slowly around the clearing and saw three shades slip through the trees to the clearing.

They were beautiful beyond description with flowing gowns of silver and gray. They smiled temptingly at him and Fedelm.

"I am Bedwine," said one, her voice husky yet sweet, as if soothed with honey.

"I am Phrysis," said another, singing the words to Cumac and Fedelm.

"I am Ioneis," said the third, her silver hair swirling around her.

They came closer and Cumac fought through the sweetness trying to overcome him and drew Caladbolg. The shapes stopped and smiled at him.

"You do not need that sword," Bedwine said.

"No. Come with us," Phrysis said. "And enjoy the pleasures that we can bring to you."

Cumac ignored them and thrust Caladbolg toward them.

"Show yourselves as you are!" he demanded.

"You threaten us?" hissed Ioneis. "You dare to threaten us?"

But then their shapes began to change into the ugliness hidden beneath the beauty. Their mouths dripped gobbets of flesh. Their breasts became dugs that leaked pus, and their legs became hairy and twisted.

"Merrows," Fedelm breathed. Quickly she sent an arrow into Bedwine, who shrieked with pain and went from them, howling into the darkness of the trees.

Two more arrows sped across the clearing, and Phrysis and Ioneis screamed and raced away on the heels of their sister.

Once again the clearing was empty. "Lucky," he muttered. "Very lucky."

A cold seemed suddenly to seep through his cloak and probe for his bones. He knelt and threw twigs on the glowing coals and blew gently until a small fire burned. He rubbed his hands over the flame, his eyes moving constantly over the clearing, still not satisfied that someone or *some thing* had not taken advantage of his lapse. But the black limbs of the trees and bushes hung silently, unmoving.

He glanced at Fedelm and saw her eyelids begin to flutter. He reached into his bag and removed two small loaves of pannin bread and munched on one. He handed her the second loaf and waited until she had bitten into it.

"Did you see anything in the *imbas forasnai*?" he asked.

She nodded soberly, her eyes large and dark, and replied in song:

The way through the Rift is grim at best.
Travel not to Ce-Aehd's Sidhe to be a guest
For Fomorians and Nightshades guard the way.
Pass to Cruachan Ai where Ailill and Queen Maeve
Are unwilling hosts to a Grayshawl whose deadly
Magic has woven a web around Cruachan's Sidhe!

"And?" Cumac asked, munching upon the bread that had suddenly became a mushy lump in his throat. "What should we do?"

She frowned and tugged gently upon her earlobe while she thought. At last she nodded and said, "If Ce-Aehd's Sidhe's is besieged, then I am certain that my own is as well. I do not think we should go through the Great Rift. If the Grayshawl and Fomorians and Nightshades have moved into Connacht, then it is certain that they are using the Rift to build an army to invade the Earthworld. We could get through—maybe. But I do not think the risk is worth trying."

She waved her hand toward the north.

"We must travel to the Sidhe of Hu Gadarn, the Keeper of the Wild, and try there."

"You think the way is clear?"

She shrugged. "It is the nearest one and closest to Emain Macha from the west. The Grayshawls will surely go to Connacht after they raise their army. Connacht has always been the enemy of Ulster, and although I am certain that Maeve will not be willing to place command of her armies under the Grayshawls, they will be certain to convince her that the time is ready for another war upon Ulster." She grinned. "And Maeve has always fumed at being thrown over by Connor for Mugain, the sensuous one. But Connor is not Ailill—he was not content to wait silently while Maeve took lovers by the dozens. I hear she needs thirty men a night to satisfy her. Or, one such as your father."

Cumac burst out laughing. "Well, then, I think our way is made clear. We go to Hu Gadarn's Sidhe and hope that he is willing to help us."

She glanced over her shoulder at the darkness of the forest. The trees looked a black wall, grim and forbidding. She shook her head. "The way will not be easy. We have no path. And we have little water and food left, I think."

Cumac nodded. "There will be water," he said.

"No. We will not drink water from Tanglewood. The waters would make us mad." She gave him a grim smile. "Nothing good comes out of Tanglewood. And we will have to watch carefully for hobgoblins and trolls, for they live in the darkest depths of the forest. But they are nothing compared to the Deag-dul, who come at night to drink the blood of the unwary. They are the most evil and difficult to kill. You must cut off their heads or send a hazelwood shaft through their hearts. And," she added, "I have a limited number of arrows and no way to make more from the twisted wood of this forest."

They finished their meager meal and rose, gathered their weapons, and moved cautiously into the dark forest at the north end of the clearing, carefully stepping around bushes and trees, their feet sinking into the rotting mulch. A great stench rose from the forest floor, and they drew the necks of their cloaks tightly over their mouths and noses, trying to keep from gagging.

They marched for what seemed hours, although they had no way of telling time beneath the thick branches of the trees. Bramble tried to snare their feet and cloaks, but they avoided the reaches of the stems and branches.

They happened upon a gurgling stream that appeared clear and clean, but Fedelm pointed where it turned black as jet fifteen feet farther where the waters ran through rotted bullrushes. They moved on, although the sound of the running water followed them and reminded them of their thirst.

Suddenly, Cumac pulled up short, raising his hand in warning.

"What is it?" Fedelm whispered.

"Something. I do not know what," Cumac said, drawing Caladbolg from its sheath. "But I feel whatever is there knows we are here and means us great harm."

Caladbolg's blade began to glow in rainbow colors. Cumac narrowed his eyes, trying to pierce the gloom, but the shadows seemed to dance and dart, and he could not be certain if they were real or only shadows. Then, he heard the sound of shuffling feet and stiffened as a hunchbacked creature stepped into view. His face was contorted as if it had been squeezed between two strong hands. His eyes gleamed yellow and large, and pointed teeth showed in the black maw of his mouth. His arms were heavily muscled and long, his legs bowed as if straining to carry the heavy weight of his torso. His skin was gray, and a doublet of gray fur hung around his waist. Heavy leather boots ended halfway up his shins. He carried an ax in one hand and a heavy sword in the other.

"Truacs!" Cumac shouted in warning as others, almost twins to the first, emerged from behind him: deadly creatures created the same time as hobgoblins, Truacs were drinkers of blood and feasted on hobgoblins and goblins when they wished.

Two shafts whistled past his ear and sank deeply into the necks of two Truacs, drawing bellows of rage from them before they toppled to the side, kicked twice, and died.

Another Truac leaped forward, swinging his ax at Cumac's head, but the youth danced nimbly out of the way and struck swiftly, Caladbolg singing through the air before it sliced cleanly through the Truac's neck. Black blood fountained from the stump as the Truac stood wavering before falling.

Other Truacs pressed forward. Cumac could smell the stench of their breath and the foul odor rising from their bodies. His blade danced and flickered in the dim light of the forest. Behind him, he became aware of Fedelm still shooting arrows into the Truacs. Then, the Truacs came too fast, howling their fury, and she was forced to draw her sword and stand next to Cumac's back, slashing and stabbing.

"Too many," she panted, swinging her sword and decapitating a Truac, whose place was taken immediately by another. "We have to get away. Somehow."

Cumac felt himself begin to shake. His head felt like an iron band was strapped around it. His muscles contorted and bulged. He opened his mouth and bellowed, the sound harsh and strident, freezing the Truacs in their tracks. Nervously, they began to back away, but Cumac pressed forward fiercely upon them, swinging Caladbolg with reckless abandon. Black blood spattered the trees and pooled upon the ground.

The Truacs turned and fled, racing into the depths of the forest. Cumac would have followed, but Fedelm shouted at him to wait.

He turned to her, his eyes glittering dangerously. A speck of foam dotted one corner of his lips. His neck muscles were corded.

"Cumac!" she said sharply. "Cumac!"

He drew a deep, shuddering breath. His shoulders slumped and a dizziness washed over him. He knelt on one knee, staring around at the carnage.

"What happened?" he asked thickly.

She shook her head. "You are your father's son. The Rage came upon you, the *riastradh*, the 'warp-spasm.' But," she said, "you come out of its grip faster than did your father."

"I feel weak," he said.

"Yes. That is the way of the Rage. We will have to rest for a while until your weakness passes."

She slipped her sword into its sheath and walked around the dead Truacs. Two were carrying leather waterbags. She raised one and took a cautious sip; the water was clean, although it carried the tang of the leather with it. She nodded in satisfaction.

"At least we have water again," she said, handing one of the bags to Cumac. "Apparently the Truacs don't like forest water either."

He took the waterbag gratefully and tipped it, drinking deeply.

"That's better," he said as he lowered the bag. He cupped his hand and poured a little water into it and splashed it on his face. He sighed and replaced the wooden stopper.

"What are the Truacs doing in Tanglewood?" he asked. "I know it is the home of hobgoblins and the sort, but there is no game here for them. Other than rats and spiders and such."

"The Truacs are eaters of flesh," she said. "Man flesh. Or," she reflected, "woman. They live on the outskirts of Tanglewood and attack travelers who try to skirt the forest instead of going through it. We must be near the end of the forest to have stumbled upon a band of them. But," she shrugged, "they may be wandering from one end of the forest to the other as we are. Tanglewood is more familiar to them than it is to us."

She glanced around them. "We could be near one of their gatherings. We should move away from here. If you are able."

He pushed himself to his feet and slowly stretched his neck, feeling the bones crack and pop.

"Yes, I'm ready," he said. He took another drink of water, then slung the waterbag over a shoulder. "Which way?"

She bit her lip, frowning. "I would think that we routed all of them. Let's try the way they came from. We may get lucky and find ourselves out of this darkness before long."

She settled the other waterbag over her shoulder and stepped forward, carefully avoiding the bodies of the Truacs, who lay in twisted heaps upon the ground.

Cumac took a deep breath and followed. Within minutes, the forest had swallowed them, and once again they were alone in the gloom.

But Fedelm was wrong. When dark fell, they still had not made their way from the forest and were forced to make camp once more in a tiny glade, the ground beaten flat from the tramping of many feet. She studied the ground and looked carefully around at the underbrush.

"If I didn't know better, I'd swear this was a fairy-ring," she said. "But no fairies would come to this place to dance and celebrate. Yet, something has been here and been here many times for the ground to be like this."

"Truacs? Trolls?" Cumac asked.

"I don't think so. But we can go no farther in the dark. We will have to make do here and wait for light. Such as it is," she amended.

"I'll get wood," Cumac said.

She frowned and shook her head. "No, I don't think we should make a fire. This place does not have a right feel to it. We do not want to bring anything to us with a flame."

"It will get cold," he warned.

"We have our cloaks," she said.

"At least, we have pannin bread," Cumac grunted, dropping his pack to the ground and kneeling beside it. He took out two leaf-wrapped loaves and handed one to Fedelm. "And water. Although I would like a mug of ale. And a roast of venison or pig. Pannin bread is beginning to wear on me."

"If wishes were horses beggars would ride," Fedelm said, shrugging. "Eat your bread and be grateful that you have that."

"You are beginning to sound like my mother," Cumac said sourly, taking a bite of bread, then softening it in his mouth with a drink of water.

Fedelm didn't answer but nibbled at her bread, watching him curiously as he ate. Despite his gift for battle and the breadth of his shoulders, he was still a youth in many ways. Brave to the point of recklessness. But, she reflected, that is brought on by the Rage.

"What are you staring at?" he asked.

She shook herself from her reverie. "Just thinking. This place has me worried."

"You think too much on what you do not know," he said, finishing his bread. He dusted the crumbs from his hands and took a long drink of water. "There is no sense worrying about what might happen."

"There's no sense in not being prepared for what *may* happen, either," she said dryly. "You sleep first. I'll take watch."

She wrapped herself in her cloak and settled to wait until the middle of the hours, when she would awaken Cumac for his turn. She did not feel sleepy, and she glanced frequently at the youth, his face softened by sleep. A fine jaw and high cheekbones had drawn her to him in the Otherworld long before he set out for the Earthworld. Many times she had thought to make the journey in the Otherworld to the eastern shore where Cumac lived, but each time she held back, uncertain about her feelings for him. Feelings that she had never experienced before that kept churning within her, causing her to drop into a restlessness that caused others in her Sidhe, who had learned how she was taken with Cumac, to tease her for her interest in him.

And what *is* your interest? she asked herself. None of the other youths had been able to match him in swordplay and in hurley—he had often played alone against thirty other youths and never been defeated. The strength in his hands was such that no one had been able to place his shoulders against the ground in wrestling—not even those gods who had tried him after he had defeated all others. Horses loved him and, she thought grimly, so did most of the women who saw him. And today, she had seen the Rage unleashed, so terrible that for a moment she had frozen in horror herself. But unlike his father, he had been able to pull himself from it alone.

She smiled as she remembered a story of the young Cucullen

when falling into the warp-spasm. The Red Branch knights had watched his approach to Emain Macha with fear that the youth would wreak havoc upon the fortress. Wily Connor remembered how shy the young man had been around the women of the fortress and ordered all of the women to strip themselves naked and go out to the young warrior.

At first, the women were reluctant to follow his order, but after they learned the warrior was Cucullen, they tore their clothes from their bodies and raced through the gate, laughing and calling to Cucullen. Mugain, the wife of Connor, the large-breasted woman with shapely thighs who brought lust into the hearts of all men, led the way. The women danced around him, and Cucullen immediately hid his face from them. The warriors of the Red Branch then seized him and plunged him into a vat of cold water to clear the battle-lust from him. The water had boiled and the vat burst from the great heat, as did the second vat. It was only with the third vat of cold water that Cucullen emerged from his rage, saw that he was naked with naked women, and tried to cover his naked frame, much to the amusement of all.

For a moment she wished that she could have been one of those women, then snapped away from such thoughts, scolding herself for letting her mind wander from her watch.

"You are lucky that no one or nothing came while you were woolgathering," she said severely to herself. "There is no time in Tanglewood Forest for thoughts to wander from the forest. Danger waits for such moments. You must remember this!"

She straightened and lowered her cloak a bit so the cold made her flesh pebble to remind her to keep watch. But the time passed without a worry, and soon it came time for her to wake Cumac.

"It is time," she said softly, shaking his shoulder.

He snapped awake, sharp and clear-eyed at once. Gracefully, he rose and walked around the clearing while she snugged herself within her cloak and stretched out upon the ground. In an instant, she was asleep, breathing deeply, and Cumac pulled his cloak around him and dropped cross-legged upon the ground, resting his sword over his thighs.

Uneasily, he let his eyes roam around the edges of the forest pressing in. Instinct told him that something was near, although he did not know what. His hand toyed with the hilt of his sword, senses straining to pierce the darkness.

MANY miles north of where Fedelm and Cumac traveled, Bricriu made his way through the clammy and cold Forest of Malden who had been cast from the Pantheon when he had tried to rape Boand of the waters. Bricriu carried the Bladhm Callis carefully wrapped in a leather pouch. From time to time he would touch the pouch, reassuring himself that the Chalice of Fire was still safe.

Wet branches slapped against his face as if they had minds of their own—and they might have, as the forest was an ancient one, where trees talked with each other in low murmurs that sounded like the susurrus of a soft wind.

Through our forest
Comes Bricriu Poisontongue
Without pausing to rest.
His breath rattles in his lungs
And he does not pause to ask
Our leave to be with us
So let us give him a hard task
As he tries to move between us.

He looked fearfully around him as the dark began to close in upon him, but still he refused to slacken his pace. Indeed, he increased his pace, hurrying forward, hoping to come to a house or even a woodsman's hut where he could rest assured that he would be safe for the night.

But he found nothing, and his legs were beginning to ache so fiercely that they trembled with the effort of pushing his way through the branches that seemed to close in around him on the path. Even the bushes seemed to have a life of their own, stiffening when he tried to pass around them.

At last he came to a small creek running through the woods and bent to take a long drink. When he had finished he lay back upon a bed of moss under a canopy made by elm branches.

Here. I will stay here. It is not a house or hut and I will be cold and miserable, but at least it is a place to rest and I am certain that no Sword-wanderers are near, he thought.

And he set about making himself comfortable the best that he could by gathering dead leaves and heaping them on the ground for a bed. He spread his cloak over the leaves so he could roll into it when he was ready to sleep. Then he gathered some dried branches and carefully built a small fire.

His eye fell upon the pouch that contained the Chalice of Fire. On impulse, he drew it from its pouch and looked at it, reading the legend engraved upon it.

I am made of Air, Fire, Land, and Sea
Only the Just may drink from Me.

Only the just, eh? he thought. Why not me? Why couldn't I drink from it before? Have I not taken justice upon the Red Branch for the way in which they have treated me? And does that not make me just?

He dunked the Chalice into the stream and held it aloft studying. A red glow began to surround it and Bricriu took heart in that, thinking that the Chalice was telling him that this time things would be different and to try and drink and gain immortality.

He lifted the Chalice to his lips and drank deeply, then gasped and dropped the Chalice to the ground as a terrible pain ran through his stomach. He bent, grabbing his stomach against the pain, and lifted his face to the sky. Then hot flame built in his stomach and raced up the trunk of his body and spewed into the sky, rising high, a blistering deep-red flame that seared the very dark around him.

He gasped and fell to the ground, curling himself into a ball as he held his hands against his belly, afraid that the flame would burn its way through. His heart began to pound like sledges splitting rock deep within a mountain, and Bricriu was certain his heart was going to burst through his chest. He screamed from the pain, and tears came to his eyes as he bawled like a hungry babe wanting to eat.

Again, the flame began to race up his trunk and spewed out through his mouth, scorching his cheeks and tongue. He cried out from the pain and began to flop around on the ground like a salmon taken from water.

At last, the flame simmered down, flickered, and went out, leaving Bricriu so weak that he couldn't raise his head.

The Chalice lay close to his head, and he reached out, taking the cup and turning it to read again the legend. *Only the Just may drink from Me.* Angrily, he threw the Chalice into the fire, yelling, "Then burn, damn you! Burn!"

For a moment, the Chalice lay on its side upon the hot coals. Then suddenly a pillar of fire thrust up into the sky, and flames of each rainbow color spread up alongside the pillar of fire. He cowered before it, drawing back as far as he could until his back was against the elm, but the fire grew hotter and hotter and sweat poured from him in greasy runnels, and he knew that he was melting before the Chalice's wrath.

Then, a roaring came through the forest and gathered around him like the hood of a cloak, smothering him, and he screamed and pressed his hands tightly against his ears, trying to press the pain away. His heart began hammering in his chest until he feared that it would break through his breast and burst.

Weakly, he pulled a stick to him and fished the Chalice out of the fire. Slowly, the colors flickered from the Chalice and died, and the roaring disappeared into the night while his heart slowed.

He touched the sides of the Chalice and found them quite cool. Angrily, he threw the Chalice from him toward his leather pouch and pressed his fingers hard against his temples. Slowly the pain eased, and he closed his eyes and fell into a weary sleep.

6

No sun, but a gray light slowly came over the forest to mark the rising of morning. Cumac rose stiff-legged from his place in the middle of the clearing and gently shook Fedelm by the shoulder.

Her eyes snapped open, watchful, then she stretched and yawned and leaped gracefully to her feet, shaking her hair free so it flowed over her shoulders. She took the piece of pannin bread Cumac handed her and washed it down with a long drink of water.

"I hope we can find food sometime today," Cumac said. "Pannin bread is beginning to grow hard upon me."

She smiled at him. "Better than nothing or have our flesh fill a pot for the Truacs."

Cumac sighed. She was right, but that still didn't keep him from wishing for a meal rich with meat and fish and ale.

"Do you have any idea where we are?" he asked.

"In Tanglewood," she answered.

"I know that," he said, annoyed. "But which way do we go?"

She shrugged. "One way or the other. But not south, and not back the way we came."

"Which way is south? I can't tell in this gloom. There is no sun."

"We use what we know. That way"—she pointed back along the direction they had come—"is north. I think," she amended. "But let us use it as north. That means to continue traveling the way we have been would be heading south. So let us go that way. Which should be west."

"And if that way isn't north?" Cumac asked, doubtful.

"If we come to the Great Rift, we will know we chose wrongly," she said. "And then, we'll have to make new plans."

"It's good that you are certain," Cumac said smartly.

She frowned. "Do you have a better plan? If so, speak!"

He shook his head. "It doesn't matter. One plan is as good as another at this time and place."

He slipped Caladbolg over one shoulder, the leather bag over the other.

"Let us see what lies ahead," he said.

He tried to make his words light, but a vague uneasiness made them sound artificial and false to his ears.

She grinned knowingly.

"I feel it too," she said softly. "But in Tanglewood, uncertainty may save your life by keeping you aware of what is around you. Here, we must always guard against laziness and feeling at ease. And the forest will try hard to make you feel this way. Tanglewood is an ancient forest. It has been here long before the Children of Danu came and was old before the Fomorians came.

"But there is much knowledge here if one could only understand the trees," she said thoughtfully. "There would be a price to pay for all of that, though, I think. And the price would be formidable."

"Then let us concentrate on not paying the price," Cumac said, impatient to be off. "Are you ready?"

She nodded and gathered her bow and quiver. "I'm ready. Who leads?"

"It's your plan," Cumac said. "You lead."

He didn't add that leading would be the easiest traveling. If danger came from the front, she would be aware of it immediately. Behind her, he would have to prepare for threats not only ahead but from where they had been.

Without a word, she led the way from the clearing and into the wood. The trees closed quickly, silently, behind them.

THE faint path disappeared and Fedelm stood, frowning at where the path had ended. Cumac stepped up beside her and shook his head, perplexed. Huge roots bulged up from the earth and blocked their way, but they could see beyond the roots, and no path emerged on the other side. The light seemed murkier here and the trees closer together than they had been hours before. Brambles, laced with spiderwebs, grew tightly alongside the path. The air had a moldy stench about it, and the silence bore down heavily upon them.

"We seem to have come to the end," Cumac said softly. The hackles rose on the back of his neck, and he glanced warily around them.

"Or the beginning of something," Fedelm said, equally soft. "And I don't like it. Can you feel it? Something rank and evil?"

Cumac nodded. "Yes. I can feel it. I've felt like something was following us for some time, getting closer and closer, but I haven't seen anything and thought I was simply being overcautious."

"There is no such thing as being overcautious," Fedelm answered. "There is only being wary."

"Then what is it?"

She shook her head and nibbled on her lower lip. "I don't know. Something. Of that, I am certain."

"Then we have no choice but to go on," Cumac said. "The path must continue on the other side of those roots and brambles." He pointed. "We'll have to chance it."

"I don't know," Fedelm said doubtfully. "It could well end here after drawing us deeper into the forest. The light is less here, almost as if dark was following us. I do not like it. We shall have to be careful when we move along. More careful than before."

A fetid stench as of rotting meat drifted to them. Cumac whirled around, Caladbolg leaping to his hand. Beside him, Fedelm nocked an arrow to her bow.

A black mist began to creep toward them, following the path.

"Hold!" Cumac snapped.

The mist ignored him and continued to creep closer.

Fedelm released the arrow, shooting into the middle of the mist.

A howl came from within and the mist folded back like a cape caught in the wind, revealing a scaled creature with baleful eyes.

"A Black Baggot," Fedelm gasped.

Cumac gritted his teeth. They lived in the ancient forests and preyed on strangers, eating their flesh raw. They approached their victims by weaving a black mist around themselves, but their breath smelled like rotted meat, and the wary person discovered their coming by smell. They were shape-shifters, but their normal appearance was frightening: tall, broad-shouldered, with large, muscular arms and legs. Their bodies were covered with black scales so hard that man-made weapons were useless against them. Their weapons were maces and swords forged in the Great Rift, the metal pitch-black.

Quickly, Fedelm nocked another arrow and sent the shaft toward the Baggot. The arrow sunk into the Baggot's neck. A bubbling scream rose from thick lips drawn back and away from teeth shaped like daggers.

Cumac leaped forward, swinging Caladbolg at the Baggot's knees. But the Baggot leaped back nimbly and swung its mace at Cumac's head. The youth dodged, and another arrow from Fedelm's bow lodged in the Baggot's chest.

The Baggot screamed again and, eyes blazing red with fury,

swung the mace again at Cumac. Cumac blocked the mace, feeling the jolt sweep up his arm and into his shoulder. He gritted his teeth, and his sword became a sweeping rainbow, flashing in the clearing. He stepped inside another swing of the mace, ducking and driving his sword through the hard scales and into the Baggot's stomach. The Baggot howled, and green blood gushed out of the wound as Cumac withdrew his sword.

A great black mist leaped from the Baggot, and Fedelm stepped forward, grabbing Cumac's cape and yanking him back and away from the mist. A red flame began to burn within the mist, and then the Baggot was gone.

Cumac leaned upon his sword, panting.

"A Black Baggot?" he asked.

Fedelm nodded grimly. "An ancient being. We were lucky to escape. No man-made weapons can harm it. The black mist engulfs and strangles its prey. There is no escaping it once it comes over you.

"And," she added, "where there's one, there's another or more. We'd better leave now."

"To where?" Cumac asked, straightening and pulling a swatch of dead grass to wipe Caladbolg's blade.

"Forward," Fedelm said. "The unknown is better than the known now. I don't like it, but to stay here is foolishness. More will come soon. At least we may be able to lose them in there." She pointed toward the forest at the end of the path.

"And ourselves," Cumac muttered. "Well, if we are going, then let's go. Talking about it here accomplishes nothing."

"Stay close," Fedelm warned. She started forward, but Cumac gripped her shoulder, staying her.

"My turn," he said firmly. "Let me lead into the unknown. You had the path."

Fedelm shrugged, resigned. "Stay as straight as you can," she said.

Cumac flashed her a smile, then turned and leaped nimbly over the massive roots blocking the way. Fedelm grinned and followed, and within moments, they had moved into the deep.

* * *

THE forest seems to be moving, Cumac thought, looking warily around him. He paused in the gray light that hung like a shawl around them and studied the trees. They *seemed* stationary, and no wind blew to bend their branches, but he knew that in Tanglewood to assume natural happenings was to delude oneself and invite disaster. He *felt* the trees were moving—subtly, but moving nonetheless, as if they were guiding his and Fedelm's path by blocking other choices they could make.

"What's wrong?" Fedelm asked softly, moving quietly up to him.

"I don't know," he answered. "Perhaps nothing. Then again—"

He left the rest unsaid and loosened Caladbolg in its scabbard. Carefully, he searched around them but saw nothing save the way between the closed trees that lay in front of him. The ground looked black and rich, made for planting, but the smell around them reminded him of rotting leaves and—smoke! he thought suddenly. Smoke! Like when leaves were burned in the fall and honeymead was being drawn from oak casts where it had been readying itself for Lughnasa, the celebration of the harvest.

He grimaced and shook away the thought. You thirst and think there is smoke because you thirst, he admonished himself. Nothing more. There is nothing here but death and more death, and you are life in this prison of death.

A soft breeze blew gently against his face, surprising him. Then, a voice came upon the breeze.

"Who comes?"

He glanced at Fedelm and saw that she too had heard the voice. Her eyes darted around warily and she frowned as she tried to find the source of the words.

"I am Cumac," he said aloud. "Son of Cucullen and grandson of Lugh Lamfada, the Long-Armed! Name yourself!"

A grim laugh followed his words.

"I am Dubh, the Bringer of Night."

Cumac took a firm grip on Caladbolg. Dubh was originally created for lovers and peace. Ragon, however, managed to send evil into night, forcing Dubh to change from a lover to a warrior as he fought to drive the evil out of the Otherworld.

"Show yourself!" Cumac demanded.

A soft gray light gathered in front of them and parted, showing a figure of a man dressed in black, his face pallid and solemn, dark eyes brooding. He carried a blackthorn bow with a quiver of blackthorn arrows slung over one shoulder. His arrows, Cumac recalled, had the power of denying those Dubh slew their journey to Teach Duinn and left them, instead, wandering aimlessly and helplessly through the darkness, suffering terrible pain from the arrow wound. Those slain would never enjoy light unless Maliman brought the wanderers out of the night.

"You are wondering where you are going and from whence you have come," Dubh said moodily. "This is not the way."

His face grew grimmer. "You must turn aside from the path you are creating and make your way toward the north. That way."

He pointed to their right.

"You are coming closer to the Great Rift and Maliman, who has been freed from the seal holding him and the Grayshawls and Nightshades captive. The Fomorians even now are making weapons for war with the help of the Grayshawls. Maliman is rebuilding Dun Asarlai, his fortress of sorcery northwest of the Mountains of Mourne. The fortress is impregnable as long as Maliman is on Earthworld. There, Maliman will gather his forces and the Nightshades and Grayshawls. The fortress is surrounded by walls three hundred feet high. Inside the fortress is the Keep where Maliman lived and worked his magic before he was sent into the Great Rift. A deep dry moat lined with iron lances surrounds the Keep. The only way to reach it is across the Criostal Droichead, the Crystal Bridge. From the Keep, he will sweep down over Ulster and Connacht and the rest of Erin before making his way across the seas. He will welcome Bricriu and the Bladhm Caillis."

"Then, if Maliman has not left the Great Rift as yet—"

"He has," Dubh said softly. "But there are others left behind who do his bidding. That is where the great forges of the Fomorians are. You cannot make your way through the Great Rift. No matter"—he held up his hand to stay Cumac's protests—"how strong you feel you are in your youth. You must go to Emain Macha to find Seanchan. But even that way will be difficult and dangerous. It will," he reflected, "be just as hard traveling from here to there. But for now, you must make your way north and from there, decide which way you go. I would suggest the Sidhe of Hu Gardan, the protector of travelers."

He gestured at the forest and grimaced.

"You can see the magic of Maliman here with the changing of Tanglewood. This was done in the First Battle, before you were born, and still Cernunnos, the horned god, has not been able to bring the forest back to the way it once was. The very ground has a black spell within it. It was here that the last battle between Seanchan and Morimag was fought. The ground could not withstand the evil unleashed that day. But, in time, perhaps. In time."

"Seanchan is at Emain Macha?" Fedelm asked.

Dubh shrugged. "Who knows? He comes and goes on a whim. But that is the place to start. He and Cathbad, Connor's Druid, are good friends. If Seanchan is not there, Cathbad will know where he is. Now, you must go."

Cumac gave a short laugh and pointed at the trees.

"Through there? Easier said than done. It seems the trees do not want us to travel any way but toward the Great Rift. If," he added, "the Great Rift lies ahead."

"Oh, it does," Dubh said. "And as for the trees, well, that much I *can* do. Go now."

He slowly disappeared back into the mist. Cumac turned toward Fedelm.

"What do you make of that?"

A groan came from the forest as if a great pain had been inflicted upon it, and slowly, grudgingly, the trees moved apart, great pieces of bark slipping from their trunks, to reveal a narrow path.

"We must hurry!" Fedelm said. "Quickly, before the trees fold back again. We must be near the edge of the forest."

7

Dubh did not prove false. By eventide they had passed the edge of Tanglewood Forest and were standing in a meadow of lush grass. A crystal spring bubbled through the center of the meadow. Bees buzzed from flower to flower and back to their hives in the middle of the meadow. Wrens and meadowlarks sang and small deer stood in the field, staring at Cumac and Fedelm as they emerged from the forest.

Gratefully, they dropped their packs next to

the spring, drank deeply, and fell back onto the grass, reveling in its freshness. Cumac took a deep breath, smelling honeysuckle and wild roses, and smiled. Bees buzzed around him, and he raised his head to study their flight.

"We made it," he said.

"We're a long way from being safe," she cautioned. "We are still on the edge of Tanglewood. And I feel the Great Rift is not far from here. We cannot relax our guard too much."

She nibbled her lip, frowning.

"I think it would be better if we moved away from here."

"Where?" Cumac asked, levering himself up on his elbows.

"To the high ground," she said, pointing at a craggy hill rising up at the edge of the meadow like a warty thumb. At the top stood the ruins of a keep that had been built for watchers. A narrow path snaked back and forth along the face of the hill. "Up there. If we are attacked, they can only come to us one at a time. We may be safe there."

Cumac heaved a deep sigh and wiggled his toes in his knee-high boots. It would have been good to take them off and soak his feet in the cool spring. But one look at the set of Fedelm's jaw told him to object would be fruitless. In the end, they would go to the top of the hill anyway, and to argue now would just be a waste of time.

"All right," he grumbled. "If we're going there, let's go. I don't fancy the climb after the light goes. And I'm hungry. Pannin bread wears thin on a man after a steady diet of it. We can shoot a deer and take it up."

"No," Fedelm said. "This is the Field of Cernunnos. We do not want to anger him. All that is here belongs to him."

"Surely he would not refuse us hospitality. The laws—"

"Mean nothing to him," she finished. "Yes, he *might* prove hospitable. Then again, he might not. Cernunnos does not tolerate visitors well: to take anything without his permission would be to invite disaster. And he *would* know," she added grimly. "Cernunnos always knows. He's a shape-shifter and might even be one of those deer. We shall have to be cautious. Try not to step on any of the flowers."

She rose and shouldered her pack and set off, stepping lithely around patches of flowers.

Cumac groaned and stood. He looked hungrily at the deer, then sighed and gathered his pack to follow her, stepping awkwardly around patches of flowers that seemed to spring up in his path. Here and there a clear path opened, only to close behind him after he had walked a few yards. Field roses and ground honeysuckle seemed to pop up at will when he least expected them and were followed by pink and blue and yellow buttercups and indigo and white daisies.

He lunged awkwardly from side to side, often in the middle of a step. He was panting from exertion by the time he reached the base of the hill where Fedelm waited patiently, tiny beads of perspiration dotting her forehead and below her lips. She grinned.

"The easiest part will be the climb," she said, pointing up.

He craned his head and followed the steep trail. In several places, the trail had crumbled, leaving gaps or narrow footing.

"I'm not a mountain goat," he complained, wiping the perspiration from his eyes with the sleeve of his tunic.

"Where is the man who can make the salmon-leap?" she teased. "Surely you can do that, son of Cucullen."

He made a rude noise and began climbing, leaping over the crumbled sections like a salmon swimming upstream against rapids..

She laughed and followed him, moving effortlessly up the trail to the top of the hill.

"Now," she said. "That wasn't so difficult, was it?"

He ignored her, turning slowly to view the surrounding area. Sunlight was beginning to fade, and the blood-red moon slipped up over the horizon. A bad omen, he thought. He could see the bleak and black Tanglewood. A cold gray light began to move over the land, making the distant hills look bleak and forbidding.

"This keep was old before the Fomorians came. It was old before the gods drank from the Chalice to become immortal. We should be safe here," Fedelm said, amending, "safer, at least."

"I don't like it," Cumac said with misgivings. "Yes, we have the advantage of anyone coming up the path, but they will have the advantage if we try to go down the path. We do not have enough food and water to last long. All anyone has to do is wait at the bottom of the path until we are forced to go down."

"Night is coming. Do you want to go down?" she challenged. "If so, we had better do it now rather than risk the path in the dark."

For a moment, Cumac almost said he did want to go down, but a quick study of her face and the grim set of her jaw made him hesitate and then shrug, sigh, and say, "Sticks and thorns! We'll stay here. But," he added, shaking his finger at her, "we leave at first light. We are not that far from the forest that we can afford to dawdle. And no fire."

"It will get cold up here in the night," she said. "And the fire can be hidden behind the stones of the tower."

Cumac turned and studied the crumbling keep. In places, the mortar still held strong and the stones still bore the marks of the sledges and chisels that had hewed the stones from a quarry far away. In places, the stones were three feet thick, and he wondered what sort of creatures had been able to drag such stones up the hill to this place. The inside of the tower had tumbled in, leaving only a few rooms, roofless now, usable. Lichens covered the stones, but nothing else grew on top of the hill.

"All right," he said grudgingly. "We shall have a fire. But a small one behind the rocks, where the light cannot be seen."

Fedelm crossed to the outer wall of one of the rooms and there, where three rocks had fallen to form a crude and small fireplace, she set a fire, using dry wood from the timbers that had once formed the inner scaffolding of the tower. The fire caught quickly, and soon a small blaze threw out warmth.

Cumac sat at the edge of the heat, reluctant to move closer and give Fedelm the satisfaction of realizing that he had wanted the fire as much as she and that he was glad that he had lost the argument.

Still, he could not shake a misgiving, a premonition that something was wrong or *would be* wrong soon, being drawn to the fire as sure as a ship is drawn to a beacon over a black sea. The night was filled with strange senses and all of them were nudging him, making him uneasy. Time and again he touched the haft of his sword, easing it back and forth in its sheath to make certain that it would slide smoothly free if he needed it. *When* he needed it, he thought.

Fedelm caught the small movements of his hand but kept from smiling. She sensed something too, but she felt secure on top of the hill and shook off her misgivings.

Then, Cumac frowned and rose, straining to see through the night. He gripped the haft of Caladbolg and began turning, searching for whatever had made him wary.

Suddenly, a cold wind came and on the wind a low moaning that raised the hackles on the back of his neck. Cumac slipped Caladbolg out of its sheath while Fedelm nocked a black-fletched arrow. They moved automatically to each other's side, each facing the opposite direction, slowly turning, looking for the source of the sound. Feldem glanced over the edge of the hill. Shadows moved slowly upward on the path.

"Nightshades!" she said, alarmed.

A dark fog slowly rolled toward the top of the hill. A foul smell of putrid meat settled over the top. Cumac swallowed heavily to keep from gagging and tried to breathe through his open mouth.

Fedelm loosed the arrow. It sped through the nearest Nightshade. A scream rose that made their flesh pebble and shiver. But the Nightshade continued climbing.

Fedelm drew another arrow and thrust it into the fire. The wooden shaft began to blaze. She drew it and sent it through the Nightshade. Instantly it burst into flame. A terrible scream rose, and the Nightshade leaped from the path, falling to the ground below, where it writhed and twisted in agony.

Quickly she fired flaming arrow after arrow, aiming for the other Nightshades. They turned and ran down the path, black cloaks flowing behind them. Her shoulders sagged from relief. She turned toward Cumac.

"I think—" The words caught in her mouth.

The fog opened and a black flame began to flicker and slowly form itself into a narrow face. The lips spread in a grimace that appeared to be an attempt at smiling, but no smile could lift the frozen features of the face. A phosphorous green burned deep in black eyes, and unkept long black hair snapped like tiny whips in the wind.

"Maliman!" Fedelm whispered.

Black lightning whipped out at her, but Cumac stepped in front of her, raising Caladbolg. The lightning glanced off the rainbow blade and cracked back toward the fog.

The face changed and the eyes stared murderously at the pair.

"*Bricriu!*" the voice hissed.

"Show yourself!" Cumac demanded. He felt Fedelm fit another arrow to her bow.

"*. . . want . . .*"

"Show yourself!"

The fog slowly began to gather around them. Cold spider filaments slid over their flesh.

Fedelm released her arrow, but it burst into flame before it went far and ashes fluttered to the ground.

"*. . . go back . . .*"

"Come and fight!" Cumac shouted.

The face began to fold itself within the fog. Then it disappeared, and the fog began to slip down the sides of the hill and stars appeared.

Cumac turned and frowned at Fedelm.

"What happened?" he asked.

She shook her head. "I do not know. I suspect that Maliman hasn't regained enough of his strength yet to do more than give warnings. But that will change. He will grow stronger in time, and his magic will become more and more powerful. We do not dare tarry. We must reach the Sidhe and Emain Macha as quickly as we can."

"But which way?" Cumac said. "If Maliman has the strength to show his face, then surely he will be able to watch us."

Her brow furrowed in thought. She began to gently rub the finish over her bow. A soft golden glow shone from the highly burnished surface, and within that surface, Cumac could see strange shapes and forms that the bow had slain.

"We are not far from Erewon, the city of the Ashelves," she said.

"At least we could rest a bit there. So far, Rowan Oak has not been invaded by Sword-wanderers or the Dark Forces. The Ashelves keep their forest safe."

"Will we be welcome there?" Cumac asked.

The Ashelves were famous for their fierce protection of Rowan Oak. Travelers through the forest had first to wait until they were granted permission by the elves before they could enter the forest. Even then, the twistings and turnings of the paths often left the unwary hopelessly lost in the depths of the forest. Erewon lay deep within the forest. Few outsiders were allowed in Erewon, and those who were could not leave, as the elves jealously guarded the secret paths to the city.

She shrugged. "No one knows if they will be welcomed or not. The Ashelves are unpredictable. But, I *think* that we will be welcome. They will know that the Great Rift has been opened and that Maliman is free. The Ashelves are not unknowing about what happens in the Otherworld. Or the Earthworld, for that matter."

"How far?"

"Two, maybe three days. We shall have to pass near Mount Niav, where we must be on our guard against warggads and sumaires."

Cumac shuddered and remembered the tales told by the seanachies who visited his mother's homeland. Stories of the sumaires who ripped the throats of their victims. They wore tunics made from thirty layers of human skin. They carried swords made from iron with a paralyzing poison worked into the blade.

The warggads were the worst of the werewolves, with hides so thick that they were vulnerable only through their eyes or when beheaded. Anyone wounded even with the slightest bite had to be treated immediately with wolfsbane.

"Warggads and sumaires? I thought werewolves and vampires had been slain by my grandfather Lugh."

"Believe me, they still exist," Fedelm said grimly, "the warggads and the vampire sumaires"—she shook her head—"who may come in your dreams or in man-shape. Their horses, the Memans, will feast on your flesh."

"At least we may be away from the Nightshades."

"Maybe," she said. "Maybe. Now, rest. I'll take first watch. It would be best if we are on our way at false morning."

Cumac didn't argue but laid his sword close at hand and rolled in his cloak as close to the fire as he could get. A great weariness fell over him and he slept.

SLEEP did not come to Bricriu. Sleep had not come to him for days as he doggedly made his way toward Cruachan Ai to claim the Laws of Hospitality from Maeve, which she would have to observe, even to protecting him against harm

He touched the Chalice in its leather bag, and a great bitterness fell upon him. He loathed the Chalice, had done so since he had tried to drink from it. It seemed a burden that grew heavier with each day, leaving him cramped and hump shouldered. He both hated and loved it, but now the hatred was rising more and more to the surface. Still, he could not bring himself to throw the Chalice away.

He swallowed against the bile rising from his stomach.

He took a tentative step onto a narrow path that led from the edge of the forest into a marsh. Stinking gas rose, burning the inside of his nose, and strange noises came from the water. He looked fearfully from side to side as the noises came closer, then retreated, then came closer again and again retreated.

He picked up his pace, hoping the gray clouds gathering overhead would not release a downpour of rain. But he didn't think there was much chance of that. Bad luck seemed to follow him every day. He couldn't remember ever having good luck since stealing the Chalice. If the truth were known, Bricriu had never had good luck, due to his poison tongue, but it seemed to him that things were much better before he had taken the Chalice that was beginning to hang like a rock around his neck.

Suddenly he saw a small hut built on stilts a short distance away. Smoke curled from a hole in the roof. He quickened his pace, hoping to find shelter where he could rest for a while.

He climbed a short ladder to gain the porch, then pounded on the door. He heard a shuffling from inside, then the door opened a crack and an eye peeped out from beneath a shock of filthy gray hair above a face covered with deep ruts.

"What do you want?" she rasped suspiciously.

"Shelter," Bricriu said.

"Go away. There is no shelter here for you."

Bricriu slid his foot between the door and jamb as the old hag started to close it. She opened it again to stared balefully at him.

"I claim the Law of Hospitality," Bricriu said darkly. "That you must give."

"If you know what's good for you, you won't," the old lady said. "But I can see you are a determined man and rain is coming—I can smell it—so come in. Come in."

She threw the door wide on its old leather hinges and turned to hobble back to a bench in front of the fire.

Bricriu entered and carefully closed the door behind him. He walked to the hut's only window and looked out.

Lightning blasted over the darkened sky, followed immediately by a crash of thunder that shook the little hut.

Bricriu flinched. That was a close one, he thought. It sounded as if it was just overhead.

Another jagged bolt of lightning jigged across the sky, and thunder again shook the hut. Bricriu shook his head, left the window, and crossed the wood floor of the hut to where the old lady sat. Another bench stood beside her and Bricriu took it, moving it a respectful distance from her. He sat, taking the pouch from around his neck and carefully setting it on the floor beside his bench.

The old lady glanced at it, then up at Bricriu. She smiled a toothless smile, her lips seeming to sink in.

"I am Bricriu," he said.

"Bricriu Poisontongue," the hag answered. "I know who you are. And I know what is in that pouch."

"How—" he began to ask, but she waved him away with a bony hand not far from being a skeleton's.

"Do you think that only a precious few know what you have done—or who comes after you?"

She turned and looked into the flames.

"The omens are not good for you. It would be better by far if you returned the Chalice to the Red Branch. If not, only evil days lie ahead for you."

"Who *are* you?" he demanded.

She cackled. "I am Bui, the Hag of Beare."

"And you can read fire?"

"I can."

"Then who is following me?"

"Cumac, son of Cucullen, and Fedelm of Rath Cruachan. But there will be others who will join them."

Bricriu slumped on his bench and stared at the fire, trying to read the flames and coals for himself, but he could not, and he raised his eyes to meet those of Bui.

"You can do nothing," she said, anticipating his next question. "That is why it would be better for you if you returned the Chalice to its rightful owners."

He shook his head and said, "How did you come to be here?"

"Ah, but that is a long story," she said.

"It seems we have the time," Bricriu said, "for I do not mean to go for a while."

She gave him a bitter smile and began a song:

The tide has ebbed from the sea
And old age has yellowed me.
Although I may grieve its coming,
It approaches its food joyfully.

I am Bui, the Hag of Beare.
A new smock I used to wear
But today my estate is so poor
I don't even have a used smock to wear.

It seems only riches you love.
There are no men that you love.

But when I lived young
It was men that we loved.

We loved the men whose plains
We rode over. Those plains
We loved, too. And the people
Boasted little who lived on the plains.

Today you make many claims
From people. But you do not give claims.
Though you do give little
You boast about receiving claims.

Swift chariots and steeds carried
The prizes away. A flood of them buried
Hatred then. A great blessing on the King
Who allowed them to be carried.

My bitter body seeks a home
Where the afterlife is known.
When The Dagda picks the time
Let him come and take me home.

Look: my arms! All bony and thin!
Once they practiced pleasant loving.
Many times they were placed
Around willing and happy kings.

But now, my bony arms
Are not worthy of my charms
And I do not any longer seek
Youths to favor with my charms.

Maidens are joyful when Beltaine
Comes their way. But grief deigns

To be my lover. I am miserable—
An old woman is not for Beltaine.

No honeyed words are for me.
My wedding will be the sea.
My hair is scant and gray,
I need a full veil to cover me.

I do not grieve if a veil of white
Covers me. I once wore white
And many other colors when
We drank ale to our delight.

I envy no old one—except the Plain
Of Feimen. I have worn the same
Old people's clothes for years.
Yellow crops are on Feimen's Plain.

The Stone of Kings in Feimen,
Rónán's Dwelling in Bregun,
Both are long from storms
But they are not old and withering.

The great sea's waves are loud
And raised high by winter's shroud.
Today I do not expect I will see
A nobleman or slave's son around.

I know where they go
Off Áth Alam's reeds they row.
The dwelling where they sleep
Is cold in winter's blow.

Alas! I will not sail on the sea
Of youth. My beauty has deserted me.

My great, wanton ways
Have long deserted me.

I rue the day when the sun
Demands I cover myself. The sun
Is no friend to age.
I recognize the old ways are done.

The youthful summers were lovely.
Even autumns were good to me.
And now the age of winter overwhelms
Everyone, including me.

I wasted my youth in the beginning
But I am satisfied with that beginning.
When I finally left my home to roam
A ways, it was not that new a beginning.

I am old indeed, and my day
Is spent as the acorns begin to decay.
After feasting with bright candles,
The oratory darkness is like bright day.

I once sat with kings drinking wine
And mead and although well we dined,
I now live on whey and water.
Poor porridge in place of good wine.

Now my ale is a little cup of whey
And I think that is The Dagda's way,
His will. I pray, however, that The Dagda
Does not make anger my way.

My cloak bears the stains of age—
Reason has left me. I am no sage.

My gray hair grows through my skin
Like when an ancient tree has aged.

Three floods near the ford of Ard Ruide:
A flood of warriors, a flood of steeds,
And a flood of swift greyhounds,
All owned by the sons of Lugaid.

What the wave of one flood brings
Is taken by its swift ebb that brings
Only emptiness to your hand.
I must live with what the flood brings.

The flood and the ebb and flow
Have become familiar to me. So
I now know how to recognize
The flood and the ebb and flow.

May my cellar's silence stay
A secret to the flood-wave.
In the dark I feel a hand
Coming upon me like day.

Had The Dagda known
What seeds He has sown
Beneath the house-pole in my cellar.
I have been liberal: I said "no" to none.

Oh, the pity! Man is the most base
Of all creatures. The case
Of the flood is reason enough.
He has not seen it, not a trace.

My flood has guarded well
That which was given me. I dwell

With what The Dagda,
Has left me. I am not sad where I dwell.

It is well for upon the great sea
I find an island that has come to me.
The food comes after the ebbing.
I expect no food later to come to me.

Today I cannot find a place
I can recognize. The space
Of time has taken that from me.
What was once flood ebbs from the place.

She fell silent, staring again into the fire while Bricriu squirmed uneasily upon the bench. He looked around the room with new eyes, registering things he had not seen before. Herbs, tied and dried, hung from the rafters. A kettle hung on an iron arm that could be swiveled. A long bench, its surface covered with pots and cups and knives and big meat forks, ran along one wall under the window. An oak table, its top white from many scrubbings, stood in the middle of the room with an oak bench on either side. Her bed, a simple wooded frame lashed together with rawhide, stood at the far end of the room with a handmade quilt worked in a curious design covering it.

Bui noticed him and again smiled her toothless smile. "You are wondering where you will sleep, Bricriu? Well, you may have my bed as I must be gone during the night to care for an old friend. Nevertheless, I shall return before dawn to fix you a meal."

"I thank you," Bricriu said, but his mouth pulled down at the corners as he thought of his luxurious bed back in his own fortress. Before, that is, Cucullen had lifted the corner of his fortress to let his wife, Emer, enter before the wives of Conall Cernach and Leogaire.

The thought of what had happened to him and his wife after his mischief-making came back to him, angered him so that a vein came out on his forehead, pulsating like a thick worm.

Bricriu had built a magnificent feast hall that rivaled that of the Red Branch, and he went to the Red Branch warriors to invite all to a celebration feast. But the warriors would not come until Bricriu promised that he would not be present to create strife among the men.

This chafed Bricriu. He exercised his mind as to how he should contrive to get the women to quarrel instead. It chanced that Fedelm Fresh-Heart came from the stronghold with fifty women in her train, in jovial mood. Bricriu observed her coming past him.

"Hail to you tonight, wife of Leogaire the Triumphant! Fedelm Fresh-Heart is no nickname for you with respect to your excellence of form and wisdom and of lineage. Connor, king of Ulster, is your father, Leogaire the Triumphant your husband; I should deem it but small honor to you that any of the Ulsterwomen should take precedence in entering the hall; only at your heel should all the Ulsterwomen tread. If you come first into the hall tonight, the sovereignty of queenship will you enjoy over all the ladies of Ulster forever."

At that, Fedelm took a joyous leap over three trenches from the hall.

Then came Lendabair, daughter of Eogan mac Durthacht, wife of Conall the Victorious.

Bricriu addressed her, saying, "Hail to you, Lendabair! For you that is no nickname; you are the darling and pet of all mankind on account of your splendor and luster. Your husband has surpassed all the heros of mankind in valor, and you distinguished yourself above the women of Ulster." Though great the deceit he applied in the case of Fedelm, he applied twice as much in the case of Lendabair.

Then Emer came out with a half hundred women in her train.. "Greeting and hail to Emer, daughter of Forgall Monach, wife of the best man in Erin! Emer of the Fair Hair is no nickname for you. Erin's kings and princes are jealous of you. As the sun surpasses the stars of heaven, so far do you outshine the women of the whole world in form and shape and lineage, in youth and beauty and elegance, in good name and wisdom and address."

Though great his deceit in the case of the other ladies, in that of Emer he used three times as much.

The three women thereupon went out until they met at a spot three ridges from the hall. None of them knew that Bricriu had incited them one against the other. They straightway returned to the hall. Even and easy and graceful their carriage on the first ridge; scarcely did one of them raise one foot before the other. But just before reaching the hall, their steps became shorter and quicker. On the ridge next to the house it was with difficulty each kept up with the other; so they raised their robes to the rounds of their hips to complete the attempt to go first into the hall. What Bricriu had said to each of them was that whoever entered first should be queen of the whole province. The noise of their running was like the noise of fifty chariots approaching. Confusion reigned and the warriors, thinking they were being attacked, seized their weapons and barred the door.

Then the women began to race around the hall, each crying to her husband to open the door that she could enter first and be given the same respect as what was due the greatest champion in all of Ulster.

Immediately Conall and Leogaire began to battle at the door, each trying to open it for his wife. Cucullen, however, brought the warp-spasm upon himself and lifted a corner of the hall so his wife, Emer, could slip beneath and be the first woman to enter the hall. When he dropped the hall, it sank three feet into the ground and threw Bricriu and his wife off the balcony where they had been watching the events with great glee. They landed in a soupy pile of horse dung and became the butt of jokes among the Ulstermen from that time on.

"Ah, I see you remember the past," Bui said. Her black eyes glinted with humor. "And that is why you stole the Bladhm Callis."

"How did you know that?" Bricriu demanded, his face flushed red with embarrassment.

"I have lived a long time," she answered. "I have heard many stories, and when I saw the backward look in your eyes, I knew you were thinking of what befell you. It was quite humorous, don't you think? You walking into the hall with dung sticking to your clothes and wet hay lying over your head? But, never mind."

She heaved herself to her feet, crossed to the counter, and brought back bread and cheese and a mug of ale and placed all upon the table.

"This should hold you until I return in the morning. I am sorry for the fare, but it is the best I can do on such short notice."

"It will suffice," Bricriu said grumpily. He sat at the table and began to cut the bread into slices for the cheese.

"Then I'll leave you on your own," she said. She gathered a shawl around her and stepped to the door, opened it, and walked out into the rain. Bricriu did not notice that the rain never touched her, so busy was he with the sparse meal.

At last, he finished and drained the ale. He went to the bed and sighed and stretched out upon it. The bed was not much, but it was better than sleeping outdoors, he thought drowsily. Then he fell asleep.

He awoke as the door opened and a beautiful woman walked in, her hair golden and her face blemish free. She was clothed all in white in a dress that fell from her neck to the tops of her feet. Her lips were ruby-red, and a high color was in her cheeks. Her eyes were blue and twinkled when they fell upon Bricriu, who stared speechless at her.

"Ah, the brave Bricriu!" she said. "Not many would have the courage to steal the Bladhm Callis from the Red Branch storeroom. Your name will soon be all over Earthworld."

"As well as it should," he said, sitting up. He smoothed his hair over his head with the palm of his hand. "And what is your name?"

She laughed. "Whatever you wish."

He frowned. "Well," he said slowly, "I have always liked the name Baine."

"Then Baine I am."

She walked over to stand beside his bed. She reached down and tousled his hair. He felt his mouth go dry.

"Wouldn't you like to give me a kiss?" she teased.

"I should like that very much," he said.

"Then kiss me," she said.

Rising, he took her by the shoulders, closed his eyes, and kissed her.

He sighed and drew back and opened his eyes to look down upon her. But it was Bui that he was holding, and she laughed at the look of revulsion in his eye as he drew away from her.

"I thank you for that, Bricriu," she said, cackling. "For now, I am free to leave this marsh and take my rightful place in Munster, where that witch punished me for the spell I placed around her husband in order to seduce him. She sent me here to languish until I could get one to give me a kiss. Alas, I am what you see. But illusion is everything, Bricriu. Or haven't you learned that yet?"

A gust of wind blew open the door, and in the twinkling of an eye, she was gone.

When he arose the next morning, there was bread and cheese and ale waiting for him on the table. But he had to spit five times to get the taste of her lips off his own.

8

Day came with frost covering the ground and light bouncing from the crystals clinging to the leaves of grass. Cumac yawned and stretched, arching his back to get the night kinks out. His nose felt clogged from the cold night air and his hands were stiff. He flexed them, working them until they were supple and came easily to the haft of his sword. He glanced over at Fedelm, still asleep. The long hair that framed her face had slipped out of the cloak she used as a blanket.

He turned hastily away and busied himself by rekindling the fire. He rubbed his hands over the tiny flames for a moment, then sighed and took two pieces of pannin bread from his pack. He looked back at Fedelm and saw her watching him.

"Good morning," he said. He leaned over and handed the piece of pannin bread to her. "I'm sorry it isn't more, but it's all that I have."

He nibbled unhappily upon his piece while she sniffed hers cautiously and took a tentative bite with even, white teeth. A crumb remained on her full lower lip. She licked it away. The gesture made her look vulnerable for a moment and made him feel that he had to protect her. He caught himself staring and averted his eyes so she would not see what he was thinking.

She laughed. He looked over. Her eyes danced with wicked lights.

"You do not hide your thoughts well, Cumac," she said teasingly.

His face flamed red, and he coughed on some crumbs of pannin. He reached for a leather skin of water, drinking deeply.

"We'd better get moving," he managed after the coughing attack eased. "If we get caught while we're in the open, we would be sorely pressed to get away."

She sobered, swallowed the last of the pannin bread, and nodded, rising.

"You're right," she said. She took a small piece of beeswax from a pouch around her waist and carefully waxed her bowstring. "Out there"—she nodded—"we'd be very vulnerable."

She laughed grimly. "Maliman may not be able to come himself. Yet. But if he can appear in spirit-form as he did last night, he is able to send others to do his work. Yes, we'd better leave."

Cumac nodded and rose, stamping out the fire. He slung Caladbolg over his shoulder, adjusting the sheath and the leather pack that hung by his left hip.

Fedelm was already on the path leading down from the hill. He hurried to catch up with her and together, they reached the bottom and began running over the field with long, easy strides. This time, flowers sprang up beside the path they'd chosen instead of as obstacles to avoid, as they had the day before. Cumac remarked on this, and Fedelm flashed him a grin.

"Cernunnos knows we are here," she said without breaking her stride. "He will guide us across his fields and meadows so we do not harm anything."

"Good," Cumac said, then muttered, "it would also be good if he could spare us some honey for our pannin bread."

Fedelm shook her head. "Do not make demands or requests. Cernunnos works his own will in his own time."

Cumac heaved a sigh and concentrated on matching her stride for stride.

They paused at noon for a breather in the middle of a plot of ling heather that seemed clipped short, but the flowers and buds grew just the same. The sun was high and heat waves danced across the meadow. The air was full of the scents of roses and lilacs, and nearby they could hear a spring bubbling merrily. Holly Blues and Purple Hairstreak butterflies, the fly-souls, flitted from flower to flower in search of a new mother. They were followed by Small Coppers. Between Cumac and Fedelm and Rowan Oak, the green trees visible now in the distance, a light mist was beginning to rise from a grassy knoll.

"We should be at the edge of the forest by gloaming," Fedelm said. "We can hide in the fringes while we wait for the Ashelves to come. But not too far," she warned. "There's no sense in inviting disaster."

Cumac tried to keep his eyes averted from the faint sheen of perspiration dotting her upper lip.

"The sooner the better," he grumbled. "I'm getting tired of traveling and getting nowhere and making detour after detour. It is time that we get to either Ulster or Connacht. Frankly, I don't care which at this point. Just get *somewhere*!"

He swatted irritably at bees and flies buzzing around his head. The sun was beginning to burn upon his back and wrap him in a flaming cloak. He splashed water on his face and wiped it with the edge of his cloak. He sighed and pushed his long hair back off his forehead.

A shimmering green column began to pulse toward them. Frowning, Cumac half-drew his sword, watching it with misgivings.

"What is that?" he asked.

Fedelm looked at him, then glanced in the direction of his attention. The green light came closer.

"Put up your sword," she said sharply. "And remain calm. That is Cernunnos."

Cumac slid the sword back into its sheath but kept his hand on the hilt, ready to draw it again, as he was apprehensive of what he did not know. Evil, he reflected silently, does not always come in black fog and mists. Often it is disguised as beauty.

The column halted in front of them and folded in upon itself. A tan young man as slim as a hazel sapling emerged, black-haired, with red lips and black eyes that glowed with tiny lights. He wore a helmet of stag antlers and was bare-chested with a green cape draped over his shoulders and green leather boots high on his calves. His pants were white, with curious green spiral designs worked into the leather. He looked at them curiously.

"What are you doing here?" he asked.

"We are on our way to Erewon and the Ashelves," Fedelm said. Her voice was respectful but her eyes held his. A tiny smile played on his lips.

"You are Fedelm of the Sidhe of Rath Cruachan. We have met before. During Lughnasa," he said. He glanced at Cumac. "But I do not know you."

"I am Cumac. Son of Cucullen and Fand. Grandson of Lugh," Cumac said.

Cernunnos laughed, the sound tinkling crystal. A golden light appeared over his head and the helmet disappeared into it. He stood hip-cocked in front of them.

"Well, Cumac, son of Cucullen and Fand and grandson of Lugh, I am pleased to meet with you," Cernunnos said.

Cumac looked at him suspiciously to see if he was being mocked. But Cernunnos's eyes stared back innocently into his own.

"And I you," Cumac said at last. He dropped his hand from the hilt of his sword.

Cernunnos looked critically at the pair and said, "It appears to me that you are in need of hospitality. Come with me."

"We need to reach Rowan Oak tonight," Cumac said.

Cernunnos turned patiently to him. "And why must you reach the land of the Ashelves by tonight?"

Cumac glanced at Fedelm. She smiled and said, "Maliman is loose from the Great Rift. We are being hunted by his subjects."

"Why?"

"Because Maliman wants the Chalice of Fire that was stolen from the Red Branch by Bricriu Poisontongue. We mean to find it and return it to Ulster," Cumac said. "We have been sorely pressed by the Dark Forces."

Cernunnos bit his lip, studying them. Then he said, "You will be safer with me for the night. You will not be able to reach Rowan Oak before nightfall. Hazelwood is not far. Come and rest. You will be guarded," he added as Cumac started to object.

"We thank you and accept your hospitality," Fedelm said formally. "It will be good to rest."

Cernunnos nodded. "Then it shall be so. Come."

The flowers and grasses waved aside as they followed him across the meadow to a thick stand of wood where the air seemed thicker and nearly impenetrable. A sylvan stream wound through the trees and formed a small pool where trout jumped after shad flies. Two deer, a buck and a doe, lifted their heads from the water to stare curiously at the party's approach. Cernunnos hummed softly, and they dropped their heads to drink again, satisfied that no harm was coming.

The air parted as Cernunnos waved his hand negligently. He stepped into the woods with Fedelm and Cumac hard upon his heels, fearful that the opening would close behind them.

Immediately, the cool shadows beneath the trees slipped over them, and they sighed in relief. A soft fluttering whispered through the branches. In front of them, a gigantic oak, easily five wine barrels around, stood, its limbs and many-fingered hands reaching toward the sky. The trunk was deeply fissured and the ground around the tree heavy with a carpet of old leaves that lent a tannic odor to the air. Cumac looked wistfully at the carpet.

"Can we rest a moment?" he asked.

Cernunnos shook his head. "You don't want to rest beneath the Guardian. No one—not even an animal—who knows about him dares that. He is not bad, but very protective of this place. The last one who rested here did not awaken."

Cumac looked closely at the oak. Now, he could see the fissures pulsing gently, ready to swallow any who came too close. The limbs seemed to quiver in anticipation, and two thick knots midway up its trunk seemed to blink. Cumac had the feeling that the Guardian was watching him suspiciously. Fedelm tugged on his arm, and he moved thankfully away from the apprehension prickling at the back of his neck.

A sound came as of a rising wind, spreading through the branches of the oak. Eerie, as if someone had dropped a stone through the air and caused ripples of anger to run out to embrace them. Fedelm moved closer to Cumac and took a new grip upon her bow, while Cumac lifted his hand to Caladbolg. Cernunnos caught their movements and smiled.

"You are safe here. The Guardian is letting others know that we have visitors," Cernunnos said. "But don't worry. The Guardian will not harm you as long as you stay a respectful distance from him. And as for Maliman, he has never been able to come into these woods or send others to do his work for him. These woods are old, and the enchantments guarding them came from the beginning of time. The first enchantment was by Tuan Mac Cairill. Do you know of him?"

Without waiting for an answer, Cernunnos began to recite Tuan's narrative:

I am Tuan
I am legend
I am memory turned myth.

"I am the storyteller. Warriors and young boys creep away from the hearths of wine halls to hear me. Greedy for tales of honor and history, they watch my lips with bright eyes, for I give them what is more precious than gold; treasure unlocked from my heart.

"My words burn like flame in the darkness. I speak and hearts beat high, swords warm to the hand; under my spell boys become men.

"But I know both the pain as well as the brightness of fire. I am the storyteller who cannot find rest. The peace of death will never be mine. I am condemned to watch and to speak; my hand reaches in vain for the warrior's sword.

"Once I, Tuan, was a man, the chieftain of a great race, the Cesair. My warriors sat on wolf skins. They raised golden chalices to me brimming with wine. Neither evil nor harm dared cross the threshold where I sat, my throne studded with jewels, inlaid with ivory.

"But the gods envy the happiness of men. Flood and sword combined to destroy my people. Now the wine hall stands empty, ruined; doorway and roof gape wide to receive the beasts of the earth and the birds of the air. It was ordained that I alone should be saved to bear witness to my people's fate. I watched helpless while the fair land of Èireann was ravaged by the scavengers and foes. The golden cities I once loved lie fathoms deep beneath gray seas.

"For many years I wandered as a man, seeking shelter in caves and the depths of the forest. But when at last the noble race of Nemed came to reclaim their homeland I was barred from greeting them as either chieftain or warrior. Another fate was mine: to watch unseen, keeping the secrets of time close in heart and brain. The gods had singled me out for a strange fate, unfamiliar pains and pleasures, for as the years passed, they bound me within the bodies of beast and bird so that I might watch and keep the history of Èireann, unnoticed by men.

"The first transformation came upon me unaware. I had grown old as a man. The years had left my body naked and weak; my joints ached and my hair fell gray and matted over my bowed shoulders. One day a great weariness came upon me. I sought shelter in my cave, certain that death had claimed me. For many days and nights I slept. Then at last I awoke to the sun. My limbs felt strong and free. My heart leaped up within me for I had been reborn as Tuan, the great-horned stag, king of the deer herds of Èireann. The green hills were mine, the valleys, the forests, and the streams.

"As I ran free across the heather-covered plains, the children of

Nemed were driven from their homeland. Only I remained, grown old as a stag, their story locked in my heart. Then the great heaviness of change again weighed me down. Again I sought shelter in my cave. Wolves eager for my blood and sinewy flesh howled to the moon. But I slept, floating loose in dream-time. Through the heaviness of sleep I felt myself grow young again. When the low rays of sunrise touched me I awoke.

"The wolves still sniffed about the entrance to my cave. But now I was young and strong, fit to face them. I, Tuan, with joyful heart, thrust my sharp tusks out of my lair, and the wolves fled yelping like frightened dogs. I was fresh, lusty with life. I had been born again, a black boar bristling with power, thirsty for blood. Now I was a king of herds. My back was sharp with dark bristles; my teeth and tusks were ready to cut and kill. All creatures feared me.

"But while I had lain locked in dreams a new race of men had come to disturb the silence of mountain and valley. They were the Fir Bolg, and they belonged to the family of Nemed. These I did not chase, and when they chased me I fled, for their blood was mine also. The Fir Bolg divided the island into five provinces and proclaimed the title Ard-ri, that is High King, for the first time in Èireann.

"As I roamed the purple hills I would often leave my herd, gaze across to the High King's hall, and remember with sadness the time when I also had sat in council, with warriors at my feet and the bright eyes of women gazing upon me.

"Once again the ache of change drove me back to my lonely cave in Ulster. After three days fasting, another death floated me beyond dream-time. Nights circled from summer into winter until one morning I woke and soared high into the clear sky.

I was reborn
I was lord of the heavens
I was Tuan, the great sea eagle.

"I, who had been king among the heather and scented woodlands, became lord of the heavens. From the highest mountain I could see the field mouse gathering wheat husks. Nothing escaped my sharp eye.

"Motionless, feathering the air, riding the wind, I watched the children of Nemed return to Èireann. Now known as the Tuatha De Danann, they sailed down over the mountains in a magic fleet of skyriding ships, led by Nuada, their king until they came to rest among the Red Hills of Rein.

"Rather than fight their own flesh and blood the Danann offered to share the island with the tribes of the Fir Bolg, but on the advice of his elders Eochaidh, their High King, refused, and the battle lines were drawn up.

"I, Tuan the eagle, watched that fratricidal struggle; that terrible slaughter of kinsmen known as the First Battle of Moytura. I saw the same green plain drenched in blood across which I had roamed, as a stag and boar. There I saw for the last time the Fir Bolg in their fullness and their pride, in their beauty and their youth, ranged against the glittering armies of the Tuatha De Danann. The battle was fierce and ebbed and flowed like waves on a sea of fortune and price.

"The circles of my eyes were rimmed with bitter tears as I watched that dreadful carnage of kinsmen, for all who fought were bound by a common bond, the blood of Nemed the Great. The battle raged for many days; death cut down the flower of the youth on both sides.

"At last the Tuatha De Danann took the sovereignty of Èireann from the Fir Bolg and their allies. But in that First Battle of Moytura, Nuada, King of the Dananns, had his hand struck off, and from that loss there came sorrow and trouble to his people, for it was a law with the Danann that no man imperfect in form could be king. So it happened that Nuada, who had led his people to victory, had to abdicate his throne and hand the royal crown over to the elders of his race.

"I, Tuan the sea eagle, wept secretly with Nuada over the loss of his crown, for he was a noble king and a just ruler who had won back the land of Èireann for his people. His mutilation and his loss were the result of his bravery in battle. For he was a great warrior, skilled and courageous and as one with his god, the Sun.

"When the noise of battle and the wailing of women had faded into silence, when the earth had soaked up the blood, when the plain of Moytura had become a sad spirit-haunted place marked by pillars and cairns, I, Tuan, still sailed high above it. I knew that that same force of history that governed the fortunes of men had made me the winged bearer of myth. I knew that the pattern of change is never completed until the world's end. Still I would have to bear the burden of man's triumph and grief.

I am Tuan
I am legend
I am memory turned myth.
I have lived through the ages
In the shape of man, beast and bird
Mute witness to great events,
Guardian of past deeds.

"It is a good song," Cumac said politely, although he thought it too long for the moment.

Cernunnos walked silently for a few steps, then said, "Tuan's enchantment is the oldest, and because it is the oldest and made long before Ragon's fall and Maliman's coming, it cannot be broken. Of course," he added, "Maliman would have to get through the other enchantments that were laid on top of Tuan's before he could try and break the spell. Ah, here we are."

They stepped out of the woods into a large glade that had a wide sweep of grass flowing away from them. The stream seemed merrier as it bubbled over smooth rocks and across gravel that sparkled with chunks of mica. The sun slanted into the trees behind them, and great shadows from the trees began to slip around the edge of the glade.

A path of crushed shells wound across the glade and around what appeared to be planned flowerbeds—periwinkles, ground roses, old man's beard, wood sorrel, and yellow pimpernel—to a limestone house covered with mistletoe and honeysuckle. Lights twinkled merrily from the windows, and suddenly a golden beam came out of the open door, bidding them welcome. A beautiful woman with long, flowing blond hair rippling down to her shoulders and cornflower-blue eyes stepped onto the threshold and waved at them. She wore an emerald-green dress that fell down to her dainty white feet and was held close around her tiny waist with a golden belt. The neckline of her dress had tiny flowers embroidered in gold, and in her left hand, she carried a sprig of holly with bright red berries.

"Ah, Creide!" Cernunnos said with a pleased smile. He turned to Fedelm and Cumac. "It has been a long time since Creide last visited. Hello!" he shouted, waving his arm overhead in reply. "Welcome our guests!"

They hurried forward, their weariness falling from them.

"You are most welcome," Creide said warmly. Her red lips curved into a wide smile while her eyes crinkled at the corners. She glanced at Cernunnos. "I gathered some honeycomb and acorns this morning and baked bread to spread the honey upon. I churned fresh butter too." She looked back at Fedelm and Cumac. "There is enough for all. And wine from rosehips."

"A feast!" Cernunnos said with relish. He beamed at Creide. "I have missed you!"

"And I you," she said softly.

She stood on tiptoes and kissed him gently on his cheek.

"Well, then!" she said. "Come in! Come in! Don't be standing outside when there's a warm fire inside and good mead waiting before dinner!"

Obediently, Fedelm and Cumac stepped over the threshold. A golden light settled over them.

They took a deep breath and stared around. They stood in a large and airy room filled with lamps, and tiny Pillywiggin fairies flitted around, busily setting fragrant flowers on the many shelves. Cumac and Fedelm knew that the Pillywiggins brought beauty and pleasure to man and to other fairies. They did not like to see the destruction of plants, and they sometimes killed a human who did not ask permission to pick flowers. They were extremely beautiful and wore light muslin, flower petals, and tight-fitting jerkins made from velverette.

A long table of dark burnished wood occupied the center of the room before a fire dancing in a large fireplace. Many candles, burning brightly, stood in wooden candlesticks. Creide moved around the room busily setting out wooden plates and cups, a loaf of freshly baked bread, the golden crust still shiny with butter, and the honey and acorn spread that glistened invitingly in its bowl. Periwinkles seemed to appear and disappear after each of her steps.

Cumac's mouth watered as he watched her fill mugs with mead and motioned for them to take a seat by the fire. She took a poker from the fire and plunged it into each mug before handing it to them. A loud hiss and steam arose from the mugs, along with the scent of cinnamon and nutmeg and other spices.

"We'll eat in a few minutes," Creide said brightly. "First, relax and enjoy yourselves while we shut out the night." She gestured at the Pillywiggins and looked significantly at Cernunnos. "Maliman's people have been seen around the edges of the wood."

Instantly Cernunnos's face sobered and set in hard lines. His eyes tightened bleakly. A chill entered the room, and Cumac and Fedelm shivered and looked warily at each other.

"This is more serious than I thought. His strength is fast growing. Tuan's enchantment is still holding?"

She nodded. "Yes. But bending. I've sent the Old Ones to guard the boundary."

"The Old Ones?" Cumac asked. He tasted the mead and felt a soothing warmth rush through his body.

"Harwraiths," Cernunnos said. "Those who were spirits before Tuan called them back to being. They are friends, but do not cross them, for they make the most terrible enemies. Your sword will do no good against them. Barach is their leader, and he is so fierce-looking that his enemies stand frozen in terror when they see him."

Cernunnos turned back to Creide. "They are keeping to the boundaries? They are not attacking?"

She shrugged. "If some of the Nightshades come too close, the

Harwraiths send a band out to meet them. The same with Black Baggots. But the Harwraiths keep far enough behind that the wood will remain safe."

Cernunnos chewed on his lower lip for a moment, then said, "It is worse than I imagined. Maliman's power is greatly increased if he threatens Hazelwood. And I am certain he wants Hazelwood. Hazelwood contains powerful magic. But, as long as Tuan's spell holds, we are safe. The Old Ones will also fight to keep us and the woods safe. Although," he added, "some of the Nightshades might be able to slip through."

Fedelm and Cumac exchanged looks, then Fedelm spoke.

"It appears Ce-Aehd's Sidhe may be closely guarded. We must make our way to Rowan Oak as quickly as possible. From there, we should be able to travel to Emain Macha through the Sidhe of Hu Gadarn. Unless Maliman has managed to corrupt the entrance."

Cernunnos shrugged. "I cannot tell you that. But I think not. He may have gone around into the Mountains of Mourne to rebuild his fortress, Dun Asarlai. He must first have a place in Earthworld from where he can work his evil. *But,*" he emphasized, "I would not tarry long in any place. The key to conquering Earthworld is to control the Sidhes, so the armies from the Otherworld cannot come to help fight Maliman's Dark Forces. Hu Gadarn's Sidhe is a strong one, but I do not know if it will be able to keep the portal open into Earthworld if Maliman attacks. He may close it as a precaution."

"Do you think Maliman is in Earthworld?" Fedelm asked.

"A part of him is. Of this, I am certain. He has managed to send the Grayshawls, the Fomorians, and the Nightshades out. Some of the Sword-wanderers will join them. The Grayshawls are undoubtedly preparing the way for him."

"Some have been seen in the Mountains of Mourne," Creide said. "They are at Dun Asarlai. They have already repaired the walls and are repairing the Keep. I have seen this mirrored in the waters of Sylvan Pool, where the past is revealed and sometimes the present and future."

"We'd better travel fast," Cumac said.

"We *have* been traveling fast," Fedelm said pointedly.

"We'd better travel faster, then," Cumac said. "Before all the Sidhes' portals are closed." He glanced at Cernunnos, who nodded.

"Yes. I did not expect this," he said. "Although you are welcome in my house and are under my protection, it would be best if you left early in the morning. I will take you as far as I can to Erewon. At least, I can take you to Rowan Oak and the Ashelves. If we leave at false light, we should be at Rowan Oak by the gloaming before Maliman knows. From there, Iain, the leader of the Ashelves, will protect you. Not even Maliman will be ready to make war upon the Ashelves. And Iain respects the ancient covenants made between the Tuatha and the Ashelves. So let us eat, and rest."

"You will be safe in the Great House with Iain," Creide said. "He is the great king of the Ashelves. And now," she added firmly, "you must rest for your journey."

Obediently, Cumac and Fedelm joined Cernunnos and Creide at the table. Famished, they ate until their bellies threatened to bulge, then took to their beds and slept soundly for the first time since meeting in Tanglewood Forest.

Pillywiggin fairies darted hither and thither, their lacy wings fluttering like gossamer as they dropped apple blossoms upon Cumac and Fedelm, lulling them into a deep and restful sleep.

Cumac and Fedelm lay together in a dream. Gray light surrounded them, and they looked up and saw the young moon rising over the woods, turning cottonwood leaves silver. The moon seemed to hang over them, bathing them in soft white light. From close by they could smell honeysuckle and roses and red clover and wisteria. Slowly, Cumac and Fedelm felt a lanquid peace slip over them. Then, a tall man dressed in flowing white robes appeared in front of them. Light reflected from his silver hair in a soft halo. He smiled at them, and they stood.

"Who are you?" Cumac asked.

"I am Barach," the man said gently. "It is good that you are together, but you must not stay long in this dream. There is danger around, and although the wood is safe, Dreamworld is not."

A strong wind began to blow, and the smile slipped from Barach's face.

"You must go! Go now!" he said urgently.

Then on the wind-road, Cumac heard the beat of hooves galloping toward them.

"The Nightshades," Fedelm breathed.

Cumac reached for Caladbolg, but the sword was not with him, and for the first time, he saw that Fedelm also was unarmed.

A foreboding came over him, and his spirits sank. Fedelm stepped in closer to him, and he smelled the warmth of her skin like wild thyme.

An orange-red fire began to lick away from Barach, rising up in the night and spreading like a thick cloud. The moon turned blood-red.

"Run!" Barach commanded urgently.

Cumac took Fedelm's hand and, turning, began running for the cover of the trees. The sound of hooves came closer and closer. Then, a stench began to creep over them.

"Faster!" Cumac said desperately.

Silently, Fedelm increased her pace.

Then, they were in the cover of thick oak trees that draped their branches protectively over them. Fedelm and Cumac turned and looked back at Barach standing commandingly in the center of the clearing. The Nightshades rode over the tops of the trees. Barach raised his hand, and a flaming red bolt flew away into their midst. A screech of pain came from the Nightshades. Then they were gone, and Cumac and Fedelm sank thankfully to the earth. They looked at each other silently.

"In Dreamworld you are very vulnerable," Barach said. "In dreams other than your own, changes may be made for the unwary. That is why you had no weapons. The Nightshades were able to enter your dreams and remake them. You must *always* be aware of everything—even when you are in Dreamworld. Rarely will you find yourself in a place where magic is woven so tightly that you are no longer vulnerable in your dreams. And that is how the Nightshades made you vulnerable to attack. Magic webs around a force can only provide safety when you are awake. Do you understand?"

"Are we dreaming now?" Fedelm asked.

"Yes. And we were lucky—this time. The Nightshades—or perhaps the Grayshawls—failed to weave a spell around your dream, holding you tightly in your dream so there would be no escape. I do not think they will make that mistake again. But I will provide you with a Dream Guardian who will come into your dreams and watch over you while you sleep. Now, awake! You have slept long enough!"

Cumac awoke and glanced over at Fedelm, who slept peacefully, one hand under her head. She breathed gently. He smiled, and his spirit soared for a moment into the air and back to him, and he felt happy that he was with her in this room under Cernunnos's roof. Then, Cumac heard Creide's song, which had awakened him.

Morning comes and it is time for sleepyheads
To leave the warmth of their beds.
Cernunnos waits impatiently to make the journey
To Rowan Oak and you will see that many
Miles lie 'twixt there and here.
Awaken! It is now morning, sleepyheads!

Cumac swung his feet off the bed and sat up, yawning and stretching. He looked at Fedelm and caught her watching him, her eyes soft and warm. Then she laughed and sat up, running her fingers through her tousled hair, and the moment was lost.

"We'd better hurry," she said. "If Cernunnos is kept waiting long, he will be surly on the journey."

"Are you aware of what happened in our dreams?" Cumac asked.

Fedelm nodded grimly. "Yes. I am. And I should have known enough to ask for a Dream Guardian."

"You cannot expect to know or remember everything," Cumac said.

Fedelm smiled gratefully at him.

"Yes. But I should at least have known that it takes a different magic to work in the Dreamworld. I was careless."

"Well, there's nothing to willy-nilly about. What is done is in the past. We have now to worry about."

Fedelm heaved a deep sigh.

"You are kind. And right. We must hasten now, for I feel Cernunnos grows impatient."

Cumac nodded and sighed and rose, slipping Caladbolg over his shoulder and picking up his leather bag. Fedelm gathered hers and her bow and quiver and together they went out into the great room. A fire flickered merrily in the wide hearth, burning with the sweet smell of applewood. The table had been set with thick bread dripping fresh honey and mugs of cool clear water that awakened them when they drank. Pillywiggins flitted around the room, setting out fresh flowers.

The door flung open and Cernunnos strode in, his green cloak furling around him. He saw Cumac and Fedelm and laughed.

"About time you two awoke. The day isn't getting younger, and the bees have already made a comb or two of honey. If we hurry, we can be out of the woods and halfway across the plains before noon break. Are you ready?"

Fedelm nodded and they rose, Cumac looking wistfully at the remaining bread and honey. Then he took a deep breath and followed Cernunnos and Fedelm out the door. Creide stopped them and handed Fedelm a quiver of arrows.

The quiver was made from soft green leather. An ancient Ogham legend had been burnt into the front of the quiver—ᚔᚐᚋᚓ ᚓᚏᚂ ᚒᚂᚂ—I Am Ever Full. Green-feather-fletched arrows filled the quiver.

"This quiver will always be filled with arrows despite how many you use," Creide said. "I have looked again into the reflecting pool and have seen that you will have great need of this before your search is over. And it will go into the Dreamworld with you along with your bow for what is one without the other?"

"Thank you," Fedelm murmured. "I am pleased with your gift." She slipped the old quiver from her shoulders, replaced it with the new one, and handed the old one to Creide.

"It is time to go," Cernunnos said impatiently and stepped to the door.

Creide went to the threshold with them and sang them onto the path away from the house.

Be safe on your journey long
And let your hearts lift to this song.
It will not be easy for your travel
If the enchantments dare unravel
Through the work of Maliman.
Go now and be wary. Be safe!

By quarter morning they had reached the edge of the forest. Cumac looked for the Old Ones guarding the edge of the forest but saw nothing except a faint shimmer that rose from the earth beyond the last tree. Cernunnos caught his inquisitive study and laughed. *Hee, hee, hee!*

"You are looking for the Old Ones, but you will not see them until they are ready for you to see them," he said. "But they are there and here and are watching carefully."

"Can you see them?" Fedelm asked, following Cumac's example and studying the trees and bushes.

"Oh yes," he answered. "But that is only because they let me see them. No one can see the Old Ones unless the Old Ones wish."

"Not even Maliman?" Cumac put in.

Cernunnos frowned. "No, not even Maliman. But we are wasting time. Come!"

He raised his hand as if in greeting, and the shimmering parted. He ran out of the trees and set a ground-gaining pace over the meadow, and Fedelm and Cumac followed. The sun immediately came hard upon them, and within moments, perspiration ran freely down Cumac's and Fedelm's faces and backs. The air filled their lungs with heat, and they panted for breath while mirages mirrored themselves in the distance.

Cernunnos ignored their panting and kept running easily across the grass, long legs moving effortlessly. Fedelm took a deep breath and grinned wryly at Cumac.

"There's no waiting for the lackeys," she said and lifted her pace after Cernunnos.

Cumac followed them as they moved on a steady, straight path across the grass. Soon his lungs began to burn and the air felt hot in his lungs. Perspiration trickled from his hair, burning his eyes. His throat felt raw.

Then a slight cooling breeze began to waft by him, and his lungs stopped burning. His head cleared, and he saw the morning dew still sparkling like diamonds upon the blades of grass. A slight hint of rose and lavender came to him, and his muscles relaxed until running became a normal gait and effortless. He felt he could run forever.

At noon, they were halfway across the grassy plain and in the distance could see a hazy green line that was the beginning of Rowan Oak Forest. Cernunnos beamed at them as he dropped to the ground and opened his pack.

Honey bread materialized, along with leather bottles of the clear cold water that they had drunk with breakfast. The bread had a slight taste of honeysuckle to it.

Gratefully, Fedelm and Cumac ate and drank. Cernunnos nodded happily at their appetite.

"It pleases me that you like the honey of my bees," he said. "It will refresh you."

"Is there a magic in it?" Cumac asked, his mouth full. "I have never tasted anything as good as this."

"Nor I," Fedelm said, licking honey from her fingers.

"The magic is in the bees," Cernunnos said. "And the flowers they use. Roses, red clover, and other flowers that are known only to them. The magic is not from me. They . . ."

His voice trailed off. He frowned and stared into the distance.

"What is it?" Fedelm asked, twisting her head to look over her shoulder.

A thunderhead moved swiftly toward them.

Cernunnos rose. Fedelm and Cumac leaped to their feet.

"What is it?" Fedelm asked again.

Cernunnos stiffened.

"Sumaires! Vampires—of the deadliest sort. Run! We cannot fight them here!"

Turning, he ran across the grasses, his feet flashing swiftly. Fedelm and Cumac sprinted after him.

Cumac heard the sound of hooves approaching rapidly over the grasses. A faint putrid stench of old corpses breathed slowly toward them. Cumac's flesh crawled as he imagined them at his back, their swords slashing at his head. He sprinted harder, matching Fedelm stride for stride.

The sun disappeared slowly as the black thunderhead covered it. A shout of triumph came from behind them, and black lightning cracked over their heads and lanced the ground. Then, a copse of trees appeared, moving faster and faster toward them.

"There!" Cernunnos shouted.

And then they were in among the trees. Cernunnos wheeled, drew a golden torc from his pouch, held it over head, and shouted, "*Ethna meth ammas beth luis nemath!*"

The trees groaned and branches moved swiftly overhead, twining themselves into a thick canopy. At the edge of the copse, vines quickly wove themselves tightly around the trunks of the trees into a heavy mat.

Again, Cernunnos shouted, "*Amieth caith tuith shemma feroth ruith math!*"

A burst of green light rose from the torc and sped through the trees, slipping between the mat of vines as they closed. Rapidly it flared into a mist that rose up and around the trees, enclosing all.

A shriek of anger came from outside. Horses ran into the green light, and then riders and horses screamed in terror as green and orange flames licked their flesh before consuming them. An acrid stench rose toward the thunderhead. Black lightning cracked again and again, striking the green light surrounding the copse but bouncing off and ricocheting wildly among the sumaires. Howls of pain sprang from the throats of those the lightning struck. One sumaire rode hard up to the light. Cumac looked into his glittering black eyes. Foam flecked the corners of the sumaire's lips. He raised his sword and struck savagely at the light, but he stiffened as the light flickered up his blade and surrounded him and his horse with green fire, then surged and burned as fiercely as a blacksmith's forge. Agony contorted the sumaire's face, and he screeched as he disintegrated into ash. The horse shrilled and tried to gallop away, but the light held it firmly within its grasp and sparked from its mane and tail as it consumed the horse.

Then quiet came over the clearing as the rest of the sumaires turned and fled, the black thundercloud following overhead. The sun appeared again, bathing everything in a soft golden light. The trees relaxed, and the vines slipped down and away from the trunks of the trees.

"We will be all right now. For a while," Cernunnos added soberly. "The sumaires are more vulnerable in daytime. That is why the thundercloud came with them, to leave them in near dark so their strength would not be halved."

"What now?" Fedelm asked, still breathing heavily from the tension.

"To Rowan Oak," Cernunnos said. "We must take advantage of the light." He frowned. "Maliman will want to attack again and soon. This time, he may send Black Baggots after us. And," he emphasized, "there are no other woods between here and Rowan Oak. If the Black Baggots catch us in the open, we will be hard pressed."

Wordlessly, Fedelm and Cumac rose and tightened their packs and belts. Cernunnos nodded and led the way out of the copse.

It was late afternoon when they reached the fringes of Rowan Oak Forest and slipped into the cool shade. Cumac heaved a sigh of relief. He glanced at Fedelm and saw the tightness go out of her jaw and the tiny lines around her eyes ease.

"You must wait here," Cernunnos warned. "The Ashelves will find you soon. In fact, they may be watching you now. Rest. Relax. Do not light a fire, however, as the Ashelves are very protective of Rowan Oak and fires here are dangerous. Besides," he added, "the trees themselves do not like fire. Here, the trees are among the oldest—before time was known—and no one knows what they are capable of."

He glanced at the sun and shook his head. It was past meridian height and slipping toward the dark.

"I cannot wait here with you," he said regretfully. "I must hurry if I'm to get back before the dark. But you will be safe here. Remember what I said!" he cautioned. "Do not go farther into the forest until the Ashelves come for you. It may be a while. They are very cautious, the Ashelves."

"Thank you for bringing us this far," Fedelm said. "May your return be safely met."Cernunnos nodded, laughed, then in a twinkling, he was racing back across the meadow, his toes barely touching the ground. He soon disappeared from sight.

Fedelm sighed, let her pack slip from her shoulder, dropped down upon the ground, and leaned back against an oak and waggled her feet with pleasure.

Alarmed, Cumac said, "Do you think that's wise? You remember how some of the other trees were. These may be of like manner."

She gestured overhead impatiently. "You can barely see the sky here for the branches. If these trees wished to harm us, they would already have done so, and there is nothing that we can do to prevent them from doing so now if they wish. Your worry is fruitless. Now, sit and rest. You must rest whenever you can, for we don't know when we might need our strength."

"I don't know," Cumac said cautiously. "I do not feel that we are alone here. The trees"—he glanced overhead—"the trees are watching us. At least," he amended, "I *feel* the trees are watching us. As is something else. Something else."

He tugged at his ear, studying the trees in front of them, half expecting a troll or a Black Baggot to leap out at them. Then, there were the goblins and hobgoblins too, he thought. And Deag-duls, those demons who drank the blood of travelers and were much worse than vampires. Fedelm had mentioned in Tanglewood that they could only be killed by beheading them or sending a hazelwood arrow through their hearts. He shook his head—there were just too many dangers that could come upon one in ancient forests. And although Cernunnos and Fedelm were confident that Rowan Oak Forest was safe, he had misgivings. Maliman had gained more power than they thought possible in such a short while.

But while he considered, a musical voice chanted from the depths of the forest:

Welcome, Cumac, the Hound's Son
And Fedelm, Daughter of the Sidhe.
Right now, your journey is almost done
For we will take you to Ulster's Sidhe.
Beware, however, that you are still
Not safe and when you go from under the hill
Maliman will attack strongly to kill
You, Fedelm, and Cumac, the Hound's Son.

Cumac's hand slipped up automatically to Caladbolg's hilt. A green-fletched arrow sped by his cheek and disappeared out into the meadow. Overhead, the tree branches moved malevolently, threatening.

"Fool!" Fedelm hissed. "Take your hand from the sword! Do you want to get us both killed? This is no place to be playing the sword dance!"

Slowly, Cumac's hand fell away from the hilt and he stood awkwardly, looking around nervously. So far, only one wood had proven safe, and suspicion weighed heavily upon him.

The hair on the back of his neck prickled as silver shimmers made their way between the trees from all sides, and a quiet voice chuckled as a form widened from a golden light inside. Before them stood an Ashelf, golden-haired and dressed in green tunic and trousers, a green cloak sweeping down from his shoulders. He took his green cap from his head and bowed mockingly, sweeping the ground with the cap.

"Greetings!" he said. "Lorgas at your service. Welcome to Rowan Oak. We have come to take you to Erewon! But," he added, eying Cumac's sword pointedly, "you must leave your weapons sheathed.

To draw your sword within Rowan Oak and Erewon will be considered an act of war and bring the wrath of Iain, our king, upon your heads. Fedelm, you will unstring your bow as well. We are well aware of your expertise with it!"

Obediently, Fedelm slipped the string loose and draped the bow crosswise over her shoulder.

"I agree," she said.

Lorgas nodded and raised an eyebrow at Cumac.

"I agree also," Cumac said slowly.

"Then, let us to Erewon!" Lorgas said cheerfully. He laughed again and spun on his heel. For a moment he disappeared as his cloak swept around him, then reappeared already moving through the trees on a path that seemed to magically appear.

"Elves," Cumac muttered as Fedelm moved past him.

She gave him a dark look and opened her mouth to chastise him, but a voice answered instead.

"Ashelves, if you please. Our race is far older than the others, who seldom remember their heritage and dance and play by the light of the moon in clearings where they make their fairy circles. They have forgotten the way of the elves before man came. We are Ashelves."

Cumac glanced over his shoulder and saw an Ashelf eying him critically, suspicion hard upon the Ashelf's face. His fingers fiddled with his bow, which had a shaft nocked. He was dressed as Lorgas was, except his hair had a reddish gold to it. His blue eyes smoldered, and Cumac smiled sheepishly, caught in his aside to Fedelm.

"I apologize," he said. "I meant no harm."

"I am Lalin," the Ashelf said. "You will do well to remember this. And to remember to hold your tongue away from your thoughts and to rethink your thoughts before you give tongue to them."

"I meant no disrespect," Cumac said.

"We shall see," Lalin said, his eyes steady upon Cumac's.

"This is not a good start," Fedelm said softly to Cumac. "You really should have listened to your lessons in manners instead of dancing with the nymphs at Lughnasa."

Stung, Cumac started to answer, but then he remembered Lalin's words and wisely held his tongue.

"We shall see," Lalin repeated. He motioned for them to follow Lorgas. "If you don't want to trip over the roots of the trees, you'd best be following Lorgas. Trees don't like outlanders, and the paths are guarded by them."

"Yes, yes, of course," Cumac said hastily, and he stepped onto the path and hurried after the Ashelf, who was disappearing within the pale gray veil beginning to drop over Rowan Oak Forest.

I'm not certain I care for this, he thought to himself, stepping lively over roots tentatively lifted from the earth to slow his way. It seems like a lot of flummery over nothing but a couple of travelers trying to find their way. They know that much about us, I'd think that they know we mean them no harm. Flummery! And more flummery!

They passed through glades where sheep nibbled on grass and again through clearings lively with buttercups and primroses. It seemed a pale light glimmered behind the gray and followed them as they made their way around the old oak trees. The air grew warmer and the rich smell of the earth rose up to them.

Suddenly Cumac spied something white slipping through the trees. He reached out and nudged Fedelm, and when she turned, he nodded toward the apparition. She smiled.

"It is a white stag," she said. "A conductor of souls to the Underworld and Great Rift. Flidess, the goddess of the hunt and making love, has her chariot pulled by a brace of white stags." She grinned. "I should think you would have encountered her in your dances with the night nymphs."

Cumac blushed and said nothing.

I will pay more attention to Cairpre, the teacher of our poets and writers, He Who Inspires, when I return. *If* I return, he corrected grimly.

They came to a steep hill and followed the path zigzagging its way up the face until they arrived, panting, at the top, where the trees had folded back away. They moved cautiously to the edge of the hill and looked down into a lush valley. In the distance, the forest was smoking with fog. But in the valley a sparkling city rose with a soft glow surrounding its tall keeps and turrets. The houses were bright and spacious. The windows were made of crystal and the streets paved with white granite. A river ran through the center of the city, leaping merrily from stone to stone, sending a fine spray into the air.

"Erewon. Brightell the river," Lorgas said from beside them. "It begins at Dianchect's well, Slaine, the Well of Healing, and ends at the edges of the forest. You will only find the river here."

"Is there magic to the river?" Fedelm asked.

Lorgas threw his head back and laughed. "There is magic in everything, did you not know that, Fedelm, daughter of the Sidhe? Even stones have their magic, and trees die and bring themselves back from the dead. There is magic everywhere."

"Even in Earthworld?" Cumac asked, wondering.

"Oh yes. Even in Earthworld," Lorgas said. "Come!"

They followed him down the path lacing back and forth along the side of the hill until they at last made it to the bottom. Here, they had a better look at Erewon. Ashelves paused to gaze wonderingly at Cumac and Fedelm as they were led to the Great House, where Iain lived. Swallows danced and darted overhead, and mockingbirds called in answer to wrens chirruping.

"During 1533 Tír Na Og, Iain led the Ashelves in the war against the Zorgoths, who attempted to destroy Rowan Oak and our race," Lorgas explained. "It was Iain who slew the Zorgoth leader, Credac. The Zorgoths were driven from the land and fled to Noraic, the land of ice and snow. Iain's house has an immense library and is also a refuge for those who are judged worth of studying to become great wizards. Only five students, however, are allowed in the house at a time. The learning period usually lasts five hundred years. Iain was a great warrior and healer, having learned that art from Caiton Ancent, the founder of the healing arts. Dianchect, the great healer of the Tuatha De Danann, was a great-great-grandson of Caiton Ancent."

Lorgas went up and knocked on the door. The door opened, and a wizened elf stared out at them, frowning. He wore a black tunic lined with silver thread.

"What is it? Be quick about it! I haven't all day to waste standing here jibber-jabbing with the likes of you! Who's this? Strangers?" he snapped.

"Not for you to question the likes of others," Lorgas said. "We bring friends to see Iain. They seek refuge for the night."

"Come in, then! Come in, then! And wipe your dirty boots. The hall's just been cleaned."

He moved back away from the doorway and shuffled off into the depths of the house.

"You would think that Barin owns the Great House," Lorgas said to the others. "He gets worse every time we bring someone to see Iain. One of these days, someone's going to shorten him by a head."

He stepped across the threshold and carefully wiped his boots before moving down the hallway to the library. The others followed, and when they stepped into the library, Cumac and Fedelm looked wonderingly about.

The ceiling was flat and paneled in oak that had been rubbed with beeswax until it gleamed with a soft golden glow. Richly carved with elven runes, walnut beams criss-crossed the ceiling. Light poured in through crystal windows. Down at the end of the library, a fire flickered merrily in a stone fireplace, and reading in a comfortable chair covered in green with red threads running through it was Iain, blond with silver streaks in his hair and eyes of cobalt blue with a light of stars within. His face was ageless. He placed a marker in his book and laid it on a small table near his elbow. He rose as they came near him, the picture of a king of ancient legend, and well he was, for legends of his power had drifted over Otherworld and Earthworld.

"Welcome to Erewon," he said softly. "Fedelm, Cumac, you are most welcome. We have been expecting you. Your way has proven difficult, hasn't it?"

The question was rhetorical, but before Fedelm or Cumac could attempt an answer, Iain continued, "Perhaps a glass of wine to relax? We have some very good rosehip laid down by my father many years ago."

He clapped his hands and a servant, dressed in impeccable white, appeared. Iain ordered wine to be brought to them. Fedelm leaned close to Cumac and whispered, "That would make the wine over a thousand years old."

"No matter," Lorgas said, having overheard them. "It will still be a good vintage. Wine made with rosehips and honey from elven hives never turns."

"We are pleased with your hospitality," Fedelm said, bowing. Cumac hastily followed her example, echoing her words.

Iain smiled and rubbed his hands together. "And after, we shall show you to the baths so you may refresh yourselves before we eat."

"We *are* rather in a hurry—*umf*," Cumac said as Fedelm jabbed him sharply in his ribs with her elbow. He glared at her.

Iain laughed. "Do not worry, young Cumac. We shall not keep you forever. But while you are here, we must talk about what has happened and"—his face sobered instantly—"about what is happening both here and in Earthworld. But do not be hasty. That path leads to bad choices and bad decisions. The time will come when you will have to act instantly, and it would be better if you are well rested for that moment."

The servant appeared with a silver tray upon which were a slender crystal decanter three-quarters filled and four matching wineglasses. The wine was the color of rubies.

"Thank you," Iain said. He took the decanter and filled glasses, handing one to Fedelm and Cumac before taking one himself and handing the other to Lorgas. He lifted his own glass in toast and said, "May your road be a safe one, and may you always find companions among the Ashelves."

"And may your reign be a long one and filled with peace," Fedelm said formally, completing the toast.

Iain sipped from his wine and smiled softly.

"I do not think that likely at present," he said regretfully. "The theft of the Chalice of Fire affects us as well as the Otherworld. We are a mirror to what happens beyond the Sidhe. Although," he added, "we can alter some matters." His face clouded. "But Bricriu's theft will bring death and destruction with the release of Maliman and the Grayshawls from the Great Rift, not to mention the Nightshades. Here, we are safe—for the moment, but that could change swiftly as soon as Maliman gains full power."

"I thought the Ashelves could match Maliman's power," Cumac said, sipping.

Iain laughed ruefully. "Even the Ashelves have their weaknesses. Not even Erewon is impregnable. But," he added thoughtfully, "the spells that form a wall around our forest and city are old spells put down by the ancient ones before the beginning of Tír Na Og. Maliman will have to know their power and key before he can break through our defenses. For now, we are safe. For how long, I do not know."

"Speed is of the essence," Lorgas volunteered.

Iain nodded. "Yes, that is true. But that does not mean you cannot afford a day or two to rest and ready yourself for the next part of your journey." He clapped his hands again and another servant appeared. "Take them to the baths and bring fresh garments for them to wear."

The servant nodded and silently stepped aside, motioning Fedelm and Cumac to precede him.

"We thank you," Fedelm said, finishing her wine and placing it on the silver tray. Cumac hastily followed suit, then bowed awkwardly and turned to follow Fedelm.

"Cumac," Iain said.

Cumac turned.

"Do not let down your guard," Iain cautioned. "Even in Erewon. You are safe, but"—he spread his hands—"always there is evil, as it takes different forms. Always be ready."

Cumac nodded. "Thank you, Iain. I welcome your advice and shall heed your words."

"Then," Iain said to Lorgas, "take them to the baths so they may refresh themselves and wash the grime of journey away."

"May even join you," Lorgas said with a grin. He waggled his eyebrows at Fedelm, who laughed.

"Yes, I can see how you would join us," she said. "But"—she

looked roguishly at Cumac—"I think there is enough when the two of us are in the baths."

Cumac felt himself blushing, and the others laughed at his uneasiness.

"Well, Cumac!" Iain said, smiling broadly, "it appears that you have things well in hand!"

Cumac turned crimson, and Lorgas laughed and clapped him on the shoulder.

"Come on, Cumac. One thing you need to learn, my boy: women speak a big game and perform less."

Fedelm smiled wryly. "That would depend upon the woman," she said sweetly.

11

Cumac sighed and leaned back in the clear water in a natural grotto formed by a hot spring that bubbled up from hidden rocks. The walls of the granite seemed to sparkle with diamonds. Slowly, he felt the tension of the past few days slip away from him as the warmth of the water worked its way into his muscles.

He looked across the small grotto to where Fedelm scrubbed herself with a handful of deep wine-red sphagnum moss, apparently oblivious to him.

Lorgas was right, he thought. A good game promised but not played.

He took a handful of moss himself and industriously scrubbed it over himself until his flesh glowed rosily. He heard Fedelm climb from the pool and glanced her way as she picked up a linen towel and wrapped it around her.

Fedelm felt Cumac's eyes upon her, blushed, and held the towel closer.

"We'd better hurry," she said. "We have loitered here long enough."

Obediently, Cumac climbed from the bath, picked up his towel, and wrapped it around his waist.

"Well, then," he said brightly. "Let us return."

They walked into a small foyer outside the grotto and discovered their clothes had been washed and mended and hung upon on two protruding stones. By unspoken agreement, they turned their backs to each other and hurriedly dressed.

Cumac smoothed back his long hair and said, "It's good to be able to relax for a bit before continuing on to the Red Branch."

Fedelm nodded. "Yes, it is. The way may become more difficult as we travel, and we need to be well rested for that."

They left the baths and followed a narrow trail that led past soft carpets of greens and pinks of heaths and heathers, bright splashes of yellow and orange asphodel, fuchsia-pinks and ruby-reds of cranberry flowers and berries, and the delicate white and pink frothy flowers of the bog bean, all transplanted into carefully prepared beds. In the trees, they heard the songs of willow tits, nuthatches, and waxwings. Bees bumbled lazily around, pollen-heavy, to make fresh honey thick within the combs.

"I could live here forever," Cumac said dreamily.

"I think you would become bored after a while," Fedelm said. "You are not made for the idle life."

Reluctantly, Cumac had to acknowledge that she was right, but he added that it would be worth the effort to change.

"The die is cast when we are born," she said.

"Even you? I thought you were among the immortals," Cumac said.

"Weapons will harm me as much as they will you," Fedelm said. "But I do have the *imbas forasnai,* and age does not affect me as it does you. But make no mistake in thinking I am invulnerable," she warned.

"I won't," Cumac said firmly. "Did I not guard your back when the Nightshades and Truacs came?"

"Yes," she said grudgingly. "You did. And we need to do that for each other whenever we are hard pressed. Do not forget," she said, smiling wryly. "I do not wish to awaken in Teach Duinn, the Island of Donn."

The hall of Iain's house was filled with Ashelves waiting patiently upon Cumac and Fedelm at the table. At the far end, Iain sat in a great chair. A golden circlet held his long hair back, and his eyes were bright with lights from small suns. Next to him sat the most beautiful woman Cumac had ever seen, and he knew that this was the legendary Airin, the wife of Iain. She was as old as Iain but the magic of age had not yet touched her. The braids of her black hair held no hint of frost, and her face was free of wrinkles. Her gray eyes held the light of stars. She, too, wore a circlet, but hers was of silver set with precious emeralds and rubies and lapis lazuli. Her white gown was embroidered with spring leaves.

"Ah, there you are," Iain said, rising from a table laid with a snowy white cloth upon which were dishes of honey and nuts, pannin bread still warm from the ovens, and bowls of fruits and pitchers of pale red wine. Many different cheeses rested in silver salvers. The faint odor of sandalwood stood in the air. Finches sang from the beams overhead. Somewhere a harp played softly, filling the hall with soothing music.

"I was beginning to think that we would have to eat all this by ourselves," Iain laughed.

"We apologize," Cumac said. "It has been a while since we were able to refresh ourselves."

"My wife, Airin," Iain said, indicating the woman sitting beside him.

Cumac bowed. "I am sorry that we have kept others from their dinner."

"No matter. No matter," Iain said, dismissing the apology with a wave of his hand. "Come! Let us eat!"

"You are welcome to our table," Airin said softly. Her lips curved into deep dimples. Her teeth were a blinding white.

Gratefully, Cumac and Fedelm seated themselves while the servant who had brought the wine when they arrived moved silently around the table, filling the cups.

Cumac found himself seated beside an Ashelf with smooth skin and golden hair that fell down to his shoulders. The Ashelf grinned as he poured Cumac's goblet with ruby-red wine.

"You will find that the Ashelves make the finest wine," he said, eyes beaming merrily. "Drink! Drink! No one knows what the morrow will bring, and it is best that we enjoy what each day brings."

Obediently, Cumac drank, and he raised his eyebrows in astonishment as the wine slid smoothly over his tongue.

"I see you have discovered this for yourself," the Ashelf said. "I am Gavin. No need to introduce yourself, Cumac, or the lovely lady Fedelm beside you. All here know who you are and why you are here."

"I thank you," Cumac said courteously. "It is good to be able to share a table such as this with you, Gavin. Would you be kind enough to explain the Ashelves to me?"

"Certainly! Ashelves like nothing better than to talk about themselves. With those who are welcome, that is," he said. "The problem is their tongues run on. You must stop me if I begin to bore you."

"I do not believe that will be possible," Cumac said.

"We shall see! We shall see!"

With that, Gavin embarked on the long history of his people and how they fought with the Tuatha De Danann against the Fomorians and Balor Evileye, whose baleful eye gleamed with a basilisk stare that slew others with a brief glance. The defeat of Balor and the Fomorians had been celebrated by the Tuatha and the Ashelves, who then divided the land of the Otherworld between themselves. Gavin was pleased with the attention Cumac gave him, and after dampening his throat with wine, proceeded to relate the adventures of several Ashelf heroes.

As Cumac reached for a bowl of fruit, he saw the servant stealthily drop a black ball into the cup meant for Fedelm. The hackles rose upon the back of his neck suspiciously. Then his brow furrowed. The servant caught Cumac's study of him and quickly averted his eyes.

"No!" Cumac shouted, and with one sweep of his hand knocked the cup away from Fedelm as she raised it to her lips.

The Ashelves grew silent and stared, baffled, at Cumac, who rose and picked up the cup, spilling the black ball from it. Most of the ball had dissolved, leaving it pitted and out-of-round, but enough remained for Airin to recognize it.

"Nightwort!" she exclaimed. "Found only in the Great Rift! This had to be brought out by one of Maliman's servants!"

A low growl from the guests followed her words.

The servant paled and, turning, tried to run, but Lorgas was too fast for him, leaping onto his back and pinning him to the ground.

The guests stared in astonishment as the servant began to hiss and writhe. Foam poured from his lips and great shrieks that curdled the blood came from his throat as he struggled to free himself. A rancid stench came in a cloud from his mouth, and his eyes glittered with black hatred.

"Maliman has him!" Iain said harshly. "The question is, how? This elf hasn't left Rowan Oak as far as I know."

Airin spoke. "Was he part of the party that you sent out to search for evil happenings surrounding the outside of the forest?"

Iain shook his head. He gnawed on his lower lip, thinking.

"I don't think so," he said slowly. A frown pinched his eyebrows together. "And if that is true, then there is another under Maliman's control here in Erewon."

Cumac glanced at Fedelm and raised an eyebrow, questioning. She shrugged and nodded slightly toward Lorgas and the servant still pinned to the floor.

Iain sighed and scrubbed his hands over his face. "We shall have to find him. If Maliman or his agent can take control of one of my servants, then there is no telling how many others have been infected from outside Rowan Oak."

"What should I do with this one?" Lorgas asked.

"If he has been infected here in Erewon, then there is only one thing that can be done. You know what," Iain said meaningfully. "He has violated the Laws of Hospitality. Take him to Raven's Gate and send him through."

"*No!*" the servant shouted and renewed his struggle. So fiercely did he heave and writhe that Lorgas was hard put to hold him.

"Help him!" Iain snapped at the guards on either side of the door leading into the feasting hall. "Bind him and take him to Raven's Gate and cast him into the darkness."

Obediently, the guards took leather straps from their belts and bent over the servant, rapidly wrapping the straps snugly around the servant's wrists.

When they had finished, Lorgas rose, wiping his forehead with a napkin he took from the table.

"Who would have thought that a man like that would have such strength in him?" he said to the room.

"All who serve Maliman can call upon strength from others," Airin said. "That is the danger of the servants of the Grayshawls who serve Maliman. With their spells, the Grayshawls allow those servants of Maliman to drain strength from other servants who may be nearby."

She looked pointedly at Iain. "And since that strength is taken from others, the one who came into Erewon as a servant of Maliman should show the effects of struggle now. You must act quickly to find him, however. The weakness will not be long upon him."

Other guards sprang to help carry the frantic servant from the hall. Screams began to slip from his lips. His face turned the color of old liver, and the muscles in his neck corded. Slowly the sounds of his fear faded away, and Cumac and Fedelm turned back to the feast. Iain sighed and shook his head.

"This is not good," he said soberly. "I fear you must leave immediately. If one Ashelf has been infected by Maliman's servant, then there could be more. Erewon is no longer safe for you," he added regretfully. "Ready yourselves. Packs will be filled for the rest of your journey."

Cumac and Fedelm rose, bowed courteously, and left the hall, hurrying to their rooms. It did not take long for them to get ready, and they soon made their way out of Iain's house. On the doorstep rested two packs, one for Cumac, the other for Fedelm. And with them stood Lorgas. He wore pants made of green leather and a green tunic with a black leafless tree sewn into the cloth. Around his waist was a belt of black leather in which curious designs had been worked in silver. A small ax hung from the belt. A sword haft stood up over one shoulder. Crosswise over his chest hung a leather pouch tied shut with leather strings.

Iain stood beside him and spoke as Cumac and Fedelm came up to them.

"Lorgas will be going with you," Iain said. "If Rowan Oak has some of Maliman's men within it, the Ashelves should be a part of your quest. It is only right that we share the dangers with you."

Lorgas grinned at them. "Three pairs of eyes are better than two. And I have been here so long that my feet have grown restless and yearn to travel. This is a way as good as another."

"Besides," Iain said, "Lorgas knows the trails well through Rowan Oak and can lead you to the Sidhe of the Red Branch faster than you can manage without him."

"You are welcome," Fedelm said courteously. "Another blade will be needed if we are again set upon by Truacs or Nightshades."

"I too welcome you," Cumac said, stepping forward to take Lorgas's hand. He shook it firmly. "There is always room for one more on an adventure."

"Well, then," Lorgas said, nudging the two packs on the threshold with his toe. "We should not be mollygagging around here while traveling is waiting to be done."

They picked up their packs while Lorgas bowed his head to Iain. "I will not bring shame upon this house," he said formally. "My ax is your ax."

"We wait for your return," Iain said. He glanced at Cumac and Fedelm. "We wait as well for your return, for your return will mean peace has once again been restored in the Earthworld."

"May it be so," Fedelm said, inclining her head.

"And now, let us depart," Cumac said with false gaiety.

He stepped over the threshold and onto the path leading down from Iain's door. The others followed, and Lorgas took the lead. Soon, they passed out of the city and into the shadows of the trees in Rowan Oak. Branches swung aside as they hurried through the trees. The wind soughing through the trees sounded ominous, but there was an urging to it as well, and Cumac heard the trees muttering warnings to him as he passed.

Beware! Beware!

12

On the second day after leaving Erewon, they came to the edge of Rowan Oak. Before them lay a sea of rolling grass. In the distance, a hill topped with a dolmen marked an entrance from the Otherworld and the Sidhes to Earthworld. But in between, only the grass, with no place to hide once they came out upon it. The sky was a great cloudy patchwork, the clouds the color of oysters.

During their trek, the enchantments woven around the forest had kept them safe, but here and there, the walls of enchantment had been battered by waves of spells thrown at them. Outside one wall lay seven Black Baggots, their twisted bodies showing the horror of their deaths for having attempted to breach the boundary of the forest.

"I do not like the open," Lorgas said grimly, studying the long ground between Rowan Oak and the dolmen. "We cannot cross this in one day—it is too far—and we may have to contend with the Nightshades. Or others from Maliman's forces."

"What if we travel by night?" Cumac asked. "Before, we have always traveled in the daylight. Perhaps if we travel by night, we may get across before Maliman discovers we are in the open."

Fedelm shook her head. "It is still a two-day journey. Or, two-night. One way or the other, we are going to be exposed to Maliman's forces. *And* there is the chance that the night-forces will be unleashed upon us. Most of Maliman's forces travel and strike by night. By traveling during the day, we cut the possibility of being attacked by half."

Lorgas squatted on his heels and studied the open land before them. He shook his head and said, "I have misgivings both ways. But it seems to me that we should lessen the gamble of being surprised if we can. Night is the hardest to guard against, and would it not be better to limit ourselves to the possibility of being surprised only once? Therefore, I say the day."

Cumac shrugged. "I think there is value in each plan. But if the two of you wish to travel by day, then so be it."

Lorgas nodded and climbed to his feet. He studied the canopy of trees overhead.

"The trees have hidden our movement so far," he said. "Maliman and the Grayshawls have no idea of where we will exit the forest—on the side leading to Cruachan or the side leading to Emain Macha, Of course, they are strong enough that they can send people to cover both exits, but I do not sense this. How about you Fedelm? Cumac?"

Cumac said, "I do not have the sight, Lorgas. I am of no help in this."

"Fedelm?"

She squatted on her heels and closed her eyes, remaining perfectly still for a long minute before offering a song:

I see blood and I feel death
Creeping toward us with stealth.
Maliman still grows stronger
And others cannot hold much longer.
We do not dare to tarry here
For the two worlds cannot bear
The forces summoned against us.
And then we shall become dust.

She took a deep breath and opened her eyes. Her look fell upon Cumac, and he was jolted to see the sadness resting behind her gaze. A coldness descended upon him. He squatted on his heels next to her, glanced at Lorgas, then asked, "What is it? You have seen more, haven't you?"

She bit her lip and nodded slightly.

"What is it?"

She shrugged. "Something that may come; something that may not come."

The way is dark and dreary
And I have become leery
Of the way that lies before
Us as we open the Sidhe door.
The rest is murky but I see
Shadows before us. Treachery
Will come our way and
May destroy our stalwart band
But the shadows are murky
And I can only see darkly.

Cumac took a deep breath and turned to Lorgas.

"Have you seen anything, too?"

Lorgas shook his head. "No, but I feel something evil this way comes. It is a feeling, nothing more. But," he emphasized, "Ashelves learn to trust their feelings. In this way, we were able to defeat Ragon Garg-Fuath and the Zorgoths and weave the green enchantments around Rowan Oak. Well," he amended, "not 'we' today, but those Ashelves who came with time and were strong enough to tighten the weave on the green enchantments. The feeling came to the ancients when Ragon tried to slip between the weaves with his army. Ragon nearly got through, but a large part of his army was caught in the web of enchantments. This was before Nuada himself defeated Ragon and the Zorgoths and banished them to the island of Cultas Dubasarlai."

Cumac scrubbed his chin with the palm of his hand. He tried to send out thoughts to bring Lorgas's feeling to him, but his mind remained blank. At last, he gave up and rose, saying, "All right, then. Let us hurry on our way. Lorgas, how fast can you get us to the Sidhe of Emain Macha?"

Lorgas grinned. "By eventide of the second day, if you can keep up."

"And if Maliman doesn't attack us," Fedelm muttered, rising. She snugged the quiver over her shoulder and tightened her belt. "So. Let's go."

Lorgas turned and began to run toward the northeast. A gloom settled over him, as he had not told everything that he sensed. Already Maliman was moving within Earthworld toward the Mountains of Mourne, and with him came an army of Deag-duls and Black Baggots and goblins and hobgoblins, who were scorching the earth, as they traveled, using fires they had brought with them from the Great Rift.

If only we can make it to Emain Macha before they discover that we are in Earthworld. There, we will have many who will join us in battle if battle comes. And, Lorgas thought grimly, that battle *will* come.

TRUE to his word, Lorgas led Fedelm and Cumac to the Sidhe of Emain Macha and the passageway through the dolmen into Earthworld. He paused, breathing deeply to ready himself for what might lie on the other side. Beside him, Cumac and Fedelm followed suit while they checked their weapons. Fedelm strung her bow while Cumac drew Caladbolg, the great sword of Fergus, and carefully wiped his hands and the haft of the sword free from sweat.

"Someone or something evil is near," Cumac said. "But I do not know if it is on this side of the gateway or the other."

"Then," Lorgas said, "it would be best if we went through into the Earthworld. At least we will be closer to Emain Macha than we are here."

"I agree," Fedelm said, taking a firm grip on her bow. She drew an arrow and nocked it.

Cumac gave a reckless grin and stepped forward and into the gateway of the Sidhe. A wave of darkness immediately swept over him. A faint light shone at the far end of the path in front of him. On either side, a fetid odor arose, and the hackles on the back of his neck bristled. He took a firm grip on Caladbolg and ran along the narrow, twisting path toward the light waiting for him. Behind him he heard Lorgas and Fedelm following.

He paused at the end of the gateway, then, taking a deep breath, leaped through the wavering light into the twilight of Earthworld. Bright lights of rainbow colors spun and crackled around him. He crouched, looking quickly around him, but saw nothing. Behind him, Lorgas and Fedelm stepped away from the passage and next to him. Fedelm drew the arrow back to her ear. Lorgas too had a firm grip on his ax.

Fedelm shouted, "Sumaires and goblins!"

She unleashed the nocked arrow and quickly drew another shaft, and then her hands seemed to blur as she drew and fired.

Cumac crouched, looking for the enemy. Then he saw the sumaires, vampires that usually came in the Dreamworld but that now were riding hard down upon him astride Memans, their corpse-eating black horses. Black cloaks flowed behind the sumaires like night patches, their armor made from thirty layers of the tanned and treated skins of their victims.

One sumaire came hard against Cumac, mouth opened in a red grimace, bits of flesh flying with spittle from his mouth. He howled as if the fires of Donn were burning his flesh. He brandished his black-bladed sword, and Cumac knew that he had to avoid even the slightest cut, as poison had been worked into the sword by black blade-makers.

"Back to back!" Fedelm shouted, and Cumac spun on his heel, ducking under the sumaire's whistling blade, placing his back firmly against Feldem's and Lorgas's. The sumaire screamed in fury at his missed blow and pulled savagely on the bridle, spinning his Meman around to charge again. Cumac swayed to the side and Caladbolg shimmered in his hands as he sliced the sumaire's head from his body.

A goblin rose up against him, rank breath coming out of its mouth on clouds of rotting flesh. Cumac blocked his blow, then spun the blade through a circle in the Apple Feat, cleaving the goblin from breast to groin.

Caladbolg danced in his hands as he moved through the Edge Feat, the complicated Crescent Feat that left most warriors twisted and contorted on their own feet and legs, and the Scythe Feat. Goblins swayed and fell, black blood spurting from their wounds. Again, Cumac wove Caladbolg through the Crescent Feat to slay a sumaire, but another sumaire reached Cumac's side as he cut backhanded through the end of the Crescent Feat.

Cumac tried to duck, but the sumaire's blade slipped over Caladbolg's hilt and sliced into Cumac's forearm.

The sumaire yelled in triumph and pressed hard against Cumac, but Cumac swung his blade in the Edge Feat and sliced through the sumaire's arm. Foul black blood spurted. The sumaire screeched in pain and fury, but Cumac returned with a stroke, this time the Crescent Feat, severing the sumaire in half at the waist.

Fedelm kept many at bay with her arrows while Lorgas slipped the blades, chopping and hacking his way to Cumac. His ax became a blur as he wielded it.

Then the light swam around Cumac as he tried to ignore the burning in his injured arm. He forced himself to swing Caladbolg around. A wave of dizziness washed over him. Dimly, he heard Fedelm shout, and he pitched forward into darkness.

13

Dimly Cumac felt the trickle of a cool wind and gentle hands probing and washing his wound. Voices murmuring like cold brook water over worn pebbles soothed him, but he could not open his eyes, although he willed them with all his power. He heard words being chanted but could not make them out.

ᚢᛉᚨᚢᚾᚾᛚᚲᚢᛚᚴᚳᛟᚾᚨᚲᚢᛋᚺᚱᚺᚺᛉ
ᛁᛦᛉᚳᛜᚢᛉᚨᛟᛉᚨᚺᛏᛚᚲᚺᛦᛟᛉ

Days came and days went, yet the chant seemed to waver about him like gossamer threads until he recognized the old tongue but could not understand the words. Once he thought he felt cool lips upon his and another time a gentle hand wiping his forehead, but still he could not open his eyes. Then a burning like hot coals swept over him, and he screamed and heard the scream in his dream.

Sumaires gathered at the edges of his sight and swarmed toward him, red mouths open, long fangs dripping with saliva. The smell of old blood rolled over him in rank waves. Flowing black cloaks waved behind them.

Then, he sensed more then saw a woman and an elf battling the demons of his dreams. Arrows flying in small clouds, swords and hatchets flashing in the darkness as arms and heads were severed. A song came softly to him and his dreams faded away as a great peace settled over him.

I sing of hills and dales
And of soft heather blooming
And soft white clouds that sail
Through evening's soft gloaming.
And peace will come softly to you
As you rest easily on green hills
And caressing winds begin to blow
And streams run merrily in rills.

And he knew that someone, clad in white armor and armed with an ivory-handled blade and an oaken bow over one shoulder and a quiver of blackthorn arrows over the other, had entered his dreams and was now guarding him against all evil that might attack him.

A murmur of voices came to him, but he couldn't open his eyes to see the speakers.

"He will always bear that wound," someone said. "It will plague him wherever he goes."

"There isn't much hope for a full cure?"

"No. I'm afraid not. Not even if we could get him to Dianchect's well. A wound from a sumairen blade is not to be taken lightly. Perhaps if we could have been with him sooner things would be different. But as it is . . ." The voice trailed off into the dark as Cumac slipped back into sleep.

And then he awoke and looked in wonder around him. Red oak beams anchored a roof of willow thrushes woven into sheaves. An acrid taste coated the back of his throat and he swallowed painfully, trying to ease it. He smelled a sweet odor around him and recognized it as honeysuckle and something else—lavender, perhaps? He ran his hand along the bed upon which he lay and felt the softness of watersilk. Then, a face with deep wrinkles and framed by iron-gray hair and beard hovered over his sight.

"Ah. He's awake now. Do you know where you are, Cumac?"

He shook his head and tried to push himself erect, but his muscles refused to answer his call and he fell back on top of the bed.

"Water," he croaked. Then he coughed, and phlegm swept up his throat and into his mouth. He rolled his head and spat. A quiet chuckle followed him.

"That is one of the problems with vervain—it clings to the back of the throat. But it does pull the poison from a wound, and discomfort is a little price to pay for all of that. You are in the guesthouse at Emain Macha—the Red Branch—and lucky to be here at all. Wounds from a sumaire blade are seldom healed. Be thankful that you had a woman of the Sidhe and an Ashelf at hand. They managed to use club moss to keep the poison from traveling in your blood until they could bring you here."

"Who—" His words cracked like pressed-acorns.

"I am Seanchan. One of the Druids who serve Connor, King of the Red Branch," the man said. He wore a gray cloak over a white tunic that fell to his feet. His blue eyes gleamed with the same light as a wolf's. "Fedelm and Lorgas brought you here. And not a moment too soon. Do you feel well enough to drink a little broth?"

Cumac nodded and Seanchan lifted his head to spoon warm broth into his mouth. He tasted pork and chicken and . . . something . . . soothing.

Then he felt himself falling into a warm embrace within the dark.

When he awoke in the gloaming, Cumac looked around, momentarily confused by his surroundings. But the pain in his arm was gone, and his mouth no longer tasted of dried, crushed oak leaves and mistletoe. He pushed himself erect and held onto the bed for a moment until a wave of dizziness passed, then cautiously rose to his feet.

He walked unsteadily to the door of the guesthouse and leaned against the frame as he studied the compound in front of him.

The houses were thatched and the ground muddy from the fall rains. A cloud of gray smoke hung over the compound from the cook fires, and young warriors practiced their swordsmanship under the close watch of grizzled trainers, well marked with scars from the time when they rode with the Red Branch in battle after battle.

His attention settled on a tall man wearing a white robe edged in red with a long hood draped over his shoulders and sweeping down his back. In one hand he carried a staff carved with curious designs. As if sensing Cumac's attention, he turned and looked at Cumac, his blue eyes crinkling at the corners, his lips behind his long gray beard curling into a wide smile.

"Ah!" he called. "The lazybones awakes!"

He walked across the compound to greet Cumac.

"I am Seanchan. You have slept a long time. A long time. I trust you are feeling better now?"

"Yes, thank you," Cumac answered.

"You had us worried for a moment," a voice said beside him. He turned and smiled at Fedelm and Lorgas leaning against the wall beside the door.

"Fedelm! Lorgas!"

He grasped their hands and smiled warmly at them. "You must tell me what happened. I have only a little recollection."

Fedelm glanced at Seanchan, an eyebrow raising in question.

He nodded and said, "I think he is well enough to hear what happened."

Fedelm nodded soberly.

"Somehow, Maliman discovered where we were going to leave the Otherworld and sent goblins and sumaires to ambush us when we went through the portal within the dolmen of Emain Macha. You were wounded with a sumairen blade in the battle." She shook her head. "If some of the Red Branch were not nearby, we might not have made it. We can thank Conall Cernach for that. He took quite a few heads with that great blade of his. Leogaire Búadbach also was there, and between those two great heroes and Lorgas and me, we managed to drive the sumaires and goblins off. But," she emphasized, "if it had not been for Lorgas and his expertise with herbs, you still would not have made it here to the Red Branch and Seanchan's magic."

"There is little magic involved," Seanchan said. "I simply finished what you two started."

He looked at Cumac and shook his head, his face sobering. "You were beginning to wane. Death was almost upon you when you were brought here. A few more hours and there would have been nothing to bring back from Donn's world. How does your wound feel?"

Cumac moved his arm and shoulder. They were still stiff, and he winced from the soreness, but the pain was gone.

"It will do," he said. "It no longer feels"—he groped for words—"as if it is on fire."

"Good!" Seanchan said. He bent and prodded the wound with his forefinger. "I would say that it is healing nicely and you should have full use of it shortly. And a good thing too," he added. "You cannot linger here with so much yet to do."

Cumac took a deep breath and let it out slowly. "What about Bricriu? Do we know where he is?"

Seanchan frowned and chewed on the end of his mustache for a moment, then said, "We *think* he has gone toward Connacht. The Chalice is safe enough for now, as he will keep it secret from Maeve—indeed, I seriously doubt that she would welcome him at all if she knew he had it. Although she would like to defeat Ulster and the Red Branch, she knows that the return of the Chalice to her would be devastating. She gave it to your father, you know, and to have it returned by treachery would bring treachery down upon Connacht. The Chalice does not forgive thieves. It is as dangerous to Bricriu as the loss is to Ulster. Still," he said thoughtfully, "there are others who *could* put it to use. Oh yes. Indeed. There are others who would welcome Bricriu well as they would be able, to bring its will to their own. And Maeve cannot dismiss Bricriu from her house without violating the ancient laws of hospitality, else she would bring a *mallacht*—a curse upon her house and Connacht. But Maliman, well, that is another case altogether. He is strong enough to bend the magic of the Chalice to his will. Oh yes. Indeed. He could. And will if he should get his hands upon it. Bricriu knows this and wants to place the Chalice into Maliman's hands—*after* he comes to an agreement with Maliman. But Maliman does not share power. He is most treacherous, and Bricriu will know to be wary while dealing with him. But," he reflected, "Bricriu must first get to Maliman's stronghold in the Mountains of Mourne. And to do that, he must pass through the lands guarded by the Red Branch. Treachery cannot help him there, as he gave up his life in Ulster when he stole the Chalice. Now, the only thing is to find where he has gone."

"I think Connacht," Fedelm said.

The others looked at her. She nodded slowly. "Yes, I think Connacht. If Maeve doesn't know he has the Bladhm Caillis, then she would gladly defend Bricriu from any army sent to bring him back. And Bricriu knows the hatred Maeve holds for Ulster and the Red Branch. Many of her sons were slain by your father in the great cattle raid and the Connacht army nearly destroyed. If we send the Red Branch over the borders into Connacht, that will give Maeve a reason to attack Ulster. And without the Bladhm Caillis, Ulster will be very vulnerable. Yet, a small enough party may be able to enter her palace, Cruachan Ai, and steal the Chalice back." She paused. "And there is also the question of Maliman. If he attacks Cruachan Ai, Maeve will fight him as long as she doesn't know about the Chalice."

"Could we not simply tell her?" Lorgas asked. "She can keep

Bricriu and send the Chalice back to Ulster. It would do both good if they could prey on each other for a while," he added darkly.

Seanchan shook his head. "No. I may have made a grave error in thinking that Maeve would not keep the Chalice for herself. I still don't think she will try to use the power that it holds—she gave the power to Cucullen when she gave him the Chalice—but that doesn't mean she can't keep it within her borders and rely solely upon the strength of her armies. She may decide that Connacht would not be harmed with its return and simply keep the Chalice and attack anyway, knowing that Ulster's strength is halved with its absence.

"I think Bricriu knows the danger of disclosing the Bladhm Caillis to others. But he *will* press for protection. Even if the laws of hospitality did not exist, Ulster has enough enemies who would be willing to take Bricriu in for the information he could give them on Ulster's strongholds and forts and strength. At least, it is a possibility. I do not think that we can count on Connacht or any of the other provinces for help. By possessing the Bladhm Caillis, Bricriu has robbed Ulster of at least half of its strength. The Chalice must be returned to Ulster. But the others do not know that Bricriu has the Chalice. I'm certain that he will not disclose it or its properties to others until he can get it to Maliman. The fool probably thinks that once Maliman has the Chalice, he will raise Bricriu to great heights. But Maliman, as I said, does not share power. If Bricriu manages to get the Chalice to Maliman, then Maliman will have what he needs to sweep across the land with his invulnerable army. Maliman *knows* how to bend the power of the Chalice to his will. Ulster will seal all the passes to the north within its borders. But there are other ways for Bricriu to get into the Mountains of Mourne."

He shrugged and threw out his hands in frustration. "There are so many ifs and maybes that we cannot afford to not find Bricriu and return the Chalice to Ulster. Right now, Maeve is questionable, so I would say that we should try to get Bricriu in Connacht—if indeed that is where he has gone and not to Munster or even across the sea to Alba."

"We can always use my Sidhe," Fedelm said.

"No," Seanchan said. "No, that would not be wise. The fewer who know about our little group, the better chance we have for succeeding."

The three exchanged glances.

"*Our* group?" asked Fedelm.

"Oh yes," Seanchan said dryly. "You need the calming influence of a"—he cleared his throat—"mature man to keep you from leaping into harm's way. Yes, I shall go with you. I feel you will have need of me before this hunt is over."

Lorgas heaved a deep sigh. "Well, I won't say you aren't welcome, but I won't say you are, either. We shall be traveling fast, and it may be too much of a pace for an old man."

"Old man!" Seanchan sputtered and shook his staff at Lorgas. "I'll . . . I'll . . ."

"A calming influence?" Fedelm asked innocently.

Seanchan thumped his staff upon the ground and glared at Lorgas. "There's more to a search than running around helter-skelter like a wren seeking a lost nest. Old man!" He fumed as he turned and walked out, his white robe flowing behind him.

Fedelm laughed. "Well, that got his temper, Lorgas. Now, you'd better hope that he takes pity upon you!"

"Pity on me!" Lorgas sniffed. "An Ashelf is as good as a Druid—even better—any day."

Fedelm looked merrily at Cumac. "And you, what do you think?"

"I think," Cumac said drowsily, "that you all better hold an easy course before you destroy yourselves with trying to outdo each other."

14

Cumac awoke early the next day feeling refreshed and eager to leave his bed. He turned his head and saw clean clothes had been laid out for him. A curious silver brooch worked in cunning swirls and whorls and set with a blood-red stone lay on top of his clothes. He rose and washed his face in a basin of water that had been left for him on a wooden table, the joints cunningly cut to hold without nails. Then, he left the guesthouse and watched the sun come up through a purple haze and slant down through the mist, setting the dew to glimmering upon the leaves of grass. He took a deep breath and his nose twitched as he smelled cooking meat. His mouth watered and his stomach rumbled, reminding him that it had been a goodly while since he had eaten anything other than porridge while on his sickbed.

Cooking fires were carefully laid back away from the wooden houses and he walked to them, hoping that someone would give him something to eat.

He was in luck. The first fire he came to was tended by a young girl who cut a slice of meat from a cooking goose and shyly gave it to him. He thank her profusely, and her cheeks blushed rosily as she turned back to the goose.

Cumac smiled and went on his way, wolfing down the slice of goose and licking the grease from his fingers.

I could eat a whole one by myself, he thought. Now, if I could only get a slice of mutton or pork!

"There you are!" a voice shouted.

Cumac turned and saw Lorgas coming up to him, a smile wreathing his face. He wore a fresh green tunic held tightly to his waist with a soft leather belt. Green were his trousers as well and his boots the same soft leather as his belt.

"We thought you were finished sleeping, but you have slept another two days since last we spoke. Seanchan said to let you sleep as your body was probably telling you to rest more from your wound. Personally," he said gruffly, "I think you were playing slugabed!"

"It's good to see you," Cumac said. He reached out and rubbed a piece of Lorgas's tunic between thumb and forefinger. "I see that you have been well taken care of."

"You can't expect an Ashelf to run around with his clothes all a-tatter! Besides, I didn't want to hurt Connor's feelings." He lowered his voice conspiratorially. "Truthfully, Connor would give us half his kingdom if we could return the Chalice to him! Of course, we'd never go so far as to accept it," he added hastily, as Cumac frowned at him. "It was just . . . a way of explaining!"

Cumac laughed and clapped Lorgas on his shoulder. "No offense taken." He glanced down at his own garments. "And you are right. We can't go around looking like we were eating our last chickpea. Where's Fedelm?"

Lorgas shook his head. "She's with Seanchan. Out in the woods, they are, a-chanting and a-carrying on like they were going to call the very trees into helping us. Frankly, I think it's a waste of time better spent going after Bricriu."

"But we don't know which way to go," Cumac said. "We can't go off blundering through forests and over bogs directionless."

"We know he isn't north," Lorgas said gesturing. "Otherwise, we would have come on him when we left the Otherworld."

"That leaves west and south," Cumac said.

"I say west. Toward Connacht. There've been grave dealings between Connacht and Ulster for years. Ever since Maeve tired of Connor's bed and went with Ailill because he isn't the jealous sort. Poor happenings with a wife," he grumbled. "No honor in sleeping with one's enemies."

Seanchan and Fedelm came through the Red Branch gate.

"Here come Seanchan and Fedelm now. I guess they've had enough communing with trees."

"Don't Ashelves do the same?" Cumac teased.

"It isn't the same!" Lorgas sputtered. "It is our solemn duty to live in the forest and listen to the trees. What can a Druid and a woman from the Sidhe hope to accomplish? Better if *I* went."

"Why didn't you?" Cumac asked.

"This isn't Rowan Oak," he said loftily. "Our trees make their oldest look like fresh-sprung saplings!"

Cumac laughed and went forward to meet with Seanchan and Fedelm.

"Hello!" Fedelm said, adding teasingly, "I see you are finally up and about. I had about given you up for lost."

"No faith, no faith," Seanchan said sternly. "I told the both of you that he simply needed more rest. No one recovers quickly from a Sumairen blade! He's lucky he wasn't lost to one of the Memans after he was wounded. Quite lucky. Yes. Quite lucky."

He looked closely at Cumac, stroking his beard thoughtfully.

"Well, you look as good as can be expected. But I don't think you're up to running wild through the woods yet."

"And why would he want to do that?" Lorgas asked grumpily. "There has to be a reason for that, and we know the reason why he should. Just need a direction, now."

"Yes," Fedelm said, smiling. "We may have that. First, though, we must meet in council with Connor and the knights of the Red Branch. We must lay out a plan for all of us. Running around like a frightened squirrel isn't going to help us at all."

The moaning sound of a horn reached them.

"Ah, right on time," she said. "Come, now. Let us sit in council and see what we can do."

A SOFT glow shined over Emain Macha as they made their way to the thatched-roof Red Branch Hall. From somewhere a wren sang, and peace seemed to rest over the land. A false peace, Cumac decided, and he remembered as if in a distant dream the darkness that was beginning to gather outside the walls.

They walked up the rough stone steps and entered the hall and paused for a moment to let their eyes adjust to the gray light inside. Niches were carved in the thick red-oak pillars supporting the roof, and each niche was filled with a head of a Red Branch enemy. The heads seemed to consider them thoughtfully as they entered. Connor sat on his throne, a simple wooden affair on a platform that raised him above the others. Around the walls, the knights sat, some scarred horribly from battle, others smooth-faced, lacking even the beard that badged the older warriors. Beside Connor sat another Druid—Cathbad, Cumac thought automatically, he whose power was known throughout the land. Seanchan crossed over and took his place to the right of Cathbad, smoothing his robe around him as he sat. He removed his blackthorn pipe from somewhere inside his clothing and filled it with a fragrant weed and lit it.

A fire flickered softly in a circle of stones in the middle of the hall, and the scent of resin rolled to them as the smoke climbed to a hole in the roof. On the walls were old wooden carvings of the ancient gods. Between the gods were other carvings—old triskeles and spirals.

Talk ceased as the warriors considered the visitors. After a moment, Seanchan rose and said, "Here are Fedelm of the Cruachan Sidhe and Cumac, son of Cucullen, the greatest warrior who sat among us. They have made their way through great peril to join us today. Bid them welcome."

"Greatest warrior! *Humph!*" a grizzled warrior said from Cumac's left, taking a long-stemmed scarred pipe from his mouth. "He's gone and I'm still here."

"But you did lose the contest set to you by Cu Roi, Conall Cernach," Connor reminded him. He looked sharply at another warrior who started to speak. "And you, Leogaire Búadbach. If I remember rightly—and I do—did not you and Conall Cernach lose your clothes when you came to the witches, while Cucullen triumphed?"

A roar of laughter welled up as Leogaire Búadbach's cheeks burned rosy red with embarrassment. Conall Cernach busied himself by studying the heads in the pillars.

The two had not forgotten the time when Bricriu had baited the two of them, along with Cucullen, into claiming the Champion's Portion at a feast Bricriu had put together. All three had claimed to be the best warrior and entitled to the tenderloin of beef that went to the champion. One of the tests they had to undergo was to sit a vigil in a forest during the night. Witches came and stripped the three of their clothes. Conall Cernach and Leogaire Búadbach had fled naked and in terror, while Cucullen regained his clothes and captured the witches.

Connor waved his hand and leaned forward from his throne.

"That is in the past. For now, we must find Bricriu and regain your father's Chalice, the Bladhm Caillis. Otherwise, Ulster will know no peace under the sun. Already our enemies are pushing against our borders, as is Maliman from the north. Yes," he continued, as Fedelm and Cumac exchanged glances, "he has managed to regain his fortress in the Mountains of Mourne. Many of those released from the Great Rift—the Grayshawls and Nightshades among them—are making their way to his fortress. The numbers grow every day. Soon, he will have an army that will be able to roll over the land. We cannot send anyone after the Chalice as we have need of all our knights to protect our borders. And a large force would be easily detected. We must leave it up to you, Lorgas, Fedelm, and Cumac. And you, Seanchan," he added, turning to the Druid. "They may have need of your skills before this is over."

Connor looked back at the three and said, "I am certain you understand the powers of Seanchan, the wizard and Druid. He is the strongest wizard, other than Cathbad, who can stand against Maliman. Maliman and Seanchan were foster brothers and disciples of Morimag the Great before Morimag turned away from the Druidic teachings and the teachings of the Tuatha De Danann."

"Yes," Lorgas said, placing his hand on his breast and bowing his head. "We have heard of the power of Seanchan in Rowan Oak. I, for one, welcome his company."

"As do we," Fedelm said. "You are most welcome to join us."

Seanchan nodded and rose to stand by the three.

"And so we have it," Connor said, falling back against his throne. "The Band of Seekers. Fail us not, for to do so will bring damnation and ruin upon all of us. Whatever you wish for to help you on your journey will be given to you, even our treasure."

"Horses," Lorgas said promptly. "We cannot travel as fast as we must."

"You shall have them," Connor said. He motioned to a young man standing near his throne, who left immediately.

"And food for seven days," Fedelm said. "For it will take us that long to reach Cruachan Ai, the home of Maeve, She-Who-Intoxicates."

"And it shall be so," Connor said, and motioned to another young man who promptly left.

"Anything else?"

Cumac shook his head. "I don't think so," he said with a quick glance at the others. "We must needs to travel light and swift. Enough to aid us. Surplus will only hinder."

Connor nodded.

"I see you have the Dragonstone on your cloak. It was made by Goibniu, the smith-god, and given by Boand to Maeve, who gave it to your father. I took it from your father's cloak after he was slain. It has great power that you will have to learn to use, and it glows black and trembles when danger is near."

"I thank you for the gift," Cumac said formally.

"It would go to no other, for the stone picks its own owner," Connor replied.

The young man sent to collect horses came bursting through the door. Connor looked at him, frowning.

"There is something strange," the youth said excitedly. "A new horse is among the others. Black, he is, as black as a starless and moonless night. I could not come near him."

"A black horse?" Seanchan asked.

The young man nodded vigorously.

"Yes. Black as black can be."

"Interesting," Seanchan said and, turning, led the others out of the Red Branch Hall to the corral where the horses were kept.

There, a gleaming black horse watched them approach, muscles moving visibly beneath his coat. He held his head high as if regarding them loftily, and indeed, he might have been, for he grumbled deep in his throat and pawed the ground, warning them not to come near.

"The Black of Saingliau!" Seanchan breathed. "Cucullen's favorite. This is true magic," he said, turning to the others. "He comes from the gray lake at Sliab Fuait, where he and the Gray of Macha disappeared into the waters after the death of Cucullen."

He studied Cumac for a long moment, then said, "He has come to be with the son of Cucullen. You, Cumac—approach him."

Cumac slid beneath the railing of the corral and walked toward the horse. Promptly the Black of Saingliau came forward to meet Cumac partway. There, he knelt and made a soft noise in his throat.

Cautiously, Cumac laid a hand on the Black of Saingliau's arched neck and stroked it. Black turned his head and nuzzled Cumac's thigh.

"Ah, aren't you a beauty?" Cumac said softly. He threw a leg over Black's back. Black rose and stamped his hooves, throwing his head.

"He has not been seen since your father's last battle," Seanchan breathed. "Yet, here he is now. Barach of the Old Ones has sent him to you. If they are giving us protection, we are fortunate indeed."

"Cernunnos spoke of the Old Ones—the Harwraiths, he called them?" Cumac said, furrowing his brow in question.

"Yes. They have existed as spirits before memory came. They are older than Tuan and are most feared, as they are savage and give no quarter in battle and are never defeated. They help guard the ancient forests with Cernunnos. They travel by thought. Maliman has tried repeatedly to force his way past them but has been defeated each time. Spells and enchantments do not affect them. The most feared of the Old Ones is their leader, Barach, whose appearance in battle is so fearsome that the enemy stands frozen in terror. They have existed before the First Invasion, when Cesair and her father Bith brought fifty women and three men to the island," Seanchan explained.

"Then they will fight with us?" Cumac asked.

Seanchan shook his head. "No, I don't think so. The Old Ones have their own way and seldom mix with this world. Unless," he amended, "someone interferes with their world, and that is highly unlikely. Of course, they are protectors of forests, but Cerunnos usually handles those problems. With the forest, I mean. Actually," he said, rubbing his chin, "no one knows that much about the Old Ones. They are very secretive."

"Well," Cumac said, rubbing Black's shoulder, "Black is more than welcome, whoever they are. When do we start?"

"Tomorrow. Early," Fedelm said. "I would suggest that we go toward Cruachan Ai. Connacht is the sworn enemy of Ulster, and Bricriu would head for there first to seek asylum from Maeve. The laws of hospitality must be observed, and any Ulstermen who cross over Connacht's borders will be set upon by the Connacht army. Bricriu will be safe as long as he stays in Cruachan Ai. Besides," she added, "as long as the Chalice is within Connacht's borders, it is away from the Red Branch, which leaves Ulster vulnerable. Maeve may attack Emain Macha, knowing that the Chalice cannot help the Red Branch."

"I agree," Lorgas said. "Ulster is indeed vulnerable without the Chalice."

"There is logic to that," Seanchan said. "And we must start somewhere instead of going hither and thither like Sword-wanderers."

"Then it is settled," Cumac said. "We shall go to Connacht first."

"But for now," Connor said, "we shall feast. Let us go back into the hall. There are three boars on the fire and much beer and ale."

They took a deep breath, thankful for Connor's hospitality, and followed him back into the hall, where vats of foaming beer and ale stood in the center. They had just made themselves comfortable when servants began bringing in platters heaped with meat and fresh bread and bowls of fruit.

They filled their trenchers with food, and then Connor cried out, "Fedlimid! A story while we feast!"

A sorrow-eyed man of slim build came forward, harp in hand. He settled himself and strummed his harp for a moment, then lifted his voice.

"For our friends and for Cumac, son of Cucullen, our greatest champion," he said, and began to chant a tale:

"Now when Cucullen's foes came for the last time against him, his land was filled with black smoke and flame and the weapons fell from their racks in his house, and Cucullen knew from this that the day of his death was close. The evil tidings were brought to him and the ugly maiden Leborcham told him to rise and go, although he had been forewarned about fighting in defense of the plain of Murthemne, and Lendabair, the wife of Conall Cernach, also spoke to him. He sprang to his arms and threw his cloak over his shoulder, but when he tried to pin it with his great brooch, the brooch slipped from his fingers and fell onto his foot, piercing it. Then he took his great shield and told Laeg Mac Ringabra, his chariot driver, to harness the Gray of Macha and the Black of Saingliau.

" 'I swear upon all that my people swear upon,' said Laeg, 'that though Connor's warriors surrounded the Gray, they could not drag him to the chariot to be harnessed. I could never refuse you,

Cucullen, until today, but you will have to come to the Gray of Macha and the Black of Saingleau and speak with them yourself.'

"Cullen went to them, but three times the horses turned their left side to their master.

"Then Cullen scolded his horses, saying they should not behave this way toward their master. With that, the great Gray came and let fall big round drops of bloody tears upon Cucullen's feet. Then Cucullen leaped into the chariot and drove it suddenly toward the south along the Road of Mid-Luachair.

"And Leborcham met him and told him not to leave them again, and the one hundred and fifty queens who were in Emain Macha at the time gave a great cry of anguish at seeing him armed, but he ignored them and turned his chariot to the right whereupon they broke out in great screams of wailing and lamentation and beat their hands against their breasts, for they knew they would not see him again.

"The house of his nurse who had fostered him was before him on the road. He would go to it whenever he came upon it, for he knew that she would always keep a cup with drink there for him. He stopped there and took the cup and drank it, then left, bidding her farewell. He went again upon the road, galloping faster to the south, and came upon three ugly hags, all blind in the left eye, traveling upon the road in front of him. They had roasted a dog on spits made from a rowan tree and prepared it with great spells of enchantment and poison. Cucullen had a geis upon him not to eat of the flesh of a dog for that was part of his name, known as he was as the Hound of Ulster, so he made to pass them, knowing they were not there for his good. But they called out to him, asking him to stop.

" 'Stay a while with us, great Cucullen,' said one.

" 'I will not,' Cucullen answered.

" 'The only food we have is a hound,' she said. 'But I know that if this had been a great feast you would have stayed with us. However,' she shrugged, 'there is only a little here and so you will not stay. This is not honorable for you to do.'

"Cucullen sighed and when he came close to her, the hag gave him the meat with her left hand. Cucullen took the meat in his left hand, ate some of it, and put the rest under his left thigh. The hand he had used and the thigh of his left leg were mysteriously seized and the great strength seeped from them.

"Then he left them and went along the Road of Mid-Luachair around Sliab Fuait. His enemy, Erc Mac Carpre, saw him in his chariot, Cucullen's sword shining redly in his hand and the hero's halo glowing over him, and his three-colored hair like strings of golden thread streaming over a craftsman's anvil.

" 'That man is coming towards us, warriors!' shouted Erc. 'Wait for him.'

"So the men made a barrier with their shields, linking one to the one next to him, and at each corner of the barrier, Erc placed two of his bravest fighting men to fight against Cucullen along with a satirist. He told the satirists to ask Cucullen for his spear, for he knew that the sons of Caitlín had prophesied that a king would be slain if his spear would not be given willingly. Then Erc had his warriors raise a great cry of challenge and Cucullen answered, rushing towards them in his chariot, performing his three Thunder Feats as he swung his spear and sword around him, slicing heads and skulls and hands and feet in half and scattering their bones over the plain of Murthemne until they fell as numerous as grains of sand in the sea or stars in the heaven and dewdrops of May and flakes of snow and hailstones and leaves on the forest and the petals of flowers on Moy-Bray and the blades of grass under the feet of herds on a soft summer day. And gray became the field with their brains left behind after Cucullen had passed.

"Then he saw one of the pairs of warriors coming together in blows and the satirist called upon Cucullen to stop them. Cucullen leaped between them and crushed their skulls with two quick blows of his fist.

" 'Give me your spear!' cried the satirist.

" 'I swear by all that my people swear that you do not need it more than I do,' Cucullen said. 'The men of Erin are upon me here and I am one with them.'

" 'I will curse you with a satire if you do not give it to me,' the satirist said.

" 'I have never been reviled for being miserly or arrogant,' cried Cucullen.

"And with that, he drove the spear through the satirist and Lugaid Mac Cú Roi retrieved the spear. He looked at the others and said, 'What will fall with this spear, sons of Caitlín?'

" 'A king will fall by that spear,' replied the sons of Caitlín.

"Then Lugaid threw the spear at Cucullen's chariot and it went through Laeg Mac Ringabra, ripping out his guts.

" 'Ah! I have been sorely wounded!' cried the great charioteer.

"Cucullen took the spear and said his good-bye to Laeg. Then, Cucullen looked at the host and said, 'Today, I will be both warrior and chariot driver.'

"Then he saw the other two warriors fighting each other and the second satirist said that Cucullen would be dishonored if he did not intervene. Cucullen picked up a rock in each hand and dashed out their brains.

" 'Give me your spear, Cucullen!' cried the satirist.

" 'I swear by all that my people swear that you do not need this spear more than I do myself,' Cucullen replied. 'I need it for my hand and for my valor and my weapons, for it is today that I must try to drive the four armies from the plain of Murthemne.'

" 'Then I will say a satire against your name and honor,' said the satirist.

" 'I am not bound to grant more than one request a day and that I have already done,' Cucullen said.

" 'Then I will cast a satire against the honor of Ulster,' said the satirist.

" 'Never has Ulster been cursed for my refusal,' Cucullen said. 'Though little of my life remains before me, I will not let that happen this day.'

"Then Cucullen cast the spear at him and it went through the satirist's head, killing him and the nine men who stood behind him. Erc Mac Carpre seized the spear and said, 'What shall fall by this spear, sons of Caitlín?'

" 'That's easy,' they replied. 'A king falls by that spear.'

" 'I heard you say that a king would fall by the spear which Lugaid threw,' Erc said.

" 'And he did. Laeg, the king of charioteers, Cucullen's driver, fell,' they said.

"Satisfied, Erc threw the spear at Cucullen and it went through the Gray of Macha. Cucullen snatched the spear and said good-bye to his horse and the horse went into Gray's Linn in Sliab Fuait.

"Then Cucullen drove again through the host and saw another two men fighting among themselves. Again, he stopped them and again the satirist there demanded his spear and again Cucullen refused him.

" 'I will curse you with a satire,' said the satirist.

" 'I have paid the price for my honor once before this day. I am not obliged to give it again,' replied Cucullen.

" 'Then I will curse Ulster because of you,' said the satirist.

" 'I have paid already for Ulster's honor,' said Cucullen.

" 'Then I will curse your race,' said the satirist.

" 'Tidings that I have been defamed shall never reach those who live on my land, for there is little time remaining for me,' said Cucullen fiercely. And he threw the spear at the satirist and it went through his head and through the heads of nine men behind him.

" 'Grace with wrath, great Cucullen,' said the satirist.

"Then Cucullen drove again through the host and again Lugaid seized the spear and said, 'What will fall by this spear, sons of Caitlín?'

" 'A king will fall,' said the sons of Caitlín.

" 'I heard you claim the same thing by the spear that Erc cast.'

" 'That is a try,' they said. 'The king of horses fell by it, namely the Gray of Macha.'

"Then Lugaid threw the spear at Cucullen and it struck him hard in the belly and went through, spilling his bowels upon the chariot cushion. The Black of Saingliau fled, leaving the chariot and his master dying alone on the plain.

"Then Cucullen said, 'I would go as far as that lake to get a drink of water.'

" 'We will give you permission to do that,' said his enemies. 'But you must return to us.'

" 'I will come to you if I can,' replied Cucullen. 'But if I cannot, then you will have to come to me.'

"Then he pulled his bowels back into his belly and staggered to the lake where he drank his fill and washed himself. But he found he could not return to them so he called for them to come to him.

"He looked to the west and his eye fell upon a great pillarstone and he went up to it and wrapped his belt around it, snugging himself to it so that he would not die seated or lying down, for he would meet his enemies on his feet at the last.

"Then all the men in the great host came cautiously up to him, but they would not go close to him for they had seen what Cucullen could do with his great sword.

" 'Shame be upon all of you,' said Erc Mac Carpre. 'Why do you flinch from that man? Take his head in revenge for my father's head which he took.'

"Then the waters of the lake parted and the great Gray of Macha came roaring out to protect Cucullen as long as his soul was in him and his hero's halo flickered above his head.

"Three times the great horse stampeded through the army and fifty fell by his teeth and thirty by each of his hooves. This is what he slew of that army, the three great red routs he made upon them and that is why we have the saying, 'Not more terrible were the great courses of the Gray of Macha after the slaughter of Cucullen.'

"Then a raven fell upon the shoulder of Cucullen and Erc said, 'That pillar is not meant for birds.'

"And he carefully arranged Cucullen's hair over his shoulder and cut off his head. Then the great sword fell from Cucullen's hand and severed Lugaid's right hand and it fell onto the ground. For that, they cut off Cucullen's right hand.

"Then Lugaid and the hosts marched away, carrying with them Cucullen's head and his right hand. They came to Tara, and there is the sickbed of his head and his right hand and the full of the cover of his shield of mold. From there, they marched towards the river Liffey, but now came the great armies of Ulster driving furiously after them and in the lead was the fury of Conall Cernach. They met the Gray of Macha, blood streaming from him, and all were saddened for they knew that Cucullen had been slain. Conall and the Gray went to find Cucullen's body and found it at the pillar-stone. The Gray went up and laid his head upon Cucullen's breast and Conall cried out, 'A heavy care for the Gray is that corpse.'

"And then Conall followed the army for he had been placed under a vow long ago that he would avenge Cucullen if Cucullen was slain first and Cucullen would return the favor if Conall fell first.

" 'And if I fall first, how will you avenge me?' Cucullen had asked.

" 'The day on which you are slain will be the same day that I will avenge you,' Conall said. 'And if I fall first, how will you avenge me?'

" 'Your blood will not be cold upon the earth before I avenge you,' Cucullen had answered.

"So Conall sped towards Lugaid at the Liffey and found him bathing his wound. 'Keep a watch to the plain so that we will not be surprised,' Lugaid said to his chariot driver.

"The charioteer looked behind them and said, 'There is one horseman coming across the plain. Great is his speed and the ravens circle above him. You would think flakes of snow were sprinkling upon the plain in front of him.'

" 'That is not a loved horseman,' Lugaid said. 'It is Conall Cernach, mounted on the Dewy-Red. The birds you see above him are clods of dirt being thrown from his horse's hooves. The snow-flakes are the foam from the horse's mouth. Look again. What ford is he taking?'

"The charioteer looked again and said, 'He is coming to the ford that is the path the others have taken.'

" 'Let that horse pass us,' Lugaid said. 'We do not wish to fight Conall Cernach.'

"But when Conall reached the ford, he spied Lugaid and his charioteer and went to them.

" 'Welcome is a debtor's face!' he said with relish. 'You owe a great debt to a man, and I am the one to collect it. I speak of the slaying of Cucullen, my friend. For that, I bring suit against you.'

"Then they agreed to fight on the Plain of Argetros and Conall quickly wounded Lugaid with his javelin. Then they went on top of Ferta Lugdach.

" 'I wish you to speak the truth of men,' Lugaid said.

" 'What is that?' asked Conall.

" 'You should use only one hand against me for I have only one hand as well,' Lugaid said. 'It would not be honorable to do otherwise.'

" 'Then you shall have that,' Conall answered.

"He tied his hand to his side with rope and for the space of two watches of the day they fought and neither could gain an edge over the other. When Conall saw he could not gain the advantage, he called to his horse and the Dewy-Red came to Lugaid and ripped a piece out of his side.

" 'This is not an honorable thing!' Lugaid protested to Conall.

" 'I had it done only on my behalf,' Conall answered. 'Not on behalf of savage beasts and senseless things.'

" 'I know now that you will not go unless my head comes along with you since I took Cucullen's head. So take my head and add my lands to yours and my valor to yours, for if I must die, I want it to be at the hands of the best warrior left in all the land.'

"At that, Conall cut off Lugaid's head.

"It was then that Conall returned to Emain Macha, but there was no triumph in the entry, for the soul of Cucullen appeared there to fifty queens who had all loved him and they saw him floating in his chariot over Emain Macha and heard him chant a mystic song in the old tongue of the Ancients, and this is what it says in the tongue that we speak today:"

It is lucky for him before my wounding.
It seems to me I see horses of Ler's son;
It seems to me I heard that,
This great music before us.

It seems to me it is of the size
As if it were a hundred warriors weeping.

Fiethata's rough wind rose in loathing,
Until he tossed his hair across the sea.

It seems to me music was heard:
This great sound toward us from the east.
It seems to me to be of the size
As if it were a hundred warriors at food.

Fiethata's rough wind arose in loathing,
Until he tossed his hair across the army.
Alas that I followed the cattle drive,
In which I am but a war cry and an exploit.

Ferdia fell by my hand in the battle,
And Caitlín of the strange tricks.
My combat is a combat of heather,
It was not a combat of a hero after the destruction.

It breaks my own tabus.
My time has come, though you regret it.
This music overcomes my strength,
The harp of Mannoir's son playing.

It seems to me that I heard music
This great sound before us from the east.
It seems to me that it caused weeping.
On the green of the horses of Ler's son.

It seems to me I heard from the east
An enormous noise before me from the west.
It seems to me of female witches in size,
Like two hundred with food.

A gentle wind arose, fierceness of deed,
Until Fiethata moved his hair on the mountain

With a noise of warriors, a great shriek,
And a sword, then a flame of brightness.

Alas that I followed the cattle drive
Wherefore I am but a shout and an exploit.
Ferdiad fell by my hand in the fight
And Caitlín of the strange tricks.
My combat is a combat of heather;
It was not a combat of a hero after the destruction.

Today another thought occurs to me—
The rest is foolishness—
I did not know my heart was not of steel
Until tonight.
I had never gone to seek
A battle before;
I did not know my heart was not of iron
Within my breast.
I was a warrior of the frenzy of fighting
Until today
I did not know my heart was not of bone
Within my chest.
I was a warrior, staunch, curly-haired—
Good was the glory—
I didn't know my heart was not of stone
Within my breast.
Maeve pursued me,
A proud journey
On the plain until I was felled
By the armies.

Bitterly am I wounded sharply by
A great evil I speak to the fair form of Culann,
Protector of Ulster's youth, a tale with harshness,
A deed with bitterness.

He fell silent, and silence filled the Great Hall as the last notes of his harp faded away. Then Conall spoke, tears leaking from his eyes like salty streams.

"Ah, but I remember that as if it was yesterday and I didn't have frost in my beard or in my hair! And that is just the way it happened, how we lost the great Cucullen and how I avenged him!"

He blew his nose on his sleeve and wiped his eyes. He honked and groused and finally settled.

"You are a fearsome harper, Fedlimid," he said gruffly. "And my shield upon it if someone says otherwise!"

"A strange choice for a welcoming feast," Connor said. "But a tale of honor and glory nevertheless. You have done well, Fedlimid."

Fedlimid bowed and carefully laid his harp aside before filling his platter from the king's table, for as he was the king's harper and tale-teller, he was privileged to eat the choice cuts of meat that were reserved for the king.

"Have you heard that tale, Cumac?" asked Fedelm quietly.

"Yes, but not as well told as this. Truly Aengus Og, the gift-giver to man of love and song, has given him the gift of song."

"I hope that you will have the time to ask him," Fedelm said archly.

"So do I," Cumac said soberly. "So do I."

15

Gray mist had yet to be burned away by the sun when the Band of Seekers rode past Emain Macha's massive oaken gate bound with heavy iron straps and began to follow the road away from the Red Branch fortress. The pines closed in tightly around them, making Cumac feel as if they were riding through a tunnel of dark green. Puddles of water lay in the middle of the road. But all was silent, and that silence seemed to press in upon their shoulders.

They rode for what seemed like ages to Cumac, who drew his cloak tighter as clammy tendrils of mist folded cold fingers around him.

It would be wet when we begin, he thought. A bad omen if one wants to believe in that sort of thing. Sticks and stones! We should have left after this mist has been driven away by the morning sun.

"We need to put miles behind us if we hope to catch Bricriu," Seanchan said, as if reading Cumac's mind. "It is a long way to the House of Sanan, where we may find shelter and protection before we continue our journey. But," he cautioned, "we must be wary, for Sanan is deceitful and will try to encourage us to stay with him and his daughter, Buan, who kills travelers for their flesh."

Fedelm nodded. Sanan had been given nine lives by the Harwraiths for standing like a stone against the invading Fomorians. Although mortal, he was such a fierce warrior that the Tuatha De Danann welcomed him into their ranks as an equal. He carried a formidable spear, Galadrois, the Spear of Fire and Ice, which struck fear into the hearts of any who saw Sanan's fierce visage in battle. His house was a sanctuary for travelers.

"And the day may be difficult," Lorgas muttered, looking warily around them. "I feel . . . something. Something that should not be there. Or here. But something. This mist has a bad smell to it, and no birds sing in the meadow we are crossing."

"What is it?" Cumac asked.

Lorgas shook his head. "I do not know. Something evil this way comes."

"I too feel it," Fedelm said. "The air smells like old iron taken new from the sea."

Cumac closed his eyes for a moment, breathing deeply, trying to sense what the others had. But he could not. Frustrated, he loosened Caladbolg in its sheath and rode warily, looking frequently over his shoulder at their back trail.

Then, he caught the fetid odor that Fedelm had described: old iron covered with old blood.

Up ahead, Seanchan reined in his horse and sat quietly, his

attention elsewhere. Lorgas and Fedelm rode up on either side of him while Cumac stayed close in the rear.

"There is something in the air," Seanchan said, frowning. "I do not like it."

"Nor I," Fedelm said grimly. "I have smelled this before but do not know it now."

Lorgas said, "As have I."

Wind began to moan through the pines and blow coldly against them. The smell grew stronger, and then the wind cleared some of the mist, revealing the stalkers.

"Warggads!" Seanchan shouted. "Look to yourselves!"

Cumac's throat went dry as he took a firmer grip upon his sword. He heard the bows of Lorgas and Fedelm release their arrows and both shafts sped true, taking their targets in the eye. Then, Cumac found himself hard-pressed as the warggads leaped toward him. He struck a hard blow on the neck of one, knocking it down. It lay stunned for a moment, then snarled and leaped up again.

"The eyes! Strike them in the eyes!" Seanchan shouted. "Or behead them!"

Grimly Cumac struck again, the edge of his blade smashing through the bone of a warggad and into its eye. The warggad gave a yelp and fell to the ground, where its legs scrambled against the pain, then lay still as the body slowly shaped back into that of a man.

Black gave a scream of fury and rose, using his hooves to lash out and crush two who tried to hamstring him. Cumac gripped Black's sides tighter with his legs and dropped the reins to use his sword with both hands.

More and more warggads came toward them, snarling and howling death cries when an arrow or Cumac's blade found their eyes. Cumac began to weaken from the illness that he had suffered so short a time ago. His sword began to feel heavier and heavier in his hand. A warggad felt Cumac weakening and pressed forward, his claws flashing faster and faster as he tried to slip past Cumac's defense.

Then, a blinding light flared from Seanchan's staff, dispelling the mist around them, and the warggads howled with pain and fled, running into the deep shadows of the woods.

All drew a deep breath, and the light burned slowly away, leaving them in a shadowed land. Cumac panted as he pulled a piece of cloth from his pack and carefully wiped his blade free of warggad blood.

"How did they know to come for us?" Cumac asked. He wiped cold sweat from his face with the edge of his cloak.

"It is the work of Maliman and the Grayshawls," Seanchan answered. "He knows where we are."

"But how?" Lorgas asked puzzled. "When we left Emain Macha, the mist hid us. How can a man, even a Druid or wizard, see through mist?"

"There are many things that do the work of Maliman," Seanchan said gravely. "Some animals, some birds, but it doesn't matter now. We shall have to keep careful watch as we travel to Connacht. We must not be surprised."

"I wonder if it is wise that we continue to take this road," Fedelm said, frowning. "There is another way—the Ford of Uath Mac Imomain—longer but perhaps safer."

"I would not wish to go that way for Horror, the son of Terror, is unpredictable. No one can tell what mood he will be in. He may wish to kill as well as welcome us to his house. He gives judgment to those seeking settlement and is able to transform himself into any shape that he wishes. He has tremendous power and a very mercurial temper. He guards the ford which bears his name. The lake in which the waters of the ford empty is his home. He can be injured but not killed. His house is always shrouded in mist, and inside, gray rules. Even the torches burn gray light."

"I think it is better if we stay along this road," Lorgas put in. "What about you, Cumac?"

"What about detouring to the south?" Cumac asked, his breathing beginning to return to normal. "If north to Uath Mac Imomain—Horror, the son of Terror—is dangerous, would not the south be better? We know that Maliman is aware we are on this road (although *how* he knows, we cannot guess) so wouldn't our chances be better to go that way?"

"We would have to go through the Forest of Tuan, the home of Black Baggots, if we go that way," Seanchan said pointedly.

"Then either way we choose will be equally as dangerous," Lorgas said. "We might as well stay this way."

"Then," Cumac said, "let us compromise. We can go to the House of Sanan, and then at night, slip south through the Forest of Tuan."

Lorgas frowned. "Seems to me that we are spilling from the pot into the fire. It's always night in the Forest of Tuan, is it not?"

"True," Seanchan answered. "But if we are very careful, we may get through without mishap."

"I still say it might be better if we go the way of the Ford of Uath Mac Imomain," Fedelm said stubbornly. "That way we have only one to contend with."

"Perhaps," Seanchan said. "But Uath Mac Imomain can summon others if he wishes."

"But," Fedelm said triumphantly, "he *may* greet us as guests instead."

Seanchan nodded. "That is a possibility."

"And we can go north from the House of Sanan," Lorgas said. He shook his head gloomily. "Pick one, Cumac. You are the one first given the task of finding the Chalice of Fire."

Fedelm and Seanchan looked expectantly at Cumac, who bit his lip and said, "Then I say we go to the House of Sanan and swing north to the Ford of Uath Mac Imomain under the cover of night. It sounds to me as if the numbers we may have to face will be less that way."

"Still, there are dangers that do not require numbers," Seanchan said, turning the head of his horse to the west. "Although we may find refuge in Uath Mac Imomain's house, there is no guarantee that the road to it will not be guarded by those serving Maliman. And now"—he studied the sky—"rain is coming, and I think we had better travel fast if we are to make the House of Sanan before dark. I should not like to be caught on this road again. We fought off the warggads, but they can be sent again along with others under Maliman's control. The eye of Maliman carries far with the help of carrion birds and some creatures of the night."

THEY traveled swiftly, this Band of Seekers, urging their horses in a quick canter, keeping ever vigilant against being surprised again by warggads or Black Baggots or others at the call of Maliman. The forest closed in upon them, and at times, Cumac was certain that he saw the forest move, but he decided, after rubbing his eyes, that what he saw as movement was only the trick of shadows. And the shadows also made him uneasy, as he expected another attack would suddenly swoop down upon them.

On they pressed, and the day became darker and darker as the gloaming and rain clouds settled upon them. A soft wind stirred, soughing through the trees, a mournful sound that prickled the flesh as anticipation fed imagination.

Cumac watched Lorgas reach to loosen his hatchet and sword at his belt, and Fedelm slipped another arrow from the quiver slung over one shoulder. Cumac slipped Caladbolg up and down in its sheath to make certain that he could draw it quickly if worry became reality.

"I do not like this," Lorgas muttered.

"Nor I," Fedelm put in.

"It is unsettling," Cumac added.

"The imagination is the worst enemy," Seanchan said. "Sweaty palms and dry mouths, all for nothing. You cannot do anything until something arrives, and that arrival we cannot control. Relax yourselves. We will have warning if the enemy approaches."

"Easy for a Druid to say," Lorgas muttered. "We can't make light with a few words and a staff."

"Do not rely upon that to appear whenever you want it," Seanchan said. "It is very tiring work and not to be performed on a whim. I can really do very little wizardry. But I can sense things, and there are *some* things that I *can* do that might prove helpful as time goes by."

"Hmpf," Lorgas said, somewhat mollified. "I suppose we'll have to make do with what we have."

"That," Seanchan said, "is the beginning of wisdom."

Cumac was getting very nervous during all this talk about who could do what, which, as the trees became menacing instead of comforting, left him tingling with terrible expectation.

Then rain began to fall, slowly at first, then faster and faster until the road became a sea of mud that sucked at their horses' hooves as they rode hunched in their saddles.

"I feared this," Seanchan said. "The rain may have been sent by Maliman to slow us and allow Bricriu to get farther and farther away. I wonder what other magic he has planned for us?"

"Then you believe he knows about the Chalice?" Cumac asked.

"Yes, I do," Seanchan said. "And I believe he knows Bricriu carries it."

"Why doesn't he just take it from Bricriu?" Cumac asked.

"He needs to build his strength before taking the Chalice," Seanchan said. "I believe he reasons that it would be better for Bricriu to carry the Chalice until he is ready for it. Then again," he added, "I could be wrong. I dimly remember stories from when I was an apprentice with the Duirgeals that the Chalice grants immortality to those who drink from it. But only the worthy can drink from it. Those who are unworthy suffer greatly from its fire. Some sorcerers and wizards can gather great strength from its presence, but that is very dangerous indeed: the Chalice was forged with its own magic, and other magic that tries to control the Chalice will suffer Goibniu's forge-fire. The Chalice," he said, sweeping rain irritably off his shoulders, "is particular about who it serves."

"And Bricriu?" Cumac asked.

"He may carry it, but he will be harmed if he tries to use it."

They came to a bend, and as they rounded it, the trees came so close—or seemed to come so close—that the tips of the branches brushed lightly over Cumac's cheeks.

At last, Cumac spoke. "Tell me, is it just my imagination, or are the trees coming closer and closer?"

Lorgas took a firm grip on his hatchet and sword and looked grimly around.

"Not the trees, but the imagination, the illusion," he said. "It is an elfin trick, and not a very humorous one. We'd better stop here."

They reined in, and Lorgas slipped down from his horse and slowly studied the trees.

"I am Lorgas of the Ashelves, cousin of Iain, Slayer of Credac, leader of the Zorgoths sent into darkness," he announced. "Show yourselves."

A laugh came from the shadows of the trees and suddenly, elves appeared, bows notched, swords and spears held ready.

They were blond and blue-eyed, and merriment and haughtiness danced in their eyes. They wore pale green tunics and leggings with boots laced halfway up the calf. One of the elves stepped forward from the others, holding his sword negligently by his side. They were as tall as Cumac.

"And what brings you this way?" he asked mockingly.

"Name yourself!" Lorgas demanded.

"I am Bern of the Ervalians," the elf said. He bowed elaborately, sweeping his hat from his head and nearly touching the ground with it. "Brother to our queen, Lakiel. I am a Janiser, one of the warrior-leaders of the Ervalians. I carry Bisuilglas, the sacred talisman of Rindale, the Hall of Warriors, where Ervalians gather when they are slain."

He held up his hand and all could see Bisuilglas, the ring made at the beginning of the First Age by the Old Ones. It was silver with a large amber stone set into the center. Within the amber, three pine needles lay in the shape of a triangle.

He smiled mockingly at them. "You make enough noise that our youngest could find you in the dark."

Lorgas flushed and said angrily, "And you obviously do not know the laws of hospitality. On what charge do you meet us with drawn bows and weapons?"

The smile slipped from Bern's face. "We have had Swordwanderers and Nightshades come this way. And some hobgoblins, although," he added grimly, "they will not come this way again. Our forest is not as old as Rowan Oak. We do not have the spells woven around it. Nor may we. The days of the elves are coming to an end. But, in the meantime, we protect this forest as best we can."

"Do we look like hobgoblins or Sword-wanderers or Nightshades?" Lorgas asked indignantly.

"One cannot be too careful," Bern said. "Now come! We shall take you to Lakiel."

"We are really pressed for time," Seanchan said. "But we do thank you for your courtesy."

Bern smiled. "It is not an offer. You have come into this part of the forest which is ours. Now, it is up to Lakiel what will happen with you."

Lorgas took a firm grip on his weapons. Fedelm's bow suddenly appeared in her hands. Cumac automatically drew Caladbolg, and Black hunched his shoulders, ready to spring into action. The Ervalians immediately drew their bows, the shafts centering on the newcomers to the forest.

"Put up your weapons!" Seanchan said sharply to his companions. "We shall not be the ones to violate the Laws of Hospitality."

He straightened and looked sternly at Bern. "I am Seanchan of the Duirgeals. Do not make me remind you of your duty not only to your queen but to visitors as well."

Some of the Ervalians looked at each other and shifted their feet nervously. The Duirgeals were the oldest fraternity of the Druids, the one to which it was most difficult to gain admission. They were one of the few fraternities of Druids who also were wizards, although they were reluctant to use their power to benefit man—they believed that man had to serve himself before they would serve him. Their power was so great that those not only in Earthworld but in the Otherworld as well feared to make them angry. They traced their fraternity back to the First Age, when they were the servants of the Old Ones. The training of a prospective Duirgeal began at age five, when a candidate exhibited traits different from other mortal children, such as insight, an affinity with birds or trees, or the ability to perform minor magic a little more than the slight-of-hand that other children could muster. Their studies lasted twenty years, after which they were apprenticed to a senior Duirgeal, who then spent the next five years training the apprentice to be tested for acceptance among the Duirgeals. Of all those who trained as an apprentice, only a bare one percent managed to pass the testing and take his vow. Those who did not pass often entered other fraternities of Druids. The Duirgeals could control the forces of nature and bend time to their will, although they seldom used that power, as to do so was dangerous. They spoke several languages and could communicate with animals.

"We know who you are, Seanchan," Bern answered sternly. "But we still must take you before Lakiel. If you resist, then we shall be forced to subdue you or"—he paused—"well, let us not threaten each other more than we already have. Be assured that you have no choice but to go with us. The times rule the laws of hospitality, for we know that those who serve Maliman often appear as something more than what they are. Not that we think you are one of the black wizards in disguise, but one cannot be too careful. That is why all who come into this part of the forest must appear before Lakiel."

He smiled and said, "Why make things difficult? If you are who you say you are, why not accept the hospitality of the Ervalians? We have sweet wine and honey-bread and apples and other fruits that others may not have. There is always time to partake of hospitality, unless you are a Grayshawl in disguise. Now, dismount and lead your horses with us."

Cumac glanced at Seanchan, who nodded and slipped from his horse. The others hesitated, but when Seanchan looked at them with a warning in his eyes, they dismounted, Lorgas grumbling and muttering about the rude manners of the Ervalians. Bern gave a chuckle and, turning, moved swiftly through the forest, following a trail apparent only to him. Birds suddenly sang overhead where none had been before, and occasionally a white deer trotted beside them for a while before disappearing into the depths of the forest. Crickets sounded and squirrels chattered as they gathered pine nuts. A jay scolded them. Even the trees seemed to whisper to them, and Cumac glanced uneasily about him.

"Do not mind them," Fedelm said. "They are aware that

strangers are in their midst and are warning each other to watch us carefully. But they will do us no harm unless we harm them or the Ervalians. This is an old forest. True, it isn't as old as Rowan Oak, but it is old nevertheless. It was planted by the Tuatha when they first came to our shores. People say that the Tuatha even gave the trees magical powers when they put them in the ground."

"True," Seanchan said. "They do have powers that will surprise you if you are not careful. They also can be mischievous at times by sending a sudden root out to trip you up, changing the direction of a path, dropping sticky sap upon your head, other things."

Lorgas said, "Indeed. That I would like to see. Rowan Oak has the true magic. These are but happenstance plantings and—*Urk!*"

The procession halted and all turned to look at him lying on the ground, covered with sap. All broke out into laughter and the trees seemed to join them with a *hunh! hunh! hunh!*

"This . . . this is intolerable!" Lorgas spluttered. "Intolerable!"

"You were warned," Seanchan said. "You have only yourself to blame."

Lorgas tried to get up, but the sap held him to the ground as he struggled. Then a bushel of pine needles fell onto him, covering him so thoroughly that only his eyes were visible.

"Get me out of this!" he shouted furiously.

Laughing, Bern came up to him. "Well, there's not much we can do but place you on your horse and let him carry you to Alainn. There, we can wash the sap and needles from you. Just be careful not to rub your eyes, or the lids will stick together and you will not see anything until we can clean you."

Lorgas fumed as the Ervalians put on green gloves and lifted him onto his horse. They pulled their hands from their gloves, leaving the gloves stuck to Lorgas, making him even more comic. The others laughed until their sides ached while Lorgas sat and fumed. Cumac took the reins of Lorgas's horse and, shoulders shaking with laughter, followed the Ervalians as they made their way through the forest to their city of Alainn. Slim and beautifully carved towers seemed to lift almost to the sky. A soft green haze rose from the lake just beyond. The streets were paved with well-laid stones, and the houses were built of solid oak well-polished, except for one built on a high hill in the center of Ailainn, which appeared to have been built from green marble. Ervalians bustled busily through the streets, going and coming from the market on the edge of the city, carrying melons and fruits and nuts and dripping honeycombs.

"Welcome!" Bern cried as he led them into the city and to the green marble house. "Welcome to Alainn! Rest yourselves and enjoy our hospitality. Soon, we shall visit with Lakiel in the Great Hall, who will decide what is to be done with you."

Three Ervalians came forth to take the horses and Lorgas, laughing at the sight of him as they led the horses toward the stable.

"I'm afraid that Lorgas is going to be a bit sore by the time they scrape the sap from him. But we will clean his weapons and give him fresh clothes to wear. His own will have to be burned. Now, come and I shall take you to your rooms. A bath will be brought to you so that you may wash off the dust of your journey. Wine will also be brought for your enjoyment," Bern said.

He crossed the courtyard and knocked on the door, which opened seemingly by itself. He led them to the central apartment that was to be Seanchan's. The windows were open to catch the soft breeze, and multicolored cushions were scattered over the floors. Against one wall stood a bed with sheer green curtains hanging from the posts. A silver bowl filled with nuts and candies sat in the center of a well-polished table made from cherry wood. A gold bathtub in a corner opposite the bed was discreetly screened from the rest of the room. The other rooms were similarly furnished.

"If you need something, please ask," Bern said. "There will be an Ervalian just outside your door to do your bidding."

"And to guard us from straying too far, I presume," Seanchan said dryly.

"No, no," Bern said hastily. "Let's not call them guards. Let us say that they will keep you from getting lost in the city if you should care to go out for a walk."

"Very tactful," Fedelm muttered.

"We shall be very comfortable," Seanchan said, casting an annoyed glance at Fedelm. "Thank you for your hospitality."

Bern spread his hands and grinned. "The Ervalians are widely known for their hospitality. Now, I must see Lakiel and tell her that we have lordly visitors. Excuse me, please."

He gave a half-bow and left.

"Well," Fedelm said, looking around in appraisal. "At least we are not in the prison. And these rooms do seem to be well chosen for comfort."

"Do not be lulled by what you see," Seanchan warned. "Despite what he said, we are still under guard. I do not doubt that we could go out to see the city—or part of it—but our guard will go with us."

"Not very hospitable if you ask me," Cumac said. He sighed. "But we might as well enjoy what is offered to us."

The door opened and Ervalians came in, carrying buckets of hot water that they poured into the bathtub. Silently, they left, closing the door behind them.

"Now, if you'll excuse me, I shall enjoy myself in the bath before the water cools. I daresay that you will find your bathtubs are also filled or soon to be," Seanchan said.

Cumac and Fedelm left to go to their own apartments. An Ervalian, armed with a strangely curved sword with the blade engraved with curious symbols, already stood outside each door.

"At least they allowed us to keep our weapons," Cumac said.

"Yes, but don't draw your sword in the presence of them. They will attack if you do, as they will see it as a gesture of battle. Remember," Fedelm warned him sternly, "we are still captives and must tread lightly around these halls. We do not want to bring them down upon us."

Cumac left, muttering to himself as he entered his own apartment. Fedelm grinned, nodded pleasantly at the guard beside her door, and entered, closing the door firmly behind her.

The gloaming came a soft gray over Alainn when Bern came to collect the four from their rooms. All were refreshed from relaxing—except for Lorgas, his flesh bright red from the scrubbing he had had to suffer in order to have the pine needles and sap removed. He grumbled about the forest and the Ervalians and their pick of dress for him—although he did look splendid in soft green with a red stripe sewn around the hem of his tunic.

Seanchan wore clean white robes and still carried his staff while Cumac was dressed in gray with a green stripe around the hem of his tunic. Fedelm wore blue with snowflakes worked into the cloth.

"You all look rested enough," Bern said merrily. "Now, let us meet with our queen, Lakiel."

"High time," Lorgas said under his breath, then fell silent from a hard look by Seanchan.

"This is a wonderful place," Fedelm said in a low voice to Cumac. "I do not wish to put Lorgas into a miff, but I would say that it rivals Erewon in beauty."

Cumac shrugged. "Maybe. But I think we are deserving of better courtesy. Bern is pushing the edge of the Laws of Hospitality by keeping us under guard."

Fedelm grinned at him. "Those are only guards as long as you think they are guards. Otherwise, you may assume they were put there to do our bidding. And that is a much better thought than thinking they are to guard us."

"Well, maybe," Cumac said grudgingly. Then he relented a bit. "It is a beautiful city, and so far we haven't been inconvenienced much. We could have been treated worse."

Fedelm chuckled. "That is one way of looking at it, I suppose. But keep your thoughts to yourself when we meet Lakiel. The Ervalians are touchy about who comes into their woods. And if they have been attacked by Maliman as they say, you cannot blame them for being cautious. No one should take Maliman lightly. That may lead to corruption of one's spirit and life force."

Cumac remained silent as they walked down halls lit by glowing torches in sconces set with precious rings. Overhead, the arches gleamed like silver, and the marble columns shone with a soft green. Paintings of past elven kings hung between the sconces, caught in the moment of their greatest triumph. Below the portraits, their swords were placed on blue velvet on oak shelves that had been burnished to a glow. The swords themselves were marked with legends that drifted back to the beginnings of the Time of Man and were listed in the *Annals of Fire,* which had disappeared when man first came to Erin. Only when Aruadh the Wise translated *Annals of the Red Branch* in the year 369 Tír Na Og did the lost legends emerge.

They came to a door that easily stood fifteen feet tall. Intricate patterns had been carved into the door, then filled with blackthorn rubbed with beeswax. Two guards on either side of the door watched the approach of the little band suspiciously.

"Open the door," Bern commanded. "These guests seek an audience with Lakiel."

"They are still armed," one of the guards said in objection. "No one may enter the Great Hall bearing weapons."

"It will be a cold day in Teach Duinn before I give up my ax," Lorgas muttered, dropping his hand to the ax on his belt.

Instantly the guards brought their weapons to bear upon them.

"Enough!" Bern commanded in a stern voice. "I bear the Bisuilglas—the Ring of Life. There are no others over me. Open, I say!"

Reluctantly, one guard pulled the door open.

Bright light poured through the open door, bathing them in white. They blinked and then saw the interior of the room. Gray panels covered the walls, and the panels were etched with silver loops and swirls. A message in the ancient tongue had been carved into the wood panel of a wall over the throne, and only Seanchan and the elves could read it. One phrase looked familiar to Cumac, but he refrained from asking Seanchan what it meant for fear of getting a lecture.

"It says, 'I am the way to those who seek it,'" Fedelm whispered.

"What does that mean?" he whispered back.

She shrugged. "It means what it says. That is all I can tell you. What 'way' would only be guesswork on my part. I know it is important, though. We would have to ask the elves."

"And only certain elves," Bern whispered, having overheard their conversation. "Very few elves know what it means. For the rest of us, the meaning has been lost in time far longer than we have been here."

He turned his back to the room and bowed deeply, his long hair nearly sweeping the floor.

"Lakiel, I bring the Seekers to you for your pleasure," he said formally.

"Rise and name them," a voice said from the white light centered on the throne.

Bern rose and, indicating each with a sweep of his arm, said, "Seanchan of the Duirgeals, Fedelm from the Cruachan Sidhe, Lorgas of the Ashelves, and Cumac, the son of Cucullen, the son of Fand."

The light faded and they saw a beautiful woman upon the throne. Her hair was the color of polished bronze and held off her broad forehead with a simple golden band. Around her neck she wore a torc of fine hammered gold with strange symbols engraved upon it. Her neck-high dress was a simple white gown that came to her wrists and her bare feet, white and dainty.

"We welcome you," she said, and her voice trilled like spring songbirds. Her eyes were a brilliant blue sapphire, yet there was a wariness about them that suggested she was capable of being friendly or a terrible foe.

"Thank you, milady," Seanchan said, placing his hand over his heart and briefly bowing his head, as formal as a Druid would be.

Cumac followed the lead of Fedelm, bowing deeply, while Lorgas, still miffed over their reception (and, truth be told, the manner in which the trees had greeted him), grumbled but did likewise.

"And what brings you to us?" Lakiel asked politely, although all knew that she had been well informed if not by Bern then by the mumblings of the forest.

"We seek the Bladhm Caillis, the Chalice of Fire, given to Cucullen the Hound by Maeve, She-Who-Intoxicates, and stolen by Bricriu Poisontongue," Seanchan said. "The way is hard, and we would seek refuge here for the moment. We would be grateful for your hospitality."

Lakiel considered them for a moment, then said, "We have

been troubled by Sword-wanderers and Nightshades that have been released from the Great Rift, and now Grayshawls have been found at the edge of our woods as well. It is well known that the Grayshawls may appear in whatever form they choose, which makes them doubly dangerous. Unconditional hospitality is now dangerous to offer."

Lorgas glared at her and sputtered. "This is—is—intolerable! To think that an elf would not be able to recognize the truth of another!"

"We do not have the luxury of being a part of the Otherworld," Lakiel said, her eyes narrowing. "We do not have the luxury of the protection of ancient oaths and spells. Here we are vulnerable despite our weavings of spells and enchantments. We are more vulnerable than the Ashelves of Rowan Oak, who can call upon the protection of the Pantheon if need be."

"Let us not slip into harsh words for which there can be no forgiveness," Seanchan said hastily. "We are grateful for your extended kindness. We must, however, continue on tomorrow, as the longer we do not press Bricriu Poisontongue, the more difficult it will be to find him. *And* there is the danger that Maliman has seized control of some of the fortresses along the roads we must travel. If he has not, then that we should bid you a hasty farewell is more urgent than ever."

Lakiel leaned against the back of her chair and frowned, studying the group before her. Cumac felt a prickling at the back of his neck. He glanced at Fedelm and recognized his own unease in her eyes. Seanchan, however, remained relaxed, smiling.

"Yet, if you are what you say and we allow you to hurry along your way, then you run the risk of blundering into Sword-wanderers and Black Baggots. Not to mention Bocanachs and Deagduls. Then, where would you be but in Maliman's dungeon in Dun Asarlai in the Mountains of Mourne?" She shook her head. "No, that would not do. We have the responsibility of keeping you from harm. Even if it is against your wishes. What would happen if we took you to the edge of our forest and bade you farewell and then you are captured by Maliman? How would The Dagda and the Pantheon view that? No, it is better if you stay here, safe within the environs of our forest.

"Do not despair, however," she said, smiling charmingly. "The Ervalians are famous for their hospitality and for providing safety for their guests. So, I am assigning you each a protector."

She gestured, and the elves who had been outside their doors came up behind them. They had their hands upon their swords and eyed the Seekers with suspicion.

Cumac's Dragonstone brooch began to pulsate with black fire, and he saw Fedelm finger the knife at her waist.

Seanchan bowed and said, "This is all well and good. But as I said, our journey is urgent, and we must attend to it immediately. In all her wisdom, surely Lakiel can understand this."

For a brief moment, Lakiel's features seemed to shift and a loathsome face appeared, pustules dotting her face and her hair greasy and unkept. Instantly the face disappeared, but Cumac was certain that he had seen it and, glancing at Fedelm and Seanchan, he saw that they had seen it too.

Cumac straightened and slipped the thumb of his right hand carelessly into the left side of his belt and kept his features straight. He breathed deeply, and beneath the smell of spices and flowers lurked another odor, dank and malodorous, like sour soil. He took a deep breath and moved up to stand beside Seanchan.

"We accept your gracious offer, milady. Yes, we are tired and a long rest will be goodly welcome." He sensed Seanchan's swift look and Feldem's eyes boring into the back of his head. "I must say that I enjoyed the wine sent to our rooms and look forward to sampling more. It was quite delicious."

A smile played over Lakiel's lips. She nodded at Cumac and raised her hand to gesture to those standing behind the Seekers.

"Then you shall have more," she said. "And now, if you will excuse me, there are a few matters of state that I have to attend to before we can enjoy each other's company in a feast."

Cumac bowed and turned, his eyes glancing fleetingly at the others. Seanchan gave a slight nod, bowed, and turned. Lorgas and Fedelm followed suit.

Bern followed them from the Great Hall and after the door closed, offered his apologies and left, promising to meet with them later in time for supper.

"I am sorry that I cannot go with you at this time," Bern said. "But there are matters concerning a theft that I must deal with. A court, if you please." He made a face. "I hate this. I will have to banish them from Alainn if they are found guilty. And that," he added grimly, "will mean their deaths."

He bowed and scurried down the hallway away from them.

"What is it?" Seanchan whispered once they had left the Throne Room and were walking down the hall."

"Yes. What is it?" Lorgas growled. "I do not like running away like a frightened fawn."

"It's the Dragonstone," Fedelm said quietly. "It is warning us."

The others looked at the brooch pulsating blackly.

"What is the warning?" Seanchan asked, taking a firmer grip upon his staff.

"We have fallen upon evil ways," Cumac whispered back. "We must bide our time for the moment. In two hours, join me in my room, supposedly for a glass of wine and some fruit. But for now, drink only water. I do not trust the wine and fruit."

"Poison?" Lorgas asked, alarmed.

Cumac shrugged. "I don't know. I have no way of telling. But I suspect something. Things are not what they seem."

They arrived at their rooms and bade each other a good rest. Cumac laughed and said loudly to the others so their guards could hear as well, "Let us rest for a bit and then come to my room so that we might enjoy each other's company in a leisurely manner."

He looked at his guard and smiled. "Could you arrange for us to have repast together?"

The guard hesitated, then nodded slowly. "It shall be as you wish. I shall have a servant bring what you desire to your room. Enough for all."

"Thank you," Cumac said politely. "Then, let us rest for two hours and relax in each other's company."

Cumac entered his room and the smile slipped quickly from his face. He crossed to the window and stepped out onto a tiny balcony. Carefully he studied the walls and considered the drop. The walls were as smooth as glass and the drop too dangerous to attempt. He went back into his room and sat on a pile of cushions, thinking.

At the moment, escape seemed impossible. Yet, an attempt had to be made. He had no doubts that Lakiel had been corrupted by Maliman's magic and was charged with keeping Cumac and the others prisoners until Maliman could deal with them. Then a thought swept over his mind—a memory of something he had noticed in the encounter with Lakiel—and slipped away. He groped for it, but it eluded him like a shadow dancing in the light of a moving lamp.

He closed his eyes and concentrated, willing the thought back to his conscious, but it proved too elusive, and in frustration, he finally gave up and stared moodily at the ceiling overhead, idly making figures out of the designs carved into the stone and wood. He thought back to Lakiel and how the mask (for he had no doubt now that her face was covered with a mask of magic making) had slipped for an instant, revealing the corruption behind it. The question was whether *all* the Ervalians had been corrupted or just Lakiel. Or, had she been replaced by another? And if so, what or who? Certainly a creature from the Great Rift, but whether it was a creature created by Maliman before leaving the Rift or another that he had shaped from a living person—elf—Cumac did not know.

A knock came at his door, and he rose and went to open it. A servant dressed in light green stood before him, carrying a platter of fruits and honey and cheeses and breads. Cumac stood aside, and the servant entered silently and placed the platter on a low table made from polished dark walnut and edged in silver. He arranged silverware on top of snow-white linen squares. Another servant entered carrying silver cups engraved in graceful loops and swirls and a pitcher of honeyed wine. He placed them on the table and silently withdrew with the other.

Cumac eyed the food and wine, frowning. There was something about the repast that bothered him but he could not figure out what was making him so nervous and wary.

Everything, he decided, was dangerous here, now. Lakiel might have noticed the brooch pulsing on his cloak. That could explain the momentary slipping of her mask. Yes, he thought, suddenly gripping the memory he had been chasing. Yes, that was it. That was the reason. The brooch was meant to warn him of danger, but in this case, it warned him with danger watching.

Again a knock came at his door, and he opened it. Seanchan, Lorgas, and Fedelm slipped inside.

"We must be as quiet as possible when we are talking about what has happened," Seanchan said warningly. "But it would be wise if we engage in some small talk that is complimentary to our hosts. Such as they are."

"Then you saw what I saw?" Cumac said. "Lakiel's face shifting."

Seanchan made an impatient gesture with his hand. "I knew something was wrong before we entered the Great Hall. The air bristles with black magic."

"I felt it too," Fedelm said.

"And I," Lorgas added.

"This is almost a feast," Seanchan said loudly for hidden ears to hear. "The honey looks freshly gathered and the bread baked within the hour or two."

"Yes," Lorgas answered. "I would agree. The wine looks as if it is made from rosehips."

"What are we going to do?" Cumac whispered. "The way to the ground is too steep and dangerous and the walls cannot be climbed."

"You forget the Throne Room," Fedelm said softly. "Remember the words above the throne?"

"But what does it mean?" Cumac asked.

"Obviously a hidden door," Seanchan said. He reached into a small pouch he took from the leather bag slung around his shoulder and took a pinch of powder. He dropped the powder into the wine. Instantly it turned black, and an unpleasant smell wafted through the room.

"Poison," he said quietly, then loudly, "Our hosts are treating us like kings. I'll pour."

He lifted the pitcher and held it high as he poured it into the silver goblets. Fedelm took her knife from her waist and began slicing the bread.

"If this is meant to hold our hunger until dinner," Lorgas said, "then I wonder what marvels we shall have then."

"We shall have to be quick," Seanchan said. "The longer we wait, the more difficult our way will be. We shall have to take care of the guards."

"Leave it to me," Lorgas said. He gripped his throat and coughed and moaned as he staggered to the door, flinging it open.

The guards looked at him as he gasped, "Poison."

A slight smile appeared on the one appointed to Cumac as Lorgas fell to his knees. Suddenly he leaped up, his dagger sweeping into the stomach of one of the guards.

Cumac rushed forward, Caladbolg shimmering like a rainbow as he sliced through two elfin bodies. An arrow sang past his ear and lodged in the last guard's throat.

"Well done," Seanchan said. "Now, let us move quickly."

They ran down the hall and rounded a corner and surprised a company of guards moving toward them. Cumac howled with rage as the warp-spasm came upon him. The blade of Caladbolg danced in his hands as arrows flew past him from Feldem's bow. Lorgas yelled and swung his sword, carving his way into the company.

Seanchan's staff was a wooden blur as it spun in his hands, dealing death blows to heads, bones crunching.

The attack was over in an instant and the Seekers ran down the hall toward the Throne Room. Groups of elves appeared then quickly fell to the blades and arrows of the Seekers. Black blood spurted from some, and Seanchan knew that the souls of these had been captured by Maliman's magic and he paused to mumble words and phrases over them, causing them to twist and turn in agony.

Then they were at the door to the Great Hall. Seanchan threw it open and the others stumbled inside. They slammed the door behind them and dropped the brass bar into its brackets, sealing the door.

"Is this the way to accept hospitality?" Lakiel said angrily.

Cumac and Lorgas whirled to meet the attack of Lakiel's guards. A blinding blue and red light filled the Throne Room and hurled the guards back toward Lakiel's throne. A smell of brimstone was in the air, and Cumac looked wonderingly at Seanchan.

"Cairnfire," Seanchan said solemnly. "From Teach Duinn." He advanced toward Lakiel, who cowered back upon her throne.

"Judgment will be swift for you!" she shrieked.

"Be silent!" Seanchan roared. He leveled his staff toward her menacingly. "Come forth from behind your mask and be known!"

Her shoulders twisted in agony and slowly a loathsome figure emerged, bent and gray, with talons for fingers. A stench rose from her as she pleaded for her life.

"Do not harm me, Seanchan!" she begged. "I am only what I have been made by Maliman. It is he who should be punished, not me! Not me!"

Instantly, a black fire licked around her flesh, eating hungrily. She shrieked with pain and tried to slap the fire out with her hands. But the fire raced faster than her hands could cope. Cumac moved forward instinctively to help her but was pulled up by Seanchan dropping a hand upon his shoulder.

"The black fire does not care who it burns," he said. "And it can only be put out by letting it make ashes."

Lorgas swore and stepped forward, swinging his ax. Her head fell from her shoulders and bounced twice before being consumed by the black fire. Then, the fire finished burning and left the rest of Lakiel in ashes.

"Maliman is not one who takes betrayal lightly," Seanchan said. "He worked the black fire into that which was Lakiel."

"He is watching?" Fedelm asked, frowning.

Seanchan shook his head. "No. That he cannot do unless there are eyes that can see. Any eyes. Now, there are none."

Cumac glanced around automatically. Seanchan saw his movement and smiled briefly.

"But it is always better to make certain that one is alone from Maliman."

"Now what do we do?" Lorgas asked.

A rhythmic beating of hammers came hollowly from the door.

"I think the answer is here," Seanchan said, pointing with his staff at the legend above the throne. "I Am the Way to Those Who Seek It."

"Yes, but what does that mean?" Lorgas asked. "I mean, I know what it means, but how do we find what we seek?"

"That shouldn't be too difficult," Seanchan muttered as he made his way behind the throne. "There is always a key somewhere to meaning and meaning to a key. The trick is just to find it."

He studied the wall carefully, then frowned.

"Well, that's the theory, anyway," he said.

He pointed his staff at a place midway beneath the legend and intoned, "*Totar amach teindey.*"

A pale soft yellow light emerged from the end of his staff, flickered gently for a moment, then disappeared.

Again, Seanchan tried.

"*Achan belleflor jais benath.*"

And again the light appeared and again disappeared.

The banging at the door intensified.

"You'd better hurry," Lorgas said nervously. "It sounds as if the Ervalians are getting very disturbed."

"This is a grievous puzzle," Seanchan said.

Suddenly Cumac saw the answer. "What is the ancient phrase for 'I seek'?"

Seanchan's eyes lit up. "*Aalfe carmes.*"

Immediately the outline of a door appeared, lined with silver. Slowly it opened inward, revealing a rough stone passage that disappeared into the darkness. A dank smell rolled out to them, and they could hear water dripping.

"I don't think it's wise to tarry," Lorgas said urgently.

"Nor I," Fedelm answered.

"I'm certain it's unanimous," Seanchan said, stepping forward into the passage. The others followed close on his heels and turned to watch as the door slowly closed, leaving them in darkness.

A soft glow began to shine from the head of Seanchan's staff. They appeared to be in a dark cavern, the ceiling far above them where the dim light did not reach. The sides were rough-hewn by ancient picks. A squeal came from the floor and Lorgas jumped, uttering a curse when he saw a mouse scamper away into the dark. Bones lay scattered around the floor, some polished to the patina of old ivory.

Seanchan moved behind the others and muttered quietly. Silver filaments appeared in the air and wound around each other, creating a web that stretched and tightened upon the walls, onto the floor, and above the door.

"That should hold them for a while," he said with satisfaction. "Certainly long enough for us to get far ahead. Of course," he reflected, "they will try pursuit if they can unravel the web. But by then, I hope it will be futile."

"What is this? Where does this go?" Cumac asked, peering forward.

"I know this place," Seanchan said suddenly. "This is the Raven's Gate, the entrance to the world between the Earthworld and the Otherworld. It is where the lost are confined. Where does it go? To where the journey ends. No one knows where he is going when he sets foot on a new path. I have never been here before. At least," he amended, "not that I have memory of. But all unknown is an adventure. That is why we travel. Stay close," he warned. "The way may be dangerous and treacherous."

He stepped forward firmly and the others automatically followed, staying as close as they could to the pool of light that gathered around Seanchan's feet.

Without the sun's light, they could not tell when day had passed, but their feet could, and a weariness settled into their bones and their minds, leaving them stupefied and short of temper. The darkness continued to gather around them like a dirty blanket, and foul odors came to them when they passed paths that led away from the one they traveled.

At last, Seanchan called a halt. They had reached a widening in the path that appeared to have been made by the unknown miners for resting. Water trickled from nearby although they could not see the source. All licked dry lips and walked around the edge of the light, hoping they would find a small pool where they could slake their thirst.

"It might not be a good idea to drink the water here," Seanchan said. "This is an old place, and we do not know from whence the water comes or what may be in it. I think it best that we wait until we reach the end to quench our thirst. Surely it cannot be far, as others have traveled this way before us and we have not seen the bones of those who were overcome by thirst. Be patient."

Lorgas groaned and dropped to the ground, grumbling.

"Water *and* food! My stomach thinks my throat has been cut and nothing is sliding down to ease hunger pangs. We should have grabbed some of that fruit—"

"Of which we knew nothing," Fedelm finished. "They could easily have been poisoned or worse."

"What could be worse?" Lorgas said.

"We could become one of Maliman's servants," she declared. "Poisoned, yes, but there are types of poison that kill and others that change a person into a puppet whose strings are held by Maliman."

"She's right," Seanchan said. "We must watch all things carefully. We do not know what lies before us. We will rest a bit here but not for long. We cannot linger and allow what lives in this darkness to find us."

Silently, they stretched out on the cold path. Seanchan brought the light from his staff down to a soft glow and wearily, they closed their eyes and fell asleep.

Cumac did not know what awakened him, but something was wrong. He lay quietly, his hand going to the hilt of his sword that he had placed beside him before sleeping. His senses pricked and he strained to hear, but all was silent, and it was this silence that made him nervous. A stench like meat left too long in the sun came to him. Slowly he rolled his head to the side and saw dark shapes moving around them.

In the dim light, he recognized them and leaped to his feet, Caladbolg sliding freely from its sheath. He swung the sword in a blinding arch. Rainbow color swam around the blade as it sliced through necks and flesh.

"Sumaires!" Cumac shouted, swinging Caladbolg again.

The others sprang to their feet. Seanchan's staff burned with a harsh red fire. Lorgas swung his sword as he drew it, lopping off a head, while Fedelm fitted arrow after arrow to her bow, shooting rapidly at the dark forms at the rim of Seanchan's light.

A sumaire bared his fangs and snarled as he swung his sword at Cumac's head. Cumac barely leaned away in time, feeling the air as the sumaire's sword went by. He countered, cleaving the sumaire to his waist. Lorgas spitted a sumaire with his sword and ripped up, slicing through foul flesh.

"Close your eyes!" Seanchan roared.

Cumac barely had time to follow Seanchan's order before a white light cracked and thunder pressed against his ears.

Shrieks came as the sumaires cried in pain from the harsh fire that swirled around them, licking their flesh, burning them to ashes.

"Run!" Seanchan shouted.

The others needed no further urging as they sprinted down the path, spiraling deeper and deeper into the bowels of the earth, following Seanchan's light as he led the way.

Cumac's side began to hurt as he panted for air. The air grew hotter and hotter as they descended into the deep. He glanced at Fedelm and saw sweat shining on her face. Lorgas was red-faced and exhaled in sharp pants as he struggled to pull more air into his lungs.

They rounded a huge boulder and Seanchan suddenly stopped and leaned on his staff.

"Look behind us!" he gasped. "Are they following us?"

Fedelm crept cautiously around the boulder and stared up into the darkness. She relaxed her mind and closed her eyes, sending out feelers, searching. But she sensed nothing behind them. She turned back to the others.

"We are alone," she said, breathing deeply.

Seanchan nodded. "We will rest here very briefly. Do not fall asleep. We must continue on before something else sets upon us. A half hour, nothing more."

Lorgas sighed and dropped, gasping, to the hard pathway. He mopped his forehead with the sleeve of his tunic. He had already removed his leather jacket and had tied it by its sleeves around his waist.

"Why is it so hot?" he complained. "When we came behind the door, it was cool. But here"—he gestured around them—"it is like Goibniu's furnace."

"And what is that?" Cumac added, pointing at a green fire ahead where shadows danced and twisted in agony.

"You are beneath Ifreann, an island in the northern seas hidden by enchantment. It is here, a world of ice and fire above the Great Rift, where The Dagda exiled Ragon. It is here that Ragon made the Cultas Dubasarlai, the cult of black sorcerers. It is here where Credac and his Zorgoths were banished. This is the edge of the Great Rift. Those in the circles are the ones still caught in the fires of the Great Rift," Seanchan said solemnly. "They are the ones that even Maliman has no use for."

"How evil must they be!" Fedelm exclaimed. "The father of evil doesn't even want them?" She shuddered. "Of what types are they?"

Seanchan lowered himself to a boulder and sighed deeply, mopping the sweat off his face with the edge of his robe.

"All types," he said. "The ones who are the lowest down are those who betrayed their masters. No one can trust them as no one knows when deceit will strike their whim. And then there are those who manipulate others for power and again can be trusted by no one. Certain thieves, liars, cheats, and molesters are in there too. Any who cannot be bent to the evil of Maliman or who cannot be trusted by the resisters of Maliman to help them in their fight against Maliman. Look closely, you may see some you recognize."

Cumac's neck hairs bristled uneasily. He looked closely into the fire and saw the flickering face and dance of Balor Evileye who led the Fomorians against the Ashelves and the Tuatha. His basilisk eye was used only in battle and it took four men to lift the lid. A single glance was enough to cause all that it touched with sight to leap into fire. He was slain by his son, Lugh, Cumac's grandfather. Other forms looked familiar but were either too shadowed or too screened by green fire for him to make out their features.

He looked deeper to where green fire turned to yellow and then a red that was hard on the eyes, and in the center, a blackness seemed to shine through the fire.

"What is that in the center of the fire?" Cumac asked Seanchan.

"That is where these rocky steeps converge and become ice instead of stone. It is black ice you see, as that is where Ragon, the Father of all Evil, lives, half-entombed in ice forever. His minions live there as well to do his bidding, those who took the side of Ragon in the Great War for the Otherworld and cast here by The Dagda. Although free from the binding ice, they still must suffer the pain of the hoarfrost that flows into the Sea of Ice. And mind you—" He paused. "Although Ragon is partially entombed, such is his magic that he can escape in spirit to the beginning of Ifreann. But no farther. We shall travel along the edge of the Great Rift."

"This is an evil place," Lorgas said nervously, fingering his ax. "I would be happier away from here."

"Keep your voice down!" Seanchan said sharply. "We are safe as long as those who dwell in the darkness and green fire are not made aware of our passing."

Suddenly, Fedelm stiffened. She whirled to face back the way they had come, an arrow leaping to her bow as she drew and held.

"What is it?" Cumac demanded, leaping to his feet. Caladbolg slid from its sheath. He held it ready, eyes straining through the darkness to see what Fedelm saw. Beside him, he sensed Lorgas standing, ax in hand.

A chuckle came out of the darkness to them.

"You right well know who I am," a figure said, emerging slowly from the dark into the faint light cast by Seanchan's staff. "I am Bern of the Ervalians, Bearer of Bisuilglas, come to offer my services to avenge the treachery of Maliman, who stole our queen and left the imposter in her place."

He stopped and stood, relaxed but wary, with sword in hand. Bisuilglas, the sacred talisman of Rindale, the Hall of Warriors, where Ervalians gather when they are slain, glowed softly on his shoulder.

Lorgas growled and crouched, ready to leap forward, but was drawn in check by Seanchan who said, "Be silent! We cannot afford battle here, and if you attack Bern, there will be battle!" He studied Bern with narrow eyes. "But tell me, Bern, why should we trust you?"

Bern shrugged but kept a watchful eye on the others. "I cannot make you do what you are not willing to do. After you fled through the door behind the throne, I discovered what you discovered in Lakiel." He shook his head. "The ashes you left behind told us much about one who may have pretended to Lakiel's throne. Now, I ask that I be allowed to join with you while you search for Bricriu Poisontongue. I will help you find him, and in finding him, perchance I shall find where Maliman took Lakiel. *If*," he added, "that was indeed not her who was burned by the black fire."

"I hope we find her for your sake," Lorgas said, sliding his ax back into his belt. "If Maliman has her, she is in Dun Darai in the Mountains of Mourne. Or dead. If we do not find her in Dun Darai, then she is a guest of Donn."

Bern nodded grimly. "I believe that this quest for the Bladhm Caillis will eventually end either in Dun Asarlai or somewhere else where Maliman rules. And where the Bladhm Caillis is, Lakiel may be as well. Although," he added, "I have no proof of what I feel. Yet, I must try."

"I do not think she will be."

They all turned to look at Fedelm, who stood with eyes half-closed. Her nostrils were pinched and white. Tight lines were etched around her lips, her eyes. Her skin looked clammy, although a deep blush appeared in both cheeks.

"I cannot see where she is, but she is in a dark gray world, and evil is all around her."

Her eyes opened and she drew a deep, shuddering breath. "I must sleep the sleep of *imbas forasnai* to see more. But I cannot sleep it here."

Involuntarily, all looked around at the darkness and the green fire and the strange light coming from Seanchan's staff. Cumac's Dragonstone began to glow a deep black and pulse as if a dark light was threatening to explode from its depths.

"I think," Seanchan said slowly, "that it would be better if we leave now. There seems to be something in the dark. I do not know what it is, but there is a foul sense to it."

"And what about him?" Lorgas asked, nodding toward Bern. "I know what he said, but remember he tried to keep us prisoner with the Ervalians."

"Had I wanted to harm you would I have made myself known? Especially here?" Bern demanded. "I have had plenty of opportunity to do you harm and did not take it. And," he added, "I have arranged for your horses to be brought to you once you are out of this world. Although that black one seemed to have his own ideas about where to go."

"But neither did Bern come to our aid when we could have used another good sword arm," Lorgas argued. "It seems to me that we may be jumping from the cauldron to the fire. A nut is a nut, whether it is an acorn or walnut."

"Yes, that is correct," Seanchan said. "But should we not give the benefit of doubt to him now? He has come forth and made himself known. I am curious, though," he said, turning to Fedelm. "Why could you not sense him before we rested?"

Fedelm shrugged and spread her hands. "I do not know. But this I do: at the time I felt nothing. And that bothers me."

"And one thing bothers me as well," Seanchan said. He turned to Bern. "How was it possible that you could travel through my weaves of enchantment?"

"With Bisuilglas," Bern said. "With it, I may slip through enchantments."

Cumac listened to the others, but his attention was drawn to a black mist that seemed to be forming at the bottom of the Great Rift. The mist rolled and bundled and unbundled as it slowly rose from the icy sea. A strange thrill of foreboding prickled the hairs on his arms and the back of his neck.

"What," he asked, interrupting the others, "is that?"

He pointed down, and Seanchan frowned as he stepped close to the edge of the Great Rift. He studied the mist carefully, then his eyes hardened.

"It is Sollag, the Guardian of the Deep, father of all Fire-Drakes, the dragons. He has found us."

Seanchan looked around quickly. They stood on a narrow path that circled the Great Rift and slowly gyred upward.

"We cannot fight here!" he said desperately. "And my wizardry is of no use this close to the Great Rift, which is bound in Ragon's enchantments!"

"There is no place better that I can see!" Lorgas said, his eyes straining upward, following the trail. "We must go back to find a level field for battle!"

"No!" Fedelm said. "You forget the sumaires!"

"I do not think that this is a place I want to be," Bern said, drawing his sword.

"What's that? There!" Cumac shouted, pointing upward.

"Where?" Seanchan demanded.

"There! Where the trail goes behind the ragged wall before it emerges! Perhaps there is a place for battle. It would," he added urgently, "be better than this."

A roar begin to emanate from the mist, and then Sollag, the Guardian, emerged from the dark. His eyes burned with red fire while green and red fire licked from the edges of his funnel-shaped mouth. Hard copper scales, beaten into tenfold thickness, gleamed with stinking green slime. His four legs ended in black-taloned claws while a barbed tail whirled viciously like a corkscrew. Two wings like bat wings the size of sea sails drove the dragon on.

Fedelm unleashed an arrow, but the shaft struck the dragon scales covering its belly and ricocheted away.

"Run!" Lorgas shouted and sprinted along the trail. The others came hard on his heels. Sollag's fiery breath struck the edge of the trail where they had stood only moments before.

A furious roar sounded and Sollag whirled upward, turning to attack again, his long neck curling viciously.

Gasping, Cumac sprinted around a narrow corner and in behind the rock and stopped, bending over to catch his breath, his body awash in sweat. He glanced around them.

They stood beneath a rock roof, the side toward the edge of the trail dropping into the Great Rift blocked with a stone the size of two houses standing one on top of the other, end to end. The wall protected them on the other side while the entrance was protected by the sharp turn of the trail.

"We are safe. For the moment," Seanchan panted, leaning back against the wall.

A burst of furnace heat slapped the wall at the turn of the trail. Cumac bit his lips to keep from screaming as the fiery air blistered his skin.

"We won't last long here," Lorgas gasped. "Sollag's breath draws the very water from us."

Fedelm took a deep breath and said, "I will try again to kill him."

She took an arrow from her quiver and nocked it. She started around the corner when Seanchan brought her up short.

"You cannot kill him," Seanchan warned. "Only injure him enough so that he drops back into the bottom of the Great Rift."

"Then that should allow us time to escape," she said grimly.

"The moment he sees you, he will turn you to ashes with his breath," Seanchan said. "Yet, there may be a way we can confuse him. He is of the Clan of Balor, he of the basilisk eye. It is only in Sollag's left eye that you may harm him enough with your arrow to drive him away. Now wait until he is confused before stepping around the corner."

He closed his eyes and mumbled strange words that no one could understand. A shimmering mist appeared in front of him, then all gasped as a man leaped from the mist and sped around the corner.

"Quickly!" Seanchan shouted. "Now!"

Fedelm jumped around the corner. In one fluid motion, she drew the arrow and released it, then spun around the corner again.

A howl of pain as of ten thousand spirits suddenly tossed in the fire followed her around the corner. Then another howl and yet another that grew fainter and fainter.

"Run!" Seanchan said. "We must be free of this before Sollag recovers!"

Obediently, the party raced from under the protective rock and ran along the twisting path leading up hill.

A faint roar of pain followed them and they ran harder, as if the Fire-Drake was coming hard upon their heels.

Cumac's chest began to burn as he tried to suck air into his lungs. His legs ached and tried to cramp, but he fought the temptation to stop and rest and grimly drove himself forward, following Bern behind Seanchan.

Cumac could hear Fedelm laboring behind him, and behind her, Lorgas gasped for air.

Then, they were suddenly at the base of a steep flight of stone stairs leading upward. Without hesitating, Seanchan led the way up the stairs to a small level place. The faint outline of a door was in front of them.

"You'd better hurry, I'm thinking!" Lorgas said urgently. "If I'm not mistaken, I think Sollag is hot upon our trail. Pardon the pun!"

"*Aalfe ensonnis*," Seanchan intoned in a deep voice.

Slowly the stone door creaked open, old dust falling away from it, making Lorgas sneeze.

Cumac started to run through the door, but Seanchan brought him up short and said, "One should never rush into the unknown. That is when bad things happen."

Cumac glanced over his shoulder and said, "I think sometimes what lies behind is worse than what lies ahead."

"Ah, yes," Seanchan said, frowning. "There is truth to that as well. Ah, me! I guess there's nothing for it but to take a chance."

He jumped over the threshold, followed in rapid succession by the others. They could hear Sollag's roar as he came nearer and nearer, but Seanchan rose, dusted himself off, then announced, "*Aalfe carmes!*"

The door swung shut, locking itself firmly into the stone of the mountain. They looked warily around them, at the dark trees that surrounded them, and sighed deeply.

"Well," Seanchan said, looking at the others. "We seem to have emerged from that with little wear. I would say that we were very lucky."

"Lucky?" fumed Lorgas. "Lucky, he calls it! We were nearly roasted alive and he says we were 'lucky.' "

"Stop your complaining!" Seanchan said sharply. "Be thankful that we are here."

Bern shook his head, knelt on the ground beneath a willow tree, and said, "If I hear rightly, I believe there is water near."

They all listened intently. The sound of water splashing cheerfully over rocks came to them. They stepped through a small stand of willows to find bright water throwing up tiny rainbows from where it slapped against rocks.

Eagerly, they threw themselves on the mossy bank and drank thirstily until their bellies threatened to burst. Then they laid back, sprawling on the cool moss thankfully.

"I say that we've earned a rest," Lorgas said. "At least a week!"

"No," Seanchan said. "A few hours, yes, but then we must move. I do not know whose woods these are, and to be caught dilly-dallying where we do not have permission may be very costly."

They grumbled but knew he was right. All made themselves comfortable and fell asleep instantly.

17

A harvest moon rose above them, red-orange in the inky black sky as they wandered, searching vainly for a road or at least a path to take them safely and quickly through the forest. It was an ancient forest—as Lorgas was quick to inform them, despite a hard look from Seanchan to keep quiet—and ancient forests were not traveled well by those wishing to go through them. Most travelers ventured only a few yards inside before feeling the terror within and quickly retracing their steps to detour around the forest. If a traveler dared to go more than a hundred yards in, he was more than likely never to be seen again, slipping out of peoples' memories with time.

They did not have the opportunity to retreat from the forest as they had no idea how far in they emerged after traveling through the cave. Some distance, Cumac thought as he walked cautiously behind Seanchan, his hand straying nervously between the haft of Caladbolg and the tree limbs he brushed out of his face.

Just as he thought that he was a bit comfortable in the forest, a thunderstorm struck, sounding as if the very gods themselves were battling Maliman's forces. Lightning cracked and danced from rock to rock, splintering trees near them as the lightning tried to find the Band of Seekers. But by this time, the little party had begun to ascend the face of a looming cliff. They used a very narrow path that wound its way under overhangs that left the seekers dry although shivering with cold.

Cumac looked out and over the path into the forest below. Stone-giants hurled rocks at each other in some game known only to them. Lightning cracked and slammed into the rocks above them, forcing them to huddle closer and closer to the face of the cliff. And then, a bolt struck the path ahead of them, breaking it off from the cliff.

Seanchan sighed and measured the distance across to the other side of the path. It was too much for anyone to jump. He squatted on his heels and bowed his head, letting the rain sluice off his hood. The others dropped down beside him, squeezing themselves as tightly together as they could without knocking one another off the path.

"We must go back," Seanchan said at last. "Apparently we are not meant to leave the forest by going up this cliff. Why, I do not know. Although," he added, "I do not like going back. Nothing good comes of repeating part of a journey. Bad luck, I say. And while we do not need any more bad luck than what we already have had, there is nothing for it but to retrace ourselves. At least we will be better off from the rain than we are here."

That was enough for the party. They scampered down the trail as fast as they could, minding their feet when they came to a bend so they would not slide off into the darkness.

Soon, they were in the forest again and huddled up under trees despite Seanchan's warning that lightning could certainly strike their trees. But they noticed that he too took a bit of shelter beneath a leafy overhang where branches from two trees formed a tight canopy above him.

Lorgas sighed and tried to mop the water from his face with his sleeve, but his sleeve was soaked—as was the rest of his clothing—and he gave it up after a feeble try.

"We need a fire," Bern said, then paused and looked around him in bewilderment as groans of protest came from the very trees around them.

"I do not think," Seanchan said deliberately, "that building a fire would be such a good idea. The trees do not seem to like the thought of fire among them."

"Stuff and nonsense!" Lorgas exclaimed and picked up a few dead sticks and laid them neatly in a pile. When he bent over with his flint and tinder to light the fire, however, a root from out of nowhere raised itself and smacked him on his rump, sending him head over teakettle away from the dead sticks.

He lay stunned for a moment, then leaped to his feet, waving his fists furiously in the air.

"Who did that?" he demanded, looking around menacingly. "Come out! Come out! This is Lorgas of the—*awk!*"

He was lifted off the ground by another root that struck him in the same place as the first. He soared end over end to land face-first in a pile of rotting mast.

He spluttered and spat and brushed the mast from his clothes while he glared around.

"I do not think these woods are friendly," Bern said cautiously, looking around him with concern on his face. "We need to leave them. And leave them now!"

Annoyance dropped over Seanchan's face. "And just where do

you suggest we go, Bern? Left? Right? Forward (wherever that is)? Or back?"

"So help me . . ." Lorgas began, but Seanchan shut him up immediately before he could give voice to his thoughts and get himself (and perhaps the rest of them) into more trouble.

"Be silent!" Seanchan ordered.

A low moaning swept through the forest, raising everyone's hackles.

"The *gasgoth*," Fedelm breathed gently. "The Deathwind."

"It seems the very trees are talking," Bern murmured, looking around him warily.

"I believe," Seanchan said slowly, "that this is the Forest of Sanan."

"The wind grows louder," Cumac said, nervously.

"Whatever you do, do not draw your weapons!" Seanchan said sharply. "And do not let the Deathwind soothe you and seize your mind. If that happens, you are lost."

The moaning turned into a beautiful song, and the shapes of beautiful women drifted slowly through the air surrounding the Seekers.

Cumac felt a drowsiness begin to creep over his limbs and fought to stay awake. He glanced at Lorgas and Bern, whose eyes were drooping shut. Even Fedelm seemed to be under the spell of the Deathwind.

Seanchan began to chant in a low voice, a soft glow beginning to surround him. The moaning in the trees came louder, and Cumac fought hard to keep his eyes from closing. Then came a soft, soothing song from behind the trees.

Soft, now, son of the Hound
Your arms and legs are unbound.
Lightly floats your care in air
And peace together we will share.
Listen to my song, my dear,
As there is nothing here to fear.
Do not feel danger in my charms
And come and snugly lie in my arms.

"Do not listen to the Deathwind, Cumac!" Seanchan roared.

A drowsiness crept over Cumac as he listened to the promises of the Deathwind, moved by the music that begain to softly drape over him like a warm cloak. A beautiful woman slipped from behind a tree, her hair white gold and falling to her knees. She was barefoot and wore a plain white robe.

What good are promises made
When only air at your feet is laid?
You shall be given your heart's desire
When you listen to my lyre
And song and the promises I make
For peace and calm for your sake.

A stinging slap across both cheeks brought Cumac blinking out of his reverie and blissful doze. With a roar, he leaped up, Caladbolg sliding easily from its scabbard. Furiously, he swung it back and forth through the air. A painful shriek sounded and then a thunderblast that nearly leveled him.

"I should think that will do it," Seanchan declared happily. "Yes, I'm certain of it."

"Is that another of Maliman's tricks?" Cumac demanded.

Seanchan shook his head. "No. No, it was its own trick. Not even Maliman can control air, and the Deathwind is made fully of air. It was created by Nemain, whose flight across the battlefields brings terror into the hearts of men. Now," he added, "I think it would be wise to awaken the others so that we may be on our way."

Cumac looked at Bern and Lorgas, sleeping peacefully with smiles playing across their lips. Fedelm was beginning to fight her own way to wakefulness, which came with a shock as Seanchan dashed water against her face.

"Arch! Plah!" she sputtered, wiping her eyes with the backs of her hands. "What is the meaning of that?" she demanded of Seanchan.

"To bring you away from dream-charms," Seanchan answered.

Cumac dragged the two elves down to a stream bubbling by and tossed them in.

They came awake instantly, sputtering and coughing and waving their hands ineffectually as they peered around at who might have dared to toss them unceremoniously into the water.

"It was Cumac," Seanchan said. "And be glad he did. You were nearly under the spell of the Deathwind."

"Hmmpf!" fumed Lorgas. "No one can charm an elf who refuses to be charmed. I was just resting my eyes for a moment before we begin our journey again."

"As was I," piped Bern. He glared at Cumac. "No one tosses an elf into the water and gets away with it."

"Enough!" Seanchan said meaningfully.

"Well, I guess it was well meant," Lorgas muttered.

"I agree," said Bern.

"Then let us shake hands and continue our journey," Seanchan directed.

"I wish we had enough time for a fire to dry out—"

No sooner were the words away from his lips than a tree root came out of nowhere and knocked Lorgas into a small thicket of brambles.

"I warned you about that," Seanchan said. "Now get out of that bush and let's be off before you get us into more trouble!"

Muttering to himself, Lorgas managed to pull himself out of the bramble bush. Impatient to be off, Seanchan nevertheless gave a little time for the others to pull stickers and thorns from Lorgas's skin while he winced and promised darkly what the woods would encounter if he had half a chance.

At last, however, Seanchan made the party move forward despite the thorns still lodged in Lorgas's flesh.

The small group stayed close together, watching the trees and bushes around them as if expecting goblins and hobgoblins to suddenly appear from hiding, swinging axes and swords, shrieking their hatred for every living thing.

But the sound was silence as Seanchan led the others ever deeper into the Forest of Sanan until no sound penetrated the thick air around the trees.

At last, they came to a small pool of water. A small hut had been built next to the pond and lights flickered from the windows of the hut. A haze hung over the pond and hut.

"Have you noticed?" Fedelm whispered.

"What?" Cumac whispered back.

"We don't hear crickets or the folding of linnet's wings or even the hoot of an owl hunting," she whispered back.

"I don't like this," Lorgas said.

"You've said that before," Cumac answered.

"No, I mean: I *really* don't like this!" Lorgas insisted.

Seanchan ignored them and, raising his staff, knocked it against the door, a huge oaken affair with black iron-strap hinges and a strange design of interlocking circles burnt into the wood. He knocked again.

They heard footsteps, and then the latch dropped from the door and the massive oak portal slowly opened, creaking on its iron hinges.

A silent figure stood before them, hooded and cloaked in gray. Man or woman, they could not tell. But all could see eyes glowing like hot embers from within the hood. The smell of rotting onions seemed to sweep from the figure to them.

"Tell your master that Seanchan of the Duirgeals awaits his pleasure. We seek shelter for the night and food and ask that the Laws of Hospitality be observed."

"And why should he do that, Seanchan Duirgeal?"

The words came in a hiss as of steam escaping from a covered cook pot. Cumac shuddered and felt Fedelm close by his side.

"What do you bring in exchange for shelter and food?"

"He may keep his head!" Lorgas said hotly.

Cumac thought he saw the figure smile, but if so, it was fleeting at best.

"Ask rather if you will keep yours," the figure hissed.

"Silence! The laws demand obedience!" Seanchan thundered. "They were given to man from the beginning."

"To man, yes," the figure said. "But not all who live in the Earth-world are of men. And what allegiance to the laws do they need to obey?"

"There is only the law. With no exceptions!" Seanchan snapped. "We asked before; now we demand it!"

The tip of his staff began to glow and what appeared to be green fire licked around the head.

The figure stood silently for a while, then a dry laugh as of snapping dried twigs came from the hood.

"You will wait until he gives his word," the figure said and firmly closed the door in their faces.

"Now, that is about enough, by Dagda!" Lorgas swore. "I have had enough of such . . . such . . . insolence!"

His hand fingered the haft of his ax. "Come! The door is only wood! We can be through it in a heartbeat."

"Perhaps," Seanchan said. "But until we know the answer from the lord of this place, we would be better served to wait for a bit."

But the others noticed that the green fire still licked around the top of his staff and looked knowingly at each other.

18

They did not have long to wait. The gray-cloaked figure returned and gestured silently to the party to follow.

They stepped through the doorway and into a small hallway whose walls were covered with battered shields and axes large enough to have been swung by giants and would have strained the sinews of an average man. Bows and arrows, lances with shafts the size of ash trees, swords, maces, whatever weapon that could be used to kill someone or something hung on the walls. But Cumac was quick to notice that all the weapons were strung with cobwebs from disuse and the feathers on the arrows were molting. The heads of the lances and the swords were dull with rust and pitted from the passing years.

He followed Seanchan and the figure leading them into a great hall with burnished oak covering the walls, slate panels covering the floor, and a roaring fire in the fireplace upon which a wild boar, crackling from the fire, turned slowly on a spit by unseen hands.

"Strange," Lorgas muttered. "The hut we came to could fit inside this hall easily with room to spare. I think a great wizard is at work here."

"I feel magic," Fedelm added, nervously fingering her bow. "And it is not the magic that we have come upon before. There is a . . . distaste to this magic."

"I agree," Bern added. He glanced at Cumac from under bushy eyebrows. "And you, Cumac?"

"Something," Cumac whispered, glancing at the Dragonstone gently pulsing with darkness. He looked around uneasily. "I do not know what, but there is something here that should not be in a friendly house."

An oak table, nearly white from daily scrubbing, stood in front of the fireplace, surrounded by six oak chairs. Food had been laid out on wooden platters down the center of the table, and each place had trenchers and wooden goblets already in place. The room was heady with the smell of spices in mulled wine, nut-brown ale, and fragrant pipe smoke.

Seanchan sat and removed his pipe from his sack, leaning to take a candle from the table to light it.

"Ah! A man needs to enjoy a good pipe after a journey!"

They jumped as the voice boomed through the great hall. They looked around for the source but saw nothing, and then, as if he had always been there leaning up against a wooden pillar, a man laughed—*a-yuck, a-yuck, a-yuck*—and clapped his hands merrily as he came toward them. He was a bowlegged and dark-faced man with a slap of white in his hair. He was dressed in leather that had been painted with silver and gold designs in loops and whorls that made one dizzy trying to find the beginning and the end.

"Welcome to my humble house!" he said merrily, gesturing around the hall. His silver eyes gleamed with laughter. "I've been expecting you."

"And how could you know that we were coming?" Cumac asked suspiciously.

The man laughed again. "I am Sanan. The trees whispered of your coming and"—he gestured at the table—"I have had plenty of time to make you welcome and prepare a repast for you. Modest though it is," he added regretfully. Then he brightened. "But tomorrow we'll feast. Ripe meat right off the bone, tankards of foaming ale, and good weed for your pipe, Seanchan!"

"We're looking—" Bern began.

Sanan laughed and waved away Bern's words. "Now, now! Plenty of time for that later! Right now, let us eat and be merry! Your journey has been long and I daresay fraught with danger. Here, you can relax and regain your strength. And"—he looked critically at their dress—"have your clothes repaired. Or new ones, for that matter!"

Cumac frowned with misgivings at this. He glanced at Fedelm and Lorgas and noticed that they shared his uneasiness. He looked at Seanchan, waiting to see how he would meet the offer from Sanan, but Seanchan smiled and said, "We are pleased with your fellowship. Although I had my doubts when your servant came to the door."

Sanan grimaced and waved his hands. "Ah, Talin! He has been with me for a long time and has little good to say about everything when his joints ache with coming rains."

Another figure came toward them, a jeweled scarf hanging over her black hair, her face held low, a red gown covering her from neck to ankle.

Sanan beamed. "And this is Buan, my daughter! I did not expect you, Buan!"

Cumac glanced at the table and saw that a seventh chair and place had been set upon the table. He frowned.

"I welcome you to my father's table," Buan said shyly.

"And we you," Seanchan said.

The others echoed his words, but Cumac noticed that Fedelm was eying Buan narrowly, her brow furrowed.

"The meat smells wonderful," Bern said hopefully. He eyed the full pitchers on the table and licked his lips despite himself.

"Then, let us take our places!" Sanan said, pulling the chair at the head of the table out and dropping into it. He looked at the others as they stood hesitantly.

"Come! Come!" he said impatiently, waving at the chairs. "You cannot eat standing up and do merit to the meal!"

"Thank you," Seanchan said, taking his place at the other end of the table. "We have had a long journey. A very long journey, and we are weary with hunger and travel. We appreciate your hospitality."

"And the board," Bern said, reaching for a platter of pork that appeared suddenly on the table in front of him. He stabbed several pieces with his fork and dropped them with a sigh onto the trencher in front of him.

Lorgas reached for the wine, but Bern waved him off.

"The ale! The ale!" he protested. "Wine is for the morning hours. But malt beer and ale is for now. Especially," he added after jamming a huge piece of pork into his mouth, "when eating meat such as this." He sighed.

"But better," Cumac said, taking a more dignified bite from the piece he had placed on his trencher. "There seems something added to it. What is it?"

Sanan waggled a forefinger at him. "Now, that is a secret of your host! Enjoy! Enjoy!"

Seanchan reached for a bowl of apples and cherries and melon cut in thin slices.

"Those apples are snow apples from the far north. The cherries are from my own orchards and the melons from my own patches. You won't find better than they!"

"I daresay," Seanchan said softly, "that we would find few people nearby."

"This *is* the only house that we have come across in a goodly time,"

Fedelm said, ignoring Bern's praise of ale and sipping from a wine goblet instead. "Are there others you allow to live in your forest?"

"Now, that would be another secret that will reveal itself in time. In time. For now, though, enjoy yourselves. We don't get many visitors here!"

"My father misses travelers," Buan said softly, her eyes upon Cumac. "As do I."

Cumac felt himself blushing as Buan's eyes held his, seeming to pull him across the table and into them. A warmth spread slowly through him as he reached for a mug of ale and drank.

"Word of your journey has come to me," Sanan said, tearing a piece of meat from a bone. Grease dribbled from his lips and down his beard. He took a large mug of ale and drained it, washing the meat down. He belched and beamed at them. "Your way has been perilous, I daresay."

"You say correctly," Fedelm answered. She took a bite from one of the apples, the flesh snapping sharply, sending a burst of flavor into her mouth. "We have had a hard time of it."

"You will be safe here," Sanan said. "That, I promise you."

"I wonder," Lorgas murmured to Cumac.

And Cumac nodded his head as his eyes held those of Buan.

Fedelm snorted.

"Not everything is as it looks," she whispered in Cumac's ear. "Eyes are deceitful. Be wary."

But the merry mood and warm fire and food made Cumac sleepy and he yawned, then quickly apologized to his host.

"Think nothing of it," Sanan said. "I see the others are as tired. So, Buan will take you to your rooms. There, you may sleep and rest as long as you wish."

Seanchan nodded thoughtfully, as he did not share the weariness of the others. He rose and followed Buan as she led the others up a flight of stairs at the back of the hall. The others were too sleepy to notice that the stairs had suddenly appeared and that when they first found the hut in the forest, there had been only one floor and no need for stairs.

19

Cumac awoke with a start, reaching automatically for Caladbolg, which he had hung on the bedpost near at hand. But Caladbolg wasn't there, and the room began to slowly fill with a dirty gray mist that rolled on foul clouds toward his bed.

He sat up and studied the mist, feeling the coldness of death coming from the cloud. He glanced at the Dragonstone—it pulsed blackly. Quietly, he stepped cautiously from his bed and to the corner where an oil lamp burned, sending flickering light into all corners of the room. Across the room he could see where Caladbolg had been carelessly tossed into a corner.

The mist followed him steadily and from within the mist he dimly heard voices but could not understand their words. Then a black hooded figure rose up out of the mist in front of him.

"Yessss. Now issss the time, Cumac," the figure hissed. For a brief moment, Cumac thought he saw a serpent curling around an apple tree, but the illusion quickly disappeared and the hooded figure stood once again, its feet hidden by the mist. Black wings grew slowly from its back. Bright-red eyes glowed from deep within the cloak's hood.

The figure came close to Cumac and halted in front of him as the mist rose and embraced both within its cold clouds. A red smile appeared below the eyes in the hood and jagged teeth gleamed like wolf fangs.

"Who are you?" Cumac demanded.

The figure chuckled. "I am that I am. That is enough."

"Your name," Cumac said sharply. "Give it! Quickly!"

"I am Corach," the figure replied. "Look well upon me and despair!"

With that, Corach slowly slid the hood to her shoulders. Her face was as white as chalk with flesh hanging from pustules that leaked yellow pus. Her hair was gray streaked with black and the strands wiggled as if they were adders. Her mouth was a red gash, and the gaps between her teeth were filled with flesh from her victims. Red were her eyes and deep within them yellow fire flickered. Her fingers were long and bone-white, the knuckles lined with grime.

First, fear filled Cumac, then anger began to boil with him and he could feel the warp-spasm begin flooding his veins with fire. His muscles knotted like melons and his hair rose to stand like nails hammered into his head, a drop of blood appearing on the tip of each hair. His chest became a barrel and his heart boomed loudly in it.

Corach hesitated and took a step back. The flesh on her cheeks fluttered uncertainly, then she regained the step and her hideous mouth spread in a smile that dripped blood.

"You are your father'ssss sssson," she hissed. "I came for him too but he managed to escape. You are your father'ssss ssssson," she repeated, "but you are not your father."

A war-drum began to beat in Cumac's brain, and he clenched his hands until his joints snapped like ice splitting pine trees. A battle-roar came from deep within his chest and again Corach hesitated. Then a great laugh came from her.

"Do not play gamessss with me," she said.

"And do you do the bidding of Maliman?" Cumac asked.

She laughed. "What would I do with Maliman? He cannot bend my will nor seize me with his magic. I am of Air and Ice, and Death runs through me. I come from time before him and will still be in time after him. His spells are useless! There is nothing for him here. No one can stand before me."

She reached for Cumac. A cold frost seemed to fill the air between them. Then Cumac stepped forward to meet her and she stopped, her feet shifting uncertainly. Never had someone come forward; all had retreated as far as they could before she touched them.

Gathering her nerve, Corach reached out again with both hands. Then, she gave a gasp of pain as Cumac seized her upper arms and squeezed with the strength of fifty men. The flesh on her upper arms slid from the bone, and then the bone snapped like a dried twig and she howled as if a thousand demons had fallen upon her.

"Go!" Cumac said thickly, the spasm still upon him. "Go and bother us no more!"

A shifting shadow slipped from his hands and disappeared, leaving only a cry of pain in its wake.

Slowly, the warp-spasm left Cumac and he dropped weakly onto an oaken chair. His hair fell lankly over his forehead. Had Corach come then, she would have had little trouble gathering Cumac to her foul breast.

Cumach's door crashed open and Seanchan and Fedelm entered, follwed by Bern and Lorgas, all brandishing weapons, Seanchan, his staff. They looked quickly around, then spied Cumac sprawled in the chair and came slowly to him.

"What happened here?" Seanchan asked.

"Corach came. I do not know who she is, but she came to gather me and then all of you, I suspect. But she failed."

"Hmm," Seanchan said, anchoring his staff to the stone floor and leaning upon it.

"Do know her?" Fedelm asked.

"Yes, do you?" Lorgas and Bern chimed.

"I know of her," Seanchan said. "She comes from the Dark Time, when she battled alongside Ragon Garg-Fuath and fell with him after he was cast into the Great Rift beneath Ifreann. Among his followers, she came first, most beloved by Ragon, a beautiful woman with long flaxen hair and dimples carved from fresh rain. But her betrayal of The Dagda changed her into a hideous creature who craves the flesh of man and woman. Few have escaped her clutches. You are lucky, Cumac. Very lucky."

"Luck favors the bold," Fedelm said. She reached out and smoothed Cumac's hair back from his forehead. A light red stain appeared in the palm of her hand. She studied it for a moment, then gave Cumac a bleak smile. "I believe Corach escaped lightly."

Cumac shrugged. "One does what is necessary." He yawned. "Forgive me, but I am very tired now."

"Of course," Seanchan said, and he motioned the others out the door. When it had closed behind them, he whispered to the others.

"He is very weak right now, and this makes him vulnerable. We must guard his door, a quarter night for each of us."

"I have seen this warp-spasm before," Fedelm said, perplexed, "when we battled Truacs in Tanglewood Forest. But he was not tired like this after that battle."

"Each time he uses the warp-spasm, the Rage, he becomes more and more a part of it," Seanchan said. He shook his head and added, "It may mean the beginning of his end, as the Rage burns him with a deadly fire from within. Unless Cumac learns how to harness its power, I am afraid that he will burn himself away. And there is nothing we can do to help him. He must learn how to do that on his own," he said as Bern opened his mouth for a question.

"How will we know that?" Lorgas asked.

"Each time will take him longer to recover," Seanchan said soberly. He shifted his staff to his left hand. "Until his day is divided in half between awakening and sleeping." He shook his head again. "We must be very careful that he is not left alone when he uses the warp-spasm, for we must be present to watch over him while he sleeps afterward.

"I do not know how long," he muttered, more to himself than the others. "It all depends upon his courage and strength without the transformation. He is made of stern stuff, and that may help him well. We can only wait and see."

"I'll take the first watch," Fedelm said.

"No, you may have the second. I will have the first," Seanchan said. "The coming of Corach may be only the first. Or she may be alone. I do not know. But if she is the first of others to come, then we need to be ready for them.

"Now, go! Sleep. I will awaken you, Fedelm, in two hours, then you, Bern, and you last, Lorgas."

They departed and Seanchan settled himself, squatting upon the floor. Carefully, he wove an enchanted web around the door. He had deliberately kept the others from knowing about his intentions as he feared others like Corach might be watching in wisps of air. Besides, he told himself, it is enough that I know.

Cumac dropped tiredly upon his bed and stared at the ceiling. He wanted sleep, but sleep evaded him for the moment. He sighed deeply and thought about the witch-woman who had just been driven from his room.

The times are getting harder and harder, he thought. More and more of these foul creatures are appearing where they should not appear. Certainly that is a mark of Maliman's growing power, his unleashing his minions upon the land. But why do they come for me and not the others? They only come for the others when I am with them. Perhaps it is because I have no magic. More than likely that is true. Bern and Lorgas have the elfin withal, while Fedelm carries the power of the Sidhe with her. And I? He smiled ruefully.

I have Caladbolg. And the warp-spasm. But how long will I be able to control that?

He had not told the others that each time he used the warp-spasm he was weaker than before when he recovered from its effects. So tired that he could scarcely heft Caladbolg and was hard-pressed to not let the others see his weakened state.

But soon I will not be able to control that. And what if I fail to protect myself again? Will the others continue to seek for the Chalice?

Then he told himself that they would, as all knew the power Maliman would gain if the Chalice came to him.

Seanchan has the power. But he is old. He might not be able to hold against Maliman if Maliman attacks with all his power at once. After all, Maliman has been kept in the Great Rift all these years, slowly becoming more powerful, while Seanchan has been spending his time in the Earthworld. I do not know what Seanchan has been doing, but surely using his power weakens him as much as the warp-spasm does me. Then again, perhaps not. I really do not know much about wizards.

He smiled ruefully in the dark. I should have paid more attention to the lessons of Deroi the Teacher when I had the chance. Now I am all empty thought with no knowledge. But no sense in fuming about the past like a thunderstorm. You have to make do with what you have and remember that choice is the beginning of knowledge.

Thinking on this, Cumac fell into a troubled sleep. His dreams came, and he found himself walking through a dolmen gate where villages and cities were empty of people and battered by time and war. Darkness enveloped the land, but in that darkness he could sense things watching him and moving with him as he walked over the burnt earth. Then he heard them—Grayshawls, the strongest of Maliman's servants. They were all-powerful in the Dreamworld except for the Dreamwalkers, Guardians, who cast out evil entities.

His blood ran cold as he saw the gray-cloaked figures begin to emerge from the mist and hover in the air just outside his sword reach. He felt a tugging at his body, and as he tried to pull back and away from the Grayshawls he heard slow, deep breaths begin to draw his life and soul away from him.

Grimly, he fought against them, trying to reach them with Caladbolg, but the figures simply rose higher than his reach. A weakness began to come over his limbs.

Then a great light shone, sudden and strong as a thunder blast, and dreadful shrieks came from the Grayshawls as they turned away and disappeared. A smell of brimstone hung in the air, and then a white-haired man dressed in red and green came before Cumac, a grim smile upon his face.

"Who are you?" Cumac panted.

"I am Coig, the leader of the Dreamwalkers. And you are lucky to be alive after going into the Dreamland of Caer Ibormeith, the goddess of sleep and dreams, without a Guardian. Barach the Assigner saw what was happening only by accident, and he told me, as he did not have time to appoint a Guardian for you."

"I thank you," Cumac said gratefully, mopping the sweat from his brow. He swallowed, trying to wash the pain out of his throat.

"Your throat hurts?" Coig asked. Cumac nodded and Coig waved his hand. A mug of foaming ale appeared in front of Cumac.

"Take it and drink it all," Coig commanded. "It is the honey ale made by Goibniu. It will ease your pain. If we were in the Otherworld, you would gain immortality from it. But you are not in the Otherworld, and although it will heal you for the moment, it will not keep you from feeling pain later."

"Thank you," Cumac said politely, taking the mug and draining it. Instantly, the pain in his throat went away, and he nodded gratefully at Coig.

"Now," Coig said sternly, "now leave the Dreamworld and return to your bed. It is time for you to awaken. But remember: do not enter the Dreamworld without a Guardian."

"I do not go into the Dreamworld intentionally," Cumac said, feeling the need to justify his presence.

Coig leaned forward and said, "All things not guarded against are intentional. Remember that."

20

Light was seeping in through the drawn curtains when Cumac awoke. For a moment, he didn't recognize the room, then he yawned, stretched, and rose from his bed. He ran his fingers through his hair, and he scowled as memory of the night came flooding back. He dressed quickly, then took his sword and arms and opened the door of his room. Bern half sat, half sprawled outside his door, snoring softly, his face serene in his sleep. Cumac nudged him with the toe of his boot.

Bern awoke and stared vacant-eyed around him, then sighed and rose from the floor.

"What are you doing down there?" Cumac asked.

"Watching."

"Watching what?"

"Your door. We decided that you had had enough of visitors last night, so we all took turns outside your door." Bern yawned, his jaw cracking. "You sleep all right?"

"What do you think?" Cumac asked. "There is something about this house that doesn't allow travelers a peaceful sleep."

Bern came alert quickly. "What do you mean?"

Cumac explained his night and the appearance of Coig who had saved him from the Grayshawls, adding Coig's warning to avoid Dreamland unless accompanied by a Guardian.

Bern shook his head and said, "We must tell the others. They may be next for the Grayshawls in Dreamland. Of course, Seanchan does not have to worry, but Fedelm and Lorgas do. As do I," he added. "The three of us are just as vulnerable to the Grayshawls as you."

"I thought—" Cumac began, but Bern cut him off.

"Like you, when we enter Earthworld, we become mortal. Except for the Bisuilglas," he said, tapping the talisman on his shoulder. "This will allow me to return. I do not know about the others, though I doubt it. Although," he added darkly, "returning takes time and waiting. Which we can ill afford. Especially now that the Grayshawls are apparently following us. We must consult Seanchan."

Bern scurried away, Cumac close upon his heels as they went down the long hallway, pounding on doors to awaken the others.

"Up! Get up!" Bern shouted at each door. "It is daylight and dangerous to sleep. Get up, sleepyheads! Get up!"

"What is all this noise?" Lorgas asked, grumbling as he opened the door to his room. He rubbed the sleep from his eyes and yawned. "You make more noise than a hundred oxcarts!"

"We have a problem," Bern said as Fedelm opened her door and silently joined them. Seanchan was just behind her.

"A problem?" Seanchan asked, his eyes narrowing as he studied the Ervalian. "Explain yourself!"

Bern nodded at Cumac and said, "Tell them. As you told me."

The others turned their attention to Cumac and waited patiently while he related what had happened to him while he was in the Dreamworld.

"Thanks to Coig I came out of it without harm," he ended.

Seanchan pulled his fingers through his beard, his brow furrowed by thought.

"I don't think I like it here," Fedelm said. "I did not sleep the sleep of *imbas forasnai*. Although," she added, "I did not go into sleep intending to dream it. But I feel that there is something wrong. I said as much when we first came. There is a magic here I do not like."

"I feel it as well," Lorgas joined in. "I think it would be better for us if we skip our breakfast and be off. We should put a long distance between us and this place. Sanan may set a good table, but such things as your dream and that episode last night, well, that isn't the mark of a good host. What say you, Seanchan?"

The old man nodded slowly, his eyes thoughtful. "I agree that we must leave. But I think we should eat and listen to what Sanan has to say." As Lorgas started to argue, Seanchan added, "Wisdom may be found behind the falsehoods that he tells." Lorgas fell silent, but all could feel the doubt running through his mind. Then he noticed the Dragonstone.

"We still need to be cautious," he said grimly, pointing to the stone pulsing blackly upon Cumac's shoulder.

The others looked, and their faces set into hard masks.

"There is danger here," Seanchan concurred quietly, taking a firmer grip upon his staff. "We will eat, leave as soon as possible, and guard ourselves fully until we are well away from this house."

"Then let us go down and get it over with," Bern said. "We can still be polite and hurry."

Together they all went down to the Great Hall where Sanan waited in front of the roaring fire that drew the coldness from the hall. The oak table was surrounded by six oak chairs, all scrubbed clean. Again, food had been laid out on wooden platters down the center of the table and each place had trenchers and wooden goblets already in place. The trenchers were laden with fresh meat ripe off the bone, and apples and plums and snow cherries filled wooden bowls. The mugs held morning ale.

"Ah!" Sanan beamed. "I trust you all slept well? You certainly have had a long sleep. The sun rose quite some time ago—the cows are all milked and the milk already being made into cheese. Come! Come!" he cried, gesturing at the table. "You must fill yourselves before you're away. If," he added, "you must be away. You are certainly more than welcome to stay as long as you wish. In fact, I would like that very much!"

"We thank you for your hospitality," Seanchan said. "But we really must be off and down the road. We have a long way to travel before we rest again. A long way," he emphasized.

Sanan heaved a deep sigh and shook his head. "Well, you know best your business. I will not detain you. But," he said, rubbing his hands together with relish, "you must have a repast before you go. I do insist on that. What would happen if word got out that I did not set a morning table for my guests?"

"We thank you for that," Seanchan said. He gestured for the others to take their chairs. "You have been more than kind to us."

"Phoo, phoo," Sanan said, waving away Seanchan's words. But he beamed with pleasure nevertheless as he took his place at the head of the table.

"But where," Fedelm asked, as she took an apple and some cherries to add to her trencher, "is your daughter, Buan?"

"Ah," Sanan said apologetically. "She is young and sleeps like the old. She will come and join us shortly, I am certain."

He leaned forward, placed his elbows on the table, and rested his chin in both hands.

"But I detect now that the night did not go well for all. But for who?"

He pretended to study all of them, then his eyes fell upon Cumac. "I have a feeling that you, Cumac, had a restless night. What bothers you?"

Cumac stared steadily at Sanan, his eyes blue ice.

"Why, nothing bothers me," he said softly. "What makes you think that something bothers me?"

"Then you slept well?" Sanan said, but there was the hint of misgiving in his voice. "You look as if the night had been hard for you."

Cumac gave him a thin smile and shook his head. "No, I slept like the dead."

"Ah," Sanan said. "I guess I was mistaken. Now, here's Buan! Up before the sun is high! Join us, daughter."

Buan nodded, smiling tiredly, lines of pain etched around her mouth. She wore a blue dress with a red hem and red slippers upon her feet. Her right arm rested gingerly in a sling.

"But what has happened?" Sanan asked, concerned. "You have hurt yourself."

"Alas," she answered. "I am afraid I fell down the stairs in the middle of the night and broke my arm. Mel, our servant, set it for me. But it is extremely painful."

Her gaze held Cumac's for a moment, then fell to the table. She reached awkwardly for the fruit with her left hand and half filled her platter.

"Perhaps if I eat something I shall feel better."

"And drink the ale," her father commanded. "It will help with the pain."

She nodded, reached for her mug, and drained it like a thirsty warrior instead of sipping at it like a well-bred young lady.

"You know," Cumac said conversationally, taking a bite of meat, chewing as he spoke. "I would have sworn that I saw you last night in my room. But," he added, "surely that was simply a dream I had."

"I am happy to have been in your dreams," Buan said, blushing modestly. "I hope the dreams were of a kind and gentle nature."

"Better than yours, apparently," Cumac said, nodding at her arm.

For a moment, her mask slipped, and all could see what lay behind—then in an eyeblink, the smooth mask was once again in place. Yet her eyes had a venomous glint to them, and a slight hiss came from her lips.

"Amusing, isn't it," Seanchan said, taking a bite of apple and chewing happily, "what can happen in a person's dreams? There a man can be a victim or a king or a great warrior. Depending, of course, upon the man himself," he amended. "A man is only what he can dream himself to be. Of course, nightmares are something else. That's when something comes into one's dreams. Or," he said delicately, his eyes holding Buan's, "when one is in the halfworld between dreams. Then fantasy can become reality."

"Come! Come!" Sanan said hastily. "Enough talk about dreams! Dreams are only momentary. What happens in light of day is what a man should concern himself about!

"By the way," he said, "I believe your horses have shown up. A big black leading them. I had my men give them each oats and fresh hay. They are waiting for you. I think," he continued, "that I have seen that black before. A wonderful horse! So wonderful, in fact, that no one seems to be able to get near him. A fiery temper, that! It takes a special man to ride that one, I declare."

"It is my horse," Cumac said, finishing his breakfast and pushing back his chair. "At least, I am the one he has taken to. I don't think anyone can own him."

"Too bad," Sanan sighed. "I would have given much for him."

"Sometimes, it is wise not to yearn for something that is beyond one's grasp," Seanchan said. He glanced back and forth between Sanan and Buan. "The pain of wanting can destroy people. Especially if they are shape-shifters. But," he slapped the table and rose, "I think it best if we leave. We have quite a long way to go, and the sun even now is climbing in the sky. And," he said harshly, "I am one for traveling in the day and not at night."

His eyes burned into those of Sanan's and Buan's. They held his stare for a second, then their heads dropped as they looked away.

"And now," Seanchan said, motioning toward the others, "I believe we must leave. We thank you for your . . . courtesy."

Sanan muttered something as he glanced at Buan and then away.

The others smiled politely as they gathered their belongings and left.

"Come!" Seanchan said quickly, once they were outside. "We must leave at once! There is more here than we have seen!"

Hurriedly, they saddled their horses, tied their belongings behind their saddles, and were away as quick as a linnet's flight.

They rode quickly away from the house, heading deeper and deeper into the forest. A dank smell rose from the ground to meet them, and ravens began to follow them, cawing at them mockingly.

Seanchan glanced up at the ravens, then at Cumac's blackly pulsing Dragonstone, and he shook his head. "Be watchful. I do not know what lies in these woods. But whatever it is, it is evil. I can feel it pressing upon me."

"As can I," Fedelm added, slipping an arrow from her quiver and nocking it.

"We are still in the Forest of Sanan," Lorgas said, fingering his ax. "They say it is here that Deag-duls wait for unwary travelers. But other creatures as well have been seen here."

He looked apologetically at Cumac. "There are sumaires here too. And for those, we must be especially on guard."

"Being on guard means being on guard for all things," Seanchan said irritably. "One cannot separate one creature from another and pay attention to one and not the other."

"Seems a little tense, he does," Bern whispered to Lorgas. "Best to mind the p's and q's for now. We don't want to make Seanchan mad at us, lest he change us into something unnatural without thinking. You have to be careful around wizards."

"Humph," Lorgas said. "We have been travelers together long enough for that not to happen. I'm more afraid that I'll be caught up in that cairnfire of his. Seems to me that cairnfire is hard to direct."

"Yes, yes. I can see your reasoning. Still, it would be better if you minded your tongue a bit more, I'm thinking."

Lorgas sighed and nodded and they rode in silence, following a dim game path that seemed visible only to Seanchan. They yearned for a wider trail—the narrow path seemed right for an ambush to the travelers—but none had appeared in the forest.

Brambles and bushes blocked their way from time to time obliging them to dismount and lead their horses. Thorns tore at their clothes as they forced their way through.

The stench grew stronger and stronger as they made their way through the forest, and Cumac pulled a fold of his cloak up and over his mouth and nose to keep from gagging. He glanced around and saw that the others were following his lead. Even Seanchan seemed a bit pale and frequently coughed in an attempt to remove the foul taste brought by the stench.

A soft murmur came through the trees and Seanchan pulled up sharply, twisting his head this way and that, trying to locate the source of the sound. His eyes strained to pierce the darkness and caught movement, although he could not identify what was moving.

Then the moaning grew louder and a black-hooded figure, red-eyed with teeth yellow and large, emerged from the deep, followed by others.

"Deag-duls!" Seanchan shouted. "Defend yourselves!"

Scarcely had the sound of his voice disappeared when two shafts left Fedelm's bow and sped past Seanchan's ear to sink into the hearts of two Deag-duls. A shriek that nearly paralyzed all sounded from their mouths as they fell to the ground, twisting in pain and then slowly disappearing into the coming mist.

Cumac swung his sword and met the sword of a Deag-dul. The shock nearly tore Caladbolg from his hand. Grimly, he gripped the haft harder and swung again, this time beheading the Deag-dul who had tried to knock him from Black by riding his horse into the stallion.

Black let out a scream and rose on his hind legs, lashing out at the Deag-duls while Cumac fought with the Crescent Feat and the Edge Feat. Behind him, he could hear Lorgas roaring as his ax cut like magic in his hands, chopping off arms and legs and heads, while Bern gave his warrior cry and fought hard with his sword.

Still, they were forced to give ground little by little until some Deag-duls managed to work their way behind the seekers and surround them. Then, the forest became outlined in red to Cumac's eyes and the warp-spasm began to twist his joints. His hair rose with a drop of blood on each hair and his warrior cry froze everyone for a moment. Foam appeared at the corners of his mouth and Caladbolg became a rainbow whirl in his hands and heads began to fall from bodies, shrieking as they were cut away. The others turned to the sides to meet the Deag-duls as they tried to press in upon the party's flanks while Cumac raged forward madly.

The Deag-duls then gave large cries and disappeared just as suddenly as they had appeared.

"I have to say that I had my doubts there for a minute," Lorgas said, panting as he leaned on his ax. "Seemed like two took the place of every one I killed."

"I took ten at least and twenty more were there in their places," Bern said, mopping the sweat from his brow. "I would say that we were very fortunate." He looked at Cumac as the warp-spasm slowly left him. "We can thank Cumac for that, I believe."

Fedelm moved her horse next to Black and grabbed Cumac's shoulder, supporting him when he sagged in his saddle.

Cumac took several deep breaths, pulled then a waterskin from his saddle and drank deeply. He lowered the skin and drew a deep sigh. His face looked strained, edged with white lines. He managed a crooked smile at Fedelm.

"Is everyone all right?"

The others checked themselves carefully. Although their clothes were tattered, all seemed to be miraculously unharmed. Seanchan fretted about a long slash in his robe, bringing a smile to faces.

"We were lucky," Fedelm said. "If you hadn't been with us, I don't think we would have made it through the Deag-duls' ambush. That was very touch-and-go for a moment."

"Yes," Seanchan said, his attention turning from the rent in his robe. "Yes, I believe we were. But we cannot imagine we are all that more safe having driven the Deag-duls away. There are others in this forest that we must worry about as well."

He pointed to the brooch on Cumac's shoulder. It shone with a steady black light.

"That tells us we should move on as quickly as possible. We need to find a safe place that we can guard, well before dark. I do not wish to make do in these close confines."

The others looked at each other grimly, then moved away, riding close behind Seanchan as he led the way along the path.

They wound their way through the forest, into darker and darker parts where the trees were leafless and a black mold covered them. No ferns or grass grew on the foul earth. Still, Seanchan rode steadily forward, as if he had his sight set on someplace in the distance that only he could see.

At last, they came to the beginning of green, and all took deep breaths of relief. Seanchan continued onward until they came to a small glade with a sylvan pool in its center. Here, Seanchan stopped and stepped down from his horse.

"This is Greenwood. We will rest here," he announced as he

placed his hands on the small of his back and stretched. His back popped and he sighed. "This seems to be a safe place. At least your Dragonstone finds nothing dangerous here, Cumac."

Cumac glanced at the Dragonstone, glowing redly on his shoulder. He nodded at Seanchan's words.

"It appears so," he said. "But will it stay so while we rest?"

Seanchan started to answer, but a musical voice broke in from the woods around the pool.

Here you may rest your weary bones
Safe from the Deag-duls' moans.
We will guard your stay,
For as long as you may
Need to recover from your fight
With the Deag-duls' might.
We bring scones and honey
For your meal. No money
Need be given for your pay
As with Lualiens you stay.

Then a silver glow came into the clearing, and when it lifted, a host of silver-armored fairies stood around them. They held silver swords.

"We are the Lualiens," a white-blond fairy spoke. "I am Salane, your host."

He bowed gracefully, then said, "You are our guests here, for we know your quest and the need for it. And," he gestured at the other fairies, "we will guard your stay."

"We thank you," Seanchan said, bowing formally. "We have been hard-pressed on our journey and will welcome a rest."

"Make yourselves at home," Salane said. "Food will be brought for you in a short while. Here, you need not worry."

"I have heard of the Lualien hospitality and am pleased that you bestow that upon us," Seanchan said.

Salane grinned. "We will set up our guard, now. You are safe."

The Lualiens disappeared.

Lorgas sighed and stepped down from his horse, rubbing his backside.

"I know I could use a moment's peace," he groaned. "Elves are not made for horses. We are runners, and very good runners at that."

"I agree," Bern said, following Lorgas's lead. "I can't remember having spent so much time on a horse. In fact, I can't even remember being on a horse."

The others laughed at their state but admitted that they too could use a rest, as the past few days had been quite a strain on them, forcing them to sleep, as it were, with one eye open. The way had been hard and dangerous, keeping them constantly wary, even though one of the party was always on the watch. Although the seekers trusted one another, each was also aware that a sudden attack could overwhelm the watcher and be disastrous for them all.

"I believe that we can fully relax here," Seanchan said. "In fact, I do not think we need to mount a watch, what with the Lualiens guarding us. I have heard of these elves, and all have been treated as we are. It is their way of extending hospitality. Greenwood is an old forest, and the Lualiens are among the oldest line of elves. I know, I know," he said as Lorgas and Bern began to complain. "I know that you also come from a long line, but the Lualiens trace their beginning back to the time of Nuada, when the laws of hospitality were being formed. So swallow your pride, Lorgas and Bern, and take advantage of what the Lualiens are extending."

Lorgas and Bern muttered darkly as they unsaddled their horses and rubbed them down with handfuls of long grass.

Seanchan smiled at their imprecations, and he, Cumac, and Fedelm followed the elves' lead and made their horses comfortable as well. Then Seanchan went to the pool of water in the middle of the glade and bent to take a drink.

His eyes widened as clouds began to swirl in the depths of the pool, parting to reveal the future. He saw the troubled time that lay ahead of them, a fleeting image of Bricriu, smiling venomously, and an ending and beginning that he did not want to believe.

He shook his head and drank as the vision disappeared.

A scrying pool. But I must not tell the others, he thought. I believe that was meant for me alone. And who is to say that it is accurate? I might raise an alarm for nothing.

He sighed and turned back to the others as Lualiens began to arrive, bearing food and drink for the weary travelers.

Cumac awoke suddenly but refreshed. He found himself lying in a bower that had been made by trees fastening their branches about him while he slept. His bed was fern and grass, deep and soft, with a fragrant odor that pleased him.

He sighed and stretched, and although he wanted to sleep some more, he reluctantly forced himself to rise and step to the pool to wash his face. When he bent to the water, he saw himself and Fedelm again alone in red-streaked darkness.

Dangerous creatures were around them and they were riding furiously to escape. Then the sight shifted and disappeared, and he saw the party enter Cruachan Ai, where Maeve and Ailill waited. But everything else appeared obscured in dark clouds.

He started to rise, then shook his head and scooped bright water to splash on his face. He drank long and deep of the water and felt a freshness within him. Still, the vision stayed with him.

The others awoke slowly, yawning and stretching with pleasure.

"Perhaps we could stay here a little longer?" Lorgas asked.

Seanchan shook his head. "No, we must continue on. Besides, although the Lualiens are guarding us at the moment, that does not mean Maliman's dark servants will not try to break through to us. I would not wish that any of the Lualiens be slain on our account."

"Ah, me!" Bern sighed. "I was just getting comfortable, and here we are, ready to mount and ride again. How far is it to Cruachan Ai? No, no, don't tell me! Any distance is too far."

"Is there any food left?" Lorgas asked, rising.

"There is," Fedelm said, gesturing at a white linen cloth that had been spread on the green and upon which were bread and fruit and pitchers of clean cold water that made teeth ache pleasurably when drunk.

The party fell to the breakfast eagerly, eating until only crumbs remained on the linen. Then, with a sigh and a grumble, they readied their horses for the journey ahead.

Seanchan mounted and raised his voice, "We thank the Lualiens for their fine hospitality and care in allowing us to rest. Word of your generosity will be spoken when we meet others. May all smile upon you!"

Salane appeared in a silver sprinkle of light, his face smiling.

"You are welcome, Seanchan Duirgeal! We are happy to be able to make you comfortable on your journey. It will be long," he said gravely, "and you must be careful on the rest of your travel to Cruachan Ai, as danger lies ahead." He glanced at Fedelm. "I am sorry to have to tell you this, but all the gates to the Sidhes have been sealed by Barach, the leader of the Old Ones, to bar the way for Maliman's Dark Forces, who are nearly at full strength."

The Seekers looked at each other in alarm. If Maliman had grown powerful enough to threaten the portals of the Sidhes, then he had grown powerful enough to threaten the boundaries of all the kingdoms of Earthworld. And perhaps the Otherworld also, since the Otherworld was almost a mirror of Earthworld.

Salane raised his hand and said, "Your band, however, may be able to slip through to Cruachan Ai. But you must beware not only of Maliman's forces but of others as well. The forests are filled with more Sword-wanderers than before and others who owe allegiance to a king or queen or—who have broken their vows to a king or queen. These are the most detestable of all, assuring travelers they are safe and then murdering them in the dark. I would send some of my people with you, but your small band has a better chance of making it through to Cruachan Ai. It is not a time for a large band to travel and draw attention to itself."

"We thank you for your hospitality and news," Seanchan said, bowing his head. "We shall take extra caution as we travel."

"The path through Greenwood will be safe for you," Salane said. "But after you leave our border, you will be in danger every step of the way. That is the best that I can do for you. Good luck."

He smiled and nodded at them, then disappeared in a cloud of silver and gold dust.

"Well," Lorgas sighed, "I knew things had been too easy for us. Now they get much worse. I guess that good times are over."

"If you call our travel good, then you are quite mad," Bern said sternly. "What do you think, Seanchan?"

"I do not know what to think. I believe we should move rapidly once we leave Greenwood," Seanchan said. "But we shall still have to exercise caution. Other than that, I am as much in the dark as you. I do not know what to expect or what lies ahead."

"Perhaps we should send someone before us?" Cumac asked.

Seanchan shook his head. "No. That would cut our strength and leave one of us very vulnerable to a quick attack. No, we shall all travel together. But," he amended, "I believe I should visit Bracha in the meantime and see what news he has of Maliman and his minions. I will not be long, and you should be safe as long as you do not stray from the path through Greenwood." He shook his finger at the little party. "And I mean *do not* stray from the path for any reason. Do I make myself clear?"

They all nodded, and Seanchan smiled and cautioned, "Remember that evil can take many forms. It is not always ugly and deformed."

So saying, he mounted his steed and galloped off on a south path through the woods and quickly disappeared.

"Well," Fedelm said, sighing. "I think we should continue our journey. But stay alert! The time we have had to recoup our strength is over once we leave here. Although Salane has promised our path to be safe, we still must be ready for anything that may come our way. If Maliman has become as strong as Salane says, then he could well have made a way into Greenwood even while we stay talking."

"Then," said Bern grimly, "let us be on our way and stop dilly-dallying, playing if and what. When trouble presents itself, I always find that motion is better than staying one's feet."

And with that, the party mounted their horses and set out soberly on the path that had been given them by Salane, each alone with his or her own thoughts.

At first, the sun shined through the branches and leaves of the trees, laddering golden light upon the path as the party traveled warily. But by noon, the sun had disappeared, and clouds forming in the west began to turn purple, threatening rain. The way began to narrow, and soon they found themselves in a thicket where branches occasionally brushed their boots and stirrups as they rode, forcing them to slow their pace.

Sudden gusts of wind blew clouds of leaves up

into the air, and rain began to fall, at first gently, then pelting them. Then came the hail, stones as big as pigeon eggs, and they were forced to pull up under a huge oak tree for protection.

"Well," said Lorgas, trying to mop the water from his face with the sodden end of his cloak. "It looks like we have gone as far as we can go for the moment."

"One thing, though," Bern answered grimly. "I think the chances of trouble are dim indeed as long as this storm lasts."

"I agree," said Fedelm, ignoring the water dripping from her. "But we must still be on our guard."

"Then," said Cumac, "let us take advantage of the moment and have our noon meal."

They dismounted and opened their leather pouches and were surprised to find that the Lualiens had filled their pouches with pannin bread and fresh, almost sweet water in their waterskins. All happily drew out the pannin bread and settled down to munch on the repast provided.

They ate hungrily while they watched the hail come down outside the canopy of branches of the old oak tree. For a while, it appeared that the hail would last for the rest of the day, and if the truth be known, all were secretly hoping that it would, for they had stopped not only beneath the protective branches of oak but on a high hummock of sweet thick and green grass that their horses grazed on as they waited.

But then the hail stopped and the wind began to die down, although the rain still streaked down in buckets.

The travelers looked at each other and collectively sighed.

"Well," Fedelm said grudgingly, "a little water never hurt anyone. I say we move on."

"This isn't a little water," Lorgas objected. "It's a right downpour that threatens to fill the gullies and flood the lowlands and wash us away. We have an excellent place here to pause for the night, and I vote that we stay."

"As do I," Bern said. All looked at Cumac.

"You are the one given the task to find Bricriu and the Chalice of Fire," Fedelm said. "The rest of us have happened along your journey. What say you?"

Cumac looked at each and then out to the downpour, noticing the deep puddles beginning to form on the path. He shook his head.

"I believe we should do what Seanchan says. Hurry as fast as we can, that we not become content with our position and laze away. It is, after all, only rain, despite how heavy it comes down, and none of us are honey and spice that will melt away."

"Then," Lorgas sighed, "let us be on our way before our will flags and we make camp here."

Reluctantly, the little party mounted the horses and rode miserably forward as fast as they could go, over patches of grass and through thick drifts of old leaves that sent a sharp smell of tannin into the air.

The Seekers did not talk among themselves, each being huddled as deeply as possible within their hooded cloaks, trusting to the horses (for the most part) to find their own way along the path.

After a half hour or so, the rain suddenly stopped. The sun came out from ragged clouds that spit a moment's rain, and then sun and clouds disappeared slowly as eventide came and the gloaming settled over them.

They paused beneath an elm tree whose leaves were rapidly turning yellow as the other trees changed color as well—russet, brown, red. The ground at the foot of the elm was heaped with leaves, yet fairly dry and sheltered by huckleberry bushes from any sudden wind.

Cumac sprawled with his back against the elm after taking care of Black. He sighed and wiggled his toes in his boots. A tune came to him as he lay on a pile of leaves whose sharp tannic odor tickled his nose pleasantly.

I sing of things that have come to pass
And here we take time to relax
Against the day's foreboding weather

That has hindered our travel rather
Than helping us along our way.

So beneath this tree we tarry
Yet still we must remain wary
Lest we find ourselves in dire straits
That will lead us to wicked fates.

And so we should for the while be merry
And forget the road before us is scary
And Maliman furiously seeks
Among the . . .

"Hmm," he added as he groped for a rhyme.

Lorgas shook his head. "Aye, I think you are better suited for stories than for song. That is, if you pardon me, a pathetic song."

"I agree," Bern said.

"And I," Fedelm said laughing.

Cumac pretended to be hurt by their criticism, although he admitted that the song was terrible and that he was more given to making other contributions to the quest.

"Well," he said loftily, "then I will take first watch, so I may sleep fully the rest of the night without interruption by one of you shaking me awake to take my turn."

"With a song as bad as that, you are entitled to first watch," Fedelm said, smiling wickedly.

And so they settled themselves to spend the night where they were, drying as they slept, each wrapped within the warm blanket of his or her dreams.

Cumac had not been long asleep when he found himself wandering a barren wasteland covered with fallen dolmens and burnt grass as black as Maliman's ashes. He could not hear the sound of water or crickets or even linnet wings.

Uneasily, he looked around, his hand nervously fingering where the haft of Caladbolg should have been. He encountered only air. Frantically he groped and looked for the sword, but it was nowhere to be found. A hand touched him on the shoulder, causing him to jump with alarm.

In front of him stood a black-haired man, attired fully in black and leaning upon his black bow. He smiled at Cumac, his white teeth shining like freshwater pearls, and said, "Do not be frightened or alarmed. I am Cathar, the Dreamwalker assigned by Barach to be your Guardian while you are here."

"And how do I know this?" Cumac asked suspiciously.

Cathar chuckled. "Because I have not already destroyed or captured you and removed your weapons. You were fast asleep before you entered Dreamworld, and such things would have been easily accomplished had I been your enemy. No, rest assured that I am who I say I am and I am your Guardian."

"Why am I here? I gave no thought to this place. Suddenly I am here and I have no idea how I came to be here," Cumac asked.

Cathar sobered immediately and straightened, taking a firmer grip on his black bow.

"Very curious. Suddenly finding oneself within it is unusual. Usually it means that someone is calling you into the Dreamworld. Someone who, no doubt, you know or at least know of. This is bad." His brow furrowed as he looked carefully around. "This is very bad indeed. Here, everything is the opposite of Earthworld. Here, winter is warm and summer is cold and leaves fall in spring—if any could be found—and bud out in fall—again, if any could be found. I personally have never seen trees, although other Guardians claim to have seen one or two. Frankly, I believe this is all." He waved around himself.

"But what is there here that there isn't in Earthworld or the Otherworld? Why would someone want me here?"

Cathar sighed. "That is rather obvious. You have an enemy who has powers greater here than elsewhere—greater than you believe him to have. You are vulnerable here just as if you were in Earthworld, as your grandmother, Deichtine, the mother of Cucullen, was of Earthworld and you carry her blood within your veins just as you carry the blood of Fand and Lugh. But Dreamworld is not boundless: one can cross its borders into other worlds that once flourished but were destroyed one way or the other. It is these worlds that are used by some to bring the unsuspecting into them so they may be destroyed."

"Other worlds?" Cumac asked, his hand going automatically to where Caladbolg should have been. "I thought there was only one Otherworld."

Cathar shook his head. "Oh no. The Otherworld, as you know it, is what remains of the past worlds. It is not a wasteland, although someday, when there is no longer a need for the Pantheon, it will become a wasteland, deserted and empty. Unless," he amended, "the Pantheon wins the last great battle coming. Then it will simply be and remain so. The portals will be locked and closed to the Earthworld until the Pantheon is needed again. Then heroes will again be summoned by The Dagda and sent forth into battle in Earthworld's darkest hour. And the enemy may well be Maliman again, if he is not destroyed now or locked again within the lowest circle of the Great Rift with new and more powerful seals holding him there. But it is now that I am concerned with, and you should be concerned with it as well. Not the future. You have no time for the future here."

Cumac peered around him but saw only fallen stone pillars and burnt grass. "I see nothing," he said.

"Neither do I. And there should be others here. You are not the only one to be brought into Dreamworld or to dream themselves here," said Cathar. "And that worries me, as I *feel* the danger to you. It is around us like marsh gas."

Cumac took a deep breath, then hastily exhaled as the fetid odor threatened to overpower his senses.

"It stinks," he gasped.

"Of course. Marsh gas is not perfume. Surely you knew that!" Cathar said scornfully.

"Well, then, what do we do? Just wait for whoever comes and makes himself known?"

Cather chewed his lower lip thoughtfully, then said, "No, I do not like this place. It is not easily defended. We need to find another place, where we can worry about only one direction and that in front of us."

"That is all well and good," Cumac said, "but I have no weapons."

"That can be remedied," Cathar said. "Let us go. I believe we will find what you need not far from here."

Together the two left, following no path that Cumac could see but that Cathar seemed to find with little trouble. The way seemed more and more desolated as they moved across the land, and here and there, Cumac spotted the remains of Great Halls but did not find the bones of those to whom the Great Halls once belonged. The silence fell hard upon his ears. He could not even hear the echoes of their feet upon the ground.

At last, they came upon a dolmen still standing and within that dolmen a large stone with a sword embedded in it. The handle of the sword was silver and wrapped in leather to keep sweaty hands from slipping. The blade (what he could see of it) shone brightly and appeared to be made of highly polished steel. A soft golden glow radiated from the sword.

Cathar paused and gestured toward the sword. "Try to draw it from the stone. It is the sword of Nuada Silverhand, Casurairmed, the one brought from the Old Lands. The one he bore to fight and defeat the Fomorians. Following Nuada's death, Barach brought Casurairmed here and placed it in the rock, sealing it there with magic, for only the son of the greatest hero to withdraw."

Slowly, Cumac approached the sword. He bent to carefully study the stone in which the sword stood but could not find the faint lines separating the sword from the stone.

He shook his head. "This sword has become part of the stone."

Cathar shrugged. "If you do not wish to try . . ."

His voice trailed off, but the tone was one of derision and scorn, and Cumac flushed. He gripped the sword and, bracing his feet on either side of the stone, heaved upward with all his strength.

The sword came freely from the stone and Cumac staggered back from the force he had used, nearly falling.

He held the sword up and studied it. Not a single blemish could he find on the blade. Not one nick or hairline crack. He spun it in a circle and marveled at how it seemed to sing as it went through the air. It was perfectly balanced and fit itself to his hand as if it had grown from his palm.

"It's a great sword," Cumac said lamely, lacking the words to fully express his feeling about the weapon.

"It is," Cathar said, then reminded him, "But it must stay in Dreamworld when you leave. Besides, you have Caladbolg back in Earthworld, which is destined to be the sword of legend down through the ages. Unlike the four other gifts the Tuatha brought from the Old Land, Casurairmed cannot be removed to be used in Earthworld. The Spear of Lugh, the Chalice of Fire, the Lia Fail, and the Cauldron of The Dagda may be taken into Earthworld, but not Casurairmed.

"But enough marveling, let us proceed and see if we can discover why you are here."

Together, the pair moved away from the dolmen, heading in a direction that seemed no direction to Cumac, as there were no stars or sun by which to guide his way. But he felt as if he were traveling through time past, present, and future at once.

Cathar unlimbered his bow and took a blackthorn arrow and nocked it, holding it tight to the bow and waxed bowstring as they moved across the barren wasteland.

Cumac gripped his sword firmly as he followed Cathar's lead.

Fedelm awoke with a start and a gasp and looked quickly around her at the others sprawled upon the grassy hummock beneath the giant elm. Lorgas snored lightly while Bern smiled and twitched. Seanchan slept deeply, his hand grasping his staff.

She glanced at Cumac and slowly sighed, then frowned. She rose and went to his side and gently touched his forehead. It was as cold as ice. She shook his shoulder, softly at first, then fiercely, but it was rigid, as was his body.

Alarmed she cried out, "Cumac!"

The others came awake with a start. Seanchan rose and swiftly came to Fedelm's side.

"What is it?" he asked, his fingers automatically touching the side of Cumac's throat.

"I cannot awaken him!" Fedelm said. She shook him again. "See? It is as if death has taken him and left him as stiff as a walnut board."

"What? What?" Bern and Lorgas said as they joined Fedelm and Seanchan. "What?"

"Cumac does not answer our bidding," Seanchan said grimly. "There is great mischief here, I'm afraid."

He closed his eyes and softly moved his hand over Cumac's body. But nothing happened. He frowned and tried again, concentrating so hard that his fingers vibrated from effort. But still Cumac lay still.

"He is alive—I can tell you that much—but barely alive."

"But . . . but what happened?" Lorgas asked with deep concern.

"He has been drawn into the Dreamworld," Seanchan said.

"Well, bring him back, then," Bern said impatiently.

Seanchan shook his head regretfully. "That I cannot do. I do not know what spell was used to bring about this enchantment. Something evil—of that, I am certain. But without knowing which one, I am helpless. And it may well be that a more powerful wizard has Cumac in his grasp."

"Is there nothing that you can do, then?" Lorgas asked fearfully.

"I do not know," Seanchan said. "Perhaps. But I can think of nothing at this moment."

"Can you enter his dream and bring him back?" Fedelm asked.

"I could," Seanchan said, "if it is *his* dream that he is in. But I fear that someone has drawn him into another's dream, and I doubt if I can find the source. Dreams are like spider filaments unique to each individual. Whoever may have drawn Cumac into his own dream will be almost impossible to find. But what about you, Fedelm? Cannot you use the *imbas forasnai* to find the one responsible?"

"I do not know," Feldem answered. "I have used the *imbas forasnai* for only the possible future. I can enter *imbas forasnai* and the

Dreamworld, but as you said, I may not enter by the right path. There are many entrances to the Dreamworld and, indeed, if the wizard is strong enough, he may have been able to place Cumac in Dreamworld without the use of a portal."

She took hold of a braid and tugged it furiously. "All I can do is try."

"As can I," Seanchan said solemnly. "But whether we can or cannot bring Cumac back from Dreamworld, we cannot move his body. To do so would disrupt the link he does have with Earthworld, and he could be locked forever in Dreamworld. We must leave him where he is and guard him, for while he may be in Dreamworld, he is still vulnerable in this world. We must always have a guard mounted over him. I fear that this may be the work of Maliman or one of his minions, an attempt to keep us here. This has all the shades of becoming very, very dangerous."

Bern looked around them and shook his head. "This is not a good place to defend, Seanchan. We are open to attack from any direction or all directions. We will be stretched very thin to defend all ways at once."

"I may be able to give some help there," Seanchan said. He rose, his joints cracking in protest. He took his staff and limped past the horses, where he stood, mumbling for a moment. Then he began to walk a wide circle around the band, undetectable words still falling from his lips. The air behind him began to shimmer with a faint rose color.

He finished the circle and came back to the group, wiping his forehead with the sleeve of his robe.

"It has been a long time since I have done that," Seanchan said, gasping for air. "It certainly drains a Druid. But," he looked with satisfaction at the shimmering waves, "that should hold, unless another of the Duirgeals comes along. But I sincerely doubt if that will happen. All spells by a Duirgeal are linked to all the other Duirgeals, and to attempt to defeat one will be an effort to defeat another. It certainly should hold against anything that Maliman can send against us. Although I do think he will test us one way or the other. And," he continued as Lorgas opened his mouth, "we

Duirgeals are here only as a last resort. Man must work his own magic and fail before we can work ours."

Lorgas and Bern nodded.

"We know that, Seanchan. And it is only Cumac who is in danger right now. But even though you have woven a guard around us, I still think we need to stay awake, just in case. Not that I think anything will breach the spell," Lorgas added hastily, "but accidents do happen, and right now, I do not think we can afford such a thing."

"I, too, agree," Bern said. "No offense."

"And none taken," Seanchan said. "Now, let us divide the day and night into equal parts, and you and Bern can guard while Fedelm and I see if we cannot enter Dreamworld where Cumac wanders."

And with that, Fedelm and Seanchan made themselves comfortable and slept while Lorgas and Bern kept guard over all.

26

The air was bitter cold when Seanchan entered Dreamworld, warily clutching his staff. He grimaced and blew on his fingers to warm them before wrapping himself tighter in his robes and cloak. Frost covered the burnt earth, and small sprinkles hung singly in the air. Immediately he became aware of the smell of rotten meat and took dried honeysuckle from a pouch at his side and placed it in his nose. He breathed easier and sighed, then slowly sent out feelers, searching for

Cumac. But the feelers did not touch Cumac, and regretfully, Seanchan brought them back and leaned on his staff as he contemplated the broken and blackened world around him.

He did feel something hostile, but the feeling was so faint that he could not recognize it. He did, however, mark the direction and set off toward whatever was causing it.

He watched for Fedelm as he went and kept himself alert for her, but she did not appear either within his sight or within the tentacles of watch that he sent out.

He came to a dolmen that had not been toppled and saw a stone set in the middle of it. Curious, he went to the stone and studied it carefully, frowning as he tried to understand why this particular dolmen had not been toppled as well.

A quiet chuckle broke in on his reverie.

Immediately, he brought his staff up protectively as he spun around, searching for the source of the laugh.

A dark shimmer appeared in front of him and then parted to reveal a dark-haired woman, dressed in thin clothes, a black wand in hand. Her clothes seemed to whisper around her. Her mouth was a scarlet gash in her bone-white face, her eyes black and glittering like an adder's.

"Why, Seanchan Duirgeal! What could possibly bring you into Dreamworld?" she asked teasingly. "Surely you know the danger for a Druid here!"

"I know, Niav," Seanchan said calmly. "I also know that you are a sorceress who was a follower of Ragon and later Maliman and that you are dedicated to them and their war against the Otherworld and the Earthworld. You have some power, but you should know well enough to not threaten a Duirgeal!"

Her eyes glittered and she thrust her wand at Seanchan, chanting, "*Athos ma ceathas fuirma teinday mara!*"

Black fire leaped from her wand toward Seanchan, who quickly responded, "*Adoth deinadey cro ma steilth arda!*"

White fire came from Seanchan's hand and clashed against Niav's black fire.

Niav furiously tried to push her way past Seanchan's defenses, but slowly, bit by bit, her black fire was forced back by Seanchan's fire. Sweat began to fall from Niav's forehead and she tried suddenly to withdraw, but Seanchan's fire swept up and over her, imprisoning her in its center.

Niav shrieked and clawed at the fire around her as the flames began to lick slowly at the edge of her garments.

Hisses and cries came from her clothes as the white fire began to steadily consume them.

"Tell me, creature of the night, where is Cumac!" Seanchan thundered. "I will not take half answers, and beware of lies, for I will know they are lies before they leave your lips! I bear the power of the Duirgeals, forged in the furnace of Goibniu and wielded by Deiru, he of the Sacred Flame of Cullasdreu! Look upon me and despair!"

Seanchan's eyes turned fiery red, and yellow flame burned deep within their depths. Black wraiths began to whirl from his staff, moaning a terrible song that wormed its way into Niav's mind.

She screamed and clasped her hands to her ears, bending double in fear and kneeling before Seanchan.

"Have mercy!" she begged, groveling before him. She shrieked and her hands trembled as they pressed tightly to her ears, trying to keep the sound from burning within her brain.

"Mercy!" she howled.

Slowly, Seanchan brought the fire back to him, but kept it flickering at the edges of his fingers.

"You bring such matters upon yourself, Niav," he said severely. "Now, speak! Where is Cumac? I will not ask you again!"

Slowly she rose until she finally stood before him, back bent like a fishhook. Her tongue flickered in and out, a foul red against the white of her face.

"You would find Cumac? He is here. Among the dead. The dead that are here but that you cannot see!"

"What mischief is this?" Seanchan asked, scowling.

"No mischief," Niav said, giving a small smile. "These are the dead who cannot go to Teach Duinn. They have lost their honor and now must roam here. In Naraka, surrounded by the River of Wailing."

"Ah, Dubh's world, eh?" Seanchan said, pulling on his beard. He looked around at the rock-strewn landscape. "So, this is what Dreamworld has fallen to. Or is that what you wish me to believe?"

He moved his hand threateningly and Niav flinched away.

"No! This is Naraka, within the Dreamworld! The place where despair is found!"

"And Cumac?" Seanchan asked, his black agate eyes gleaming dangerously.

"He is here! With a Guardian! Sent by Coig!"

"But there is something else, isn't there?"

She fell silent, studying the ground between her and Seanchan.

"Answer me! Quickly!"

"There are others here," she said, keeping her gaze fast upon the ground. "Many others. Some even you would not wish to know!"

"Then let us find him and leave!"

A low growl came from the air around them. Seanchan whirled, his staff coming up defensively. He saw nothing, but he sensed danger, near and deadly.

"Tricked! Tricked!" came a cackle from Niav.

He spun back, but she was gone.

Naraka, Seanchan thought, pressing his lips tightly together. Once a place for lovers, replete with sparkling fountains and fresh bowers and blooming flowers, it is now a wasteland within a wasteland. If one stays too long in Naraka, he is doomed to stay here forever. I must hurry.

He turned and moved forward, sending out tendrils of seeking, hoping that the Guardian would be able to help Cumac yet knowing as well that the Guardian was only that—one who guarded against harm but could do nothing else.

FEDELM moved within the *imbas forasnai* slowly holding herself back from the edges of the Dreamworld but remaining close enough to watch over it. Carefully, she made her way around Dreamworld, searching for Cumac. She saw black creatures moving like shadows and knew them for what they were, but she kept silent, staying hidden just outside Dreamworld. She could hear the moaning of forgotten souls who were castoffs even from the Great Rift and had no place but here to belong. But she felt little pity for them, as they had had the chance to become something but had chosen to remain distant and detached from Earthworld, avoiding life.

Nor, she thought, did anyone have any pity for them, for they had not loved or hated or helped or even stolen, preferring to remain aloof from Earthworld. Now, they suffered with harsh despair of what they might have been had they only tried. Now, they embraced the darkness, and with it came a bitterness that made them savage and sent hatred rippling through the very air. At last, they had come to realize what had befallen them, but it was too late for them, as they were locked, here, in Naraka.

A tenuous filament reached out through the dark and trembled in front of her. She frowned and cautiously touched it. A warmness spread through her as she recognized a tendril from Cumac. Then she flushed as she felt Cumac's feeling for her.

She pondered what to do for a moment. She could follow the tendril back to Cumac—or, she amended, at least *attempt* to follow the tendril back, but what would happen if she lost it while in Naraka? She might not be able to extricate herself if she got lost. But, she admonished herself, that is not even a thought to be having. You must get ahold of yourself! You know what you have to do!

With a deep sigh, she took a careful look around, tightened her grip on her bow (that could now go into the Dreamworld thanks to the quiver given to her by Lakiel), then stepped forward into the Dreamworld and Naraka.

Instantly, a savage cold pebbled her flesh and she sneezed, trying to drive the stench from her nostrils. The tendril was still there, and she seized its thought and ran quickly with it, leaping over fallen columns and stones and boulders as she began to trace it back to its source. The tendril grew in size and became warmer and warmer as she ran, concentrating on it as hard as she could without leaving herself defenseless.

She could feel the evil around her, and out of the corners of her eyes she could see shadows begin to follow her, spreading out to try and embrace her, but she gritted her teeth and pressed forward harder and harder along the tendril.

A black arrow flashed in front of her. She flinched but ignored the temptation to turn away and answer with an arrow of her own. Then she heard the moaning and recognized the cry, and her blood turned cold.

Deag-duls!

How did they get into Naraka?

She could feel the coldness of them as they came closer and closer. Then, she saw Cumac and his Guardian ahead and clenched her teeth together as she raced toward them.

She saw the Guardian stiffen and spin around to face her. His face was stern and forbidding as he quickly drew an arrow, fitted it to his black bow, and released it all in one movement. Before the arrow had flown twenty feet, two more were on their way after it.

Fedelm twisted in the air to avoid the arrows and heard squeals of anger and pain as they struck the Deag-duls behind her. How many of them were there? she wondered, but she did not turn to look.

Cumac spun around, a brilliant sword in his hand, and recognized her and spoke sharply to the Guardian, who shifted his aim and sent arrow after arrow to each side of her, each shaft bringing cries of pain.

Then she was beside him, gasping for breath, her own bow coming around with an arrow fitted. She saw other Deag-duls rushing toward them, and she released bolt after bolt with almost as much speed as the Guardian.

One Deag-dul managed to escape through the hail of arrows and sped screaming toward Cumac, who swung the sword savagely. A great song rose from the blade as it sliced through the Deag-dul's head. Then another's, and another's.

Still the Guardian fired calmly, taking one Deag-dul after another, and then, suddenly, there was a loud clap of thunder and a great fire rushed over the Deag-duls. They howled with pain and tried to turn away, but the fire burned too hard and quickly turned them into ash.

Fedelm glanced wildly around for this new threat, then sighed and relaxed as she saw Seanchan coming toward them.

"A friend," she gasped quickly as the Guardian raised his bow. "That is Seanchan."

Slowly the Guardian lowered his bow and watched suspiciously as Seanchan came up to them and stopped, leaning upon his staff, his face concerned.

"Are you all all right?" Seanchan asked.

Fedelm nodded. "But it was close there for a moment." She glanced at the Guardian. "This is Seanchan Duirgeal. I am Fedelm of Rath Curachan Sidhe." She bowed her head.

"I am Cathar of the Dreamwalkers, warrior to Coig and Guardian of Cumac," he said, bowing toward both of them.

"Fedelm!" Cumac said, and he rushed forward and hugged her with glee.

Startled, she returned his hug, her face burning with embarrassment.

He reached around her and shook Seanchan's hand.

"Thank the gods you came!" he said fervently.

"You did not think we would leave you here, did you?" Seanchan asked, his eyes twinkling merrily. "That is not what friends are for. Greetings, Cathar."

"Greetings, Seanchan," Cathar said, smiling. "I take it that you have come to bring Cumac back into Earthworld?"

"Oh yes," Seanchan said. "And we probably should leave as quickly as possible before the Deag-duls return, this time with others."

"That is a curious sword," Fedelm said, looking closer at the sword in Cumac's hand. "I have never seen one like it."

"It is destined for another time," Cathar said, reaching out to take the sword from Cumac's hand. "As such, it must not leave here until then. I shall return it to its home in the stone. Meanwhile, I believe you are right, Seanchan Duirgeal. You should leave. I will return to Coig, but know this, Cumac," he added, turning toward his charge. "If you should ever need me again, I shall be there. We are linked, you and I, by Coig, and I shall be your Guardian for the rest of your days."

"My many thanks," Cumac said, taking Cathar's hand firmly.

Cathar smiled. Then a bright crystal shimmer appeared around him and he disappeared.

"Well, then," Seanchan said, spinning a golden circle around them, "I believe we shall leave as well."

In a twinkling, they found themselves under the elm where Lorgas and Bern stood watch over their bodies.

Lorgas gaped as each shook, then stretched and stood.

"Now, where did you come from?" he said.

Bern punched him on his shoulder. "From the Dreamworld, idiot. What do you think they were doing while they slept?"

Lorgas glared at him and rubbed his shoulder.

"I did not expect them to return like that!" He turned to the others. "What was it like?"

"You don't want to know," Cumac said, wiping his forehead with the palm of his hand. He glanced around and found Caladbolg on the ground beside him. He took it and drew it from its sheath and looked closely at it. Then, satisfied, he returned it to its sheath and sighed.

"I did not think I was going to get out of there so quickly," he said.

"Quickly?" Bern asked. "We have been here a week, watching over you. And thanks to Seanchan's spell, we have been safe. Although it has not been without attempts being made to battle with us."

He pointed to the ground around them. Black Baggots and goblins lay strewn around the circle, dead, stunned looks upon their faces.

"For a while there, I thought that they were going to break through," Bern said.

"We would have been enough for them," Lorgas growled, fingering his ax.

"You definitely have an exaggerated opinion of yourself," Cumac said. "We could have made them pay dearly, but I do not think we could have stood long enough to keep them away."

"It is enough that you were ready to defend us," Seanchan said. "But for now, I think it would be best if we were away from this place. Undoubtedly our enemies know where we are, and I believe they will be returning shortly with more warriors."

The others quickly made themselves ready and hurried to their horses, saddling them and mounting them, waiting expectantly for Seanchan.

Black turned his head and looked at Cumac, then nickered softly and nudged Cumac's foot with his muzzle.

"I know," Cumac said softly, patting the horse on his neck. "I too am glad to be back with you."

Seanchan unwove the spell, and together they rode forth, trotting quickly from the little clearing.

27

By high noon, the party had traveled through the deep forest and was now on the outskirts, where the scraggly trees gave way to a thick marsh with a narrow trail winding through it. Cumac wondered how war chariots managed to ride along the path, for if two were to meet, one of the two would have to back up, and backing temperamental and spirited warhorses was a most difficult task.

Marsh hens flew away at the sound of their

horses' hooves, as did the coaltits nesting on hummocks and the occasional nuthatch that lived close to where the forest merged with the swamp. Here sweet-smelling bog myrtle and wine-red sphagnum moss thrived along with lichens and deer grass. Gingerly, with Seanchan leading the way, they set off along the path, each horse's nose a scant two feet from the rump of the horse in front of it. A bird called a clear high note trying to attract its mate back to a nest. Marsh gas rose to the surface in bubbles and broke, leaving a noxious smell that lingered in the air. In the far distance, Cumac could see the green line of trees that marked the end of the marsh. He hoped that they would manage to get through before being forced to stop, as spending the night in the marsh was a dismal idea indeed.

He needn't have worried, as Seanchan quickened the pace when the sun fell lower and lower to the horizon, painting the sky purple and pink as it dropped. The gloaming was on them, however, as they finally emerged from the marsh, batting mosquitoes away from them. Seanchan led them deep into a forest of elm and oak and willow before calling a halt for the night.

Cumac slid thankfully from his horse and stretched, rubbing the small of his back in relief. Bern and Lorgas followed suit, while Fedelm leaped lightly to the ground and took her horse and Cumac's to the side of the glade where they had stopped. In minutes she had the saddles and bridles off and began to rub each down with handfuls of gamma grass.

"I think I've bruised every bone in my back," Lorgas groaned.

"And I," Bern echoed.

"Enough complaining," Seanchan said, then ordered, "Bern, you find firewood before the full dark sets upon us. I fear the night will be cold, and we will want fire to warm us and," he emphasized, "cook our dinner. Which, Lorgas, you will provide. A boar would be nice. Or a red deer."

At the promise of food, Lorgas and Bern smiled and quickly left, one going left and the other right, Bern searching for dried branches and twigs, while Lorgas stretched the waxed string on his bow. Seanchan watched them scurry away and smiled at their eagerness. He caught Cumac watching and said, "The promise of little can mean a lot to those who are yearning for relief from the day."

"I see," Cumac said. "What do you have in mind for me?"

"You are cooking."

Cumac groaned. It was a mistake for him to have made a roast from a wild boar's haunch for the party, seasoning it with wild mushrooms and wood sorrel and onions. The roast had disappeared quickly, and the others thanked Cumac with great enthusiasm.

"Well," Cumac said dubiously, "I'm not certain what is left that I can use for cooking."

"I found some wild onions and mushrooms while we rode," Fedelm said, coming up to Seanchan and Cumac. "And there may be some oddments in my bag. I'll take a look."

"I have sea salt," Cumac said. "And I'll go look for something else that I might be able to put with it. Maybe I can find some berries."

With that, Cumac rose and went into the woods, moving slowly as he looked around for something that he could use. Although he was new to cooking, he had discovered that he had a knack for it. But, he promised himself, the others are going to have to take a turn or two themselves.

He had not walked far before he heard the sound of water running, thought that he might find something along the banks of the stream, and made his way there. The sparkling water looked good, and he threw himself upon the ground and drank deeply, sighing when he rose, wiping his chin with the sleeve of his tunic. He spied more mushrooms and, using his knife, carefully sliced the caps off and put them in a makeshift pocket of his cloak. Idly, he took one and munched on it as he walked along the bank. A great lethargy came over him, peaceful and warm, and he came upon a thick grassy hummock beneath a large willow. He sighed and removed his cloak and stretched out on the hummock for a moment.

A vision of dancing pixies came to him. He delighted in their dance and strove to get up and join them, but his limbs would not obey him, and after a moment, he didn't care. He smiled happily at them and took another mushroom cap and munched on it contentedly.

And then he slept and dreamed dreams of flowers and peace and contentment.

LORGAS returned with a small red deer over his shoulders. He sighed and dropped his burden on the ground by Bern, who was carefully building a fire. Lorgas looked around the clearing, puzzled.

"Where's Cumac?" he asked.

Fedelm and Seanchan looked around as well and then at each other, frowning.

"He went into the woods to see if he could find more to go with our meal," Fedelm said.

"He should have returned by now," Seanchan said. "Unless he went too deeply back in the forest, and I wouldn't think that he would do that."

Fedelm stood for a moment, then took her bow and headed in the direction Cumac had taken.

"I'll go look for him," she said.

"And I'll come with you," Seanchan said, heaving himself to his feet. He winced as his joints popped in complaint.

Together, the two went off, walking silently through the forest to not alert anyone or thing who might have taken Cumac.

"Here's his trail," Fedelm whispered. She pointed off to their right. "He went that way."

They made their way deeper in the forest until Seanchan suddenly pulled up, stopping Fedelm.

"What is it?" she asked nervously, putting an arrow to her bow. She looked carefully around but saw nothing.

"I do not know," Seanchan said. "But I sense something. Something wrong, but I'm not sure what. Just that something is wrong."

Then they heard the murmur of a creek and walked through a willow thicket to emerge on the bank of the water. Fedelm saw some mushrooms and bent to pick some, but Seanchan stayed her hand.

"Those are dreamcaps," he said. "You eat those and nothing seems to matter anymore. You feel yourself at peace with the world."

"Fresh cuttings have been made," Fedelm said, pointing.

"Cumac's, I'm certain," Seanchan said. "Use your Sidhe eyes, Fedelm. Can you tell which way Cumac went? Upstream or down?"

Fedelm narrowed her eyes and crouched on her heels, studying the ground in front of her. She found the slight indentation of a heel and toe in a soft bank of moss and pointed.

"Downstream," she said. She rose and took a firmer grip on her bow and stepped off, following Cumac's track.

They had not gone more than a hundred yards when they found Cumac lying on a soft bed of grass, a blissful smile on his face, his eyes closed, lost in a world known only to him.

"Just as I feared," Seanchan said, peering around them into the gathering dusk. "We must get him back to the others. And soon, before night falls fully. I smell the stench of Black Baggots around but not near. Yet."

He bent and touched the end of his staff to Cumac's forehead and chanted.

No good will come of this sleep
As you fall into Dreamland deep
And find that which you desire
Within the lethargic mire
Of Caer Ibormeith's keep.

Cumac stirred and awoke, reaching automatically for another mushroom cap, but Fedelm took them all and threw them into the stream.

Cumac frowned faintly, then looked around and said, "Where am I? And where are the dancing pixies? What type of magic is this that takes them away from me?"

"A bad magic," Seanchan said, leaning on his staff. "The mushrooms are called dreamcaps and belong to Caer Ibormeith, the goddess of sleep and dreams. You are very lucky, Cumac. Had you been long in her sleep, you would have been locked in the keep of her castle."

Cumac sighed and ran his hands over his face, rubbing memory away. He struggled to his feet with the help of Fedelm and stood, swaying for a few moments before being able to stand alone. But he still had a dreamy expression, and Seanchan scooped up a handful of cold water and threw it in Cumac's face.

The dreamy expression went away as Cumac spluttered and sneezed. He glared at Seanchan and said, "What was that for?"

"To make certain that you are fully awake," Seanchan said. "Now, let us go. We will have to hurry in order to get back to camp before darkness drops fully and hides the camp from us."

They bunched closely together as Seanchan and Cumac followed Fedelm back the way they came. Bushes and brambles that had not been seen before snagged their clothes, threatening to hold them back for the arms of night to cuddle them. But they pushed through and presently found themselves back in camp, where Bern had the fire burning merrily and Lorgas had cut slices of meat from the red deer and spitted them carefully with green sticks over the fire. The smell of roasting meat came strongly to the three, and their mouths watered in anticipation

Lorgas and Bern looked at them and shook their heads.

"You look a bit the worse for wear," Lorgas said.

"What happened?" Bern asked.

"Cumac had fallen under the spell of Caer Ibormeith, the goddess of sleep and dreams," Seanchan said. He looked at the two elves firmly. "And all of us must be careful that that does not happen again to one of us. Be careful what mushrooms you eat, as there are some which will lull you into never-ending sleep. I will not always be around to bring you out of that sleep. You can tell the difference as dreamcaps have a blood-red color—crimson, fading to yellow with age—and are scattered with white to yellow flecks and white stems. Leave these alone. They belong to Caer Ibormeith."

"Can we eat, now?" Lorgas asked, looking hungrily at the roasting meat.

"All right," Seanchan said.

"And Cumac," Bern said. They all stopped to see what he had to say. "If it's all right with you and the rest, I think someone else should do the cooking."

"Perhaps so," Cumac said and stepped past Lorgas and Bern to help himself to one of the slices of meat that appeared to be done. He dropped cross-legged on the ground and began to eat.

Lorgas was dozing on watch when the Black Baggots came at the changing hour, nearly catching the party by surprise. But Cumac was finding it hard to rest after his sleep earlier and heard the Black Baggots coming stealthily among the trees behind a black mist that was creeping into the clearing.

"Awake!" he shouted, leaping to his feet and drawing Caladbolg. "Black Baggots!"

Instantly all were on their feet, their weapons in hand.

Lorgas shouted and leaped forward, his ax a blur in his hands, while Bern struck two heads from the trunks of Black Baggots.

Fedelm's arrows flew, each hitting its mark.

Cumac roared his battle cry, feeling the warp-spasm beginning to contort his frame. Caladbolg made a rainbow arch through air as Cumac struck again and again, heads flying like black spores.

The Black of Saingliau, Cumac's horse, screamed and lashed out with his hooves at the black bodies, trampling them under hoof, yellow teeth snapping hard against flesh.

Then the warp-spasm was full upon Cumac and he roared again, a more terrifying sound than before, and for a moment all movement was frozen in the clearing as the fearful creature Cumac had become waded into the Black Baggots, driving forward, Caladbolg a fiery rainbow in his hands. The rest of Cumac's party recovered from their trance and began to battle more fiercely than before.

But still the attackers swarmed into the clearing, and then the blinding blue and red cairnfire exploded from Seanchan's staff and wrapped itself around the Baggots, setting them afire.

Screams and shrieks of pain filled the air and the Baggots in front turned and tried to flee, but others at the rear continued to press forward.

Then bodies burst open and black blood fell to the ground in waves as the cairnfire lanced its way through until at last, those in the rear discovered what was happening and turned and fled into the forest, leaving the dead bodies on the ground.

Still Cumac bounded forward, hard on the heels of the Baggots, killing those in the rear. Their screams filled the forest and those in front doubled their efforts to escape from the fearful apparition behind them.

"Cumac!" Fedelm yelled. "Stop! Stop!"

But Cumac did not heed her and continued his mad slaughter. Suddenly he was clubbed to the ground, and when he tried to rise, he found he could not lift his arms and legs.

Seanchan leaned over him and said, "That is enough, Cumac.

Bring yourself back to us as what you once were. Throw off the warp-spasm, now!"

Slowly, Cumac inched his way out of the warp-spasm, his joints returning to normal, and then the fierce gleam in his eyes faded away. A weakness came over him and he tried to rise, but his legs refused to hold him. Fedelm stepped forward and took one of his arms and placed it around her neck to help him make his way back to camp.

They emerged into the clearing, and Fedelm lowered Cumac to the ground. The air had a fierce smell to it, and horrible stench rose from where the bodies of the Black Baggots lay.

"I do not think I'll be able to sleep here the rest of the night," Bern said, cupping his hand over his mouth to help filter his breathing. He winced and shook his head. "No, I am certain that I will not be able to sleep here. Or even stay. Needles and leaves, but these bodies stink!"

"I agree," Lorgas said. "We need to find another place where we can pass the rest of the night."

Black snorted and shook his head as if saying that he too wanted to be away from the clearing.

"All right," Seanchan said. "Gather your things and we will ride up the fringes of the marsh until we find someplace where we can rest."

They quickly struck camp and saddled their horses. Bern remembered the meat and wrapped it in the red deer's hide before mounting and following Seanchan and the others out of the clearing.

Seanchan glanced upward and found the north star. He moved off toward it, keeping it on his left shoulder as he brought the party along the edge of the forest.

They rode about an hour before they came to a horseshoe-shaped clearing cut in the forest. Seanchan halted and studied the clearing for a moment before nodding decisively.

"Yes, here we are," he said. "I do not sense any danger here. We should be safe for the rest of the night."

The others dropped from their saddles thankfully, for all were weary now that the excitement of the fight with the Black Baggots had worn off.

Lorgas found a neat pile of dead branches at the back of the clearing and brought them up to the middle, where Bern had pulled grass from a large round area. Lorgas neatly placed some of the wood in the center and added flame, nursing the small fire until it burned happily and gave off a bit of warmth.

"This must be a place often frequented," he said to Seanchan. "The wood has been placed in a pile for use."

Seanchan frowned and stiffened. He rose and carefully walked around the clearing, studying the dark between the trees until he returned to the fire.

"I wonder who it was," Cumac said.

"Travelers of the forest, I would imagine," Seanchan said. "But I'm not certain if they are Sword-wanderers or Foresters."

"Perhaps we should mount a watch," Lorgas said.

Bern looked scathingly at him. "And you will have the first watch to make up for what almost happened to us back there!"

He glared at Lorgas, who glared back and said, "I wasn't sleeping! I was just resting my eyes! You take back what you said!"

"Now, now," Seanchan said hastily. "Let us not—"

He went silent immediately as a faint song came closer and closer to their party.

Fiddle-diddily-dum
I sing of things that are done
With a hiddy-hiddy-hoe
I stumble with my toe
When a pretty lady smiles
At me after I travel miles
And come at last to her door.

Fiddle-diddily-dum
I sing of things that are done
With a hiddy-hiddy-hoe
And I stumble with my toe

And fall flat on my face
As a fool whose house he'll grace
When I step through her door.

Fiddle-diddily-dum
I sing of things that are done
With a hiddy-hiddy-hoe
I stumbled with my toe
And fell flat upon my face
Without very much grace
And kissed the hardwood floor
As I came through her door!

This last came as he paused on the edge of the trees and looked at the party and said, "Hallo the camp! My name is Millus the Forester, a shepherd of the forest, and these are my woods. I welcome you! May I come in?"

"Come and be welcomed!" Seanchan said loudly.

The others gave the Druid a hard look, then turned to face the man as he walked into the camp.

He was dressed all in green with an odd-looking cap made of rainbow-colored patches. His feet were encased in green leather, the tops climbing high upon his thighs. His shirt was green, the same color as his tunic and cloak and the pants that disappeared into his boots. His eyes sparkled merrily, and a smile lifted his lips into deep dimples. He was clean-shaven and his hair was cut neatly at his shoulders. Around his shoulders hung a quiver of grouse-fletched hickory arrows. His bow was long and so thick that none there would have been able to draw it. He beamed at the others.

"So you have come to my woods and helped yourself to the wood that I left at this clearing! You did not replenish it!" He looked sternly at them for a moment, then laughed. "But no one does! Why should you be any different?"

"We are sorry to have offended you," Seanchan said, bowing slightly.

"No matter! No matter!" he cried and laughed again, twirling his bow through fingers as thick as hard-packed sausage. "You may relax, my friends," he added merrily. "I mean you no harm."

Reluctantly, Lorgas and Bern removed their hands from their weapons, while Cumac slid the half-drawn Caladbolg back into its sheath. Fedelm took the arrow from her bow but held it guardedly between two fingers.

"And," Millus said, rubbing his hands together with relish, "I see you have helped yourself to a red deer. Would you mind sharing your supper? It has been a long time since midday when I came upon your track and followed it, and I am famished!"

"We have already eaten," Bern said. "And it is not time for breakfast."

Millus Sang:

Fiddle-diddily-dum
I sing of things that are done
When one should break a fast
From when he has eaten last.
Time is only a passing thing
And hunger is always the same.

He frowned for a minute. "That last was without a good rhyme, but it shows promise! It shows promise!"

Seanchan looked at the others. "I see no reason why we cannot breakfast now. If truth be known, that fight gave me quite an appetite."

"Ah, a partial rhyme. Fight—appetite!" Millus beamed.

"I could eat," Lorgas said grudgingly.

"You can always eat," Bern said.

"Well, then," Cumac said, "let us have an early breakfast. Time does not rule the stomach as much as the stomach rules the time."

"Then let us spread the feast!" cried Millus and, digging into a green leather pouch that hung over one shoulder, he removed six large salmon. "I suggest we save the meat until later, as it will keep longer than these salmon will."

Cumac's mouth watered, and he stepped into a small willow patch and began to cut green sticks upon which to spit the fish.

"Ah! An enterprising young man!" Millus said.

"I'll clean the fish," Lorgas said, reaching for them.

"But they have already been cleaned. One shouldn't carry fish that haven't been cleaned. That may end in an unpleasant odor," Millus answered. Nevertheless, he handed the fish to Lorgas, who helped Cumac spit the fish and shove the sticks into the ground at an even angle over the flame.

"Now," Millus said, dropping cross-legged on the ground. "Tell me: what was that battle noise I heard a while ago?"

"Black Baggots," Fedelm said, sitting on the ground and facing him. "We were attacked by Black Baggots just as the changing hour came. We were hard-pressed to get away from them!"

Millus's eyebrows raised at the news. "Black Baggots? Here in my forest?"

The others nodded, and Millus's face grew grim.

"We cannot have that," he said. "Now, which way did they go? Into the forest or across the marsh?"

"Back into the forest," Seanchan said.

"Ah! The fish is ready!" Millus said, clapping his hands. "Let us eat. Then, while you sleep, I will tend to these Black Baggots! Never fear," he added as the others exchanged meaningful looks. "You will be quite safe here! I will see to that!"

Lorgas rose and took the sticks from the fire and handed one to each. Cumac took sea salt from his pouch and handed it around. Soon, they were drowsy and content with full stomachs, and a great relaxation came over all.

"And now, I shall leave you," Millus said, rising and bowing. "You may sleep safely here! You have the word of a Forester! When you awake, do not go over the marsh. Instead, set your course to the north until you are free of the forest and marsh before turning to the west."

He disappeared into the forest, slipping easily from shadow to shadow.

Bern watched him go, then asked Seanchan if he thought they were safe.

"He gave his word as a Forester, and a Forester's word you may trust with your life!"

With that, Seanchan wrapped himself in his cloak and was snoring before a minute passed.

"If everything is all right with Seanchan, then it is all right with me," Cumac declared and rolled himself into his cloak.

The others followed suit, and soon all were asleep.

CUMAC awoke with a start just as the sun was burning away morning mist. For a moment he rested peacefully, wondering what it was that had awakened him. Then he heard the distant sound of frightened cries and the roar of a battle.

He clambered to his feet and fingered his sword worriedly, looking hard into the trees but seeing nothing except disappearing gray mist.

"It is our friend, Millus," Seanchan said, sitting up. "I believe he has found the Black Baggots."

"Then we should go and help him," Cumac said.

Seanchan shook his head and smiled. "It is not him we should help but the Black Baggots, and those we do not want to help. They are beginning to rue the moment that they came into Millus's forest. I do not think, though, that any of them will live to see the sun. Ah! I think the battle is over."

Cumac strained but could not hear a sound other than some songbirds beginning to sing awake the day.

"One man did that?" he asked incredulously.

"No. He is not a man. He is a Forester. They are charged with keeping the woods safe for innocent travelers. And all do," Seanchan added. "Now, I say let us have a bite to eat and be on our way. Even though Millus guarantees this place, I believe discretion is better. It is best not to look a gift horse too deeply in the mouth."

They rode north for six days. On the seventh, a downpour threatened to flood the lowlands. Grimly they continued on through the rain, looking vainly ahead for shelter. Thunder boomed and lightning flashed, momentarily lighting their trail before plunging it again into the dark. Even their horses—with the exception of Black—looked drenched and sodden by the time Seanchan spied a light burning ahead of them.

"We may have found shelter," he told the others. They could barely hear him over the pounding rain.

They quickened their pace and soon were in front of large house built of wooden logs, easily the size of a mead hall and more besides. Seanchan dismounted and waded through a large puddle to the door, pounding upon it with the end of his staff. He waited a moment, then pounded again. The door creaked open and a humpbacked gray-haired man peered out.

"I am Seanchan Duirgeal," Seanchan said. He waved back at the others. "And these are my companions: Fedelm of Rath Cruachan; Cumac, son of Cucullen; Lorgas of the Ashelves; and Bern of the Ervalians. We seek shelter from the rain and night!"

"Come in," the ancient one croaked. "And be welcomed."

He threw the door wide and bright light spilled out into the rain.

"Callem!" he called. A youth with dirty blond hair and a sullen face appeared. "Take their horses to the stables. And," he added sternly, shaking a bony finger in the boy's face, "make certain you dry them and brush them, and give them hot bran with honey and a clean bed of straw. I will be by soon to check on you."

The youth sighed and stepped out into the rain, taking the bridle reins from the hands of the riders. He turned to the right and squished through the mud around the corner of the house.

The party entered the hallway thankfully, shaking rain from their cloaks.

The old man locked the door behind them and said, "First we must make you warm and get you dry clothes. Follow me!"

They fell in behind the old man and followed his shuffling step into a large hall, the walls covered with hunting trophies—red deer, elk, boar, bear—and weapons of every type: spears, swords, maces, shields, bows, quivers of arrows, knives. And then, there were the heads on a shelf that ran around the room. Although Cumac did not like the ancient custom, he knew that collecting the heads of one's enemies and embalming them in cedar oil was a war trophy. The head was the dwelling place of the soul, the center of the man himself, and by displaying the heads, the victor was gaining protection from magical power. Here, the presence of the heads seemed ominous, not in keeping with those kept at the Red Branch or Cruachan Ai.

"First, let us warm you from the inside out."

"Ah, I would appreciate that," Lorgas said.

"Then you shall have it," the old man said. He raised his voice and called, "Seleam!"

A middle-aged woman, her lips down-turned as if she had sucked on alum, came from a door at the side of the hall. The party could smell rich foods and brown gravy when she opened the door.

"Bring us mulled wine," the old man ordered.

She nodded and left wordlessly.

"Stand by the fire," the old man said, then clapped the palm of his hand to his forehead. "I am forgetting my manners. My name is Crom."

Seanchan's eyes narrowed as the woman, with the help of two others, brought goblets of mulled wine and gave them to the party. They sipped thankfully and sighed as the heat spread out from their stomachs and seemed to warm their very fingers.

"I know of one by that name who is not so hospitable."

Crom waved his fingers as if brushing away Seanchan's words. "It is a common enough name. Especially here in Magslect, the Plain of Adoration. Siamper!" Another middle-aged woman appeared, equally unhappy. "Take our guests to their rooms and supply them with hot baths and clean clothes. Then clean the clothes they are wearing and repair them."

She heaved a deep sigh, then gestured for the others to follow her.

She climbed the stairs and walked down a short hall, pointing to one of the party and then at the door to the room that each would use. They thanked her and entered to find hot water in a small tub waiting for them and fresh clothes folded neatly on the foot of their beds.

At last she reached the room for Fedelm, who stood in the doorway and considered it. It was a simple room, with a bed, a table and chair, a stone fireplace, and in front of the blazing fire, a brass tub filled with hot water.

"I thank you," Fedelm said, turning to the woman. "But tell me: who is the master here?"

The woman shook her head.

"Surely you know," Fedelm said.

The woman hesitated, then opened her mouth wide so Fedelm could see where her tongue had been pulled out by the roots.

Fedelm paled. "Who would do such a thing?" she demanded. "Was it the servant?"

The woman nodded.

"On behalf of his master?"

She shook her head.

Fedelm frowned, then said slowly, "Is *he* the master here?"

The woman glanced around fearfully, then quickly nodded.

"But why? So you will not be able to talk with anyone?"

Again the woman nodded, then stepped in the room with Fedelm and closed the door behind herself. She pointed at the knife belted around Fedelm's waist and opened her hand. Slowly, warily, Fedelm took the knife from its sheath and handed it to the woman.

The woman pretended to cut from her rear and then, to Fedelm's surprise, raised the imaginary meat to her mouth and chewed vigorously.

"You mean he eats the flesh of people?"

The woman nodded and handed the knife back. She turned and opened the door.

"Wait," Fedelm said, but the woman shook her head and left, again closing the door behind her. Fedelm could hear the woman's footsteps slap against the floor as she hurried away.

Fedelm stood dumbfounded, staring at the door.

"This must be shared with the others as soon as possible," she said. "But first . . ."

She turned to the tub and stripped her clothes from her body to enter the warmth.

30

Cumac stared disbelieving at Fedelm. “Cannibal? Are you certain you understood the woman correctly?”

Fedelm nodded irritably. “There could be little doubt. She was very clear. I think that travelers who stop here for shelter are enslaved somehow and either put to work as servants or are used as food. I wouldn’t be surprised if Crom doesn’t eventually turn the servants into food when they become old and replace them with others. You understand, I don't know this. It is just a feeling I have."

"And one that warrants measure," Seanchan said, frowning. "I have heard of one called Crom Cruach who lives on Magslect who eats the flesh of people. I have never seen him, but it appears that those who live around him are forced to give up their firstborn to him or become victims themselves. It appears that we may have stumbled upon his house. I would suggest that we drink water from now on until we shed ourselves of this place. Ale might be how he subdues his victims, as it is thick and heavy and would hide the taste of anything that may have been put in it. And," he continued, "I would not eat any meat here. Confine yourselves to fruit and vegetables. That makes for meager fare, I know," he said, "but it is better to stay on the road than travel blindly through a forest."

"Ah, me!" Lorgas moaned. "From rain into fire. Sticks and stones! Will we never be able to rest and eat and sleep without one thing or another trying to kill us? Or worse, make us slaves?"

"You do need to get your priorities straight," Bern said caustically. "So why don't we just leave now? Isn't discretion better than challenging the unknown? Crom may think of another way or two to enslave us. In fact, I wouldn't put it past him," he added grimly. "Did you see those heads in the hall? That is a lot of heads for only one warrior to collect."

"I think we need to spend a little time here," Seanchan said. "We must decide what to do for those he still holds captive. And what should we do for other travelers?"

"A spell?" Lorgas said hopefully.

Seanchan shook his head. "There is much magic here. And if we try and do not succeed, then he will know that we are aware of his penchant for man-flesh!"

"We could kill him," Bern said quietly. "That would make things certain."

"Could we? I wonder," Fedelm said. "If he is who Seanchan believes him to be, then he is one of the ancient ones. He could only have grown stronger over the years. And he may be shape-shifter. But could we not turn his plan back upon himself?"

"I don't know," Seanchan said doubtfully. "I really have no feeling for this place. We must be on guard all the time. I cannot use magic here, as I do not know how it will be received by whatever other magic may be in place. No, we shall have to use our wits now."

"I don't think I like this place," Lorgas groaned.

"An understatement," Bern said. "But that is the way of the Ashelves."

Lorgas bristled. "And the Ervalians? Cautious where courage is needed!"

"Enough!" Seanchan said sharply. "Now, let us go down for dinner."

Together, they walked down the stairs, each treading cautiously, a bit stiff, if it be known.

They entered the dining room and discovered that the table had already been made ready for them. A platter of sliced meat roasted with piñon nuts was in the center of the table, and huge foaming pitchers of ale stood in three places down the middle. Three bowls of apples, cherries, grapes, and other fruit were beside each pitcher, and a large bowl of wheat meal and another of oatmeal flanked the platter of meat.

"Ah!" Crom cried when he saw them. "Now, let us feast, and then to bed, for I believe you are tired after traveling all day in that driving rain. I daresay you could use a good night's sleep! Sit! Sit!"

He gestured at the chairs and beamed as they took their places at the table.

"Where is the master of the house?" Seanchan asked casually. "Is he not joining us?"

"Perhaps later," Crom said, dismissing Seanchan's question. "He went hunting a few days ago and has not returned. But he will. He will. Probably late tonight or early on the morrow. I know that he wouldn't want you to wait on him."

"Are you joining us?"

"For a bit," Crom said. "Then I have some matters that I must take care of before the master returns. He wouldn't be pleased if everything wasn't running smoothly."

He took a seat to the right of the master's seat at head of the table and gestured at the meal.

"Now, my guests, do help yourselves to this simple fare!"

"We thank you," Seanchan said. He took his trencher and heaped it high with fruit and wheat meal. He took a chunk of bread and set to eating. The others followed suit, leaving the meat untouched.

Crom's eyes narrowed. "Have some meat!" he said. "This has been prepared especially for you. It is the master's own recipe. With blackberry sauce it is especially tasty!"

"I have no doubt," Seanchan said. "But I'm afraid my stomach isn't right at the moment. We ate earlier some fruit that had fallen from its tree, and I daresay that we all have a touch of stomach sickness. This is why we were so thankful to find a place where we might rest for a day or two—well, the rain, too, had something to do with it—before continuing our journey."

Crom chewed his lower lip a moment before breaking into another smile and saying, "Well, perhaps in the morning. With fresh eggs? And fresh bread?"

"Perhaps," Seanchan said. "And thank you for your courtesy. May we have some fresh water? I fear the richness of your ale may do more damage than good."

A strange look passed over Crom's face; he glared at them just for a second, then forced a laugh.

"But of course! Anything that you want! All you have to do is ask!"

He clapped his hands and Siamper came into the room. He looked closely at her, and all there could see a flicker of fear in her eyes before she could bring it under control. She trembled and bowed to Crom.

"Hmmm," he said, eyeing her suspiciously. "Siamper, bring cool water for our guests!"

"Fresh from a running stream?" Seanchan asked innocently.

"Fresh from a running stream," Crom said, barely holding in the anger that burned deep within him.

Siamper hurried away and returned with pitchers of fresh water that sparkled when poured into cups. Then she almost ran from the room.

The party ate carefully of the fruits and wheat and oatmeal, chatting amiably with Crom and among themselves. At last, they were finished, and Cumac yawned hugely, feeling the corners of his jaws crack. Others followed suit, and soon, they all sat sleepily around the table, trying to stifle further yawns. But it was no use, and finally Seanchan said, "I believe it would be best, Crom, if we retired for the night. We are quite exhausted, as you can see."

"Very well," Crom said stiffly. He clapped his hands again and called, "Siamper!"

Reluctantly the woman appeared and stopped just inside the doorway, wringing her hands and looking furtively at Crom.

"Aid our guests in retiring for the night. Then come to me for further instructions."

A look of fear swept through her eyes and she scurried to the stairs and climbed swiftly, leaving the others trying to match her speed.

Halfway down the hall, Seanchan caught her. She looked fearfully back the way they had come and tried to pull away, but Seanchan kept a firm grip upon her arm. She shook her head and looked down at her feet, making tiny noises in her throat.

"You think he knows that you told us about him, don't you?" Fedelm asked soothingly.

Tears began to trickle down her cheeks and she nodded.

"We have to do something," Cumac said to Seanchan.

"Oh, let's just kill him and go," Lorgas said, fingering his ax at his belt.

"No," Seanchan said. "There are others here like you?" he asked Siamper.

She nodded.

"Seanchan," Lorgas began.

"We have been over this before. I do not think he would be easy to kill," Seanchan said. "Remember the story of Cu Roi and Cucullen that came about because of Bricriu's challenge at his feast?"

Lorgas sighed and nodded.

One day as the Red Branch was in Emain Macha, worn out after the gathering and the games, Connor and Fergus entered the Great Hall along with other warriors, tired and hungry. Neither Cucullen nor Conall Cernach nor Leogaire was there that night. But the rest of the Red Branch warriors sat and waited for their meal to be served.

Evening was falling upon them when a big ugly uncouth man entered the hall. He wore an old hide with a dark cloak around him. Yellow eyes protruded from his head. Each finger was as thick as a person's wrist. In his right hand was an ax weighing at least 150 pounds.

Silently he went and stood beside the fire, blocking the warmth from the others.

"Stop blocking the fire," said Dubhtach Chafertongue.

The man turned and said, "I hear there are great warriors here. I bring a challenge to test their bravery."

"Tell us," Fergus said grumpily.

"Connor cannot take my challenge, as he is king and the land needs a king," the man said. "And Fergus as well. But as for the rest of you, I challenge you to cut off my head today, and tomorrow I shall cut off yours."

"I'll take that challenge," cried Munremur, leaping to the floor of the hall. "Bend down, bachlach," he said scornfully.

The man smiled, handed the ax to Munremur, and bent to bare his neck for the blade.

With that, Munremur took the ax from the man's hand and swung as hard as he could. The bachlach's head bounced across the floor as blood spurted high.

The man rose, gathered his head and ax, and left.

"Impossible," said Dubtach. "If he returns tomorrow, I don't think anyone else will stand up to him."

"Oh, let us eat," Fergus said, annoyed. "It is a childish game, foolish and accounting for nothing."

But the following night, the man returned, and when Munremur saw him, Munremur fled out the back of the Great Hall and disappeared.

The man laughed and spun his ax in the air, smirking at the rest of the Red Branch.

"Is there no warrior here willing to play the game fully with me?" he taunted. "Is there not one of thc three who claims the right to being the greatest warrior of the Red Branch?"

"I'll take that challenge," Leogaire said. He seized the ax and cut off the man's head. But when the man returned the next night, Leogaire hid from him.

Conall Cernach rose and took the challenge, but he too hid when the man returned.

This time, Cucullen was there, and when the man made his challenge again, Cucullen rose and stepped forward. He took the ax from the man's hand and cut off the man's head, and again the man rose and gathered his head and ax and left the hall.

The next night, the man returned to collect Cucullen's head. But instead of running, Cucullen bowed his head upon a block of wood that had been set there for that purpose. The man took his weapon and swung mightily at Cucullen's neck. But the ax buried itself in the block of wood, leaving Cucullen unharmed.

Then the man said, "The Red Branch was looking for its greatest hero, and now, I proclaim that hero to be Cucullen. I am Cu Roi, and to me came the demand that I choose the greatest warrior. Here he is."

And Cu Roi left the hall, and Cucullen took his rightful place next to Connor.

"Yes," Lorgas said. "I remember the story. Do you think Crom has the same power as Cu Roi?"

Seanchan shrugged. "I do not know. But we must be very careful with our plans. Anyone who leaps in wild-eyed and bushy-tailed is as foolish as a mockingbird crying that he has the power of an eagle. No, we'll wait."

"But what about Siamper?" Cumac asked. "There may be something to her fear."

Seanchan chewed the ends of his mustache and stroked his beard while thinking. Then he nodded and said to the woman, "Siamper, can you hide in the barn for tonight? Someplace where you will be safe for at least one night?"

She nodded and held up a finger.

"Yes, just one night," Seanchan said. "That should give us time to figure out how to save the rest of you."

She smiled nervously and disappeared down the hallway, ignoring the steps to the Great Hall.

"Well," Lorgas said darkly, "I still say we should just lop off his head and send him to Teach Duinn. We could be long gone away from here by the time he recovers."

"And what about the others?" Fedelm asked.

"We can take them partway with us," Bern answered. "I agree with Lorgas."

Seanchan said, "Caution. Caution. There will be time enough in the morning, I suspect."

"What," Cumac said, "about casting him into the Great Rift? Granted, Maliman could get him out of there, but it will take time."

"I do not have that power," Seanchan said soberly. "It is a good idea, but I do not have the power. Let us sleep, and perhaps one of us will have an idea in the morning. We shall meet in my room. Be early."

The others nodded soberly and each went to his or her own room, firmly closing the door and locking it.

THE rain had stopped by the time they arose the next morning, but the sun was hidden by gray clouds threatening more before the day was over. No birdsong came through the open windows of their rooms, but a smell of dank and decay rolled in, so thick that it could well have been a fog.

Cautiously, all slipped out of their rooms and down to Seanchan's room, entering as quietly as they could. Seanchan was seated in the room's chair, frowning at the floor. He appeared lost in thought, and the others quietly took their places on his rumpled bed and on the floor at his feet, waiting.

At last, he looked up, gave a brief smile, and said, "I told you that there is great magic here. I believe that Crom has that magic and has woven it around this house and himself. But, there is a chance. Not with your ax, Lorgas, or your arrows, Fedelm, or your sword, Bern. But Cumac carries Caladbolg, the sword from the Otherworld, and that might be able to cut through Crom's magic long enough for me to use cairnfire. I believe that Crom's head is where the seat of his power resides. So," he turned to Cumac, "I want you to behead him. You must be quick about it, before he begins to suspect us. All of you must think of something other than his beheading when we enter the Great Hall. Cumac, you must be as swift as a swallow's flight. Do not give him time to prepare. After you behead him, I will use the cairnfire upon his head. Now, if I'm right, he will have to go to Teach Duinn to retrieve it, and Donn is very particular about allowing things like that."

"I still want to use the ax upon him," Lorgas grumbled. "But I'll go along with you."

"Do not miss," Seanchan cautioned Cumac. "That would be deadly for all of us. You will only have time for one stroke. Remember, the web of magic must be broken, or mine will not work."

"I'll do it," Cumac said, sliding Caladbolg up and down in its sheath.

They left Seanchan's room and made their way to the stairs, coming down slowly as each tried to put thoughts in order that would mislead Crom—if indeed he could read them.

"Good morning, my guests!" Crom cried as they stepped into the Great Hall. "I trust your sleep was good? And your stomach is ready for a full breakfast?"

He swept his arm toward the table set with food as it was before. When he turned, Cumac leaped forward, Caladbolg singing from its sheath, and a rainbow arch appeared. Crom's head flew from his body, and black blood flooded down from the stump. The head landed in a corner of the room.

"Ah, but that is no way to treat your host," the head said.

You have discovered my name
And think that you have won the game.
You have struck me from my shoulders
And thrown me like boulders
Thinking that this will do for me.
But there is more to me, you'll see.

"And what did you plan for us?" Seanshan said. Blue and red fire leaped from his hands and wrapped around Crom's head. A smell of brimstone came into the room. The head gave a shriek, then burst apart, spilling Crom's brains onto the floor seconds before they too burst into flame.

"Well, that worked," Lorgas said, rubbing his hands together.

"You have a keen grasp of the obvious," Bern said caustically.

"Come!" Seanchan commanded. "Hurry and gather the others and let us leave this place!"

Within minutes, they had gathered the servants and were leaving when Callem came through the doorway, stopping them. He smiled evilly at them, his eyes black and full of contempt.

"Did you think that I, Crom Cruach, would allow you to go so easily?" he said, his voice sepulchral and hollow. "You burnt me with cairnfire, but I am here as well."

"The partitioned soul," Seanchan whispered, more to himself than the others. "Very uncommon."

"Oh yes, Seanchan, very. And now, if you please, return to the hall, and we shall see what to do with you."

But Fedelm was quick, and within a second, an arrow appeared in each of his eyes.

He screamed and pulled them out, the orbs coming with the barbed ends of the arrows. He screamed again, staggering away from the door, groping blindly. They stepped aside as he made for the Great Hall.

"Quickly," Seanchan said, opening the door.

The others sped outside and discovered their horses saddled and ready. Siamper grabbed Fedelm's arm and smiled gratefully. Then she pointed at herself and the other servants. The men held weapons, and the women carried packs filled with food and what they might need as they traveled. Siamper then turned to the east and pointed in that direction.

Fedelm shook her head.

"That is not the way we are traveling," she said.

Siamper nodded and pointed again urgently, this time.

"You mean to go to the Red Branch!" Cumac said suddenly.

Siamper clapped her hands and nodded.

"Then stay to the northern edge of the forest," Seanchan said. "When you come to the House of Boand of the Waters, tell her that I sent you. She will see you safely to the Red Branch."

Siamper nodded, and tears leaped from her eyes.

"You are welcome," Fedelm said. "But now, you must hurry. We do not know what other magic might be here. Travel for a day and a night, and then you should be far enough from here to rest."

She glanced at Seanchan, who nodded.

Siamper turned and ran after the others, looking over her shoulder and waving once more before she disappeared into the forest.

"And now," Seanchan said, climbing up into his saddle, "I think it would be prudent if we followed their example and put distance between us and this house."

The others mounted and lifted their horses into a trot as they rode away, heading once again to the northwest.

They continued their journey toward the northwest, making a camp on a rocky plateau where the wind whipped mercilessly at them, tugging at their clothes so fiercely that they feared the garments would be torn from their bodies. They could not light a fire because of the wind and stone, so they rested as best they could until gray light appeared in the east.

They hurried across the plateau and came down into a valley rich with green grass and elm and oak mixed with aspen. Gratefully, they pulled their ponies into a soft lope and breathed deeply the scent of meadow flowers while red grouse and rabbits scurried from their approach. Once they saw a kestrel drop and seize a small rabbit, and another time a hump-backed shadow moved in the trees, paralleling their course, but they could not make out what it was. The land wasn't desolate enough for hobgoblins or goblins, but there were other enemies the thought of whom made the little band uneasy.

At night, they camped in the open after clearing grass away for a fire. Better, Bern commented, than camping in the woods, as here in the open they would see the enemy before it managed to get close enough to make things harrowing.

But nothing came during the night, and the next day, they breathed easier as they rode, letting the horses pick their speed alongside Black, who moved tirelessly until evening, coming finally to a tiny copse of beech trees around a crystal pool of water. Here, they made camp and relaxed idly, passing small talk while Fedelm hunted and brought back a brace of heavy conies for their meal.

Bern cleaned them and mixed them with some shaved horseradish and herbs, and soon a mouthwatering aroma rose from the blackened pot. He added a bit of water and began to make brown gravy that soon had all sighing with hunger.

Cumac took pannin bread from his pouch and cut equal slices for all, while Lorgas took a torch from the fire and disappeared into the wood, returning shortly with combs so thick that heavy honey rolled off his palms.

They set to with relish, and soon the meal was finished and all were lounging back drowsily, yawning and visiting among themselves until night had fully fallen. Then, they rolled in their cloaks and fell asleep almost immediately. They had slept almost through the night when a hallo awoke them.

Instantly all were awake, facing in opposite directions, weapons in hand, eyes trying to pierce the dark. Seanchan blew the fire awake with his staff. All looked around for the source of greeting but saw nothing.

Then a man dressed all in black appeared suddenly out of the trees to stand at the edge of the firelight. Long black hair fell to his shoulders, and his eyes were anthracite. His mouth was a thin line. The black hilt of a huge sword with a blade easily four feet long peeped over one shoulder, and at a black belt around his waist hung a large knife in a black sheath. An empty leather waterskin hung slackly from one shoulder and a leather pack from the other. A breath of chill air seemed to flow from him and over the others. Cumac felt a coldness settle in his stomach.

"I seek your hospitality," he said.

"Come into our camp," Seanchan said. "And welcome. We cannot offer you much, although there is some honey left and pannin bread."

"For a hungry man, it is enough," he said as he moved into the firelight.

"Give us your name!" Lorgas said sharply. The others looked quickly at him, then back to the stranger, for demanding one's name before it was given was considered unlucky and rude.

The stranger eyed them coldly for a long moment before answering.

"I am Tarin and would share your fire, for it is coming a bit cold before morning."

"I am Seanchan Duirgeal. And this is Fedelm of Rath Curachan, Bern of the Ervalians, Lorgas of the Ashelves, and Cumac, son of Cucullen."

"Who do you serve?" Bern asked politely.

The smile slipped a bit from Tarin's face. "I serve no one. Not anymore, at least. The Great Hall of my liege was destroyed by Deag-duls and hobgoblins and goblins a fortnight past."

"Together?" Seanchan asked sharply.

Tarin nodded.

"Yes, together. There were Nightshades as well. We fought well, but it was hopeless, and when there were only a handful of us left and our liege dead, we slipped away from them and made our way into the forest. There, we split up, as we thought it would be harder for the invaders to find us if we were by ourselves. Not all made it to safety, however. I could hear their cries and screams on the wind and now believe I am the last alive."

"A Sword-wanderer," Cumac said disgustedly. He drew Caladbolg as Fedelm fitted an arrow to her bow.

Tarin stepped in closer, the black-hilted sword slipping easily into his hand before the others were aware that he had drawn it.

"Aye, a Sword-wanderer. But not all of us are ill-meaning to travelers. Put up your weapons. I mean you no harm."

"Do what he asks. Put up your weapons," Seanchan said. "Tell me, Tarin, what are your plans now?"

Tarin shrugged. "I know not. I have no family, no place to go. I do not wish to sell my hand and sword to another, for it is hard to tell friend from foe these days. As I'm certain you have discovered, if you have traveled far. I don't blame you for greeting me as you have. It is right to be cautious."

"Will you sit and eat?" Seanchan asked courteously.

"Gladly and my thanks," Tarin said. He replaced his sword, then took the scabbard from his shoulder. He removed his pack and waterskin and carefully placed them on the ground near him.

Cumac eyed Tarin's sword carefully. Tarin caught his look and handed his sword to Cumac. Cumac drew it from its sheath and studied it carefully. The handle was ridged, wrapped tightly in black leather strips, and made for two hands. The blade shone brightly and bore curious shapes. He frowned and looked at Seanchan for an answer.

"That is a rune-blade," Seanchan said softly. "You rarely see them anymore. Those marks upon the blade are the marks of long use and made in the dragon days."

"My father's and his father before him, as far back as I can count," Tarin said, taking a comb of honey from the hand of Lorgas and placing meat between two slices of bread. Fedelm took his waterskin, filled it from the pool, and set it beside him. He gave her a quick nod of thanks.

"It is a very long time since I have had gracious company," he said.

He took a big bite of honey and wiped some drippings off his chin. He ate hungrily, quickly devouring what they set before him. At last, he finished, looking around hopefully for more, but nothing was left. He drank deeply from his waterskin and sighed.

"You have been more generous than I thought you would be," he said. "But what brings you here?"

They shared a quick look among themselves, then Seanchan spoke, saying, "We seek Bricriu Poisontongue, who stole the Bladhm Caillis—the Chalice of Fire that brought peace—from the Red Branch. We must find it before Maliman, who has escaped from the Great Rift, is strong enough to claim it. With the Bladhm Caillis, Maliman might be able to turn its power into his. Then sorrow and bleakness will sweep over the land, imprisoning all and turning them to servants of Maliman. We are the Seekers of the Chalice."

Tarin's eyes shot upward and he said, "I have heard of the Fire Chalice and know somewhat of its power. I would join you if you wish. I have no other place to go, and this sounds like an earnest quest."

"You're Tarin the Damned," Bern said suddenly.

Instantly Tarin's thin face tightened. His eyes went flat and cold.

"Some call me that," he said harshly. His hand dropped to his sword beside him. The blade slid smoothly from its scabbard as he leaped to his feet.

The others reached for their weapons, but Seanchan motioned for them to keep their weapons down.

"You are the Damned," he said. It wasn't a question, but Tarin treated it as if it were.

"Yes. I am," he said quietly. "And now, I imagine you wish me to leave."

"No, you are welcome," Seanchan said, and he looked sharply at the others as they started to protest. He silently stretched his hand to Tarin. After a moment's hesitation, Tarin took it.

At this cue, Fedelm said, "You are most welcome."

The others echoed her sentiment.

"Where are you traveling?" Tarin asked, taking his place once again beside the fire.

"To Cruachan Ai," Cumac said. "We believe that Bricriu is headed toward Maeve's court."

"Maeve! She-Who-Intoxicates! I have always wanted to see that minx, to find out if she lives up to her legends. But why there?"

"She is the one who gave the Chalice of Fire to Cucullen. And since Connacht is the sworn enemy of Ulster, I imagine Bricriu would think that there he will receive protection." Seanchan shrugged. "At least, it's a beginning for our search."

"Yes, I can see that," Tarin said slowly. "But what about the rest of you?"

"We are of the Otherworld," Fedelm said. "All of us except for Seanchan. And he is of the Duirgeals. Maeve will not wish to gain their wrath."

"And me?" he asked. "Do you think that she will welcome me?"

"A chance. But you will be with us, one of the Seekers of the Chalice. I cannot see her harming you," Fedelm said. "What say you, Seanchan?"

"He will be safe. And now, let us sleep. We shall have to find you a horse along the way, Tarin. We will worry about that in the morning."

And so they made themselves comfortable around the fire and wrapped themselves in their cloaks for warmth.

"Why is he called the Damned?" Cumac whispered to Bern when they stretched out together on a soft grassy hummock.

Bern cast a swift glance at Tarin wrapped in his cloak across the fire from them. Bern leaned closer to Cumac.

"The way I heard it, he was called to Culhane's court in Munster. At the time, he was the champion of Munster, much in the same way your father was the champion of Ulster," Bern whispered. "He was only three miles from his fortress of Dun Scathe when one of the traces on his chariot broke. He returned home to repair it and discovered that his wife, Galata, had left soon after his departure for the fortress of Ganach. At a feast held by Culhane the month before, she had behaved boldly with Ganach, and Tarin had cut their visit short to return to Dun Scathe.

"Anyway, Tarin followed her to Ganach's fortress, and what

happened there is anyone's guess. A few days later, however, a traveler, seeking hospitality, discovered all had been slain. Blood spattered the walls of Ganach's fortress, and Ganach's head along with Galata's had been chopped off and placed on spears surrounding the fortress of Ganach's Great Hall. No one could prove Tarin's guilt when he was brought before the Brehons for trial. Since then, he has been a Sword-wanderer and called the Damned."

Cumac chewed his lower lip for a moment, then asked, "Do you think he did it?"

"I don't know," Bern said, looking again across the fire at the sleeping Tarin. "But I know one thing: I am not going to ask him. His feats with that rune-blade match those of your father's."

With that, Bern rolled himself in his cloak and went to sleep.

Cumac studied Tarin's figure for a long moment, then muttered, "If so, he will be either a friend or foe. I don't know which."

He curled up in his cloak, and after a short while, his muscles relaxed from the day's travel and he felt fast asleep. He dreamed of a threatening dark figure swinging a blade furiously against foes. But Cumac could not tell who the black figure was fighting, and he slept restlessly through the night.

Frost sprinkled the ground when they awoke, stiff and sore from the overnight drop in temperature. Breakfast consisted of cold water and honey spread over thick slices of pannin bread—which did nothing to ease their tempers.

Cumac went to saddle Black just as Black came into the clearing, nipping the flanks of a saddled horse in front of him.

Cumac stared in disbelief as there now were enough horses for all, Tarin's horse being a white-maned chestnut with fine lines. Cumac grinned and patted Black and said, "You continue to surprise me, Black of Saingliau. I thank you for bringing the other horse that we needed."

Black made a snuffling noise in his throat and looked pleased with Cumac's praise. He bent his head so Cumac could ruffle the mane between his ears.

The others came into the clearing to saddle their horses and stopped dead still when they saw the chestnut, already saddled. They looked around in amazement for who had brought the horse.

"How—" Lorgas said, pointing at the chestnut, at a loss for further words.

"Black," Cumac said, bending to pick up his saddle and place it gently on Black's back. "He brought it to us."

"That is one of the most amazing things I have ever seen," Tarin said, his eyebrows raised nearly to his hairline. "How—well, that is, how did he know I needed a horse?"

Cumac patted Black on his neck. Black preened. "He is the Black of Saingliau. One of my father's horses. He comes from the lake of Sliab Fuait."

"You mean 'around,' " Tarin said.

"No, I mean from the lake. When my father was killed, Black and the Gray of Macha returned to the lake from whence they came."

"Truly a magical steed," Tarin said.

"You have no idea," Lorgas said, grunting as he saddled his horse.

Soon they were off, hunched deeply within their cloaks against the cold.

They crossed the valley and entered the forest that stood at the far end. The sun had not shone in the valley, and they knew that it would not shine here either. The trees held brown, yellow, and russet leaves edged with hoarfrost so thick that even if the sun did shine, it would not penetrate. The trees seemed to close like a wall around the path leading through them. Stalky and faded hemlocks, wood-parsley, and fireweed stood between the trunks of the trees. It grew colder as they rode deeper and deeper into the forest, and so silent was it that the thud of their horses' hooves seemed to echo.

"Where are we?" Cumac whispered, trying not to disturb the quiet.

"This is the Forest of Morphia. No one knows how old it is. Few who enter it are heard from again," Fedelm said.

"Who lives here?" Cumac asked.

Fedelm shrugged. "Bears, deer, honeybees who travel far to collect pollen, rabbits, although I hear their meat is black and foul-tasting. Carp live in the waters of the ponds, but their flesh makes travelers sick. We shall not find much to eat while we are in this forest. Only what we carry."

"Pannin bread," Lorgas said grumpily.

"Yes," Bern said. "Pannin bread. But what about water?"

"It is best that we drink only what we are carrying," Fedelm said.

Her words were greeted unhappily by the others, who huddled deeper within their cloaks.

The path wound around and around, and Cumac could have sworn that he saw trees moving to block their path. Mist filled the hollows, and it was in the hollows that they heard the only birds they had encountered: the cawing of ravens.

A fold in the earth appeared in front of them, but the sides were so steep that they could not ride down to the bottom. And even if they did manage to reach the bottom, they would not be able to climb out of it.

Dejected, they turned to what they thought was west and followed the fold as it turned back and forth upon itself like a series of oxbows.

Soon the frost lifted from the ground and leaves, allowing the travelers to slip their cloaks from around them. But then steam waves seemed to rise from the ground, and they huddled miserably on the backs of their horses, who walked head down along the faint lines of what might be a path. Then they took heart as they came upon an old path that led across a shallow dip of the fold. Pines and firs began to replace the ash and oak trees, but there were other trees in the forest that none had ever seen before. Even Seanchan could not name them, and it was these trees that seemed to gather close to them as they traveled.

Then, to make matters worse, the path seemed to twist eastward. Brambles and undergrowth picked themselves up and blocked the path, so the Seekers had to climb down and force their way through the undergrowth. Each time they made it through a patch, the trees grew thicker and thicker and the way darker and darker.

By now, all realized they were simply following a path that seemed to have been chosen for them, but whether it was the work of the trees and bushes or of others they could not tell.

It grew hotter, and blood flies and horseflies began to buzz around them, biting furiously until at last they had to halt and build a smudge fire to keep the insects away.

They sat for what seemed like hours, until a wind came up and blew the flies away and they were able to mount their horses once again.

Finally the gloaming came upon them, and they were forced to stop for the night. They made a small fire, and though the forest seemed to stiffen angrily, they kept it burning and all huddled around it. They took the pannin bread from their packs and washed it down with cautious sips from their waterskins, conscious that they had to preserve their water until they managed to leave the forest.

Sleep slowly came to them, a drowsy sleep that made their limbs feel heavy and their eyelids close despite all efforts they made to stay awake. Soon, all were slumbering, despite half-hearted plans to keep a guard during the night.

Dreams came to Cumac, restless dreams and evil dreams. Suddenly, he jerked awake and discovered a sumaire kneeling on the ground beside him. Startled, the sumaire drew back and Cumac rolled frantically away, clawing for Caladbolg and shouting, "Sumaires! Upon us! Awake!"

The others were swiftly up, lunging to their feet, weapons in hand. The sumaires gave a triumphant howl and fell upon them, trying to get past the party's defenses. Slowly, the party was forced into a circle, each parrying black blades and axes and slaying sumaires. But still the Sumaires came, more and more, until it seemed that for every sumaire felled, two others took his place.

Cumac found himself heavily pressed, and then Tarin was beside him, his long blade flashing and singing as it sliced through the sumaires.

Then came a roaring from the forest, and the sumaires screamed in fright and tried to flee but couldn't. A huge black bear came upon them, powerful paws pounding the sumaires to jelly, long claws ripping their necks and bellies open. More and more sumaires fell, yelling in agony, twisting and turning, their hands held tight against their stomachs, holding themselves together until at last a handful managed to escape and ran crashing through briars and brambles.

The bear sat on his haunches, carefully checked his fur, and, nodding with satisfaction at having emerged unharmed, looked at the others with a curious expression on his face.

"Good evening, Seanchan," the bear said pleasantly. "It appears that you were at a disadvantage for a while."

"Until you came, Reaggus. Thank you. It was touch-and-go there for a bit."

"A *talking* bear?" Tarin asked no one in particular. Reaggus scowled.

"And why not? Many of us do. We just chew words as others."

"Thank you," Seanchan said, casting a warning glance at Tarin and the rest.

Reaggus waved a heavy paw nonchalantly. "It was my pleasure. But what brings you this far into Morphia?"

"The trees," Seanchan said. "They have been most unaccommodating."

"Hmm? Well, we should be able to take care of that. Where are you going?"

"To Cruachan Ai," Seanchan said. "The Chalice of Fire has been stolen from the Red Branch, and we are trying to bring it back to Ulster."

"Ah, you are the Seekers of the Chalice," Reaggus said, licking his paw and scrubbing it over his face and muzzle. "I have heard about you, and I daresay others have as well. But Cruachan Ai," he shook his head and frowned, his voice dropping into a deep growl. "That Maeve is one I hope to meet somewhere in my forest. Alone. The last time she saw me on the forest edge where I was 'liberating' a hive of honey, she tried to have me killed for my skin. Filthy woman!" The frown disappeared from his face. "I hear that it is Bricriu who has taken the Chalice. Is this correct?"

"It is," Seanchan said. "Bricriu Poisontongue. We think he may be heading to Cruachan Ai, as it was Maeve who gave the Chalice to Cucullen and he to the Red Branch." Seanchan shrugged. "We had to pick a direction."

Reaggus scratched his head with a heavy claw. "Seems pretty weak to me. But I guess you have to start somewhere. Well." He clapped his paws together. "Do you have any food?"

"No," Lorgas said. "And my stomach is glued to my backbone."

"A curious thing," Reaggus said, looking at Lorgas's back.

"He means he's hungry," Bern said, scoffing. "It's one of those things with Ashelves to overexaggerate."

"Oh," Reaggus said, puzzlement still showing on his face. "Well, it must be something unique to you. Let's see: I can get you some honey and nuts and berries. Would that be all right?"

"And water?" Cumac asked.

"Of course," Reaggus said. "But you will have to travel a short way with me. The water in this part of Morphia is not good."

"Of course," Fedelm said. "I do not think that would bother us at all. At all."

"Well, then, gather your things and follow me!"

"The trees—" Cumac began pointing uncertainly.

"Oh, yes. The trees," Reaggus said. "I had almost forgotten about them."

He stood on his hind legs and stared at one, an oak. At first nothing happened, then the oak began to tremble. A few leaves loosened and fell to the ground. Lorgas swore later, it seemed that the oak began to whine.

"Now," Reaggus demanded, keeping his stare focused upon the oak, "who forced these fine fellows off their course? Tell me!"

Still upon the morning breeze
Moving easily through we trees
As if we were his private stand,
The black friend of Maliman.

"I see," Reaggus said. "But that does not excuse your conduct. What would other people say if they heard about how unfriendly you were? Never mind! I'll tend to you later. *And* the black friend of Maliman!"

"Do you know who he is?" Cumac asked.

"Oh yes. I know. For the sake of keeping the peace, I allowed him to stay on the northern reaches of Morphia. But now no more," Reaggus said grimly. "I will be showing him his way. Come on! Come on! Enough dilly-dallying! We don't want to be talking the hours away. Stay a day and night with me to rest, and then I shall have a guide lead you to the west and back upon the road to Cruachan Ai."

They hurriedly packed and mounted their horses. Reaggus stalked toward the wall of trees, grumbling deep within his throat, and the trees parted, showing a path that had been well-taken. They traveled nervously behind him (except for Seanchan, who knew Reaggus well) but had no more problems. At last, they came into a large glade. In the middle of the glade was a huge house with a pair of doors so large that two men on horses could ride abreast through the entrance and never have to bow their heads. The house was cheerful-looking and neatly painted in green and yellow. ("The colors change with the season," Seanchan reported later.) The roof was cleanly thatched, and at the back of the house was a warm and friendly cave where they could stable their horses.

Inside the house, the Seekers halted in awe. A fire blazed cheerfully in the stone fireplace, and the walls were richly paneled in oak that had been continually rubbed with beeswax until the wood had obtained a mellow gold like honey. A pump stood upon a wooden counter in the corner, and the tables and chairs were of polished bird's-eye maple. The main table had already been set with fresh bread and bowls of berries swimming in heavy cream, and pint mugs had been filled with honey-mead that, they discovered soon, had a taste so sweet that it slid down the throat with great ease.

Pallets had been made all along one wall, and Cumac said, "But how did you know we were coming?"

Reaggus smiled and laid one heavy paw aside his nose and said,

In the Forest of Morphia, many things
Are not what they seem and other things
Are what they seem but here you may stay
For a restful and long night and day
Safe from any harm. I promise you.
Now, I am afraid that I must leave you
To settle things in the north but I
Will be back in morning before you open an eye.

And with that, he left, his ponderous bulk moving lightly across the glade and into the woods, leaving them alone in the house.

"Well!" said Lorgas, rubbing his hands together while he eyed the table. "I don't wish to seem rude, but here is food fit for a king and I'm eating."

"Maybe a prince," Bern said. "We Ervalians are a bit more picky than Ashelves."

But Lorgas did not rise to the jab. Instead, he plopped himself down on a small bench and helped himself happily to the mead.

"Do you really think we are safe here, Seanchan?" Fedelm asked.

"Oh yes. Oh yes indeed! Reaggus keeps his woods safe." He frowned. "Had I known that we had gone this far into Morphia, I would have tried to let him know. But, I didn't. I would, though, like to know who he is going to visit. But for now, let us join Lorgas before he has eaten everything!"

With glad hearts, they pulled out benches and settled in, eating and drinking merrily.

During the night, Cumac thought he heard a bear roaring, but he decided he was dreaming and rolled back over and went to sleep.

33

The sun was shining and buttercups were fully open upon the grassy glade. The air had a hint of smoke to it, but it was the smoke of autumn, a rich tannic smell that made one think of apples floating in a wooden tub of water and pumpkins and rich fall ale and platters full of every kind of food one could want.

The table had already been set before they awoke, and the house was just as cheerful as when they had arrived. They rose happily, and

Cumac went out to check on their horses. The stable was warm and clean, and fresh hay had been provided for the horses in addition to fresh water and a bran rich with oats. Cumac went to Black and rubbed his mane along the back of his neck. Black grunted with pleasure and gave Cumac a gentle nudge with his nose.

Cumac laughed, slipped an apple that he had taken from the table out of his pocket, and held it for Black, who took it daintily.

"I can see you are content, my friend. Rest, for we will not leave until tomorrow morning. But early, then, I should think."

Black vigorously nodded and went back to his feed, while Cumac made his way back to the house where the others had already sat down to a breakfast to match the night meal.

"I take it that you are all happy," Seanchan said, then looked at Cumac. "And did you find our horses well cared for?"

"Our host is very kind," Cumac said, settling on a bench. "They are quite content."

"They'd better be," Tarin said, his mouth full of bread and honey. "Or else I have a hunch that big black of yours would take matters into his own . . . er . . . hooves?"

The others broke out in a peal of laughter, and even Seanchan had to grin at Tarin's momentary confusion about whether "hands" or "hooves" would be more appropriate.

"But where is our host?" Cumac wondered.

"I imagine that he is up on the northern skirt of Morphia," Seanchan said soberly. "He does not tolerate meddlesome fools, and anyone who would meddle with Morphia is a fool indeed. A very big fool."

"Will he be back tomorrow morning when we leave?" Tarin asked.

Seanchan shook his head. "I do not know. But I doubt it. If there is one fool on the northern edge of Morphia, there may be others on its boundaries, and Reaggus will probably patrol around the edge to make certain that all things are as they should be."

"But we will have a guide, certainly," Fedelm said.

"Oh yes. Of that I am certain," Seanchan said.

"Then let us put that out of our minds," Lorgas said.

"A fine woodland elf you call yourself," Bern said and was rewarded with a slap in his face of a huge slice of bread flooded with honey. He sputtered and pulled the bread off, glaring at Lorgas who was eating with an innocent look, as if it was common practice for Bern to receive a slice of bread and honey in his face.

"Why, you . . . you . . ." Bern choked as a piece of bread slid down his throat, causing Fedelm to pound his back vigorously.

"If I may say so," Seanchan said, "and I will, you have had that coming for quite a while, now, Bern. Lorgas has been very patient with you."

"I'll . . . I'll . . ." Bern sputtered. The others laughed at him as honey dripped off the end of his nose, until finally Bern had to laugh himself. He acknowledged that he had indeed been very caustic of late toward Lorgas and asserted that all was well and good.

Toward midday, the Seekers were lounging sleepily in the warmth of the sun and finding the tension of the past days slipping away from them like water off a wet rock. Bees buzzed lazily around the glade, and bluebirds sang as squirrels scampered among the trees, laying in stores of walnuts, acorns, and chestnuts against the coming winter.

"Seanchan?" Cumac asked.

"Hmmm?" the wizard responded, his eyes closed, enjoying the sun's heat upon his joints.

"How far are we from Cruachan Ai? And how do you think we are going to be received once we are there?"

"Received? Why, with honor, I expect. But that will depend upon Maeve. Ailill is of an easy mind, but Maeve?" He clucked his tongue. "One never knows from one day to the next what her mood will be."

"I mean, if Bricriu is there, how will she treat us?"

"The same as if he were not," Seanchan said, opening his eyes. His bushy eyebrows twitched. "She might be unpredictable, but she is no fool. It is not, however, *being* at Cruachan Ai but *getting* to Cruachan Ai that may be the problem. Between here and there the land is Connacht, and Connacht, as you all know, is no friend to the

Red Branch. I would not be surprised to find Sword-wanderers hired to keep us away and kill us if necessary. There is no honor among them. I beg your pardon, Tarin," Seanchan apologized.

"No need. You are right." Tarin levered himself up on his elbows and looked around at the others. "You are from the Otherworld. Things are different there, I expect, although I hear what happens in Earthworld is a mirror to the Otherworld. Or is it the other way around? No matter. The beginning of famine is upon the earth, and Sword-wanderers are little trained to be farmers or herders. The way of the sword is all that they know. And if they are hungry enough, they will sell their sword to whoever has the money to buy it. If there is no money, even a promise will buy them," he added grimly. "These are bad times, and I do not think that things are going to get any better. Soon, I believe, farmers will have to leave their land and try to find food for their families elsewhere. And herders will find their stock losing weight as the farmers run out of food to sell.

"I do not think that you all are aware of what is taking place in Earthworld. No offense—you have no way of knowing unless you have traveled in Earthworld for long. But when people are hungry enough, they will do anything. Even if it is to disobey custom. And that makes everyone treacherous or potentially treacherous. When we leave this forest, then we will be unprotected by the trees until we reach Cruachan Ai. And that is when we need to be especially alert. Seanchan is right—I do not think our passage across the Great Plain will be without difficulty."

The thought was sobering, and they all rested uneasy with their thoughts. So far, things had been bad enough. The idea of more trouble than they had yet seen was disheartening.

"Is there any way around the plains?" Cumac asked at last.

Seanchan shook his head. "No, not that I know. Fedelm? This is your country."

Fedelm shook her head regretfully. "No, ahead lies the Plain of Cruachan, and there is no other way to reach Maeve's city. There are no portals, no Sidhe except one, and that one has not been opened for ages. I am certain that it wouldn't be opened for us now.

Ready yourselves, because we must cross the plains the best that we can."

"Then," Bern said, "I suggest we travel by night and sleep by day. Fires at night are easily seen, but we can hide the smoke during daylight with little effort. And there is less chance of being seen under the cloak of night."

"I agree," Lorgas said. Bern cast him a swift look. "You're not always wrong, Bern. And I know you are no fool, although being with this band is not necessarily the mark of a wise man. After all, I am here, so that should be proof enough. But," he said, standing and turning toward the southwest, scratching his head, "I have heard of an old band of Ashelves who have a small forest to the southwest. I have not seen it, and I have, until now, taken the account as a story to frighten children into behaving. Those Ashelves—if any remain—fought among the other Ashelves, my people, and were driven away from Rowan Oak. I do not know if they would greet us with friendship or weapons. But, if we cannot cross the plain, we might try that way. It is, if I recollect the stories well, only two days ride from here."

"Are you speaking of the Forest of Turgain?" Seanchan asked. "If so, I would not go into that forest unless it is absolutely necessary. Nothing good lives in that forest, and there will be no Reaggus to help us out of trouble if we are hard set upon. *And*," he emphasized, "after the Forest of Turgain, we shall have to go through the Valley of Shadows."

"What is the Valley of Shadows?" Cumac asked.

"A gathering for all that is feared and loathed by man and the Otherworld," Fedelm said softly.

"I do not know of any who have entered the Valley of Shadows who have returned. Or gone out the other side," Tarin said.

"But what really *is* in the Valley?" Cumac asked.

Tarin sighed. "The dishonored dead are there, as well as warggads and trolls. Goblins and hobgoblins live there, as do sumaires and the Deag-duls and others who feast on the blood of travelers who enter the Valley near the home of the Black Wizard. . . ."

"Who once was a student of the Duirgeals," Seanchan added

darkly. "He challenged Deroi, the leader of all teachers, and was cast out of the order when he was defeated. Until then, he had been the best student and had gained great magical powers. But he turned all that he had learned to black magic and evil ways."

"Do you know him, Seanchan?" Tarin asked.

"Yes. I know him," Seanchan said grimly.

"Others may have gone into the forest to join him as well," Tarin said. His face had turned to stone, and although questions stood on the tips of the tongues of the others, a quick look at his countenance made them bite back their words. He fell silent, and a sorrowful look slipped over his face. He slumped and stared brooding into the distance at something that only he could see. His fingers toyed with the haft of his sword.

Lorgas shrugged and looked at Bern. "What have you heard of Turgain, Bern?"

Bern shook his head. "What you have just said and what Seanchan has just said. That forest is an evil place. A *very* bad place. I have not even heard of a path through it, such are the stories of the Ashelves who live within it. If indeed there *are* Ashelves still there, after all this time. Some stories say they eat the flesh of their victims in there."

"I have heard those stories as well," Fedelm said. "They were often told to make the young ones of the Sidhe behave. And even among those of the Sidhe, no story of a party emerging safely has come down. If we must go that way, we will probably have to force our way through, yard by yard. I would not like to go into that forest unless we have no choice. It may be only two days out of our way to the forest," she added, looking at Lorgas, "but it will certainly add more than a week to our travel to Cruachan Ai. Even if we could avoid the Valley of Shadows."

"I have heard of this place. Sword-wanderers stay away from there," Tarin said, rubbing his shoulder, massaging his fingers deep into the muscle. "And Sword-wanderers have nothing to lose. If any good might be in that forest, the Sword-wanderers would have found it. Of this, I am certain."

Seanchan pulled on his beard with tiny jerks as he fell into deep thought. The others waited patiently. At last, he spoke gravely, "Then, let us indeed try the Plain of Cruachan and move south only with great reluctance. Maybe we will be able to cross the plain without being seen. I don't know. But we have had much trouble since we left the Red Branch, and I do not think that I want to trade the possibility of familiar trouble for the certainty of unknown trouble. The only thing about your forest, Lorgas, that recommends itself *is* the unknown. No one knows what lies in that forest, and we might, *might* make our way through *if* we cannot cross the plain."

The others nodded agreement, and all lay back down in the glade, trying to recall the contentment they had felt before the rest of their travel had been laid out before them.

THE afternoon, evening, and night passed peacefully enough, but when morning arrived, Reaggus still had not returned, although their breakfast was laid out carefully for them and their horses had been curried and saddled and waited in front of the house.

"What are we going to do now?" Tarin asked, finishing his breakfast and looking out the great door into the glade. "Reaggus has not returned. How are we going to find our way through the forest?"

"Reaggus promised us a guide," Seanchan said. "He did not say it would be him. But one will be provided. Of that, I am certain."

"It doesn't look promising to me," Lorgas said.

"Nor me," Bern echoed. He looked at Fedelm. "Fedelm, you have the vision gift. Can you see anything?"

She shook her head. "No, but like Seanchan, I believe that a guide will be provided."

"Well," Cumac sighed, rising from his place at the table, "let us be on our way. Standing here batting our teeth together isn't going to get us from here to there. We simply will have to place one foot in front of the other and trust to luck."

"Luck," Lorgas muttered. "It has been a long time since we had luck."

But when they left the cottage and gathered their mounts, a

white deer came to the clearing and walked up to Seanchan fearlessly. The deer bowed to Seanchan and shook his antlers at the others.

"Are you the one sent to guide us?" Seanchan asked.

The deer bowed but said nothing and turned and waited patiently for the Seekers to mount their horses. He pawed the grass impatiently, then walked off toward the wall of trees that surrounded the glade.

He was almost to the edge of the glade when the trees parted, leave the Seekers ample room to ride without danger of being snagged by brambles or briars or having a branch from an oak or aspen slap them across their faces.

"How far to the end of the forest?" Cumac asked.

Seanchan shrugged. "I do not know. I just know that we have a ways to go, and I hope we will be out of the forest before nightfall. Even with our guide, these woods are not safe unless Reaggus is with us."

The stag glanced back at Seanchan and shook his head. Then he increased the pace.

They passed through stands of trees black and barren. Brittle grass snapped and appeared in tiny clouds around the hooves of the horses. Ravens cawed and eyed the group with suspicion. Dead vines clung to piles of rocks and boulders, and black squirrels scampered across their path. Branches of bramble and chokecherry bushes snapped like dried twigs.

For hours and hours they crossed the wasteland until dark fell so black that they saw the person in front only by motion. And still the white deer led them forward, a wondrous glow appearing around him that gave them comfort. Strange night sounds spoke from the sides of their path, and unconsciously they huddled closer and closer together.

Bern stirred uncomfortably and fingered his sword nervously, wondering if it would be best to draw it from its sheath and ride with it across the pommel, keeping it ready for anything that might fall upon them. But, he decided, if he did so, the others, especially Lorgas, might make jokes about his fear.

The moon appeared, edged in black, and within the crescent of the moon shone Sirius, the Dog Star, burning brightly. Clouds laced through with purple passed in front of the moon, and although they heard the sounds of running water, they could not see it.

At last, they came to the edge of Morphia, and the white deer halted and nodded at the wide expanse of plain lying before them.

"I take it that our path lies ahead of us?" Seanchan asked.

Again, the white deer nodded.

"Well, we do thank you for bringing us here. We would have bungled our way through Morphia without your help."

The white deer nodded again and, turning, disappeared back into the trees.

The others drew deep breaths and looked at each other as the tension slipped away from their bodies.

"I have never seen that," Bern said. "Of course, there are a lot of things on this trip that I haven't seen before, but that was one of the strangest."

"Not counting Reaggus," Lorgas said.

Bern nodded. "Not counting Reaggus."

"I suggest that we look for a place to camp until night, when we will travel across the plain. Keep a sharp eye out. We are looking for a gully or at least a fold in the land which will keep our fire from being seen—although," Seanchan said, "I think it would be best if we did without a fire at all as we cross this plain."

"How far?" Cumac asked.

Seanchan wrinkled his forehead. "I'm not certain. It all depends where we are, exactly. Fedelm?"

"About five days," she said. "And we do not travel straight west for the entire distance. We will come upon a large river and a marsh that we will have to cross, and once we do that, we must bear northwest. We will see Cruachan Ai long before we arrive. But," she emphasized, shaking her finger, "we will also be seen a long time before we arrive."

"Then," Seanchan said, "I suggest we move away from here and rest a bit until night falls. Which," he added, eyeing the sky critically, "is not far off, I believe."

Silently, the Seekers moved out onto the plain, traveling slowly, keeping a wary eye on the horizon and on the land around them, for they were not familiar with this part of the Plain of Cruachan, and any hollow or fold in the ground might conceal the enemy. The plain was deceptive and not the flat tabletop it appeared—this, they knew.

They had not traveled far when they found a hollow cut by wind and rain and rode into it gratefully, unsaddled their horses, and rubbed them down with handfuls of grass. They rolled into their cloaks for a brief nap before arising in the dark at moonrise to begin crossing the plain.

34

For three nights they made their way across the plains made silver by the moon, and so peaceful was the riding that they began to relax and breathe easier. Yet they still kept the discipline of travel, foregoing fire and resting during the day. Even Seanchan seemed to be a bit more at ease, as they saw nothing on the plain except birds that flew away at their approach and a rabbit or two that scampered away. One time, in the distance, they saw a wolf paralleling their course, but he was gone when they pulled up for morning. They kept looking for the path, but it did not appear, and Tarin wondered aloud if maybe they had missed it in the dark, but Seanchan put his worry at ease by telling him that the path was actually a road hammered solid by the passing of many chariot wheels.

Tarin rode out a ways from them, making a wide circle around the group as they traveled, watching carefully for a sign that the enemy had crossed in front of them, but found nothing. Not even the sign of large game.

Near morning of the fourth day, they found a gully surrounded on three sides by a heavy thicket and gratefully made a dry camp. As false light appeared in the east and they started to relax fully, large screams rent the morning air.

"*Maliman! Maliman!*" and great howls from the throats of warggads brought chills to the blood of the Seekers.

Tarin was the first to recover from the surprise, leaping to guard the opening through the thicket with his great sword that stabbed and slashed as quickly as an adder's tongue. The blade of the sword shone and emitted a strange moan as Tarin stubbornly refused to give ground.

Then Lorgas was beside him, his ax cutting through heads mercilessly, causing the warggads to howl even more as they pressed closer to the attack. Arrow after arrow sped through the air to lodge in the eyes of the beasts, felling them, while Cumac and Bern stood ready to fight those who managed to slip past Tarin and Lorgas.

One such creature came baying between the two defenders and leaped toward Cumac. Caladbolg sang and a rainbow arched through the air to cut off the head of the warggad, who fell to the ground, writhing, then lay still. Bern took another head while Seanchan's fire caught others, searing them to black ash.

"Cairnfire!" Cumac shouted.

"Too close!" Seanchan shouted back.

"Maliman! Maliman!" bellowed the warggad battle cry, and the front line pressed forward, try to dislodge Tarin and Lorgas from the opening. The line could not make their way through the pair,

but more and more individuals were managing to slip through the sword and ax to press upon those in the clearing.

With a shriek that made the warggad blood cold, Black came forward, nose breathing fire, his eyes a furious red as his hooves trampled one warggad after another. He rose on his hind legs, his forelegs flashing swiftly, and the warggads tried desperately to get out of Black's way. But they could not, and Black's hooves hit heavily, stomping to a pulp those warggads who had the misfortune to come into range of his hooves.

And then the sun came over the horizon, touching the clearing with light, and the warggads gave a last angry howl and disappeared.

The defenders leaned on their weapons, panting heavily. Seanchan looked at Tarin's sword and said, "Most astounding. Warggads cannot be slain by any weapon made by man unless an arrow is sent through an eye. I can understand Lorgas's ax and the blades of Bern and Cumac, as they were forged in the furnaces of Goibniu and not in the forges of man. But your sword is not."

Tarin shook his head as he pulled a clump of grass free to carefully clean the blade.

"I do not know where the sword came from, although my grandfather and father told how this sword was made by the Old Ones from fiery steel that fell from the sky when they still walked Earthworld. Hence, the runes upon the blade. Of course, that is a nice story, but," he shrugged, "it is only a story."

"I don't know," Seanchan said doubtfully, taking the sword from Tarin's hand. He studied the runes as he had before. He shook his head and handed the sword back to Tarin.

"There is old magic there and of the kind that no one can read or understand. Perhaps in the Duirgeal library, deep underground where the old texts and scrolls are kept. But it is good to know that our weapons are such that we have no weaknesses with them. Well now!" he said, changing the subject. "We are in a fine fettle! Maliman has discovered that we are on the Plain of Cruachan, and we are two days ride from Cruachan Ai. The warggads will be back, and this time, I believe they will come in the night, when the Deagduls and the Nightshadows can accompany them."

"I do not want to go down into the Forest of Turgain," Tarin said firmly. "I would rather take my chances here on the plain. We may not find another defensible place like this, but I would still rather travel across the plain."

"The sun is up now," Fedelm said. "We might as well travel during the day: Maliman's minions have found us, and we can better see them coming far better now than we can at night. And it's possible our attackers will think that we will travel in daylight, as we haven't so far. Besides, we can go much faster. And, I think within a day and a night of riding, we should be in sight of Cruachan Ai." I do not think Maliman's strength has yet grown strong enough to attack a city the size of Cruachan Ai. Do you, Seanchan?"

The wizard shook his head and chewed on the ends of his mustache. "No, I don't think so either. But traveling like that will tire us immensely, and we would be fair game for those who search for us."

"The Forest of Turgain is out as far as I'm concerned," Tarin said firmly. Bern nodded in agreement. "I vote we follow Fedelm's advice. Our horses are fairly rested, and I do not think that the warggads or others will believe that we will press on after this attack. I do think, however, that if we don't leave this place, we will be attacked in the gloaming. And like you said, Seanchan, we are weary from the last battle, and I suspect we will still be tired in the evening, even if we rest now."

"We do have nothing to lose," Cumac said. "Either way, we have a good chance of being set upon again. But we may, as Fedelm says, get close enough to Cruachan Ai that we would fall under her protection." He looked at the others and shook his head. "Either way, it is a gamble. But I'd rather take this one than go through that forest, given what you have had to say about it."

"Then resaddle your horses," Seanchan said, "and let us be off. And perhaps this time, Lorgas, we will have some luck."

"I doubt it," Lorgas grumbled. "We haven't had much of that since leaving home. And I don't see it getting any better soon!"

"Then," Cumac said, "let us not waste time. I would put this behind us as swiftly as possible. If we are fortunate, we should get to Maeve's stronghold without being forced to swing south toward the Forest of Turgain."

"Ride, ride, ride," sighed Lorgas going toward his horse. "My rump is getting sores upon sores."

"But," Bern said, following him, "at least you have your head."

"It is not only the land that we must watch but the sky as well," Seanchan said, ignoring the elves. "And watch for birds flying by the dozens. They are more than likely in Maliman's grip, as well as other beasts. The birds are his eyes."

DETERMINEDLY, the Seekers set off, riding through the morning and afternoon without pause. When night fell, Tarin suggested that they detour a few miles toward the north under cover of darkness to confuse any of Maliman's creatures from following the path that they had made during daylight.

The others agreed and quietly, they rode north until Sirius appeared, then turned once again to the west, raising their tired horses into a lope. Tarin lagged behind, dragging a heavy willow to wipe out marks of their traveling.

The night passed uneventfully, and by mid-morning, they could see the fabled city of Cruachan Ai gleaming whitely, high on a steep hill that fell away on three sides into cliffs. The plain was flat here, providing no hiding place for enemies.

Tiredly, the Seekers made their way slowly across the plain. When they were halfway across, a horn sounded, and the huge gates, sheathed in bronze that glittered brightly in the sun and almost blinded them, opened, sending a party of horsemen and another of chariots riding out to meet them.

Seanchan held up his hand quickly and said to the others, "Keep your hands away from your weapons lest the Connacht men believe we come as unfriendly ones."

"There are only six of us," Tarin muttered. "No one should believe that we come on a mission of war."

"Nevertheless," Seanchan said sternly, "follow my lead."

He reined in his horse and sat calmly, waiting. The others surrounded him as the Connacht chariots ringed them, creating a protective wall for the approaching horsemen. After a moment, a horseman, dressed in black armor, his black cape outlined with three threads of red, rode between the chariots and halted in front of the party.

"I am Maine Daire, son of Maeve. Who are you who come to Cruachan Ai? Speak! And speak quickly!" he said. His lips were drawn thin and his blue eyes were flint-hard. His long blond hair flowed over his shoulders.

"Not a very friendly sort, is he?" Tarin murmured to the others.

"I am Seanchan Duirgeal. And this is Fedelm of Rath Cruachan; Bern of the Ervalians; Lorgas of the Ashelves; Cumac, the son of Cucullen; and Tarin. We come to seek hospitality from Maeve and Cruachan Ai. Our business is our own and for Maeve's ears alone."

Daire looked closely at Cumac and said, "I did not know the Hound of Ulster had a son. Other than the one he slew by mistake."

"I am from the Otherworld," Cumac said, steadily eyeing Daire. "My mother is Fand, wife of Manannan Mac Lir. I am a grandson of Lugh Longarm."

"The Otherworld," Daire said slowly. He glanced at Bern and Lorgas. "Elves from the Otherworld? And I know you, Fedelm."

"And you should, Daire," Fedelm said. "And yes, these are elves from the Otherworld. As Seanchan has told you, unless you have too much wax in your ears. Now, take us to Maeve or suffer the consequences for ill manners!"

A sneer slid across Daire's face. "You need to have a lesson in manners yourself."

Instantly, Cumac's sword sang from its sheath and the point lodged at Daire's neck.

"And who are you to teach manners to a woman of the Sidhe? It is not for you to break the Laws of Hospitality," Cumac said, pressing gently with Caladbolg. "That is for your mistress. Now take us before her and quickly, or your head will roll in the dust!"

Instantly, there was the sound of weapons being drawn from the

Connacht men. But Daire's face grew whiter and whiter as Cumac continued the pressure on his throat.

"Hold!" Daire commanded. But the command lost a little of its force as his voice climbed higher than before. "He will kill me."

"You are not as dumb as you look, Daire," Cumac said softly. "Now tell the others to put up their weapons."

"Do it!" Daire ordered.

Weapons were lowered, although hostile looks were turned upon the Seekers. A soft glow began to shimmer around the Seekers as Cumac withdrew his sword. Daire looked as if he would like nothing better than to slice his way through the party, but when he put his hand out, it met the glow, and blue sparks snapped from it, stinging him.

He drew back with an oath and looked at the palm of his hand, where a blister the size of a walnut was beginning to form.

"Now," Seanchan said calmly, "let us go meet your queen."

Reluctantly, the Connacht men drew back from the Seekers, opening a path through the chariot wall. Daire rode in front of the Seekers and led them across the plain and through the gates. Seanchan released the soft glow as they entered the city.

Tarin looked with wonder at the size of the bronze gates and the huge walls surrounding Cruachan Ai.

"A chariot could be driven around the ramparts," he breathed. "And that gate will never be breached with fire or ram. This is a formidable place."

"It is," Fedelm said. "The defenses have never been breached, although many have tried. Even sieges have been defeated here."

They halted before a ramp leading up to a large hall that overshadowed the rest of the city. Daire gestured for them to dismount and follow him up the ramp.

A stableman reached for Black's reins and almost lost his hand as the warhorse snapped at him. Cumac smiled.

"I would not handle Black," he said. "Tell him where you wish him to go, and perhaps he will. Or perhaps he will not. He is the Black of Saingliau."

The stableman's eyes opened wide in disbelief as he stared at Black.

"The Black of Saingliau," he breathed. "This is an honor. I have heard much about this horse."

Black arched his neck and preened at the stableman's comments. Cumac laughed.

"You seem to have made a friend," he said. "But still, ask him to go. Do not try to command him."

"As I live and breathe," the stableman said. He bowed his head before Black and said, "Will you honor me by coming to the stable?"

Black tossed his head and nudged the stableman, causing the poor fellow to stumble.

Cumac hid a smile and turned to follow the others inside the Great Hall.

Torches burned cheerfully from the walls and the wooden floor beneath their feet shone glassily. Heads were mounted along the top of the wall, and long tables stood at either side, leading up to the elevated throne where Maeve sat next to Ailill.

Tarin gasped at Maeve's beauty. She had red-gold hair that spilled over the arms of her chair. Her face was free of wrinkles, with red eyebrows that arched over azure-blue eyes. A dimple appeared in each cheek. Her teeth were like white pearls and her lips were full and sensuous, inviting a man to drink deeply of their wine.

Beside her, Ailill sprawled in his seat. He was clad all in black to match his hair and eyes. His face was thin and chalk-white, his lips red and thin and pulled down in a petulant pout.

Then, the Seekers froze as they saw the man sitting at the bottom of the three steps leading up to the thrones of Maeve and Ailill.

Bricriu.

35

Cumac hissed and started forward, only to be pulled back by Seanchan.

"Do not be a fool!" Seanchan said sharply, softly. "He is under the protection of Ailill and Maeve. You attack him now and your life will be forfeit. As will all of ours." He turned toward Ailill and Maeve and said, "Hail, king and queen of Cruachan Ai. We come begging your protection and care."

"Granted," Maeve said, waving her hand grandly. "But why do you enter the land of Connacht?"

Bricriu grinned maliciously at them.

"Who is that man?" Tarin asked quietly, nodding toward Bricriu.

"That is the one we seek," Fedelm said. "He is Bricriu."

"Let us do our business and be off!" Lorgas said.

"No," Fedelm said. "We must not. Yet."

"We seek the one who sits at your feet," Seanchan said, using his staff to indicate Bricriu.

"And why, may I ask, is that?" Maeve asked, her lips trembling in a smile.

"He is a thief and a blackguard!" Seanchan said loudly. "He has stolen the Bladhm Caillis, the Chalice of Fire, given by your own hands to Cucullen, the Hound of Ulster, to recognize the greatest hero of the Red Branch. As a gift, once given, cannot be taken back unless given by the owner, we claim the right of the Red Branch to the Chalice."

"Hmm. A most perplexing state," Maeve said. She looked at Bricriu. "And what say you, Bricriu?"

"I claim the Laws of Hospitality for myself and all goods in my possession," Bricriu said.

Maeve turned her attention back to the Seekers and shrugged and spread her hands. "As you can see, there is nothing that I can do to aid you. He is as much under my protection as are you while you all remain in Cruachan Ai. But I see that you are weary with travel and would undoubtedly like to bathe while your clothes are cleaned—or," she added, eyeing them critically, "replaced. I will have fresh tunics and pants brought to your chambers along with food. Later, tonight, we shall visit once again about your quest that brings you to Cruachan Ai."

She clapped her hands, and servants appeared to lead the Seekers away.

Reluctantly, they followed the servants through the winding halls of the Great Hall and to their chambers. The servants opened the doors and waited for them to enter.

"We should rest," Seanchan said to the others. "Maeve will do nothing until this evening, and by that time we will be ready to present our case in more depth."

"What can we possibly do?" Cumac asked. "As long as Bricriu is here, he is under protection."

"There are ways," Seanchan said, but he refused to comment further as he turned and entered his chamber.

"Ah, me," sighed Tarin. "Well, at least we can relax for a change."

"Yes," Fedelm said, "but Maeve is wily, and Ailill is no fool either. Do not let your guard fall too far. Remember that Connacht is a bitter enemy of Ulster."

"Nothing," Lorgas said mournfully, "comes easy anymore."

And with that, all entered their rooms and gave themselves up to a welcome hot bath and light fare before tumbling tiredly into their beds as the servants pulled curtains closed and quietly left with the Seekers' clothes.

EVENTIDE was upon them when the Seekers awoke to find fresh clothes laid out for them in the patterns of those clothes which they had worn. They dressed and, leaving their weapons behind at Seanchan's order, were taken through the maze of hallways until once again they arrived in the Great Hall where torches burned so merrily that the light seemed almost the light of day.

The tables had been set with a great banquet in their honor. Heaping salvers of meat and breads made from many grains and fresh apples and other fruits stretched the length of the tables. Pitchers made from green marble and foaming with the fabled honeyed wine and ale of Cruachan Ai stood within three feet of each other down the middle of the tables. Plates and goblets matching the pitchers were set four feet apart.

The greatest heroes of Connacht sat on benches according to their rank from the doorway up to the three stairs that led to the thrones of Ailill and Maeve. A separate table had been placed crosswise in the center for Ailill and Maeve and the six Seekers, three on each side of the royal pair.

Bricriu sat with the Connacht champions at the table to the left of Maeve and glowered at the six Seekers as they entered the hall. In front of him stood the Bladhm Caillis, the Chalice of Fire, shining brightly with a golden glow surrounding it. He smiled evilly at the Seekers as they paused, looking at the Chalice, their faces suddenly grim.

"Ah!" said Maeve. "Our honored guests have arrived. Welcome to the Great Hall of Cruachan Ai and to the feast that has been made for you! It has been a long time since such heroes have been honored in this hall. The last were Conall Cernach, Leogaire Búadbach, and the greatest of the Red Branch warriors, Cucullen, the Hound of Ulster! Then, we feasted greatly, and now, equally as greatly for the Hound's son, Cumac!"

The Connacht heroes banged their hands upon the table in welcome as the Seekers walked slowly between the two rows of tables and halted in front of Maeve.

"Greetings, Maeve!" Seanchan said. "We are grateful for your hospitality as seen by such a great feast. Seldom have I seen such a wonderful display of welcome! Not even at the Red Branch, or," he said, a slight grim smile upon his face, "at that feast which was given by one for mischief-making!"

Bricriu blushed furiously and leaped to his feet, outraged, but Maeve caught his words before he could speak them.

"You will sit down, Bricriu, or lose the gift of hospitality which has been extended to you!" she said sharply. "I do not tolerate ill will at my table! Especially from my guests!"

Chastened, Bricriu sat, glaring sullenly at Seanchan, daggers leaping from his eyes.

"You speak well, Seanchan Duirgeal. And I am quite pleased with your compliments. Would you and your company join us?"

"We are greatly honored," Seanchan said.

He crossed in front of the table to the dais and took the chair to the right of Maeve. Cumac sat beside him and Fedelm beside Cumac. Tarin, Lorgas, and Bern sat right of Ailill. Maeve rose and stood regally, facing the Great Hall.

"Now, we are all here! Let the feast begin!"

Hidden harpists began playing, accompanied by soft flutes. A seanachie, a teller of tales, took his place at the foot of Maeve's table and began a story.

Hear, now, the dream of great Connor,
Cathbad's son, the most fair and great,
Who returned safely from his great foray,
And rules again Ulster's state.

One night when Connor lay in Emain
With deep sleep enfolding his frame,
A woman approached the sleeping man
And slipped quietly into his dream.

Her robe was red and sewn in gold
And the rest of her garments were fair
And a golden crown was shining bold
Upon her silken and braided hair.

Then the noble woman said to him,
"Connor! To you I will sing
"A song of luck and valor without sin
"For the noblest and greatest king."

"So tell me what the future holds,"
Spoke the royal Nessa's son.
"When shall the battle bold
"Be fought by me and won?"

"Seven years from this day
"Your ranks will number boys and wives
"And glory shall sweep them low, I say,
"As for the great Brown Bull they strive."

"But who will come to drive the Bull
"From Cooley? Who dares begin the war?"
"Ailill in Connacht will make his armies full
"With men from all Ireland near and far."

"No, this I do not believe," said Connor,
"For an evil path you have foretold

"That must be fought without honor.
"Who will dare to be so bold?"

"Do not fear a lie from me. Already
"Fate has set in motion the days
"As Ailill's son comes forth boldly,
"The one the bards all praise.

"Gerg's daughter Ferb waits for him.
"For the two a wedding is planned.
"A hundred fifty men come with him
"To guard against treacherous plans.

"Nine hours from noon to night
"The wedding feast will be
"In Glenn Geirg will be the fight.
"This, Connor, you'll see!"

"Now, if we wisely plan the raid
"How many men should I take?"
"Fomorians, an army of a hundred
"Fifty is the army you should make."

"Connor, you have been great in war
"And victory shall follow you again.
"But you must not miss this war,
"Or your name will bear a stain."

Then, Connor awoke and swiftly rose
And awakened his queen Mugain,
And told her the tale of woes
That in his dreams he had seen.

Then spoke the gracious Mugain,
The sagacious wife of Connor,

"This is much to trust. Again,
"You must consult Cathbad, Connor."

Connor listened to wise advice
Although he wished for battle's roar,
"Connacht brings to us the strife
"By coming to great Ulster's door."

The queen said, "Since fate wills this
"And you cannot without dishonor stay
"Away despite my slumbrous kiss,
"I wish you safe return from your foray."

Then Connor took the Fomorians
In numbers the queen foretold,
And marched to great Rath Ini,
The place of Gerg's abode.

The castle was dressed in splendor
When Connor's great band
Arrived. Quietly they made to enter
The castle, but there Gerg made his stand.

A hundred fifty warriors waited
When Connor approached alone
While outside his army awaited
His command like pillars of stone.

To the Great Hall gates went Connor
With his great warrior's stride,
And watching his approach was Mani More
Along with Ferb who would be his bride.

Then the Druid who upon Gerg attended
Cried out his fear, "This I see!

"That in that beaker to me extended
"Is the broth of battle to be!"

Then, great Brod, the charioteer,
Hurled his mighty spear that day
And through Gerg passed that spear
And so began the great foray!

Through the feasting house Connor
Led his mighty warrior band,
And a hundred forty men were slaughtered
And from Mani was struck his head.

Behind him, in that house, he left
All the troops who fell in battle
With the exception of Brod the Deft
Who also escaped death's rattle.

Then to the west the fairy woman flew
To bring Maeve the battle news.
"Listen to me," she said. "Only a few
"Have escaped Connor's crew!

"Your son has been slain by Connor
"In this hour when he was to take a bride.
"Now you must march with honor!
"Gather your men to make your ride!"

From the west came Maeve to battle
With seven hundred men in her ranks.
Like a great stampede of cattle
Came Connor with his battle ranks.

Upon the plains of Ulster Maeve slew
Many with her warrior's might

And Connor's two sons fell upon the dew
Along with seven heroes in that fight.

Yet, Maeve's army was driven back
And away to Cruachan Ai she fled
And left behind in her track
A hundred forty warriors bled.

Then proudly marched the Ulstermen
To the ancient home of Gerg,
And swarmed the walls to plunder
And capture Gerg's daughter Ferb.

A bloody battle then was waged
With Gerg's men stoutly resisting
The triumphant Ulstermen's rage
But without glory they were subsisting.

Many noble men were killed
And the castle defenders died
And the cries of Ferb were stilled
As thirty fell at Fergus's side.

Thirty more heroes in battle fell
With Muredach their death they found,
Falbe, thirty more, as with Donnell
And thirty more with Fland.

Cobthach thirty, and Cond led thirty,
Corpre thirty, and Dubhtach thirty,
Ross led thirty and Angus thirty,
All died in bands of thirty.

One cannot speak of their valor
For in that there is no truth.

They were among the weak in valor
And to Ulster's swords they came to rue.

Loudly rose their cries of terror
And pleadings came in vain
For the warriors led by Connor
Fell upon them and they were slain.

This battle was to be a prelude
To the great cattle raid of Cooley,
Mani was slain in a manner crude
To set the stage for another story.

Mighty deeds have been unfolded
With the Vision that terrified
Gerg's people. This story's told,
Now, and its truth verified.

Home came Connor with banners flying
From victories gained on the battlefield.
Connor's glory will remain undying.
This the Vision has revealed.

The seanachie fell silent and silence filled the hall. At last, Seanchan rose and said, "We thank you for giving us a story about one of the glories of the Red Branch." He turned to Maeve. "And we are most honored, gracious queen, by your allowing this tale to be told in this hall. But tell me: why *did* you allow such a tale to be told instead of one concerning Connacht's triumphs?"

Maeve smiled, lights dancing in her eyes, and said, "We cannot always avoid the truth, Seanchan. There have been many Ulster losses, but I doubt if Connor would allow those stories to be told in his Great Hall. Here, in Cruachan Ai, we have no need to avoid the truth, for the truth is as great a weapon as the Caladbolg Cumac carries. And this story reminds all here of what we must do the next time to win. It is a story that is taught to our boy-warriors to instill within them the wisdom that they need to make certain such a history does not repeat itself to the defeat of the Connacht army. Look around you."

Obediently, Seanchan turned and saw the disgruntled faces of the warriors at the table. Some were speaking angrily to each other. He turned back to Maeve.

"This is great wisdom, and I daresay that when the Connacht warriors are once again loosed upon the world they will win great honor."

Maeve smiled, pleased with Seanchan's answer, then said, "But that is *all* that will be said or sung of Ulster's glory in this hall! Whatever else is provided will be of Connacht's glory. And, if you recall, we have had some. The great cattle raid of Cooley, a story of Cucullen's glory, was not a victory for Ulster despite the heroics of its great warriors, but a victory for Connacht, as we took the great bull back into our lands."

"Yes, that is true," Seanchan said. "But let us hear a tale now of Connacht while we eat."

"Very well," Maeve said. She nodded at the seanachie and said, "Give us a tale and not a song. For songs ease the mind and are good for digestion, a tale is such that relaxes the mood."

The seanachie nodded and thought a moment, then began:

"Now, Flidais was the wife of Ailill Finn, whose name means "the fair-haired," who ruled in Kerry. Although she remained faithful to Ailill, she came to love Fergus Mac Roich after she heard the tales spun by the bards who visited Ailill's court. She began to send secret messages to him by people she trusted at the end of each week, declaring her love for him.

"When it came about that Fergus fled from Ulster and made his way to Connacht, he brought the matter of Flidais to Ailill, for he was much perplexed about what he should do since he was now a refuge in the very land that he used to raid.

" 'What should I do so that I do not heap dishonor upon you and betray your hospitality? Not long ago, I was laying bare your lands and stealing your cattle and women,' Fergus said.

" 'Hmm,' Ailill pondered, laying his chin upon the heel of his hand. 'Yes, this is a matter of great importance. Let us consider the matter with Maeve and listen to her counsel.'

"Together, they went to see the red-haired beauty of Connacht, seeking her advice in this matter of great import. After Maeve heard the entire story of how Flidais was in love with Fergus and had been pursuing him with messengers for quite some time, she said, 'I suggest that one of us go to Ailill Finn and see if the Laws of Hospitality provide us with sound advice.'

"She turned to Fergus, grinning wickedly. 'And, I see no reason why you yourself shouldn't be the one to go to him. After all, it is your reputation with your mighty sword that has caused her heart to swoon.'

" 'You've the tongue of a shrew,' Fergus growled, but he noticed how Maeve's eyes always had hungry fires behind them when they fell upon him. 'But this is good advice from a beautiful and dangerous queen.'

"And so it was that Fergus left Cruachan Ai with thirty men, including himself and Fergus Mac Oen-lama and Dubhtach. They traveled lightly and were soon at the Ford of Fenna in the north of Kerry. From there, they sent word to Ailill Finn that they wished to have an audience with him. The request was returned promptly to them and they were brought before the king.

" 'What is it that I can do for you?' asked Ailill Finn. But they noticed a dangerous sheen in his eyes that suggested he had it good in store what they wanted with him.

" 'Well, now,' Fergus said, pulling vigorously at his ear with heavy thumb and blunt knuckle, 'we thought we might be staying a while with you, given that we've had a bit of a quarrel with Ailill, the son of Magach.'

" 'If it had been any of your people save yourself making that request, it would be granted,' Ailill said. 'But you will not stay here, as I will not put the man my wife loves under my roof. Do you take me for a fool? If a man invites a fox into his bed, sure it is that he will get bit at one time during the night.'

"Miffed, Fergus glared murderously at him and said, 'Well, then, if you are so lax with hospitality, then we require a gift of cows from you. There's a great need that lies upon us for food and drink. There are many others who have gone into exile with me, and they must be fed.'

"Ailill shook his head, refusing Fergus's request with pleasure. 'There's no present coming from me for the likes of you,' he said. 'I have already explained that you will not be remaining in my house for a visit. If I gave you the gift that you want, people will say I did it out of fear that I might lose my wife to you and bribed you to go away. But'—he held up his hand, to stop an angry retort from Fergus—'I will give your company an ox and bacon to satisfy their hunger and beer to satisfy their thirst. If that is good enough for your pleasure,' he added sarcastically.

"Fergus's eyes burned like overheated furnaces. 'I will not eat a single bite of bread you have offered, as there's no honor in your gift but the back of your hand.'

" 'Then get out of my house! All of you!' fumed Ailill.

" 'As you say, and welcome to what will happen when we leave,' Fergus said. 'We won't lay siege to your house, but there will come a reckoning.'

"With that, he turned on his heel and stormed from the house of Ailill with his troops in tow.

"Once outside, Fergus directed his men to stand aside while he drew his sword and planted his feet defiantly like two sturdy oaks in the earth.

" 'Now!' he bellowed toward the castle. 'Let a man, the best of you, come and fight with me beside the ford at the gate of this place of dishonor!'

"Ailill stood above the gate to his home, staring hotly down at Fergus.

" 'I will not send another in my place to save my honor,' Ailill said. 'Instead, I shall come down myself and do battle with you. Or, if you wish, another of your choosing!'

"With that, Ailill donned his armor and went down to meet with Fergus.

"When he saw Ailill approaching him, Fergus laughed and

turned to Dubhtach and said, 'Well, which of us will go and meet this angry cock?'

" 'I'll go,' Dubhtach said. 'I'm younger and a bit sharper than you right now.'

"With that, Dubhtach gathered his spear, and went against Ailill. With his first thrust, he sent his spear through both of Ailill's thighs.

"Gasping with pain, Ailill unleashed a javelin that pierced so deeply that the head came out the other side of Dubhtach.

"Dubthach's shield clattered on the ground, and Fergus, seeing his helplessness, threw his own shield over Dubhtach. Ailill again struck, thrusting his spear at the shield of Fergus so fiercely that he drove the shaft clean through it.

"At that, Fergus Mac Oen-lama ran forward and held his own shield over Fergus Mac Roich. Again, Ailill struck at the shield and drove his spear through it. Then, he leaped high and lay on top of his comrades.

"When she saw the fury of her husband in his attack upon Fergus and his friends, Flidais ran from the castle and threw her cloak over the three of them.

"Under the cloak of secrecy, Fergus and his men flew from Ailill's wrath. But Ailill was not finished with them as yet and pursued them, slaying those he could catch. Twenty fell by his blade and only seven managed to escape to Cruachan Ai and tell the whole of the story to Ailill and Maeve.

"The behavior of Ailill the Fair-Haired infuriated Ailill and Maeve, and they rose, calling the nobles of Connacht to their side along with the exiles from Ulster. Together, the army marched into Kerry as far as the Ford of Fenna.

"Meanwhile, Flidais was caring for the wounded men in the castle, using her skills to quickly promote healing.

"The Connacht force then came to the castle, and Ailill Finn was summoned to Ailill Mac Mata in order that Fergus and Ailill the Fair-Haired might hold conference on neutral ground outside the castle. But Ailill Finn refused to go, saying, 'I will not sit or stand in conference with a man who has such a great pride and arrogance about him.'

"It was, however, a peaceful meeting that Ailill Mac Mata sought, in order to save Fergus and keep Ailill Finn from warring with Connacht. He did this in order to appease the nobles who had followed him to Kerry.

"The wounded men were then brought on wheelbarrows from the castle that the Connacht people might care for their own.

"With that further breach of hospitality, Ailill ordered his men to attack the castle. For a full week, the Connacht forces stormed the castle, yet each time, they were beaten back and one hundred forty warriors fell in their attempt to breach the castle walls.

" 'This was not a good idea of yours,' panted Bricriu to Ailill Mac Mata. 'I don't think taking this castle is one of the best you've had.'

" 'That is one of the truest things an Ulsterman has spoken,' Ailill said. 'You have a keen grasp of the obvious. Yet, I would like to point out that this does not speak well for the Ulstermen as well, as three of their heroes lie wounded by the same warrior's hand and they have yet to take revenge for that! And where are these heroes of yours? Lying under wisps of straw, moaning about their cuts and bruises. That is scornful, that one man should wound those three.'

"When he heard this, Bricriu shook his head and said, 'Woe! Oh, woe! That such a man as Papa Fergus has been laid low by one lowly man!'

"When they heard the poisonous words of Bricriu, the men rose naked from their beds, shaking in their rage. Seizing their swords, they hacked their way through the armies until they forced the outer gateway and ran into the middle of the castle with the Connacht men close on their heels. They stormed the castle and such was the rage of Fergus and his men that a wild and pitiless battle was waged with no thoughts to taking prisoners, only heads.

"Then, they wearied of battle and the defenders of the castle were overthrown. The Ulstermen alone slew seven hundred warriors in the castle, including Ailill Finn and thirty of his sons. Amalgaid the Good fell, as well as Núado and Fiacho Muinmethan (the Broad-Backed) and Corpre Cromm (the Crooked One) and Ailill Brefne and the three Oengus Bodgnai and the three Eochaid of Irross and the seven Breslene from Ai along with the fifty Domnall.

"Those of the Gamanrad with Ailill and each of the men of Domnan who had come to his aid assembled in the castle, for he knew that the Ulster exiles and Ailill and Maeve would use their army to demand the surrender of Fergus to them, as Fergus was under their protection.

"The Gamanrad were the third race of heroes in Ireland, known as the Clan Gamanrad of Irross Donnan. The other two were the Clan Dédad in Temair Lochra, and the Clan Rudraige in Emain Macha. But the other clans were destroyed by the Clan Rudraige.

"But at this time, the Ulstermen rose along with the warriors of Maeve and Ailill to lay waste the castle and take Flidais out with them, along with other women as well into captivity. They also took all the riches they could find: gold and silver, horns and drinking cups, keys, vats, all the garments of various colors, a hundred milch-cows and a hundred forty oxen and thirty hundred head of other cattle.

"After this had been accomplished, Flidais went to Fergus Mac Roich in accordance to the decree of Ailill and Maeve in order that the Connacht men might have food on their raid across Ulster's borders to Cooley. Every seventh day, Flidais would give what her cows produced to the men of Ireland during the cattle raid of Cooley in order that they might live. This, then, became the Herd of Flidais.

"Flidais went with Fergus to his home and later to his new home when he received the lordship of that part of Ulster known as the Plain of Muirthemne which once had been in the hands of the great Ulster warrior Cucullen, who was the son of Sualtam.

"And after a while, Flidais died at the shore of Bali, and by this time, the state of Fergus's household was none the better for that as she once supplied all of the needs and wants of Fergus.

"Sometime later, Fergus died in the land of Connacht, after the death of his wife. He had gone to Connacht to obtain a story to cheer himself and to bring home a grant of cows that had been promised to him by Ailill and Maeve. There, however, he found his death through the jealousy of Ailill, for by this time Maeve had taken to the great and scarred warrior.

"But this is another story entire of itself and is not concerned with the tale of Flidais."

"Well, that is what it is," Seanchan said, placing a thumb beside his nose. "A song and a tale all in one feast, one to the glory of the Red Branch and another to Connacht, is good for easing the rancor that might exist between the two. Especially," he added with a grin, "seeing as how you have us at a disadvantage."

Maeve laughed and lifted her goblet and said, "To the honor of Ulster and Connacht. May peace be with us—and in war, Connacht victory!"

The others raised their goblets, draining them to the dregs, then slammed the goblets back upon the tables with a roar of satisfaction.

Maeve sat and glanced at Ailill, her husband, then back to Seanchan.

"Well, Seanchan, what is more that Cruachan Ai can do for you besides offering you hospitality?"

Seanchan ran a thumb and forefinger along his mustache and said, "A joining of forces. Maliman grows steadily stronger, and together, Ulster and Connacht would provide a more formidable front to him. I know that bad blood does exist between Ulster and Connacht, but these are dangerous times, for Maliman does not share power with any, not even those who aide him. No, it is time for Ulster and Connacht to unite to face this scourge."

"And who," Maeve said, "would lead such a force? Connacht or the Red Branch? Such an army as you have suggested must be led by one person, for one leader is victory, while two are losers. Tell me, friend Seanchan, who would lead us?"

"It cannot be one from Ulster or Connacht," Seanchan said slowly. "For if a leader was chosen from one, the other would resent him. No, it would have to be someone outside the pale."

Fedelm cleared her throat. "Perhaps it should be Scathach Buanand, the Woman of Victory, who lives on the Island of Shadows. She is a warrior-woman who has taught many of the Red Branch heroes as well as Connacht heroes. She has never been defeated in battle."

"What man would allow himself to be ordered by a woman?" Ailill said scornfully, speaking for the first time. "Men must lead men."

Maeve colored with indignation and said, "And you, Ailill, my precious, who do you lead when I am sitting upon this throne? The Connacht men will follow me—and not you—into battle, as they have several times in the past."

"You only lead with our will," Ailill said. "And as for this Scathach Buanand, well, although she is regarded by many to be the best warrior in the world, she is still a woman. She may teach warriors, but not lead them."

Maeve flared and turned back to Seanchan and said, "If the Red Branch will agree to be led by Scathach Buandand, Connacht will follow."

Ailill leaped to his feet and glared at Maeve. "We shall talk about this later in private, where ears will not hear us argue."

"We shall," Maeve said to Ailill's back as he stormed away.

She turned back to Seanchan, her nostrils white and pinched with anger. "Do you think Connor will follow Scathach?"

"I don't know," Seanchan said. "There is little love lost between you and Connor, although at one time you were in love."

"True," Maeve said. "But I will never live with a man who places me lower than himself. Connor did that and more." Her eyes shined brightly with anger. "But that is the past. I have found a man who is not jealous and will allow me to live equally. Now. But, tell me, Seanchan. What else can Connacht do for you?"

Seanchan looked at Bricriu, sitting still pleased with himself after hearing himself worked into the story just finished. He stared mockingly back at Seanchan, daring him to try and claim the Chalice.

"There can be no peace between the Red Branch and Connacht as long as the Bladhm Caillis is not in Ulster's hands. At least, not as long as you allow it to remain in Connacht."

Maeve looked long and hard at Seanchan, then said, "You know the law as well as I. You know that as long as Bricriu remains here, I must extend him the same courtesy I extend to you."

"I know," Seanchan said. "But I also know that Connacht and the

Red Branch must come to terms with each other before a mighty and united army can be formed. That will never happen as long as Bricriu remains here."

"Ah, Seanchan!" Bricriu said with savage glee. "You would have the law one way for you and another for others. But here I am, and here I shall remain, for there is nothing that you can do. Or the Red Branch either."

His words hissed from his lips like water poured over hot coals.

"The question," Seanchan said, "is whether you are *allowed* to remain here. A bear will not tolerate a wolf in his den." He turned to Maeve. "There is one way. If a man wishes to challenge the right of another to the Laws of Hospitality, it may be granted to him *if* he emerges successfully from a task given him by the host. I now claim that right for one of my party to fulfill any task that you give to him."

Maeve frowned. "I don't remember that. Are you certain of this, Seanchan?"

Seanchan drew himself up and looked sternly upon Maeve. "I am Seanchan of the Duirgeals, the oldest order of the Druids and wizards who use our power to benefit man. We serve man only after he serves himself. We trace our order back to the First Age, when we were the servants of the Old Ones. I was taught by Deroi, the mightiest of the Druids and wizards, and from him was made a Brehon, one of the lawgivers to man."

"No offense meant," Maeve said hurriedly. "Yes. Very well. I shall give your chosen one a task to fulfill. If he can."

Bricriu leaped to his feet, face black with anger. His voice shook as he said, "You would give me over to these . . . these . . . defilers of the law? I claim the right of hospitality. I have heard of no law to deny the right of hospitality to a person. Nor did you, Maeve, before Seanchan claimed that one exists. How do we know he is not lying? How do you *know*? He may be playing puppetmaster and pulling your strings!"

"No . . . one . . . controls . . . Maeve," she said through her teeth. "And Seanchan, as a Duirgeal, is sworn to the truth with an oath that is terrible in punishment if broken. Surely *you* know that,

Bricriu Poisontongue. The law was not created alone for you. Nor was the world."

She turned back to Seanchan. "Go! We will meet again tomorrow night, when your chosen one will enter the Cave of Cruachan and face the three lions of Connacht! And that, Bricriu, should give you ease. No one has ever left the cave except Cucullen—and Conall Cernach and Leogaire, who he brought out with him!"

Seanchan bowed to Maeve and said, "Yes, my queen. We shall return tomorrow with our champion alone bearing those arms he will carry with him into the Cave of Cruachan."

"Now," Maeve said, "enough of this needling. Let us enjoy what remains of the feast!"

Bricriu looked as if he would argue the matter, but a sharp look from Maeve made him sit back on his bench in silence. Even an acid tongue like that possessed by Bricriu knew enough to be silent when faced with an angry host.

"AND what are the lions of Connacht, Seanchan?" Tarin asked when the Seekers met in Seanchan's room after the feast.

"They are lions who have killed all those who faced them. Except for your father, Cumac. The last time anyone was sent into the Cave of Cruachan was when Conall, Leogaire, and Cucullen were sent to Maeve by Connor for her to choose which one was the greatest champion of the Red Branch. The lions were the test that she gave them.

"On the night of the test, the three heroes were led to the cave, where a table had been set for them with plenty of food for them to eat. They fell to with relish, but while they were in the middle of the meal, a faint scratching noise came to them. Conall called for quiet, and then growls rumbled from the back of the cave and three huge lions leaped into the room where the heroes sat. Slobber dripped from their long yellow fangs, and their claws, as sharp as a barber's razor, scratched over the floor, leaving huge gouges in the stone. They crouched and began to stalk the heroes.

"Conall and Leogaire leaped for the rafters high overhead while Cucullen took up his arms and shield to face the lions. When one attacked him, he swung hard at the lion's head, but instead of the head falling from the lion's shoulders, his sword rebounded from the lion's neck and struck the stone floor, ringing a high clear note like a golden bell.

"The other lions came to the attack, and Cucullen backed into a corner to keep them from getting behind him and fought to keep them away. They could not be slain with Cucullen's sword, as it had been made by man. Still, it was enough to keep the lions from pressing the attack for the rest of the long night. Early in the morning, however, Cucullen's sword broke, and the lions came forward eagerly while Conall and Leogaire watched from their places high in the rafters. One sprang at Cucullen, but with his fist, he drove the lion back. And then, the cock crowed, bringing forth the day, and the lions disappeared back into the cave from whence they came.

"For that, Cucullen was awarded the Chalice of Fire as first among all champions, while the other two were given lesser chalices."

"Sounds like an impossible task to me," Tarin said. "But I'm ready for it."

Seanchan shook his head. "No, the task is not for you, Tarin, as willing as you are to undertake it. The task must be taken by Cumac with his sword Caladbolg. Caladbolg was not created by man but forged by Goibniu, the smith of the Pantheon. With that, Cumac may have a chance. Indeed," he continued, his bushy eyebrows moving like white worms on his forehead, "I think that he will not have as great a task as seems to lie before him. And once you have bested the lions, Cumac, you are free to make any demand of Maeve that you wish."

"And that will be Bricriu," Cumac said.

"No," Seanchan said. "Not Bricriu, but the Chalice. The Chalice does not come under the Laws of Hospitality. Now that it is once again in Cruachan Ai, it is once again within the order of Maeve, although she may not reclaim it. She can, however, demand that

Bricriu surrender it to Cumac. Then, perhaps, Connacht and the Red Branch may unite against Maliman and his forces."

"Then let us hope that you are successful tomorrow, Cumac," Lorgas said feelingly.

"Yes. Let us hope that," Cumac said.

36

Word had apparently gone around Cruachan Ai that one of the guests recently arrived was going to enter the Cave of Cruachan that night. When the Seekers arrived in the Great Hall, it was bursting with people.

"It looks like they are waiting for some tragedy," Cumac whispered to Seanchan.

"That is the way of humans," Seanchan said. "They all want to watch something bad happen to someone. They will even postpone a journey to see such a thing. That is their nature."

The Seekers strode up to the dais, where Maeve and Ailill sat. Seanchan stepped forward and knocked his staff against the floor for order.

"My queen," he began. "We have held counsel and have agreed upon the member of our party who will enter the Cave of Cruachan tonight."

"I don't see Bricriu," Lorgas whispered to Bern.

"Nor do I," Bern whispered back. "You would think he would be here. It is his presence that is being decided upon."

"And who is this brave one?" Maeve asked.

"Cumac, the son of Cucullen, who was the last to enter the Cave of Cruachan and return."

Maeve's eyebrows rose as she considered Cumac standing before her.

"Hmm. But is the son like the father?" she asked. "I have known few who could equal their father's feats. No matter. I accept your decision."

She waved a hand and a herald stepped forth. "Mac Chect, conduct this brave heart to the Cave and wait upon his return or his death."

"Won't he have to enter the Cave to tell if Cumac is dead?" Lorgas asked.

"I think he will wait until daylight," Bern said. "Remember Seanchan's story? The lions retreated into the Cave when daylight came. He should be safe at that time."

Mac Chect bowed to Maeve and, turning to the Seekers, said, "The time has come, and it is now that I shall conduct you, Cumac, to the Cave. All others will remain here in the Great Hall."

A groan came from the huge audience, but Mac Chect raised his hand for silence and said, "This is the way of things, and tradition will be upheld. From time unknown, this has been the manner of testing."

He motioned to Cumac, and together they left the Great Hall and made their way to the Cave, a short distance away.

The Cave was halfway up a mountain to a small shelf. Torches burned redly at the opening of the Cave, and from the dark beyond, a fetid stench rolled out to greet them. Cumac wrinkled his nose at the smell and turned to Mac Chect.

"Does no one come up here? This smell is horrible!" he said.

Mac Chect grinned grimly and shook his head. "There are few willing to come this far, let alone enter the Cave to draw the remains of the brave out. If you can last until sunlight, the lions will leave you alone and you may return here. I shall be waiting for your return."

"Or not," Cumac said wryly. He drew Caladbolg, took a deep breath, and entered the Cave, taking one of the torches with him.

He stood for a moment in the dark, letting his eyes adjust to the deep darkness, then moved forward gingerly, senses alert, hand holding Caladbolg so hard the muscles in his forearm stood out like ropes.

Slowly, he moved deeper into the Cave, feeling the stone sides and ceiling begin to close upon him. His mouth was dry and he swallowed repeatedly, thinking, Why is it that when man is ready for battle his hand sweats and his mouth goes dry? You would think it would be the other way around.

He followed the twists and turnings of the Cave passage, winding deeper and deeper into the mountain. The stench grew stronger and stronger, the silence bearing down hard upon his ears.

Then, faintly, he heard a stealthy tread and the scratch of claws upon the floor as chilling as long fingernails being drawn across slate. He shivered and held the torch as far in front of him as he could.

He came to a place where the passage widened into a small room. The roof disappeared into the darkness high overhead. Unlit torches had been placed in sconces set into the walls.

This is the place where the battle will occur, he thought.

Carefully, he made his way around the room, lighting the torches, then withdrew to the entrance, holding Caladbolg ready.

It would be best for you to stand here where one of the lions will not be able to get around to your back. Here, they will be forced to come to you one at a time. Be alert! Be quick! Be accurate with your strikes! he told himself.

And then, a lion slowly entered the room across from him.

Cumac felt his blood chill at the sight of the lion. As tall as the mast of a ship, the lion stood at the shoulders. His mouth opened into a red snarl. His teeth were yellowed spikes. His claws shone like pounded steel. Scales seemed to cover his body, and tufts of fur stuck out from around the edges of the scales. Its eyes flashed green, and Cumac would swear later that blood dripped from the corners of the lion's eyes and mouth.

The lion crouched as it moved into the room, and behind him came his twin and then a third, alike as pomegranate seeds. Their growls were low and rumbled threateningly. Their tails twitched with excitement.

Two lions moved slowly away from the first, trying to edge along the wall to get closer to Cumac's sides, but Cumac took a small step backward into the entrance through which he had come.

At this, the first lion roared in anger and leaped toward Cumac, great paws clawing to dig the warrior out of the opening, but its claws scraped uselessly along the sides of the room.

In frustration, the lion crouched and extended a paw into the opening, trying to seize Cumac and drag him out into the room for the other lions, but Cumac swung Caladbolg hard against the paw, severing the paw from the lion's legs.

The lion roared in pain and withdrew into the center of the room, licking the stump where its paw had once been. It looked in confusion back at Cumac.

"This is Caladbolg, the Rainbow," Cumac said ringingly. "Forged by Goibniu deep within the fires of his mountain. It was not made by man!"

Another lion came, its head coming first into the opening. Cumac struck hard, slicing the jaw away from the lion's head, sending blood gushing into the lion's great maw.

And then the third came, more cautious than the first two, standing just beyond the opening. It crouched, tale whisking furiously back and forth, eyes flashing fire.

Come out little man and battle
Until one of us hears death's rattle.
You may harm us, this we know
With your sword's swift blow!
But you will not leave here
As your body dies here
And leaves your bones
Lying among these stones!

"Then come and take me," Cumac said, his voice seething with anger. The lion laughed and motioned for Cumac to come out into the room.

Come then and fight
In this room and torchlight
To see if you are indeed the one
To stay here until the deed is done.

It was at that moment that the warp-spasm came upon Cumac. An iron band was strapped around his head. His muscles contorted and knotted like huge stones, and his hair stood straight up with a drop of blood upon the end of each hair. His chest widened and his heartbeat came like a great drum. Cumac felt himself begin to shake. He opened his mouth and screamed his battle rage and the lions stopped and took an involuntary step backward. A hero's pillar of blood flew upward from Cumac's head.

Cumac made the salmon-leap into the center of the room, Caladbolg flashing in his hand, a bright rainbow arching through the air. Huge chunks of fur flew from the bodies of the lions. But this was what they wanted, and they leaped toward Cumac.

As they did so, Cumac bounded high in the air, and the lions slammed into one another. Cumac fell upon one lion's back and, with an enormous sweep of Caladbolg, cut the lion's head so fiercely from its body that the head rebounded three times off the walls of the room before rolling to a stop.

He didn't wait to see the result of his blow but leaped again, dropping onto the back of another lion and decapitating it with one strike. Its head rebounded six times off the walls before rolling to a stop.

Cumac dropped lightly to the floor and faced the third lion. Slowly the lion paced around Cumac, green eyes glowing like a furnace. A harsh rumble came from its throat.

"Let us finish this," Cumac growled, turning with the lion's pace. "Come! Join your brothers!"

In mid-stride, the lion suddenly pounced, its huge paw striking Cumac and knocking him into a corner of the room. Caladbolg flew from his hand, and the lion roared in triumph and hurtled toward him.

Cumac stepped inside the lion's paws and gripped the lion's jaws in both hands. Slowly, he spread the mighty jaws until a loud *crack!* sounded as he ripped the lower jaw from the lion's mouth and struck the lion mightily with its jaw.

The lion fell away, and Cumac seized Caladbolg and leaped forward lithely, swinging the sword with all his might. The lion's head flew from its body and rebounded twelve times from the walls before coming to rest beside those of its brothers.

Cumac wiped the sweat from his forehead with the sleeve of his tunic and leaned back against a wall, drawing deep, shaky breaths to calm his beating heart.

Slowly the warp-spasm left him. Then he sighed deeply and squatted on his heels to rest a moment.

"Well," he said to himself, "this was a good night's work finished." He lifted Caladbolg and eyed it critically. "You have done well by me this night. I thank you."

He rose and staggered shakily to the last lion and wiped the blood from the blade of Caladbolg with a handful of fur he pulled from the lion's body. Then he turned and entered the passage and made his way back to the Cave's mouth.

Mac Chect stared in shock as a blood-spattered Cumac appeared before him.

"The lions?" he asked.

"Dead," Cumac said.

"You truly are a great champion," Mac Chect said in awe.

"Let us return to the Great Hall," Cumac said grimly. "Now, I wish to see Bricriu!"

Together the pair made their way back down the mountain and to the Great Hall.

When they entered, a great hush fell. The warriors nudged one another and stared disbelieving at the bloody Cumac as he made his way to the foot of the thrones.

"Good job!" bellowed Lorgas, leaping to his feet and pounding Cumac between his shoulderblades.

"Indeed," Seanchan said, a smile parting his mustache from his beard.

Fedelm smiled and patted Cumac on the shoulder, while Tarin joined Lorgas and pounded Cumac on his back.

"And now, Maeve," Cumac said. "I wish to see Bricriu. I have finished your task, and the Lions of Cruachan are no more. Fulfill your promise!"

Maeve rose slowly from her throne and stepped down to Cumac and drew a deep breath. Her eyes stared admiringly into his as she grasped his hands in both of hers.

"And so it shall be," she said. She turned to her herald and said, "Mac Chect, fetch Bricriu and the Chalice of Fire to me."

Mac Chect bowed and left.

"Tell me all," she begged Cumac. "You have even surpassed your father, the great Cucullen! He could only survive the night, not kill the lions."

"In a way, he was there," Cumac said. "In spirit, with me."

"The warp-spasm," Fedelm breathed.

Cumac nodded. "Yes. That which came from my father to me."

A warrior came forth and thrust a goblet of mead into Cumac's hand, saying, "You must feast with us, Cumac. No one could match your feat tonight. Or ever will," he added.

At that moment, Mac Chect hurried into the room, his face hard-planed with anger.

"Where is Bricriu?" Maeve demanded harshly.

"Gone, my queen. He has fled Cruachan Ai with the Bladhm Caillis."

"Send a party to bring him back. He cannot have gone far."

Mac Chect bowed his head and went among the warriors, tapping those he wished upon the shoulder. Together they rose and left the Great Hall.

"I do not believe they will find him," Seanchan said slowly. "I fear he is lost into the night. By the time it is light enough to find his path, he will have traveled even farther."

"And now?" Cumac asked.

Seanchan shook his head and heaved a great sigh. "We begin again."

The next morning, the Seekers rose early and, after a quick breakfast, left Cruachan Ai with Maeve's blessing, following a road to the south that, according to the patrol Mac Chect had sent out, Bricriu had traveled during the day and night. It led toward the Forest of Turgain and the Valley of Shadows.

"Will we catch him soon?" Tarin asked.

Seanchan shrugged, his face a grim mask. "I do not know."

"I see a cloud of black smoke rising in the East," Fedelm said. "This I saw last night when I slept the sleep of *imbas forasnai*. Maliman has regained his strength. His armies are gathered and begin to march upon these lands once more."

"Our task grows even more urgent," Seanchan said.

They raised their horses into a ground-gaining lope, each lost in his or her own thoughts, riding due south toward the Forest of Turgain and the Valley of Shadows.